ESSEX - TUDOR REBEL

TONY RICHES

COPYRIGHT

All rights reserved. No part of this publication may be reproduced, stored in a retrieval system or transmitted in any form or by any means, electronic, mechanical, photocopying, recording or otherwise, without the prior permission of the author.

This book is sold subject to the condition it shall not, by way of trade or otherwise, be resold or otherwise circulated without the consent of the publisher.

Copyright © Tony Riches 2021
Published by Preseli Press

ISBN: 9798735406532
BISAC: Fiction / Historical
Cover Art by Gordon Napier

ALSO BY TONY RICHES

OWEN – BOOK ONE OF THE TUDOR TRILOGY
JASPER – BOOK TWO OF THE TUDOR TRILOGY
HENRY – BOOK THREE OF THE TUDOR TRILOGY

MARY ~ TUDOR PRINCESS
BRANDON ~ TUDOR KNIGHT
KATHERINE ~ TUDOR DUCHESS

DRAKE - TUDOR CORSAIR
RALEIGH - TUDOR ADVENTURER

THE SECRET DIARY OF ELEANOR COBHAM
WARWICK: THE MAN BEHIND THE WARS OF THE ROSES
QUEEN SACRIFICE

ABOUT THE AUTHOR

Tony Riches is a full-time writer and lives with his wife in Pembrokeshire, West Wales, UK. A specialist in the history of the early Tudors, Tony is best known for his Tudor and Brandon trilogies.

For more information visit Tony's author website: www.tonyriches.com and his blog at www.tonyriches.co.uk. He can also be found at Tony Riches Author on Facebook and Twitter: @tonyriches.

For my wife
Liz

HIC TVVS ILLE COMES GENEROSA ESSEXIA NOSTRIS
QVEM QVAM GAVDEMVS REBVS ADESSE DVCEM.

1

NOVEMBER 1576

The excited barking of the dogs interrupted Robert's answer. The crunch of hooves on gravel, and a deep voice calling for a groom, was too much for him after a long morning of Latin. He clambered on to the velvet-cushioned widow seat, and cleaned a leaded pane with his sleeve to stare into the courtyard.

Master Wright muttered under his breath as he closed the leather-bound Latin textbook they'd been studying. Robert had turned eleven the previous week and was a gifted student, fluent in Latin and French. The problem wasn't lack of talent, but ease of distraction.

There'd been few enough visitors to Chartley Manor since Robert's father left for Dublin, and his mother to her friends at Kenilworth Castle. His sisters, Penelope and Dorothy, needed their mother, and little Walter seemed an unhappy child. Master Wright counted himself fortunate he only had to worry about Robert.

'Who is it, Master Robert?' His voice carried a trace of irritation at his lesson being interrupted.

'I hoped Father had returned early, Master Wright. It's not

him, but it *is* someone important.' Robert beckoned his tutor to come and look. 'He has a fine black horse.'

Master Wright joined him at the mullioned window. 'That's Ned Waterhouse, your father's secretary.'

'Should we go to welcome him?'

Master Wright agreed they should. Herodotus, and his history of the conflict between Greeks and barbarians, would keep for another day. In his bureau was a short letter from Ned Waterhouse, sent all the way from Ireland. He'd been asked to keep the contents confidential; the news would change them all forever, and he followed Robert with a heavy heart.

Edward Waterhouse carried the distinctive odour of horse sweat and looked grim-faced as they led him into the great hall. The grandest room in the manor house, with French tapestries decorating the walls, the great hall was also the coldest. The cavernous Italian marble fireplace stood empty, except for a dusty bouquet of dried cornflowers.

The family used the smaller rooms, which were easier to keep warm in autumn and winter, and ate in the refectory when their parents were away. Edward Waterhouse peered up, his eye resting on cobwebs in the corner of the hammer-beamed roof, as if passing judgement.

He ran his hand over the polished oak table, and stood for a moment, staring at the earl's high-backed chair at the head of the table, before choosing one of the burgundy velvet upholstered chairs arranged around the fireplace. He gestured for Robert to be seated opposite, and turned to Master Wright.

'Would you send for the other children? I have grave news to share. It's better done with them all together.'

Master Wright gestured to the waiting housemaid, and gave Edward Waterhouse an apologetic look. 'We may have a little wait.' He glanced at Robert. 'Robert's sisters will wish to look their best.'

As if to prove him right, young Walter, known as 'Wat', appeared alone and stood in the doorway. Seven years old, he wore oversized hand-me-downs from Robert which made him look small for his age. He stared, wide-eyed, at Edward Waterhouse and shuffled into the chair next to Robert without speaking.

Penelope and Dorothy finally entered, in matching gowns of embroidered brocade with satin sleeves and high lace collars. Skilled seamstresses, their kirtles and bodices fitted so well no one would guess they'd been crafted from their mother's cast-offs.

People told Robert he had his father's good looks, but his sisters had their mother's beauty and striking red-gold hair, curled in long ringlets. Penelope's dark eyes shone with self-awareness. She would be fourteen in the new year, and confided to Robert that their father planned her betrothal to the handsome and wealthy courtier, Philip Sidney.

Dorothy would soon be as tall as her sister, with a confidence which belied her twelve years. She wore a pear-shaped pearl pendant on a gold chain, woven into her hair. Her necklace of small diamonds, a gift from her father, sparkled in the light.

They bobbed a graceful curtsey to their visitor, the hems of their gowns swishing on the tiled floor as they crossed the room and sat by their brothers. Edward Waterhouse seemed surprised, as if unused to such formality. His face reddened as he bowed to the girls.

He cleared his throat, and glanced at Robert before speaking in a sombre voice. 'It is my sad duty to tell you that your father has died in the service of Her Majesty in Ireland.'

It sounded as if he'd rehearsed the words many times, yet could still scarcely believe them. He sat back in his chair, and allowed them to take in the news. 'I am deeply sorry for your loss.'

A gasp from Penelope broke the silence as their lives changed in a heartbeat. Robert put his arm round Wat, who looked close to tears, as his mind raced with questions. He bit his lip.

'Was our father killed in a battle with the Irishmen?'

Edward Waterhouse shook his head, but hesitated a little too long before answering.

'Your father fell ill at a banquet held in his honour at Dublin Castle, and died three weeks later of a fever and the flux.'

Robert recalled Master Wright's account of how the warrior king Henry the Fifth died of the flux in France, after the long siege of Meaux. He put the dreadful image from his mind, and struggled to compose himself. As the eldest son, he was master of the household now, and must set an example.

'Will our father be brought back from Ireland for his funeral?' His voice wavered.

'He asked to be buried in St Peter's Church, in Carmarthen, in a week's time. I was to escort you there, but the journey is long, and storms make the ride challenging at this time of year.' His tone softened. 'I shall be honoured to represent you, and your uncle, Sir George Devereux, will be chief mourner.'

Robert glanced across at Penelope, and saw a tear glisten on her cheek. 'What is to become of us, Master Waterhouse?'

'Your father spoke of you all with great affection and, in his last hours, asked me to ensure you are all provided for as well as possible.' His eyes met Robert's. 'You are now the second Earl of Essex, Viscount Hereford and Lord Ferrers. Your father's wish is for you to become a ward of Sir William Cecil, Lord Burghley, the Lord Treasurer.'

'I'll have to leave Chartley?'

The thought filled him with apprehension. Chartley Manor

was his home. He loved to ride in the fields and forests of the Chartley estate, and the ruined castle on the hill was their playground. Although his sisters were old enough to look after themselves, he couldn't leave little Wat behind. He glanced again at Penelope and saw her cautionary look.

'Lord Burghley agreed you can remain here until after Christmas, then he wishes you to continue your education. Your father's lawyer, Master Richard Broughton, is to be your trustee, and Master Wright will accompany you to Hertfordshire to continue as your tutor.'

He turned to the girls. 'Your mother has been sent for, and I am sure will have plans for your future.'

Robert heard the hint of disapproval in Edward Waterhouse's voice as he spoke of their mother. Their father seemed troubled by something at his last brief visit, and Robert guessed it concerned their mother's poorly kept secret.

Cold November rain trickled from the gutters into the deep green moat, and a bitter wind kept them all in the house. Penelope, in her temporary role of mistress of the manor, kept busy overseeing the army of servants scrubbing and cleaning every room in preparation for their mother's imminent return.

Covers were pulled from furniture, wooden floors polished, and windows cleaned until they shone. Robert watched groundsmen sweep autumn leaves from the courtyard, and heard his sister scold a footman for walking into the hall with mud on his boots.

Robert also heard Dorothy, normally mild-mannered, snap at Wat to keep still while she made alterations to the seam of one of his oversized doublets.

'You'll have one of these pins in you if you're not careful!'

'I don't want to wear Rob's old clothes.' Wat's reedy voice carried a new edge. Their father's death changed them all, as if something of their childhood had died with him, and they all knew their family life at Chartley would soon come to an end.

Robert returned to the dark-oak desk in his late father's study, where he'd begun drafting a letter to Lord Burghley. Several failed attempts lay torn up in a pile. He dipped his quill in fresh ink, but the new sheet of parchment in front of him was blank, except for the salutation: *My very good Lord*.

Before he left, Edward Waterhouse had given him a letter with an impressive wax seal, written in Lord Burghley's neat hand, expressing his condolences. It seemed only right that he should write a sincere reply.

In truth, Robert was relieved to be excused attending his father's funeral in Wales. He wanted to remember his father raising a hand in a wave of farewell as he left for Dublin, not the stark truth of a wooden coffin. There would be plenty of time, when he was older, to visit his father's grave at St Peter's Church in Carmarthen, but for now he needed the space to grieve.

His father had promised to take him hunting when he returned, and to teach him how to shoot a pistol. He'd been looking forward to that day, and bit his lip as he struggled to overcome a wave of sadness. He didn't understand how or why his father had died, and his many questions were still unanswered.

Master Wright was a Fellow of Trinity College, Cambridge, and seemed to know everything except that which mattered. He'd never led a cavalry charge, or commanded one of the queen's great sailing ships. If asked how to plan a battle, he would talk of how the ancient Greeks fought the Persian kings. Robert doubted he'd ever held a sword in his life.

He decided to write an apology for not being able to ride to Wales for the funeral. '*I would be willing to do my Lord and father not only this service but any other in my power, if that my weak body could bear this journey.*' He could think of no other excuse, and wished Lord Burghley good health before signing the letter with a boyish flourish: *R. Essex.*

The queen had visited Chartley Manor on a royal progress the previous year, and his mother's return reminded Robert of that grand occasion. A lookout waited for hours to alert them of her approach, and all the servants formed a line, while the children waited in their best clothes.

He'd been in awe of the queen as he gave his well-rehearsed bow. His mother warned him only to speak if Her Majesty asked him a question. The worry kept him awake that night, but the queen simply stared at him with sharp eyes that bore the intensity of a fox deciding whether to eat a chicken.

Robert took an involuntary step backwards as the queen's smile revealed yellowed and uneven teeth. The queen's smile vanished and, for a moment, he thought she might be angry, but she merely frowned and moved on to his older sister.

The night after the royal party left, he overheard his parents arguing in their bedchamber. His mother shouted something about their debts, and Robert remembered his father's terse reply. *The queen has ruined me, and no man will give me credit for any money.*

He told Penelope, and she'd said the royal visit must have cost them a fortune. The queen's travelling household, of over a hundred, were all fed at their parents' expense. She'd also told him their father's debts were due to the cost of his ventures in Ireland, and at times they'd struggled to pay the servants' wages.

If his mother worried about saving money, she showed no sign of it. She arrived in a fine new coach pulled by a team of fine white horses, and a retinue of lady's maids and liveried servants to rival the queen herself.

They hadn't seen their mother since July, and Robert couldn't understand why she hadn't returned earlier, or even sent a letter when she'd learned of their father's death. He recalled Edward Waterhouse's words. *Your mother has been sent for, and I am sure will have plans for your future.*

He watched as liveried coachmen helped their mother from the high coach. She wore an ornate ruff of pleated lace as wide as her shoulders, and long strings of pearls around her neck. More pearls decorated her brocade kirtle, and her puffed sleeves glistened with embroidered gold and silver flowers.

'Welcome home, Mother.'

Robert caught the exotic scent of her perfume as she embraced him. She studied him with an appraising look, as if seeing him for the first time.

'You're going to be a handsome young man.' She kissed him on the cheek, an empty gesture without affection. 'I'm sorry I wasn't here for your birthday, but I have a wonderful present for you in my baggage.'

He'd almost forgotten his birthday, which seemed long ago, so much had changed. His sisters had sewn him two shirts of white linen, and persuaded the cook to make his favourite venison pie, with sugared fruits and marchpane comfits. They'd shared it at a mock banquet, with watered wine, and small beer.

Their mother embraced each of the others in turn, whispering something he couldn't hear to Penelope and Dorothy, and comforting Wat. Robert had lectured his brother not to cry in front of their mother. 'You must take care of our sisters when I leave for London. Be strong, and make our mother proud.'

Robert always wanted to make his father proud. He'd expected his father to introduce him at court, and prepare him for his inheritance. Looking at his mother, he realised they'd become strangers, another thing that would have to change. He needed his mother more than ever, and there was little enough time left.

Penelope took her mother's hand. 'You must be tired after your journey. You must come and see what we've done with your rooms.'

She led their mother away, followed by Dorothy, while Robert and Wat watched their servants unloading their mother's mountain of baggage. At least it seemed she planned to stay longer this time.

Later that evening, after Dorothy and Wat retired to bed, their mother sat with Robert and Penelope to talk about their future. She told them nothing about where she'd been for the past three months, and listened while Robert explained what their father's secretary, Edward Waterhouse, had told them.

'He said we could only stay here until after Christmas. Why is that, Mother?'

'You both need to know the truth. We can't afford to live in such a grand place, with so many servants. I've no idea of the extent of your father's debts, but I fear he's made you the poorest earl in England.' Her scathing tone showed no hint of regret at the loss of her husband.

Robert resisted the urge to defend his father's good name. Everything his father had done had been to advance their family, and he'd been intensely proud of their Devereux heritage. Their mother squandered his money on new gowns and overlong visits to Buxton with her frivolous friends.

Penelope echoed the question Robert had asked Edward Waterhouse. 'What is to become of us, Mother?'

'Your grandfather has kindly agreed we can live with him at Greys Court in the new year.'

Robert liked his grandfather, Sir Francis Knollys, who told him stories of knights and gallantry. A strict Puritan, he'd been sent to guard Mary, Queen of the Scots, at Carlisle Castle, and said he'd taught her to read and write in English to pass the time.

He lived alone, as their grandmother had died seven years ago. Their mother, Lettice, was Sir Francis Knollys' third child and, she liked to say, her father's favourite. Robert couldn't remember his grandmother, but his mother once told them she'd comforted Queen Anne Boleyn before her execution, and witnessed her horrific fate at Tower Green.

Penelope finally spoke. 'It will be good for Wat to get to know his grandfather.'

Their mother didn't seem to notice the sadness in her daughter's voice. 'If this is to be our last Christmas together at Chartley Manor, we must make it one to remember.' She looked up at Robert. 'That reminds me, I have your birthday present.' She opened her bag and handed him something heavy, wrapped in dark-blue velvet, tied with a plaited cord.

Robert guessed what it might be from the weight and shape, but gasped when he saw the fine silver-handled dagger, in a scabbard engraved with the Devereux motto: *Virtutis comes invidia*. A wave of emotion swept over him as he turned the sharp steel blade in the light and guessed this was more likely to be his father's gift than his mother's.

It hadn't escaped his notice that she'd not mentioned his father's death, or said anything about the funeral in Carmarthen. He guessed it might be his mother's way of coping with her loss, but it seemed to him she cared little that their father was no longer around.

'Thank you, Mother. I shall carry this always.'

'Take care never to draw it in anger.' His mother smiled. 'I should tell you this was your godfather's idea, and he commissioned it to be specially made for you by a London bladesmith.'

'My godfather?'

'Your namesake, Sir Robert Dudley. He's agreed to join us for our Christmas celebrations.'

Robert exchanged a look with his sister and saw her dark eyes narrow. She'd once expressed her suspicions and it seemed she'd been right. Sir Robert Dudley, Earl of Leicester, would not continue to be their mother's great secret much longer.

2

JANUARY 1577

Chill winter winds drove stinging flurries of snowflakes into Robert's face, making the hundred-and-fifty-mile ride to London the hardest he could remember. As well as Master Wright, Robert travelled with his groom, Tom White, and his valet, Anthony Bagot, leading two packhorses laden with their luggage and his tutor's precious collection of books.

Tom White, an easy-going Irishman, had followed Robert's father back from Dublin, and remained as head groom at the Chartley stables. Anthony, known to everyone simply as 'Bagot', was the son of their neighbour. With his sister Anne, he had joined the Devereux household more as companions to Robert and his sisters than servants.

All Robert owned in the world fitted in one leather bag, but everything he cared about was left behind. He would miss his sisters, particularly Penelope, who'd helped him cope with their father's death. He worried about how little Wat would manage without him, although their grandfather would no doubt spoil him.

He'd inherited Chartley Manor, including the acres of deer park, the castle and tenanted farms. His father's Welsh lawyer,

Master Broughton, arranged to keep Chartley in trust until Robert came of age, to avoid it being sold to pay off the family debts. He guessed many years might pass before he could return.

There were few travellers on the London road, so he passed the time asking Master Wright questions about Lord Burghley. He knew from Edward Waterhouse that, even on his deathbed, his father had been determined to persuade the Lord Treasurer to accept his wardship.

'Why did my father choose Lord Burghley?'

Master Wright turned in his saddle, his eyebrows raised in surprise that Robert would ask the question.

'Lord Burghley is the most important man in the country, and the right hand of the queen. He's also Master of Wards, responsible for the welfare and education of nobles such as yourself.'

'Will there be other boys like me?' The thought hadn't occurred to Robert, and cheered him a little.

Master Wright cursed and steadied his horse as the road turned to slippery mud. 'You are in a position of great privilege, as you will be tutored with his lordship's own son.'

'I thought Lord Burghley was old. I didn't expect him to have a son my age.'

'I've been corresponding with Lord Burghley about the arrangements, and believe Robert Cecil is only a few years older than you.' Master Wright gave Robert a knowing look. 'I understand he also has two daughters. Anne is married to Edward de Vere, the Earl of Oxford, but his daughter Elizabeth Cecil is closer to your age.'

'Do you think I'll be allowed to see her?'

'I'm certain of it. Lady Cecil has a reputation for believing girls should have the same schooling as boys.'

Robert brightened, despite the cold wind which froze his

fingers, and smiled to himself. He'd imagined a lonely future with an elderly lord, not a whole family much like the one he'd had to leave behind. He looked forward to meeting Robert and Elizabeth Cecil, and hoped they would become friends.

They rode through the city gates in fading afternoon light. He was shocked to see an overwhelming confusion of narrow, crowded streets, stinking of waste, with an air of danger about them. Beggars dressed in ragged clothes reached out with grubby hands. They pleaded for money, and shouted curses as Robert passed by.

'How do we find our way, Master Wright?'

His tutor scowled at the stench from the open sewers.

'I have directions to Lord Burghley's residence in the Strand, one of the finest parts of London, but we must get a move on. There's a city curfew from dusk in winter, and fines for anyone found in the streets.'

As they drew closer, Robert was grateful to see the cobbled streets were wider and clean, and the air fresher. They found Burghley House halfway along the Strand, one of the grandest, with a paved forecourt and high wrought-iron gates.

He peered up at the towering red-brick chimneys as Tom and Bagot led the horses to the stables. Master Wright rang the bell. A liveried servant showed them into a wood-panelled room. Tapestries of Old Testament scenes decorated the walls, and they warmed their hands on a welcome log fire, blazing in a marble hearth.

The door opened and a middle-aged woman with a kindly face entered, wearing a white lace coif over her grey hair. Robert noticed the large ruby set in a gold ring on her finger, and the gold embroidery on her gown. He guessed she must be the Lord Treasurer's wife.

'Welcome.' She smiled. 'I'm Mildred, Lady Burghley.'

Master Wright bowed. 'My lady, this is Robert, Earl of Essex.'

Robert found it strange to hear his new title, and bowed. 'It's my pleasure to meet you, Lady Burghley.'

'You must be tired after your long journey. My husband will be home soon, God willing, so you no doubt wish to change for dinner.'

Master Wright nodded. 'Thank you, my lady.'

Robert followed a servant up a grand staircase and along a panelled corridor to a high-ceilinged room at the rear of the house. His leather bag waited next to an inviting four-poster bed. Crossing to the tall mullioned windows, he peered out, surprised to see well-kept, formal gardens, and green fields beyond.

An elegant washstand with a jug of water and a basin stood to one side of the window, and a dark-oak writing desk and chair to the other, with a quill and parchment, and a silver ink bottle. Robert decided he must write to his mother in the morning, to tell her he'd arrived safely. He'd seen the look of concern in her eyes as he'd left, and suspected she sensed his resentment.

Sir Robert Dudley had arrived at Chartley soon after his mother, and sat in their father's chair at the Christmas celebrations. Robert didn't understand what was going on, but his sister did. Penelope explained that their mother and Sir Robert were both widowed, and would be free to marry after a suitable period of mourning.

He scowled at the thought as he poured cold water from the jug into the basin, and washed his face. He changed into a fresh linen undershirt and his best silk doublet and wide breeches. He glanced longingly at the comfortable bed, and would have preferred to sleep than have to meet the most important man in England.

. . .

A dozen beeswax candles lit the long oak dining table, their warm yellow light reflecting in Lord Burghley's intelligent blue-grey eyes. He had a silver beard, and wore a deeply pleated ruff, with a doublet of dark-red velvet. The glint of a square green gemstone in a gold ring on his little finger caught Robert's attention.

Lady Mildred sat to Lord Burghley's right, and his youngest daughter, Elizabeth, to his left. Robert and Master Wright sat opposite them, with Robert Cecil, who had a deformity which caused him to sit hunched in his chair.

Robert noticed Elizabeth's shy smile as Lord Burghley said grace. She reminded him of his sister Dorothy, and looked uncomfortable in her tight-fitting satin bodice, buttoned all the way up to her throat. He turned to Lord Burghley.

'I must thank you for your hospitality, my lord.'

'Your father, God rest him, gave his life in the service of his country.' Lord Burghley studied him with an appraising look. 'It's our Christian duty to do what we can for you.'

Robert watched Elizabeth wash her fingers in her silver bowl and dry them on a square of white linen. He did the same, thinking he had a lot to learn. They'd forgotten such refinements, and dined like unruly servants in the refectory at Chartley.

Lady Mildred seemed to sense his awkwardness. 'How was your journey to London?'

'Very long, my lady, and cold enough, so I was most pleased to arrive in the city.'

Lord Burghley signalled to the servants and they brought silver platters of roast pheasant, pigeon pie, and quails in a sweet peppered sauce. A young serving girl filled Robert's goblet with mulled wine, but he waited to watch the others before touching the food.

Robert Cecil carved the meat from a breast of pheasant with his knife, and turned to him. 'Have you been to London before?'

'No. I'm looking forward to seeing the Tower of London, and the abbey of Westminster. My father—' He stopped himself, recalling Master Wright's warning about listening more than talking. 'I've heard they are the greatest sights in England.'

Robert Cecil gave a wry smile. 'I fear we have little enough time to visit the sights of London.'

Lord Burghley looked across as he dismembered a roasted quail. 'You should visit Westminster Abbey, and learn what you can from those who rest there.' He gave his son a cautionary frown. 'As for the Tower, I find it a bleak place.'

Robert smiled as Elizabeth rolled her eyes at him, the first sign of what he hoped would become their friendship. He was going to have to work hard to impress Lord Burghley, and Elizabeth might help him win her father's approval.

Master Wright welcomed Robert to their new study early the next morning. 'I'm afraid I'd become somewhat lax with my tutoring at Chartley.' He shook his head. 'His lordship has provided a timetable for your daily studies.'

Robert frowned as he read the list. 'Dancing? Before breakfast? Then French, Latin, and writing before prayers?' He gave his tutor a puzzled look. 'Why do I need to learn to dance?'

'You will be expected, as an earl, to partake in dancing at court.' He glanced at the door, then lowered his voice. 'I will only tutor you in Latin. You shall have French lessons with Robert Cecil in the mornings, and cosmology each afternoon.' Master Wright smiled. 'You'll not be surprised to hear that I'm no dancer.'

'Who is to teach me?'

'Lord Burghley tells me he has retained the best dance tutors in the country.'

Robert studied the timetable again. 'The last lesson ends at half past four.'

'And then you are expected to study the Bible. His lordship told me his children read the entire Psalter, Old and New Testaments each year.'

Robert's initial excitement at his new life was replaced by a pang of homesickness for his easy existence at Chartley. He missed his sisters, and even little Wat, and resolved to make time at the end of his busy day to write to them all, as well as his mother.

Elizabeth came bounding into the room, wearing a pale pink bodice and farthingale. She looked younger with her long hair loose, closer to his own age, and smiled at him, a twinkle in her eyes.

'Time for our dance lessons, Master Robert,' she twirled on the spot, 'and you are to be my new partner.'

He left Master Wright to sort out his pile of Latin textbooks and followed her down the corridor, his homesickness forgotten. His new life in London might not be so dull after all, and the prospect of learning to dance with Elizabeth Cecil put a broad smile back on his face.

Robert soon settled into taking his lessons with the others, after so long studying alone. He was surprised to find he was more fluent in Latin and French than either of them, and was pleased when Elizabeth was impressed. Robert Cecil was competitive, which spurred him on to work even harder.

He'd still not seen Westminster Abbey or the Tower, but they could walk down to the River Thames after they'd finished their studies. Wherries jostled for trade at the wharf, and there were more white swans than Robert could count. Elizabeth called after him as her brother began climbing down the ancient stone steps to the muddy foreshore, exposed by the low tide.

'Take care! We promised Mother we'd not go down to the water.'

He ignored her, and beckoned Robert to join him.

'There are treasures hidden in these stones.' He grinned. 'Boys our age can earn a living from what they find.'

Robert clambered down the steps, which were slippery with green slime. Elizabeth followed as far as the bottom, lifting her hem to keep her gown from the foul-smelling mud. At first, he only saw stones and rubbish, then Elizabeth pointed out an inkpot, half buried in the ooze.

He washed it in a puddle, pleased to see it looked undamaged, although very old. Robert looked up as howls and cheers rang out from a round building further downriver, on the opposite bank. The sound carried well across the water, and he could tell there must be quite a crowd to make such a noise.

'Bear-baiting.' Elizabeth scowled. 'Father says it's a barbaric sport.'

'They make bears fight?' It seemed unlikely to Robert.

'Only one at a time.' Robert Cecil bent to pick a coin from the mud as he spoke, and swilled it in the water. 'The bear is chained by its leg in a pit, and bulldogs attack it while people make bets.' He studied the coin with a frown, then showed it to Robert.

'Look – HDG. Henry by the grace of God.' He rubbed the coin on his sleeve. 'The queen's father was called old copper nose, because he debased the coinage. The silver is so thin it rubs off, and you can see it's only copper underneath.'

Church bells clanged, and Elizabeth called to them. 'We should go back, before the curfew.'

Robert looked along the river. 'There's much I want to see.

My father told me tales of the Tower of London. Can you show me, another time?'

Robert Cecil shook his head. 'The Tower is a good three miles downriver – and we'll be moving to the country now.'

'I thought we'd be staying in London...'

Elizabeth smiled. 'You'll like Theobalds.'

Robert didn't understand. 'When are we going there?'

Robert Cecil seemed surprised he didn't know. 'We've only been waiting for the building work to be finished.' He glanced up at the threatening grey sky. 'And for the weather to improve.'

With extensive parklands and a deep green moat, Theobalds reminded Robert of Chartley Manor. In the Hertfordshire countryside, a morning's ride from the city up the main north road, Theobalds was a magnificent statement of Lord Burghley's wealth and importance.

Elizabeth and Robert Cecil seemed happier and more at ease away from their father's strict routine. Robert found he looked forward to his dancing lessons with Elizabeth, and was beginning to gain confidence with more complicated steps.

Elizabeth looked pleased when he took her hand and complimented her on her silk dress, which flared from the waist with hoops of willow. They'd moved on from the pavane, where he had to touch only the tips of her fingers, to the more difficult galliard. Their lute player was joined by a young fiddle player, and a man with a drum.

Their cheerful dance tutor counted out the steps, clapping his hands in time to the rhythmic drumbeat. 'Right, left, right, left, cadence!'

After three quick hops with alternate feet, on the word *cadence*, Robert jumped, landing with one leg ahead of the other, in a move called the posture. At first, Elizabeth laughed at his attempt, but together they mastered the steps, and now he looked forward to the day he might dance for the Queen of England.

Exhausted, they sat together to catch their breath before joining Elizabeth's brother for the day's lessons. Robert Cecil didn't dance, due to the problem with his spine, which had a sideways curve, and one foot which turned at an odd angle. Although older than Robert, his hunched posture made them about the same height.

'I asked your brother about his back yesterday.' Robert watched for Elizabeth's reaction, and saw her eyes widen in surprise. 'I've seen how it makes him sit awkwardly in the saddle.'

'What did he tell you?'

'He said he was most likely born with it, and with God's grace, it will not grow worse.'

Elizabeth looked thoughtful. 'I dare not mention it. He can be angry when people do.'

'He didn't seem bothered by my question. He said it only hurts when people stare and make comments.'

Elizabeth frowned. 'I used to call him names – but only when we were small.'

'You are lucky to live with your brother.'

She seemed to pick up on the regret in his voice. 'You must miss your family.'

'In truth, I haven't had time to miss them, but I thought they would stay together, with my grandfather.' He frowned. 'Instead, my family are spread further apart. My mother's letter said my father wished my brother to become the ward of his cousin, Sir Henry Hastings, Earl of Huntingdon. I worry about Wat, as he's been sent to York on his own. Mother says he's lucky to join such a family. Sir Henry has a claim to the throne, and is President of the Council of the North.'

'I'm sure your brother will be fine.' Elizabeth smiled. 'Does Sir Henry Hastings have other children?'

Robert frowned. 'No – and his wife is Sir Robert Dudley's sister.'

'That's a good thing for your brother. I've heard my father talk of Sir Robert Dudley. He's a favourite of the queen.'

'My sister thinks he is trying to take our father's place.'

'I forget you have sisters. Where are they now?'

'That's the thing I don't understand.' He looked up at Elizabeth. She was a good listener, and he was glad to talk about his family. 'My mother has taken Penelope and Dorothy to a place called Coleshill in Warwickshire, but gave no reason in her letter.' He frowned. 'I wonder if we will ever be together again.'

Robert's tutor asked to see him in his study. The spring term was at an end, and they looked forward to the summer when Elizabeth and Robert Cecil's parents were to come to Theobald's for the summer recess. There was even a rumour the queen might include them on her royal progress.

'Take a seat, Master Robert. I have some good news.' His tutor looked pleased with himself, and Robert guessed he knew the reason.

'Is my mother coming to London?'

Master Wright smiled. 'She well might when she hears your news.' He gave Robert a conspiratorial look. 'I am pleased with your progress, and the Master of Trinity College, Cambridge, John Whitgift, has agreed that you should be admitted to study for your degree.'

Robert hid his disappointment. He'd learned Coleshill Manor was some hundred miles away, yet Theobalds would be on his mother's route to London. She always visited court, and said that with Queen Elizabeth, 'out of sight was out of mind'. She'd even suffered the long journey from Chartley in midwinter to deliver the queen's New Year gifts.

A thought occurred to him. 'I would have to ask permission from Lord Burghley, as his ward.'

Master Wright produced a letter, with a distinctive signature, and handed it to Robert. 'Lord Burghley has consented, and wishes you success with your studies.'

Robert recalled what Master Wright had taught him about *rota Fortunae*, the wheel of Fortune. The Greek goddess Fortuna spun her wheel, changing fate, to the misfortune of some and good fortune of others. The wheel had turned again. His mother was unlikely to visit him in Cambridge.

'When do I have to leave?' With a heavy heart he knew he'd have to say farewell to Elizabeth, his closest friend, and that he might never see her again.

'I've arranged with Lord Burghley that, because of your age, I shall accompany you to Cambridge.' He looked pleased at the prospect. 'It's fifty miles due north of here, and we should make the journey while the weather remains fair.'

3

JUNE 1578

Robert trimmed the point of his goose-feather quill, holding it to the light to inspect the tip, before dipping it in ink. He smiled to himself as he recalled the day he'd found the inkpot on the muddy banks of the Thames. He believed the old pot brought him luck, and it reminded him of Elizabeth Cecil, the only person he counted as a true friend.

His letters to Elizabeth were short and formal, as Robert feared they might somehow fall into her father's hands. He never wrote to her of his worries, but told her about the kindness of Doctor Whitgift, Master of Trinity College, who oversaw his studies of ancient Greek and Hebrew, arithmetic and astronomy.

Robert described the tranquil River Cam, which flowed close to his college and had become part of his life. He didn't mention the stink from the king's ditch, an open sewer that emptied into the river, or the feral pigs and honking flocks of wild geese roaming the town.

Two years older than him, Elizabeth would turn fourteen in July. He missed her company, and longed to return to Theobalds and see her again. The problem was that his mother had been right when she said he was the poorest earl in England. Robert believed he might also be the poorest student in Cambridge.

He'd written to Elizabeth's father in his best Latin. He'd spent long hours on the wording, thanking him for his place at the university, wishing him good health and hoping a gentle reminder might bring further funds. There had been no reply from Lord Burghley, and no increase in his allowance.

His valet, Anthony Bagot, suggested an idea which appealed to Robert. Although older, Bagot was about the same height, and a little thinner – perfect for their plan. The clothes Robert wore to his meeting with his tutor were the worst they could find.

His breeches were threadbare, his coat frayed at the collar and too small to fasten at the front, and his shoes wouldn't see Bagot through another fenland winter. If other students noticed, it might even help if they judged him for it, especially if they failed to keep their observations to themselves.

The key to success was to convince his tutor. Robert climbed the worn stone steps to Master Wright's rooms in the masters' lodge. In the oldest part of Trinity College, the lodge had thick oak beams, tall red-brick chimneys, and windows of leaded glass.

He took a deep breath and rapped on the door with the iron knocker, hoping his money worries would soon be over. Master Wright appeared in the long black gown of a cleric, as worn by the masters at Trinity. He apologised as he moved a pile of books and papers from the only spare chair in his cramped study.

'I'm glad you've come to see me. There's talk of plague returning to Cambridge with the hot weather. I thought you might be well advised to visit your mother.'

'I'd like to, Master Wright, but I'll need money for new clothes and my expenses.'

'Is there still no reply from Lord Burghley?' He sounded

surprised, although he would be the first to know, as his duties included keeping a 'reckoning' of Robert's monthly expenses.

Robert shook his head, and showed his tutor the worn soles of his shoes. 'I've grown a good four inches taller, and my clothes no longer fit. I'm grateful for Lord Burghley's allowance, and it pays for my food and lodging, but little else. I imagine he believes my mother sends me money.'

'I can tell you he does not. Lord Burghley mentioned that your mother has written to him repeatedly, requesting his assistance with her finances.'

Robert frowned at the news. 'Will you write to him for me? You could tell him I shall soon have to sell my horse, and let my groom and servant go.'

Robert Wright sat back in his chair, stroking his well-trimmed beard as he thought. 'I think it's best if I write to your trustee, Master Broughton. He lives in London, and is well placed to put your case to Lord Burghley in person.'

'Thank you.' Robert smiled, a weight lifted from his shoulders. 'I would prefer not to have to write to Lord Burghley again asking for money, but he'll listen to Master Broughton. Can you tell him I need two new doublets, as well as a jug and ewer?'

Master Wright took his quill and a scrap of parchment. 'I'd better make a list.' He looked up at Robert. 'You should have a new gown as well.'

'And a riding cape for the holidays.' Robert counted them on his fingers to make sure nothing was missed. 'Three pairs of hose, two pairs of nether stocks, new boots – and a new hat.'

'You said you need a jug?'

'Yes, and a basin and ewer for washing – as well as some goblets. Do you think we should say silver, not pewter?'

'I don't see any harm in asking.'

'In that case, will you ask for silver plate, a salt cellar, and some candlesticks?'

Master Wright smiled. 'I shall add this list at the end of my letter. If I know Richard Broughton, you'll have the money in time for your visit to your mother.'

He didn't tell his tutor he had no idea where his mother might be living, or that it had been some months since her last letter. His sister Penelope wrote to let him know she'd been sent with Dorothy to join Wat at the King's Manor in York.

Penelope chose her words with care, but Robert knew her well enough to read between the lines of her apparently innocent letter. His sister didn't like Sir Henry Hastings, or his childless wife, Katherine, Countess of Huntingdon, and believed their mother wanted them out of her way, no doubt for good reason.

Robert whistled to himself as he made his way back to his attic room, a new plan forming in his mind. The threat of plague in Cambridge provided the perfect excuse to secure an invitation to return to Theobalds for the summer. God willing, he might soon have the money to ride back to Hertfordshire and surprise Elizabeth.

Master Broughton secured enough funds for much-needed new clothes, as well as a fine collection of silverware. As an earl, and the eldest son of a knight, Robert could wear velvet, and bought a doublet and breeches in popinjay blue with silver fastenings. He also bought a ruff of Dutch lace, a felt hat and a black riding cape, as well as new black leather boots and gloves.

He wore his fine dagger at his belt for the first time. The gift from his mother had been kept in the bottom of his wooden chest, still wrapped in a square of dark-blue velvet. He'd thought it tainted by association with Robert Dudley, but believed wearing the silver dagger made him look like someone of importance.

Master Wright, his groom, Tom White, and his valet, Anthony Bagot, rode with him to Theobalds in bright summer sunshine. The roads were busy with people heading south to avoid the threat of plague, and drovers with flocks of sheep and cattle. They broke the fifty-mile journey south overnight at an inn in the bustling market town of Bishop's Stortford, and arrived at Theobalds by mid afternoon the next day.

Elizabeth had grown from a shy girl into a confident young woman. She wore a satin gown of soft lemon yellow, with wide sleeves and a high lace collar. A gilded circlet, set back on her dark hair, glistened with pearls. Robert hoped she would remember their friendship. Then their eyes met, and he sensed her longing.

He smiled with relief. 'I've missed you.'

He held their eye contact for as long as he dared, just a few short seconds, aware her parents and brother waited to greet him.

He bowed to Lord Burghley. 'Thank you for your hospitality, my lord.' He bowed again to Elizabeth's mother. 'My lady.'

'Welcome back, Earl Robert.' Lord Burghley smiled. 'I've heard encouraging reports of your progress. Master Whitgift tells me you are one of his most hardworking students, and he's putting you forward for your Master of Arts. Well done!'

Robert glimpsed a look of jealousy in the eyes of Elizabeth's brother, and recalled the Devereux motto, engraved on his dagger. *Virtutis comes invidia*. Envy is the companion of excellence. He wondered why Robert Cecil hadn't been sent to Cambridge with him.

Elizabeth's mother seemed to notice Robert's hesitation, and glanced at Master Wright. 'You must be thirsty and hungry after your ride. Allow me to arrange some refreshments for you both.'

. . .

The sun began to cast long shadows before Robert could be alone with Elizabeth. They escaped to her mother's garden behind the house, where the delicate scent of roses filled the still summer air. The only sounds were the sleepy buzz of honeybees, and the trilling song of a skylark high overhead.

The stifling atmosphere of Trinity College, with its strict rules and relentless routine of study and prayer, seemed a world away. Robert no longer thought of Chartley Manor as home. His childhood seemed a different life, and Theobalds was where he was happiest.

Elizabeth smiled at him, her eyes twinkling with amusement. 'Now you can tell me what it's really like at university in Cambridge.'

'I've learned some important lessons during my first year.' He returned her smile. 'They will serve me well, but are not what I expected when I first entered Trinity College.'

They'd reached her mother's wooden bench seat. Shaded from the setting sun, the secluded spot had a good view of the garden, yet allowed them some privacy. Elizabeth sat and arranged her dress to stop it from creasing, then gestured for him to join her. 'Tell me what you've been doing. I want to know everything.'

Robert wasn't sure where to begin. 'I've found my studies interesting enough, and my tutors are kind and encouraging, but I have to say after a whole year I have few real friends. Master Wright does his best for me, but I miss your company.'

Her cheeks reddened, and her voice softened, as if something had changed between them. 'There must be other students your age?'

'Some seek me out in the belief I'll be of use to them.' He shook his head. 'They pretend friendship, yet only because I have the title of Earl of Essex. Much worse are those who do their best to unfairly provoke me.'

'What do they say?' She placed her hand on his arm.

'They call down the corridors, like the cowards they are, "Your mother is a harlot, Essex!"' Her eyes widened as he mimicked their harsh shouts. 'One said she had my father poisoned.' The comforting warmth of her hand rested on his arm, and he was glad to be able to tell her. 'I try to ignore them, but their taunts trouble me, and one name keeps returning to my mind.'

'Your godfather, Sir Robert Dudley?' Elizabeth looked serious. 'You told me your sister Penelope didn't trust Dudley. She suspected your mother was seeing him while your father was away in Ireland.'

Robert nodded. 'She said rumours begin from a grain of truth. Did you know Robert Dudley's wife died in a fall down her stairs one day, while he was with the queen?'

Elizabeth's hand went to her mouth. 'Do you think he might have had his wife murdered?'

'Who can know? I've been thinking about the day my father's secretary, Edward Waterhouse, told us what happened in Dublin. There could be something about my father's death he kept back, perhaps for good reason.'

'You must find out, for your father's sake.'

Robert agreed. 'I shall write to Edward Waterhouse and ask about my father's last days.'

The sun turned the sky a soft peach as they walked back to the house. He'd worried the bond between them might have changed – and it had, but for the better. Robert saw how her eyes shone when she laughed, and liked the feel of her hand on his arm. For the first time, he found himself wondering if they might marry, when he'd earned his degree and reached his majority.

He put the thought from his mind for now, and turned to her. 'Why didn't your brother attend university?'

Elizabeth looked serious. 'My brother is being groomed to one day take our father's place.'

'To become the most important man in England?'

She nodded. 'He will be well suited to it, as his private tutors prepare him for a life of court politics. There is talk he might go to Oxford.'

'You sound as if you envy him?'

'And you, with the Master of your college, Doctor John Whitgift, as your personal tutor.'

'I'd not thought how it must be for you.'

'I'm more fortunate than many girls my age, who learn little more than needlework and hope for an early marriage; my mother makes sure I have the best tutors. But it's not the same.'

They reached the house. Robert silently rehearsed an apology for being so preoccupied with his own problems. The moment passed, but he'd glimpsed the resentment behind Elizabeth's smile, and there was nothing he could do about it.

Dry autumn leaves swirled in the courtyard at Trinity College like a swarm of bees. The nights were drawing in, and Robert was glad of the thick woollen coat he'd bought in the town. For once, Cambridge escaped the scourge of the plague, but those who knew about such things said they should prepare for a harsh winter.

He'd found life easier since returning from his idyllic summer break. He struggled to cover his expenses, but hoped to return to Theobalds next summer. He looked forward to the letters from Elizabeth, which were longer now, with messages in their secret code for him to decipher.

The letter delivered that night to his attic lodgings, however, was not from Elizabeth. He'd hoped it might be a reply from his father's secretary, Edward Waterhouse, but he stared as he recognised the red wax seal, and took a deep breath. The first letter from his mother for many months raised questions in his mind. He broke the seal and began to read.

His eyes filled with tears. He loved his mother and missed her, yet for the first time he cursed her. Robert lay her letter down on his writing desk and held his head in both hands as he wept, his body shaking with sobs as he finally surrendered to his grief for his father.

At the end of her official mourning, his mother had married Sir Robert Dudley, and was living with him at their new home, Wanstead Manor in Essex. Robert's mind filled with questions, yet in his heart he knew this had been his mother's plan all along. His sister Penelope had guessed correctly.

He picked up the letter and read it a second time. Something troubled him, but he couldn't work out what it might be. She said she was married in the sight of God, and her father, Sir Francis, had attended with her brother as witnesses. Robert guessed his grandfather insisted on the marriage to end the threat of scandal.

Robert lay back on his pallet bed. His mother's money worries would be over. She would now be the Countess of Leicester, with fine houses and her new husband's fortune. It seemed strange to think he was now Sir Robert Dudley's stepson.

His mother's new marriage might end the insults called down dark corridors. He'd never found out why people shouted such things, but it could only mean the rumours had reached Cambridge. He doubted the cowardly troublemakers would dare risk the anger of Sir Robert Dudley.

He sat up as an idea occurred to him. He took a fresh sheet

of parchment and dipped his quill in ink, then hesitated. This was not something to be trusted to a letter. He would travel to York and see his sister Penelope.

Master Wright shook his head. 'I'm sorry to disappoint you, Robert. York is a ride of some hundred and sixty miles north of here.' He frowned. 'We can travel there next summer, if you wish, but I fear it would take you away from your studies for too long to make such a journey now.'

Robert decided he would have to explain. 'I've received this letter from my mother.' He took the folded parchment from his pocket and handed it to his tutor.

Master Wright's face looked grave as he read. Then he refolded the letter, and stared at the broken seal. 'It looks as if your mother has married in secret, and might not have permission from the queen.' His eyes filled with concern. 'There would be consequences, if I am right.'

'My mother could be banished from court?'

'I'm afraid people have been sent to the Tower for less.' Master Wright gave him a puzzled look. 'What is it you think your sister can do?'

'Penelope told me Robert Dudley was Her Majesty's favourite, and the queen would never let him marry our mother. I thought it would help to talk to her – and, in truth, I miss her.'

Master Wright looked thoughtful. 'I understand. I have a sister of my own, who I haven't seen for more than a year, but as a ward of Lord Burghley, it's to him you should turn for help.'

Robert's pulse raced at the prospect of returning to Theobalds and seeing Elizabeth, but then he realised the danger. 'Lord Burghley is the queen's advisor. He might tell Her Majesty. I wouldn't wish to be the cause of my mother being locked up in the Tower.'

Master Wright stroked his beard. 'You were right to come to me. My advice is to heed Epictetus. Make the best use of what is in your power, and take the rest as it happens.'

'I don't understand...'

He gave Robert a kindly smile. 'You must reply to your mother, and wish her good fortune with her new marriage. Both your mother and the Earl of Leicester know Her Majesty as well as anyone. They might have already told the queen, and there's no point in resenting their choice, now it's made.'

4

APRIL 1581

Robert raised his cap and joined in as the crowd gave a rousing cheer. The gilded royal barge, rowed by nine pairs of red-liveried oarsmen, was followed up the Thames by the barges of a delegation of French nobles. He craned his neck for a sight of Queen Elizabeth, an apparition of white silk and pearls under a canopy of cloth of gold, and called out, 'God save the queen!'

Lord Burghley had given permission for Robert to attend the St George's Day gala, and he wore a new satin doublet and velvet hose, and a crimson jerkin with silver buttons. He escorted Elizabeth Cecil, who would be seventeen in July and turned heads in her new silk gown and fur-trimmed cape. She would make the perfect wife for him one day, yet he wanted a taste of adventure before settling down to start a family.

His sister Penelope, now eighteen, was to marry Lord Robert Rich. She'd told him she'd been in trouble for protesting against her betrothal, and called Lord Rich an ugly little man, churlish, uneducated, and short. The grandson of Sir Richard Rich, who'd made his fortune from the dissolution, he'd visited Cambridge to win Robert's support, but bragged of how he evicted his tenants when they objected to his increased rents.

The visit proved a near disaster for Robert, as word reached Doctor Whitgift that he'd been seen out riding in the countryside with Lord Rich when he was meant to have been at his studies. He sent a backdated letter to Lord Burghley asking permission, but it fooled no one, and he'd thought he might be expelled. Instead, Master Wright was unfairly blamed for lack of supervision.

Robert had been at Trinity long enough, and wanted to see the world outside the college walls. He dreamed of making his fortune, and pictured himself at the head of an army, commanding a fleet of warships – or, like Sir Francis Drake, exploring exotic foreign lands, and claiming new territories for the queen.

After the deafening, two-hundred-gun salute from the royal armoury, Elizabeth took his arm. 'We must find my brother and take a wherry upriver, or we'll be late for the reception.'

Robert was enjoying the spectacle on the Thames, but she was right. He spotted the familiar hunched figure waiting in a black coat by the steps to the jetty, and gave Elizabeth a questioning look. 'Your brother hardly passes the time of day with me. Is it because of my mother?'

Elizabeth frowned in concern. 'I doubt it. How is your mother, since being banished from court?'

'Banishment seems to have made little difference to her, although she thanks God for the queen's mercy.'

'Well, your stepfather must be back in favour, to be hosting such an important banquet.'

'Your father told me it's on condition he keeps my mother out of sight.' Robert grinned. 'I doubt the queen knows my mother is in her confinement.'

'Half of London knows.' Elizabeth smiled. 'The Earl of Leicester has many talents, but discretion isn't one of them. He's telling everyone the child will be his heir. It doesn't seem to have occurred to him that your mother might be carrying a girl.'

They reached the crowded jetty to find Elizabeth's brother had a waterman waiting. Robert helped her aboard, and they set off on the short journey upriver. She might have to stay out of sight, but his mother was now a neighbour of the Cecil family. Leicester House was a short distance from Burghley House in the Strand, and equally as impressive.

They stood as the queen swept into the grand banqueting hall to a fanfare of trumpets. Robert hadn't seen his father-in-law since his last Christmas at Chartley. Lucky not to be sent to the Tower dungeons, Sir Robert Dudley now escorted the queen as her host, smiling to his guests as if he'd never done anything wrong.

Queen Elizabeth looked tired as she took her seat, and sounded annoyed as she spoke in French to one of the ambassadors. Her ladies-in-waiting followed behind, and Robert saw his sister's dark eyes scan the guests. Penelope smiled and raised a hand when she spotted him. A younger version of their mother, her red hair glittering with jewels, she clearly enjoyed being the centre of attention.

Robert was disappointed he couldn't sit with his sister, but now he understood. Penelope told him she only had to take care of the queen's gowns, yet he could see she'd been chosen to charm the French nobles, who made her laugh with their flattering compliments. He turned to see that Lady Burghley had changed seats with Elizabeth.

'Your sister is the prettiest and cleverest of all the queen's ladies.' Lady Burghley's eyes twinkled. 'You would never guess she is new to the court.'

Robert glanced across at Penelope. 'My mother employed a

Cambridge tutor, Mathias Homes, and my sisters are fluent in French, Spanish and Italian.'

Lady Burghley gave him a conspiratorial look. 'Your mother is shrewd, and your sister is a credit to her.'

He managed to catch Elizabeth's eye once or twice during the endless courses and overlong speeches in French. He found the banquet dull without Elizabeth's company. He supposed her mother was trying to make him feel welcomed by their family, yet her brother was cold towards him. His mother's actions hadn't harmed Penelope's reputation at court, so there must be some other reason. He had a lot to learn.

Robert lay awake on his pallet bed, staring at the silvery cobwebs festooned across the beams of his attic room, and thinking about his future. In two months his years at Trinity College would end with his graduation. He must bide his time until he reached his majority, and had yet to decide what to do.

His mother's child was due in less than a month, so he planned to visit her in London when he graduated. He looked forward to spending the summer exploring the city, and still hadn't seen the Tower or Westminster Abbey. Robert smiled to himself as he thought of Elizabeth Cecil, and the growing bundle of letters which kept his spirits up during the college examinations.

There was a cursory knock and the door banged open. Anthony Bagot entered carrying a laundered shirt, his ewer and basin, and a towel. 'Soon be time for your meeting with Master Wright, my lord.' Bagot handed Robert the linen shirt, then hummed to himself as he slopped the water into the basin. 'Will you dispense with breakfast?' His tone suggested he knew the answer.

Robert clambered out of bed. 'Needs must, Bagot – but I shall want a hearty dinner at noon.' He scowled at the shock of cold water as he splashed it over his face. He dried himself with the towel and pulled on the fresh shirt, then turned to Bagot as a thought occurred to him. 'Did Master Wright say why he wants to see me?'

Anthony Bagot shook his head. 'I believe he's had a letter from Master Broughton.' He gave Robert a curious glance. 'Did you ask him for more funds?'

'No – but I should have. Life in London will be costly, and I won't rely on my stepfather's charity.' He pulled on the hose, nether stocks and breeches Bagot had laid out for him. 'I also hope to see my sister at the Palace of Westminster while I'm in London – then travel north to visit my brother and sister in York.'

Anthony Bagot helped Robert on with his boots.

'It's been a few years since we've seen little Wat – and he won't be so little now.' He made a calculation on his fingers, and looked at Robert in surprise. 'I reckon he'll be twelve years old, and no doubt as tall as I am.'

'Penelope is the only one who bothers to write, and says my brother and sister have a dull enough life in York.' Robert frowned. 'Countess Katherine, the wife of their guardian, Sir Henry Hastings, is making plans to find a suitable marriage for Dorothy.'

Bagot raised an eyebrow. 'Like she did for Lady Penelope?'

Robert couldn't miss the note of scorn in his valet's voice. He suspected Bagot was secretly in love with Penelope. She was only four years younger than him, yet forever beyond his reach. Bagot had been appalled when he met Lord Rich, and said he wasn't worthy.

'Neither of my sisters will take kindly to choices made for them.' Robert smiled at the thought. 'They both have our mother's spirit, and are not afraid to speak their minds. I fear for any man they are made to marry.'

Robert hurried to the tranquil peace of the chapel in time for prayers, then made his way in the early morning sunshine to the tutors' lodge. Master Wright would only have sent for him so early if he had important news. He hoped the news was good, as he needed to settle his debts.

Master Wright welcomed him, and produced a letter from his desk. 'Master Broughton says that as you are still a minor, your grandfather, Sir Francis Knollys, has agreed you can live with him at Greys Court when you finish here.'

Robert frowned as he saw his plans unravelling.

'I want to visit my mother in London.'

'We can visit London first, if you wish.'

'You're coming with me?'

Master Wright gave Robert a deferential look. 'I'd like to remain with your household. I have no future here.'

Robert nodded. 'That matter with Lord Rich was my mistake, not any fault of yours.'

'Well, I look forward to being of further service.' It seemed he still resented being given his notice. He handed the letter to Robert. 'Master Broughton also mentions that your father left Lamphey Court, and the guardianship of yourself and his other children, to his younger brother George Devereux, along with a pension, and the sum of three hundred pounds.'

'We spent summer at Lamphey once, before my father first went to Ireland, but I've no memory of meeting my uncle.' Robert frowned at the letter in his hand. 'What does this mean?'

'It means your uncle has a duty to take care of you, as your guardian. He invites you to join him, when you wish, at

Lamphey Court, and is sending a man named Meyrick to join your household.'

Two letters waited on his desk when Robert returned after a long day of translating Aristotle's treatise on the art of persuasion from ancient Greek. He was relieved to see one was from Elizabeth. She'd not replied as quickly as usual, and he'd worried she might be unwell. He recognised his mother's flamboyant hand on the other letter, her first for many months.

He broke the wax seal and began to read. His joyous mother had given birth to a healthy son. She gave thanks to God there had been no complications, and told him his half-brother had been christened Robert, after his proud father, who called his new son his 'noble imp' and had already granted him his title of Baron Denbigh.

Robert hadn't thought of the dangers his mother faced from childbirth at the age of thirty-seven. He had mixed feelings about visiting his mother now as, in some strange way, it seemed she'd replaced him. He refolded her letter and frowned at the thought of having to accept charity from Sir Robert Dudley.

He lay his mother's letter on his desk, and opened the one from Elizabeth. She began formally, as if she expected it might be read by others. '*My dear Earl of Essex...*' Robert gasped as he read her news, and cursed her betrayal of their friendship. He read her letter a second time, but there was no mistake. Lord Burghley had agreed Elizabeth's betrothal to William Wentworth, eldest son and heir of Baron Thomas Wentworth.

He decided to visit Theobalds, and persuade her to change her mind as soon as he could – then realised he was too late. He'd kept his feelings about Elizabeth secret for too long. Robert had never heard of William Wentworth, or his father, and crossed to the tutors' lodge, his mind in a whirl.

Master Wright scowled at the mention of the baron's name. 'I'm surprised you don't know the story. Baron Wentworth is infamous for surrendering Calais to the French, and was sent to the Tower, charged with treason. There were calls for him to suffer a traitor's death. He was eventually forgiven – but not by many.' He gave Robert a curious look. 'Why do you ask?'

'Why would Lord Burghley choose Baron Wentworth's son as a husband for his daughter, Elizabeth? It makes no sense.' He heard the edge of despair in his voice.

'You thought of her for yourself?' He smiled. 'Rest assured, as Earl of Essex you will have the pick of the young ladies at court.'

Robert's cheeks reddened, and he admitted the truth. 'I thought there was plenty of time to tell Lord Burghley.'

'Then let this be a lesson to you. How old is Lord Burghley's daughter now?'

'It will be her seventeenth birthday in July.'

'Then it's time she was married. I confess it's a mystery to me why Lord Burghley would choose Wentworth, but there's nothing to be done about it now she's betrothed.'

Robert was struggling with the wording of a reply to his mother, when there was a confident knock at his door. He opened it to see a dark-eyed stranger of about twenty-five with an iridescent peacock feather in his cap. The man removed his cap to reveal an untidy mass of curly black hair.

'My lord of Essex?'

Robert recognised his accent, and was reminded of his

father, whose voice had the same Welsh lilt. 'You must be Meyrick, from Lamphey. I've been expecting you.'

'Everyone calls me Gelly, my lord.' He grinned. 'They can't say Gwyllyam.' He exaggerated the guttural sound of his first name, as he'd no doubt done many times.

'Come in.' Robert gestured towards the wooden chair at his desk, and sat on his bed. 'How is my uncle?'

'He's well, my lord, and he sends his best wishes.'

'How long have you worked in his household?'

'Since I was a boy, my lord. My father was Bishop of Bangor, but he died of the sweating sickness when I was nine years old.' He frowned at the memory. 'We moved back to my mam's place in Hasguard.'

Robert was struck by Meyrick's matter-of-fact tone, then realised he probably hadn't been born when Meyrick was nine. He'd had plenty of time to come to terms with his loss, yet he understood the note of regret in the otherwise cheerful Welshman's voice.

'Isn't it unusual for a bishop to have a son?'

'I have three younger brothers, so my father wasn't one to stand on ceremony.'

'My father died when I was ten. I'd like to visit his tomb in Carmarthen, to pay my respects, when I can.'

'I rode through Carmarthen on the way here, my lord, and will be happy to show you the church.'

Robert sensed Gelly Meyrick was a man to be trusted, and the thought of returning to Pembrokeshire appealed to him. He would like to spend time in the place which meant so much to his father. He would also like to meet his uncle, who might tell him more about his father's last days.

The decision not to visit London was easily made. He didn't want to see his new stepbrother, the 'noble imp', or face Elizabeth Cecil. Now he understood why the Cecils had been behaving as they had. He should have asked Robert Cecil what was wrong. Elizabeth's brother would have told him the truth.

Robert didn't miss his attic room in Cambridge, which was freezing in winter and stiflingly hot in summer. He also had no regrets about leaving the strict regime of Trinity College. He'd been awarded his degree of Master of Arts yet, in truth, had learned nothing of the world, or gained any useful skills.

His grandfather greeted them when they arrived at his manor house, Greys Court, in the southern Chilterns near Rotherfield Greys. A strict Puritan, Sir Francis Knollys dressed in black, apart from his starched ruff. His well-trimmed beard had turned pure white, yet his sharp eyes studied Robert with an appraising stare.

'How old are you now?' He made it sound like a test.

'I'll be sixteen in November, sir.' Robert wasn't sure how to address his grandfather, but needed to stay on the right side of him.

'You're welcome to stay here at Greys until you are of age.'

'Thank you, sir.' He decided not to mention staying with his uncle at Lamphey Court, as he sensed he must pick his moment. Robert recalled his mother saying her father disapproved of George Devereux.

Robert didn't expect much in the way of presents on his birthday, so his grandfather surprised him when he handed him a heavy purse. 'As you've reached your sixteenth birthday, your trustee, Master Broughton, has provided you with the sum of fifty pounds.'

He knew what to do with the money. He'd always wished to see his brother and sister in York, and now he had the opportunity. He wrote to Sir Henry Hastings, and secured an invitation to spend Christmas at King's Manor in York. Master Wright drew them a map, marked with suggested stopping places, and reckoned the trip would take them about a week.

They set out for York in the first week of December. Gelly rode at Robert's side, and Bagot followed with their packhorse. The winter storms arrived before they were halfway to York, so they broke their journey in the sprawling town of Nottingham.

Robert enjoyed his first chance of freedom; two weeks passed, and much of his money was spent, before they reached the city of York and rode through the impressive four-storey gatehouse, known as the Micklegate Bar.

Sir Henry Hastings didn't look like the most powerful man in northern England. He wore his Garter chain when he greeted them, as if worried someone might mistake him for a commoner. Although mild-mannered in appearance, his voice carried a stern edge as he laid out the rules for Robert's stay in his home. 'You will attend prayers three times a day, and not indulge in drinking or gambling in the town.'

Dorothy, now seventeen, was a grown woman, and made Robert smile as she rolled her eyes behind Sir Henry's back. His brother Wat, now twelve, looked pale but pleased to see him. Penelope was right – the strict Puritan regime had taken its toll on them.

Robert was surprised to find that Countess Katherine seemed pleasant towards him. Penelope said she'd been betrothed to Sir Henry when she was only twelve, and married at fourteen, but warned him to remember she was Robert Dudley's sister, and not to be trusted.

After supper, Robert contrived to have some time alone with Dorothy, who wanted to know everything he could tell her about his time at Cambridge, and all the details of Penelope's wedding and her life at court.

'I want to get away from this dreadful place, and become a lady-in-waiting to the queen.' She smiled. 'Wat wants to be a soldier, like our father – but Sir Henry says Father left fifty pounds a year for his education, and he's to be sent to Oxford to gain his degree.'

Robert decided to take her into his confidence. 'Our grandfather is kind to me, but I'm learning nothing of the world at Greys Court, and plan to live with our uncle in Lamphey as soon as I have the means to do so.' A thought occurred to him. 'Why don't you join me?'

Dorothy frowned. 'What if Uncle George proves to be more insufferable than Sir Henry?'

'I'll write to you, and you can make your choice.'

'It will have to be soon. Lady Katherine is determined to marry me off.'

'Who to?'

Dorothy gave him a nervous smile. 'I believe she has a list, although she refuses to discuss it with me.'

Robert frowned. 'I think they mean to do their best. Penelope's husband will ensure she's well provided for, yet even Bagot thinks the man is a weasel.'

Sir Henry's regime at King's Manor left no time to explore York, even if Robert had the money to do so. He liked Dorothy, but worried that Wat had become even more withdrawn. There was nothing to lose by asking Lord Burghley to send money. He trimmed the nib of his quill with his knife, and began.

'My very good Lord, I hope your lordship in courtesy will pardon my youth, if I have, for want of experience, passed the bounds of frugality. I cannot but embrace with duty your lordship's good coun-

sel, whose love I have effectively proved, and of whose care of my well doings I am well persuaded.'

Robert decided he should come to the point and ask for money to be sent so he might visit his uncle. After several attempts, which littered the floor at his feet, he continued.

'I do beseech your good lordship, notwithstanding the lapse of my youth, still to continue a loving friend unto me, as I will acknowledge myself in all duty bound unto your lordship. Thus I humbly commit your L. to the tuition of the Almighty. York this 13th day of December, 1582. Most humbly at commandment, R. Essex.'

Robert read his letter aloud to Dorothy after evening prayers. 'I believe Lord Burghley will appreciate my honesty, and I shall leave for Wales as soon as I have the funds.'

5

FEBRUARY 1582

The bustling market town of Carmarthen on the River Towy was a welcome sight after their long cold ride. Robert stared up at the grey stone towers of the castle his father would have known so well. The narrow, cobbled streets were thronged with people, and the marketplace buzzed with the shouts and chatter of vendors in Welsh.

Funds had arrived as a New Year gift from Lord Burghley, although winter snowstorms kept them in York for longer than planned. Robert promised to write to his sister Dorothy once he'd reached Lamphey, and to look after his brother Wat – who, as second son, had no inheritance – as well as he was able to.

St Peter's Church proved easy to find, but the tomb they'd come so far to see proved less so. Robert studied the impressive effigy in the north-east corner of the chancel. An inscription said that Sir Rhys ap Thomas had fought at the Battle of Bosworth, but there was no sign of Robert's father.

Hungry and tired, Robert forgot where he was and cursed. 'He must be here. Edward Waterhouse told me.'

Gelly went in search of the church warden, and returned

with a worried-looking elderly man in the robes of a cleric. Gelly led him to Robert as if he were a prisoner under arrest.

'Kindly tell his lordship what you told me.'

The man bowed his head. 'I regret to say there is no memorial to Sir Walter Devereux.'

'My lord.' Gelly nudged the man.

'My lord.'

Robert scowled. 'Yet he *is* buried here?'

The man pointed. 'I believe your father rests under the chancel floor. Many nobles, including Sir Rhys ap Thomas, were moved here after the monastery of Greyfriars was torn down in the dissolution. Their names are listed in the church records, but not the locations of their graves.'

Robert heard the regret in the man's voice. 'I will arrange for a memorial when I can.'

Master Wright studied the chancel paving stones. 'I suspect your uncle might not have had the funds to take care of a memorial and, of course, your mother—'

'Has had her own problems.'

Robert crossed to kneel in front of the altar. He clasped his hands, and prayed for his father's soul. In life, they had never been truly close, yet he sensed his father's presence. He'd wanted to make his father proud of him, and now his duty was to ensure Sir Walter Devereux was not forgotten.

A chiffchaff's rhythmic song rang out from an apple tree in the grounds of Lamphey, the only sound to break the tranquil silence. Robert remembered their young family making the exhausting, two-hundred-mile journey all the way from Chartley, yet only now did he understand why.

His father had lived at Lamphey for ten years after his own

father died, restoring the deep fishponds and watermill to create a rural sanctuary. Ancient byways led through peaceful woodlands stocked with wild deer, reaching the coast, and a wide, sandy beach some two miles away.

Within the privacy of the high stone walls, well-tended gardens provided a rich harvest throughout the year. The chiffchaff's apple tree was in an orchard of pear and plum trees, with medlars and rare quinces from Brabant. Cobblestone paths linked the great hall to the family chapel, where his uncle's chaplain, Rhys Prichard, led the daily prayers.

The library of ancient and precious books, collected by generations of Devereux lords, had become Master Wright's study, and the old manor house provided rooms for them all. The crotchety old cook complained of having so many mouths to feed, but the young scullery maid seemed glad to have more to do.

George Devereux had been Sheriff of Pembrokeshire, and was now Sheriff of Carmarthen. A younger echo of Robert's father, he couldn't have been more different, and dressed more like a farmer than a lord. He joked that his unruly temperament was the reason no lady of quality would marry him, but he made them feel welcome, and was keen to continue Robert's education.

'Lamphey was home to the queen's great-grandmother, Margaret Beaufort. King Henry the Seventh was conceived in this house, when his mother was thirteen.' He frowned. 'She nearly died when he was born, but lived to see her grandson crowned King Henry the Eighth – then passed away within a week.' His uncle gave Robert a wry look. 'Just as well, if you ask me. Lady Margaret would turn in her grave to see what he did.'

. . .

Robert enjoyed the rustic charm of Lamphey, and for the first time in his life, felled a tall rowan tree with an axe and cut it into logs. Gelly told him rowans were magical, and the logs burned slowly, with more heat than oak. Afterwards, Robert joined his uncle at the roaring fire in the manor house, with a jug of the strong local ale as reward for his hard work.

His uncle filled an old pewter tankard with the foaming beer, waiting for it to settle before handing it to Robert. 'Your father used to sit in that chair, and we'd tell each other tall tales until the small hours.'

Robert took a drink and caught a mouthful of warm froth, which he wiped on the sleeve of his shirt. He saw his chance to ask the question that had been on his mind since he'd arrived. 'Can you tell me about my father's last days, in Dublin?'

George looked apologetic. 'I have a confession to make. Your father's secretary, Ned Waterhouse, forwarded your letter to me, as he was unsure how to reply.'

'All I want is to know the truth.' Robert heard the edge to his voice. Ned Waterhouse had treated him like a child.

George frowned. 'I doubt we'll ever know the truth. I told Ned Waterhouse to wait until you'd graduated. Like you, I was sent up to Cambridge, to St John's College.' His face became serious. 'I had no wish to distract you from your studies, and there were, shall we say, complicating circumstances.'

'You mean the rumours my father was poisoned?'

His uncle raised an eyebrow. 'I can tell you the sad facts, if you wish?'

'I need to know.'

'Your father was first unwell after he dined at his house in Dublin, at the end of August. He spent the next few days travelling with Ned Waterhouse. He had pains in his stomach, and his doctor diagnosed the flux.'

'I know what that is.' Robert grimaced. 'A slow death.'

'It seems your father's strength faded fast, and he began talking about putting his affairs in order.' George looked across at Robert. 'He said, "Within this month I was well and strong, and now I am ready to die."'

Robert liked his uncle, who reminded him so much of his father, and knew he told the truth. 'Why do people say my father was poisoned?'

'His manservant, and an Irish guest at his house, who drank with your father the night he fell ill, also suffered with the flux – the same day.'

'Did they die as well?'

His uncle shrugged. 'You'd have to ask Ned Waterhouse, but Robert Dudley's enemies saw the opportunity to tarnish his reputation.'

'Do you know where Edward Waterhouse is now?'

'The last I heard he was in London – Richard Broughton will know.' He threw another heavy log on the fire, sending a shower of sparks into the air.

'I don't have the money to go back to London.' Robert drained his tankard, feeling the strong ale making him light-headed. 'I don't wish to ask Lord Burghley, and won't have charity from Sir Robert Dudley. Can you help, Uncle?'

'I have the Devereux curse.' He grinned. 'A talent for my expenditure exceeding my income.'

Robert didn't understand. 'Master Wright told me you were left three hundred pounds.'

'Long gone, I'm afraid. My only income is my stipend as sheriff, a pension of a hundred pounds from your father, and the modest rent from our tenant farmers – when they can afford to pay it!' He smiled. 'Your father granted me Lamphey Court until you come of age, on condition I did everything in my power to stop you suffering the Devereux curse.' He raised his tankard in a toast. 'Together, we will honour your father's wishes.'

Robert frowned. 'It would have been easier if my father had left me an allowance. Master Broughton said I don't inherit anything until I'm twenty-two.'

'Your father's only care was for his children. He did something for you which money can't buy. He sent a letter to the queen, asking her to be a mother to you.'

'I have a mother...'

'He meant care for you, as a mother would.' His uncle George stared into the red embers of the fire, deep in thought. 'Her Majesty has a vacancy for a handsome new admirer.' The orange light from the fire flickered in his eyes as he turned to Robert. 'Do it for my brother, your father. No one can stop you, not even that old goat, our Lord Treasurer, Sir William Cecil.'

Robert was surprised to hear the bitterness in his uncle's voice. 'He showed me great kindness, and met the costs of my time at Trinity College.'

'Your father asked him to care for your education. As Master of Wards he had little choice.' His uncle frowned. 'Lord Burghley is the reason we have no money. He tricked your father into taking huge loans for the campaign in Ireland, then charged him ten per cent interest. Did you know your father had to sell off half your inheritance because of Lord Burghley?'

'I did not.' Robert frowned.

'Your father asked Her Majesty to cancel the debts he'd incurred for the Crown.' He gave Robert a meaningful look. 'I can never prove it, but I believe the Lord Treasurer stopped her. Whatever happened, it cost your estates in Cornwall, Essex, Wiltshire and four parks at Middleham in Yorkshire.'

'Mother said my father made me the poorest earl in England. I've no idea what's left of my inheritance.'

'You can rest assured that Richard Broughton and Richard Bagot look after your best interests in all such matters.'

'Richard Bagot? You mean our neighbour at Chartley – the father of my valet?'

'You must know that Richard Broughton is married to his daughter Anne? He appointed his father-in-law to oversee your remaining lands, including the Chartley estates.' His uncle smiled. 'Anthony Bagot was sent to Cambridge to keep an eye on you, and make regular reports to his father.'

'Anne Bagot is a friend of my sister Penelope – and I've always thought of Anthony Bagot as my friend.'

'Which he is, even though you treat him as a servant.'

Robert watched as his uncle topped up their tankards with beer. They had all been keeping an eye on him, because his father asked them to. He'd never suspected a thing, but their plans for him were flawed.

'I don't think the queen likes me.'

His uncle laughed. 'What makes you say that?'

'I've met her three times. The first time, she came to Chartley and was cross because I refused to kiss her. The second time was one Christmas, when she shouted at me in front of everyone, for not wearing my hat, and the last time was the St George's Day gala, last year.'

'What did you do that time?'

'Nothing. That's the point. The queen ignored me.'

His uncle leaned forward, an earnest look in his eye. 'Well, we're going to prepare you. By the time you reach your majority, the queen will love you as if you were her own dearest son.'

Robert doubted it. 'I have a lot to learn.'

Bright yellow daffodils announced the start of spring, and they all joined in the work to prepare the walled gardens for the new season's planting. Robert's hands blistered as he dug the hard earth, but he breathed fresh country air, and the muscles in his arms grew firmer.

He heard his name called and turned to see Anthony Bagot with a letter in his hand. He stuck his spade into the freshly turned soil and took the letter, frowning as he recognised Master Broughton's seal. He opened it. After the usual formalities came the news Robert had known was coming.

Elizabeth Cecil had been married to William Wentworth in February. He'd secretly prayed Elizabeth's mother might encourage Lord Burghley to see sense, but now that last glimmer of hope was snuffed out, and his heart hardened against the Cecil family.

Bagot gave him a curious look. 'Bad news?'

'No.' He'd been more guarded since he knew the truth about Bagot. 'Nothing I wasn't expecting.' He thrust the letter into his pocket, and returned to his digging.

He recalled Master Wright's advice. He could have his pick of the queen's young ladies, although he doubted he would allow any as close as Elizabeth Cecil. He'd told his uncle he had a lot to learn, but he'd been taught more about the world since arriving at Lamphey than in all his years at Cambridge.

Gelly Meyrick showed him how to set a snare and skin a rabbit, and his uncle gave him lessons in how to fire a gun. One day he would buy a pair of the expensive new wheel lock pistols, which could be fired with one hand. In the meantime, he practised with his uncle's terrifying old arquebus. The blast from the powerful gun made his ears ring, but his aim was improving.

Master Wright had been teaching him the mysteries of court etiquette, and how men of influence used the rules of law and politics to their own advantage. Robert found he enjoyed learning everything he could about the queen and those around her.

Master Wright produced a deck of playing cards, and placed

a queen, three kings and three knaves on the desk in front of them. He tapped his finger on the queen of diamonds. 'A lonely queen, even though she surrounds herself with ladies, and has three kings.'

Robert smiled at Master Wright's game. 'I'll bet Lord Burghley is the king of spades. He acts as if he is her king – but I've no idea who the other two are.'

'The royal palaces are full of spies, listening to the most innocent gossip, and reporting back to the queen.' Master Wright lowered his voice, as if they might be overheard. 'At the centre of this web is the queen's spymaster, her principal secretary, Sir Francis Walsingham.' He tapped his finger on the king of clubs.

'Then I must take care what I say, and to whom.' Robert thought it seemed easy enough.

'The spy might be the serving girl who smiles at you as she refills your glass of wine. It's thought Walsingham has an informant in the household of every courtier. You can be sure at least one of your mother's servants is on Francis Walsingham's payroll.'

'Why would the queen care what my mother has to say? Is it not enough that she's banished from court for doing nothing wrong?'

'Your mother married the queen's favourite without her consent.' He gave Robert a wry look. 'You must learn from that, and not make the same mistake.'

'Is the king of hearts Sir Robert Dudley?'

'Well done. I used to think the rumours that she loved him were nonsense – but look at how he's survived unscathed, and as important as ever.'

Robert tapped the three knaves. 'I'll guess one of these is Philip Sidney. My father said he was destined for great things. He wanted my sister Penelope to marry him.'

'Right again. He's a good man – perhaps too good for the royal court.' He tapped the knave of spades. 'This is someone else you know. Robert Cecil.'

'I should have remembered. Elizabeth told me once that her brother was being prepared to take his father's place.'

'That only leaves the knave of diamonds.'

'I have no idea...'

Master Wright picked up the card and laid it alongside the queen. 'The only one of the same suit as Her Majesty.' He smiled. 'It's you, of course. The son she never had.'

Robert breathed fresh sea air and looked over his shoulder to see Gelly chasing behind. He urged his new horse into a brisk gallop as they raced across the deserted foreshore of Freshwater East. A gift for his sixteenth birthday from his stepfather, his horse was a fine charger, bred and trained for stamina. He'd named him Perseus, and made the short ride from Lamphey Court to the secluded beach most days.

'An easy win!' he called out to Gelly, and allowed his horse to amble in the surf, tasting the salt spray, as another rolling wave broke against the shore.

Gelly joined him at the water's edge and grinned. 'He's fast, I give you that one.'

Robert patted his horse. 'I've been thinking I'd like to learn how to joust. My sister Penelope said the queen enjoys watching a tournament.'

'I'll make a tiltyard in the meadow field.' Gelly looked thoughtful as they rode back home. 'You'll need a lance, and armour.'

'I can fashion a lance easily enough from a young pine tree –

and my stepfather might be persuaded to buy me some armour. I shall write to him.'

Gelly agreed. 'We should build a quintain. All you need is a weighted sack that swings round when you hit it, and whacks you in the head!'

Robert left Gelly to take the horses to the stables, and went to consult Robert Wright about the wording of a letter to his stepfather. He found him working in his study, sorting through the letters recently arrived from London.

He looked up at Robert as he entered, his face unusually serious. 'There's some sad news from London. I'm afraid William Wentworth has died.'

It took Robert a moment to recall the name. 'Elizabeth Cecil's husband?'

Robert Wright nodded. 'I don't know the details, only that it was at Theobalds, and quite unexpected.'

'Do you know how Elizabeth is?'

'I imagine she's devastated. I understand she is carrying his child.'

Robert had done his best to put Elizabeth from his mind. He'd flirted with Bethan, his uncle's attractive young scullery maid, and she encouraged him with her smiles. But the news rekindled old feelings and now he hoped there might be a chance of seeing Elizabeth again. This time, he would not keep his feelings secret.

He could raise the child as his own, and was even prepared to forgive Elizabeth's father. It might mean having to return to Theobalds, but he might persuade her to come to Lamphey Court. All thoughts of writing to his stepfather were forgotten as he rehearsed his letter of condolence.

. . .

Robert had to wait for some time before Elizabeth Cecil's reply, and was disappointed to see how formally she thanked him for his condolences on the sudden and unexpected death of her husband. Then a glimmer of hope. Elizabeth explained she was in her confinement, so it would not be possible for him to visit Theobalds, for now. The promise of her last two words set Robert's pulse racing, and under Elizabeth's confident signature was her secret mark for a kiss.

He spent hours wording his reply, stopping short of promising to care for her unborn child as if it were his own, but hinting as much. Elizabeth hadn't offered any clue about when the birth was expected, but Robert had time on his side. He would reach the age of majority next November, and now he had much to look forward to.

6

APRIL 1583

Robert wrote to his younger sister as he'd promised, inviting Dorothy to join him at Lamphey. He'd been unsurprised when she didn't reply, and imagined his letter was intercepted by her guardian, Sir Henry Hastings. Dorothy told him how Katherine, Countess of Huntingdon, was determined to marry her off.

The last thing he'd expected was a messenger to arrive one afternoon with a formal invitation to dine with Lady Dorothy Perrot at Carew Castle, only four miles north-east of Lamphey Court. His uncle read the note and looked equally surprised.

'Your sister has married Sir John Perrot's son.' He frowned. 'I've known John Perrot for years, but never trusted him. He claims to be one of old King Henry's bastard sons. I doubt it, but he has the luck of the devil. He was a companion to young King Edward, and carried the canopy at the queen's coronation.'

Robert had heard of their neighbours the Perrots, although he'd never met them. 'Didn't they serve with my father in Ireland?'

'Sir John Perrot caused no end of trouble by hanging over eight hundred Irishmen as rebels.' His uncle scowled at the memory. 'His son Thomas is a hothead. The last I heard of him, he'd been thrown into the Fleet prison for challenging Sir Walter Raleigh to a duel.'

'It would be typical of Dorothy to marry someone like that. She would do it just to spite her guardian.'

Robert's uncle agreed to accompany him on the short ride to the village of Carew. The river in front of the castle had been dammed to create a large millpond. Home to a pair of mute swans, the still water reflected the high, mullioned windows of the castle as Robert approached.

An impressive tiltyard filled the field adjacent to the castle. Much better than Gelly's makeshift tiltyard at Lamphey Court. Long red banners streamed in the light breeze, and canvas canopies protected the raised wooden viewing stands.

His uncle turned in his saddle. 'Sir Thomas Perrot is an accomplished jouster. He's made quite a name for himself, competing in the royal tournaments.'

Robert brightened. 'Do you think he might be persuaded to teach me to joust?'

His uncle shrugged. 'Jousting in tournaments is a dangerous pastime, best left to the experts.'

A steward in red-and-gold livery led them through a gatehouse to the great hall, where Dorothy waited to greet them with her new husband, a sharp-eyed man with a pointed black beard. Dorothy looked happier to Robert than she had in York, and older than her nineteen years, in an emerald satin gown with a high lace collar.

'Welcome to Carew.' She smiled, as if enjoying the look on Robert's face. 'This is my husband, Sir Thomas Perrot.'

Robert removed his hat and shook hands with Sir Thomas. 'Congratulations, Sir Thomas. I believe you knew our father?'

Sir Thomas nodded. 'A good man.'

'You also know our uncle, Master George Devereux?'

'Of course, we've been neighbours for some years.' He

smiled. 'Pembrokeshire is a small enough county. We all know each other.'

Dorothy smiled at her uncle. 'You remind me of our father.'

'And you have your mother's spirit, to defy the queen.'

She looked surprised. 'Has word reached here already?'

Her uncle shook his head. 'A lucky guess.'

'It wasn't so lucky for us.' Dorothy glanced at her husband. 'Tom was locked up again in the Fleet.'

Sir Thomas looked unconcerned. 'A token punishment, that's all. Better the Fleet prison than the Tower, thank God. There are mostly debtors in the Fleet, so the jailers were easy enough to bribe to ensure I was treated well.' He gestured to a servant to bring wine. 'Come through to the parlour, and we can tell you what happened.'

Robert was surprised how small the parlour was for such a large castle, but the beeswax candles gave it a warm aroma of honey. His chair was comfortable, and covered with dark-red velvet. Sir Thomas noticed Robert looking at the Perrot coat of arms – a red shield with three golden pears.

'The Carew estate was granted to my ancestor, Sir Stephen Perrot, as reward for helping William the Conqueror win the Battle of Hastings.' He smiled. 'Sir Stephen married the daughter of Marchion ap Rice, Prince of South Wales, so my father likes to say we are the last true Welsh royalty.'

A dark-eyed serving girl filled their glasses with wine while they washed their fingers and dried them on linen towels. A servant brought a simple meal of cured ham, and several different cheeses, with trenchers of manchet bread, still warm from the oven.

Robert's uncle cut a slice of ham with his knife. 'Tell me, how did you two meet?'

'My sister Penelope was the matchmaker.' Dorothy smiled. 'I

was new to court, and totally in awe of the queen, so Penelope took me under her wing.'

Sir Thomas helped himself to a slice of ham and passed the platter to Robert. 'I was visiting my father when your sister caught my eye.' He smiled. 'Our family motto is *Amo ut invenio*. I love as I find. I warned Dorothy she'd be married off soon enough, no doubt to someone twice her age and even worse than Lord Rich!'

Robert sipped his wine. 'I don't understand why you didn't ask the queen's permission to marry, after what happened to our mother.'

Dorothy gave Robert a conspiratorial look. 'Her Majesty always seems to be in a bad mood – and shouts at her ladies for no good reason.' Her eyes twinkled and she glanced at Sir Thomas. 'I didn't want to risk her refusal.'

Robert frowned. 'Why would she refuse?'

Sir Thomas glanced at Dorothy. 'I had better explain. The problem is, I have no money of my own, and live on a small allowance from my father. Dorothy's guardian made it clear she thought she could do better.'

'We ran away, and married in secret.' Dorothy made it sound easy, but Robert suspected it had taken courage, given the consequences.

'Our chaplain warned us of the great risk we were taking.' Sir Thomas shook his head. 'The poor fellow was locked up in the Fleet prison with me for his troubles.'

Robert's uncle turned to Dorothy. 'So now you are also banished from court?'

Dorothy nodded. 'I appealed to Lord Burghley, and he persuaded the queen to free my husband, and our chaplain, on condition we remain here in Carew.'

Robert laughed and raised his glass in a toast. 'Well, here's to your new life in Wales.'

Sir Philip Sidney cantered into Lamphey on a magnificent white stallion, at the head of four yeomen and his travelling household, like the commander of an invading army. Handsome, heroic and charming, he'd been a frequent and welcome visitor to Chartley Manor, and was everything Robert aspired to become.

Robert's father had taken Philip Sidney on his campaign to Ireland, and said he was like a son to him. Master Wright told Robert that Philip Sidney had been knighted in January, not for what he'd done, but because the queen wished it.

'My Lord Essex!' His voice rang out across the courtyard as he spotted Robert. 'I've come to teach you how to joust!'

Robert grinned. 'How did you know?'

'Your uncle wrote to me, and said I'd best come soon before you did yourself an injury.' He swung easily from his saddle, as if he'd not ridden any distance, and gestured towards his yeomen. 'I've brought swordsmen and musketeers.' He slapped Robert on the back. 'I shall show you how to use a pistol and, between us, we'll make a soldier of you.'

Supper turned into a special occasion to honour their guests. Lady Dorothy and Sir Thomas Perrot were invited from Carew Castle, and Gelly sent for musicians from Pembroke, with the offer of as much beer as they could drink.

Bagot helped to slaughter and roast a whole pig, which took most of the day to cook, and Robert's uncle opened a cask of red wine from the undercroft. His chaplain, Rhys Prichard, said grace, and the musicians struck up a lively tune. The roasted pig, sizzling on the spit, was carried in by Gelly and Bagot, to cheers and applause.

Philip Sidney stood to propose a toast, and raised his glass of wine. 'To the memory of our dear departed friend, father and brother, Sir Walter Devereux.'

Platters of hot pork in a rich sauce were followed by a crusty dove pie and baked fish, fresh from the Lamphey fishponds. Even their long-suffering cook seemed charmed by the presence of Sir Philip Sidney. She served sugared fruits, which she only prepared for special occasions, with comfits of ginger and spice.

Robert's uncle turned to Sir Philip. 'We've not had letters or visitors for some weeks – what's the latest news from London?'

'There's sweating sickness in the city again, with the usual panic and disorder, so I was glad to come to Wales.' Sir Philip smiled. 'The best news is that I'm betrothed to be married to Lady Frances, the sixteen-year-old daughter of Sir Francis Walsingham.'

Sir Thomas Perrot raised his glass. 'Congratulations, Sir Philip – and do *you* have Her Majesty's approval?'

'I would have to say Her Majesty's *grudging* approval.' He smiled. 'My forthcoming marriage unites my uncle, Sir Robert Dudley,' he nodded to Robert and Dorothy, 'your stepfather, with Her Majesty's private secretary. It seems the queen dislikes the thought of us rallying together – but there is nothing she can do about it.'

Robert's uncle laughed at the thought. 'What of our friend, Lord Burghley? Did he not try to secure you for his own daughter once?'

'He did. Anne Cecil, the one that got away.' A hint of regret echoed in his voice. 'We were engaged, but she married Edward de Vere.' He gave Robert's uncle a wry smile. 'That turned out well.'

'The Earl of Oxford was lucky to be released from the Tower. I for one would have bet against his chances, yet I heard he's reconciled with Lady Anne.'

'That may be so, but Lord Burghley looks a beaten man, and there's talk he'll hand over to his son sooner than he'd planned.'

'Why is that, Sir Philip?' Robert was curious. 'Is Lord Burghley ill?'

Sir Philip took another drink of wine and his face became serious. 'He recently lost his youngest daughter, Elizabeth, in childbirth, and it's left him bereft.'

Gelly's musicians played a melodic Welsh folk tune, while Robert stared at Sir Philip in disbelief. He heard his uncle ask the fate of the child, and saw Sir Philip shake his head. The music gave it all a surreal, dreamlike quality. Robert muttered an excuse and stumbled into the cold night air, Sir Philip's words echoing in his head. He wept for Elizabeth until the tears would come no more.

Robert threw himself into his military training with a ferocity that alarmed them all. He fought with the long, narrow rapier until his sword arm ached and sweat ran into his eyes. Sir Philip watched with the critical eye of an expert swordsman, and shouted advice.

'Watch your guard!' He shook his head as his yeoman scored yet another point. 'When you use a rapier to lunge against someone, it's not just to kill them. You have to defend yourself at the same time.' He stepped forward to demonstrate. 'The lunge is fast, but leaves you vulnerable. The pass keeps you upright, and in a strong position. Strike, and parry your opponent's blade with a single action!'

Robert learned to use the rapier in one hand, with a basilard – a double-edged, long-bladed dagger – in the other. He practised the feints and cuts of swordfighters, sometimes against two opponents at once, over and again until he didn't have to think about it. The secret was in the footwork, which had to become instinctive.

'Don't put your left foot forward – it reduces the coverage of the sword to your body, and means you can't lunge. See how much easier it is? With your right foot forward, you can lunge and pass.'

The flintlock pistols were harder to use with accuracy than the new musket Sir Philip brought with him. Robert learned to reload and prime them quickly, but cursed when his shots went wide of the mark. Sir Philip's musketeer, a thick-bearded man with dark eyes, who'd fought in Ireland, took one of the pistols and reloaded it.

'Have a firm grip with your hand, and place your feet in a good stance, like this. Don't try any tricks like holding your breath or closing one eye.' He brought up the pistol, his arm outstretched. 'The slower you pull the trigger, the better your shot will be.' He fired, his bullet smashing the earthenware pot Robert was using as a target.

Most afternoons were spent at the tiltyard. Gelly helped Robert fasten the leather straps and buckles of the armour sent from London by Sir Robert Dudley. They'd spent hours taking measurements, but when the armour arrived it consisted of a collection of mismatched pieces. The old steel breastplate was dented and scored, and the helm restricted his vision, but the gauntlets had seen little use, and were a good fit.

Sir Philip had come to see Robert's progress. 'Men often fail to score a hit due to poor control of their lances – or lack of determination. Keep your eyes fixed on your opponent until the point of impact.'

Robert took his words to heart, and charged down their makeshift tiltyard with a reckless disregard for his own safety. More by luck than judgement, he struck his opponent in the shoulder, shattering the tip of his lance in a spray of sharp splinters. The yeoman called for assistance, and cursed as he pulled off his helmet.

Sir Philip gave Robert a stern look as he took the reins of his horse, and glanced back at his yeoman. 'Jousting is for show. No one needs to be injured for the amusement of the court, or to entertain the crowds.'

Robert didn't tell him that the shock of the impact had numbed his arm up to the shoulder. He took off his gauntlets and helmet, and frowned as he ran his fingers through his hair. 'I thought we were making me into a soldier.'

'We are – but not at the cost of my men.' Sir Philip patted Robert's horse. 'You ride well, and show real promise, but you must learn to control your aggression, or it will be your downfall.'

The day before he left, Sir Philip accompanied Robert on his regular ride to Freshwater East. The tranquil, slate-grey sea sparkled in the early morning sunshine, as if sprinkled with shimmering diamonds. A flock of orange-beaked oystercatchers took to the wing with their shrill, high-pitched whistle as they heard the thump of pounding hooves.

The beach always raised his spirits, but now Robert saw it as desolate and empty, like his life at Lamphey. A gull pecked at a dead crab, washed up on the sand. He'd learned a lot in a short time from Sir Philip Sidney and his men; when they left he would struggle to keep improving.

Sir Philip brought his horse to a stop, and turned in the saddle. 'You seem troubled. What do you plan to do with your life?'

Robert shrugged, then decided to confess the truth. 'I once

thought I might marry Elizabeth Cecil, and settle down to have a family.'

'I'm sorry.' Sir Philip frowned. 'I didn't know you were close.'

'No one knew.'

Sir Philip nodded in understanding. 'I was supposed to marry your sister Penelope, and had your father's blessing ... but it was not to be.'

'How is Penelope?'

'Lady Penelope Rich has become a favourite of the queen, and lights up the court like a bright star in a winter sky.' He smiled at the thought. 'Your father would have been proud of her.'

'I worried about her when she married Lord Rich. I hope he treats her well?'

Sir Philip gave a scornful laugh. 'Lord Rich doesn't have any idea what he's taken on. Penelope moved in with your mother to avoid him, and has her own life now – at her husband's expense.'

'I might visit them in London. I'm eighteen in November, but don't inherit until I'm twenty-two. Once I have money of my own I want to travel, and see the Continent.'

'I was about your age when I first went to Paris.' Sir Philip stared out to sea, as if remembering a different time. 'I had no idea what I was letting myself in for.'

'What happened?'

'I was with the Protestant Huguenots during the marriage celebrations of Henry of Navarre and Margaret of Valois.' He frowned. 'A Huguenot leader, Admiral Gaspard de Coligny, was shot and wounded. He only lost a finger, but the Huguenots demanded justice. We heard church bells ringing at midnight, too early for matins. Later we learned the bells were the signal for the massacre of thousands of Huguenots.'

'By the Catholics?'

'By the French king's mercenaries. They knew they were setting a spark to dry tinder. The Catholics had been waiting for their chance to crush the Huguenots. They stabbed the admiral in his bed, and cut off his head. The atrocities spread through Paris, then France, like a wildfire.' He glanced at Robert. 'Wars of religion are the worst kind. Men were executed without trial, the women raped and murdered.'

'Were you involved in the fighting?'

Sir Philip shook his head. 'There was nothing I could do – in fact, I was lucky to escape. My future father-in-law, Sir Francis Walsingham, served as ambassador to France at the time, and had to run for his life.'

'Do you still think it's a good idea for me to visit the Continent?'

'I do.' He smiled. 'Just take care who you trust – and who you choose to become acquainted with.'

Robert wondered if Sir Philip had somehow learned of his flirting with Bethan. His uncle warned him to be discreet, yet the attractive young maid encouraged his attention. It was impossible to keep anything secret in Lamphey – and now he'd lost Elizabeth, he cared less about the consequences.

7

MAY 1584

Robert's uncle rode at his side on the familiar road to Carew under a cloudless, cornflower-blue sky. Pale yellow primroses and purple-pink foxgloves brightened the hedgerows, and the rhythmic clip-clop of iron-shod hooves mixed with the soft bleating of spring lambs.

Behind them rode Gelly, carrying the flag of St George, and Bagot with the Essex banner. His uncle's maidservant, Bethan, rode at the side of Robert's Irish groom, Tom White, who drove the wagon laden with their tent, a keg of ale, freshly baked bread and oatcakes. The long lances, painted in the Essex orange and white, lashed to the side, were a clue to the purpose of their outing.

Wearing a scarlet cape over his jousting armour, Robert was appearing in public as the Earl of Essex for the first time since he'd come of age, and wished to look the part. He'd borrowed his uncle's sword, and also wore his silver dagger at his belt.

The Carew May Day tourney attracted spectators from all over the county, and offered Robert his chance to show what he'd achieved with the long hours of practice. He smiled as he heard the lively music of fiddle players. The shrill shouts of excited children and the scent of woodsmoke from cooking fires reached them before they saw the tournament field.

His uncle turned in his saddle as they approached.

'Remember Sir Philip Sidney's advice.'

Robert grinned. 'Not to kill anyone?'

His uncle smiled. 'Whenever I believe you've grown from a boy to a man, you like to prove me wrong.'

'I'll not forget Sir Philip's training. They've come for entertainment, and that's what they shall have.'

The tournament field was decorated with banners and bunting, and the crowd cheered as Robert and his retinue paraded past the tiered viewing stands. Robert raised a hand in salute to his sister Dorothy, seated with a group of young ladies in colourful silk gowns.

One of the ladies caught his eye and smiled. She looked about his age, and he felt an unexpected frisson of attraction. He returned her smile, and saw her turn and say something to his sister. He still missed Elizabeth and resolved to choose his own wife, and not allow a match to be forced upon him.

He made his way to the row of canvas tents in the competitors' area, where Sir Thomas Perrot greeted him.

'Are you ready to defend the honour of Lamphey, Lord Essex?'

Robert laughed. This was all part of the show, and he called out, over the noise of the music, so everyone could hear. 'I trust *you* are ready for a new challenger, Sir Thomas!'

Gelly and Bagot hammered in the wooden pegs and soon had their tent ready, with a seat and table, and the Essex banners planted each side of the entrance. Robert handed Perseus over to Tom White to be caparisoned in orange and white. Bethan poured him a cup of ale, and he took a drink while Gelly checked the buckles on the leather straps securing his armour.

His uncle appeared at the entrance to the tent. 'Best mount up when you're ready. They're waiting for you.' He gave Robert a look of concern. 'Take care. I'll count it as a good result if you stay in the saddle.'

Robert mounted Perseus, who looked magnificent in his flowing caparison, reaching close to the ground. Tom led him to the grassed arena in front of the stands, where the other riders were assembled. Gelly followed as Robert's squire, carrying the first of the long wooden lances over his shoulder, and they stopped to listen as the herald called out the rules.

'Each rider will charge up to four times with lances, and only three lances are allowed. If there is no decisive winner, the judges will vote, giving points for skill and accuracy, making deductions for foul strokes.'

The order of riding had been chosen by lots, so Robert had the chance to assess his competitors while waiting his turn. Most made the mistake of riding too slowly, dipping their lance and raising it too late to make contact. The crowd didn't seem to mind, cheering each failed pass with the same enthusiasm.

Robert was grateful his first ride was against the son of a merchant from Haverfordwest, rather than an experienced man like Sir Thomas Perrot. He rode to the end of the tilt rail and fastened his helmet. Gelly handed him his lance and wished him luck. The eye slit in his helmet meant he had to turn his head to see the herald's signal, then he charged.

The months of rehearsal for this moment meant his lance was firmly couched under his arm. Perseus had never galloped faster, and Robert thundered down the list, repeating Sir Philip Sidney's advice: *Keep your eyes fixed on your opponent until the point of impact.*

His lance struck the other rider and shattered into splinters on impact. Gelly had spent hours sawing part way through the tip, and hiding the cuts with paint. The result must have looked convincing, as the crowd erupted with a roar of applause.

Robert's second pass was another clean hit, breaking the tip of his second lance, so now he only had one remaining. He frowned as he realised his final opponent was Sir Thomas Perrot. He'd watched as his brother-in-law unhorsed one rider and injured a second when his lance struck a glancing blow on the man's helmet.

Gelly handed him his final lance. 'I've saved the best until last.' He smiled 'The balance is perfect.'

Robert peered through the slit in his helmet and saw Sir Thomas signal that he was ready. Taking a firm grip on his lance, he spurred Perseus into a charge, and raced forward. The sharp crack made the crowd gasp as Sir Thomas's lance smashed into his shoulder, twisting him backwards in the saddle.

Robert's arm went numb, and he cursed at the shock of the impact. He dropped his lance in surrender and Gelly rushed forward to bring Perseus to a stop. Robert's shoulder throbbed as the feeling returned, but the crowd were on their feet again, cheering. Gelly took his gauntlets and helmet, and handed Robert a cloth to wipe the sweat from his eyes.

'Well done, my lord.'

'I lost.' Robert looked back to see Sir Thomas being awarded the champion's ribbon by Dorothy.

'That's what I mean, my lord.' Gelly grinned. 'You let him win. Sir Philip Sidney would be proud of you.'

Robert rubbed his aching shoulder and smiled. He would have liked to win, but Gelly was right. This was the best result, for now, and no one would think any less of him for losing to Sir

Thomas Perrot, a more experienced rider. He'd moved one step closer to competing in a royal tournament for the queen, but when the time came he would give no quarter.

Robert woke to the metallic click of the latch on his door, and sensed a shadowy figure standing in the doorway. He sat up in bed and rubbed his eyes. He had no idea of the hour, but a sliver of moon sent a shaft of yellow light through the leaded window.

'Who's there?' His first thought was that someone was playing a trick on him. 'Show yourself.'

He hardly recognised the woman who stepped into the moonlight. Instead of being tightly braided under a linen coif, Bethan's long auburn hair flowed around her shoulders, and her dark-brown eyes sparkled with mischief.

'I wanted to thank you for taking me to the tourney, my lord.' She closed the door behind her, the scrape of the bolt an unmistakable sign.

Robert lay back on his comfortable bed, his pulse racing as he watched her unfasten the lacing at the front of her woollen gown. He'd dreamed of this, yet now he didn't know what to do or say. He pulled back the coverlet of his bed.

Bethan understood his invitation. She took off her gown, then pulled off her thin cotton shift, standing naked for a moment, before climbing into his bed. She stroked her hand over his chest and frowned when she saw his bruised shoulder. 'Does it hurt?'

'I'll live.' He smiled as he turned on to his side and looked into her eyes. 'I must confess, you are more beautiful than I could ever have imagined.'

She raised an eyebrow. 'Do you imagine me often, my lord?'

'All the time.'

She laughed, and kissed him with a longing that took his breath away.

Robert lay awake with Bethan sleeping in his arms. He'd had no idea how wonderful it would be, or how easily she could seduce him. He'd seen the coupling of horses in the field, and laughed at the stable boy's lewd talk, but no one ever told him why men risk everything for love.

He stroked Bethan's long hair away from her face, and wondered what the future could hold for them. He caressed the soft, flawless skin of her back, and remembered Master Wright telling him he could have his pick of the young ladies at court. They'd formed a special bond, and she'd opened his eyes to a whole new world of possibilities. He still had a lot to learn, but she would be a willing teacher.

'Don't you think it's time you showed your face at court?' Master Wright held up the stern letter which had arrived from Robert's mother. She made it clear she thought he was wasting his life in Lamphey, and should start to make a name for himself.

'In truth, I don't want to.' Robert smiled. 'I'm happy here in Wales, and don't miss the noise and dirt of London. I shall wait until I'm twenty-two and have my inheritance. I don't want my stepfather's charity.'

'Do you remember what I said when your mother married Sir Robert?' Master Wright used a tutor's trick, and held the silence to force him to answer.

Robert frowned. Their time at Trinity seemed a long time ago, but he had a good memory. 'You quoted Epictetus, and told me to make the best use of what is in my power.'

Master Wright gave Robert a kindly smile. 'You must reply to your mother, and thank her.'

Robert grudgingly took the quill and ink from Master Wright and retired to a quiet corner of the library to gather his thoughts. He had nothing to lose, and hoped he might see his sister Penelope. She hadn't written to him for a year but, then, he'd not written to anyone, and the thought of Wat alone in York troubled him.

He took a sheet of parchment and began formally, as he'd been taught: *My very good Lady and Mother*. He read his mother's letter again, and couldn't ignore her insistent tone. He dipped the quill in fresh ink and wrote.

'*If I find by your ladyship's displeasure conceived that I am thought in sort to have offended, so I desire to deliver myself, either wholly or in some part from the same fault. The which some will hardly term undutifulness to your ladyship, others carefulness of my own good.*'

He thought of Master Wright's admonishment. It seemed unfair, yet he hadn't written to his mother, or anyone, for as long as he could remember. Robert frowned with the unfamiliar effort of appeasing his demanding mother, and dipped his pen in fresh ink.

'*Many think me inconsiderate, in not making your ladyship more acquainted with my determinations. The name of undutifulness as a son I utterly abhor, my purposed course to do well I hope shall deliver me from the suspicion of carefulness of mine own estate, and if in your ladyship's wise censure I be thought inconsiderate, I plead as a young man pardon for that fault whereto of all others our age is most subject.*'

He read his letter through as he waited for the ink to dry, then took it to show Master Wright, who tutted as he read. 'Do you think this letter will result in an invitation to London?'

'My mother writes to me as if I were a foolish boy.' Robert

smiled. 'She must have good reason to demand my return after so long.'

'We shall see.' Master Wright handed the letter back. 'I should like to accompany you, if you go to London.'

'You are most welcome. I should take my household, such as it is, and you as the master of it.'

He dipped his quill in ink and signed his letter. '*Humbly craving your ladyship's blessing, I daily pray for your ladyship's most honourable and happy estate. Your most obedient son.*'

The reply, when it came, was a summons from Sir Robert Dudley, which turned the peaceful world of Lamphey Court upside down. Robert's father-in-law proposed to present him to the queen, and sent a messenger with the funds for the journey to London.

He was invited to stay with his mother at her house in the Strand and, as well as Master Wright, Robert decided to take Gelly, Anthony Bagot and Tom White, as his travelling household. He found his uncle in his study and explained his plan.

'I am grateful for everything you've done for me, Uncle, and when I've settled, I hope to return.'

His uncle smiled. 'I shall miss you, Robert. Lamphey will be a good deal quieter once you're gone.'

'I hope to travel, and visit the Continent, when I can. Would you come with me?'

'It would be an honour.' His uncle seemed to reach a decision. 'It will not be long before you inherit. As you know, I'm a man of limited means, so I wondered—'

'I shall do whatever I can for you, Uncle.'

'I was thinking we could combine households. I'll miss Gelly and Bagot – and would you have a place for my chaplain, Rhys Prichard?'

Robert nodded. 'He's a good man, and is welcome.'

'What about Bethan?'

Robert's face reddened. He'd never discussed his poorly kept secret with his uncle. His affair with Bethan had soon become common knowledge, like everything within the walls of Lamphey Court. 'I worry about unfairly raising her expectations.'

'Well, she won't be the first, and I'm sure she won't be the last, but you should be a gentleman and speak to her before you leave.'

He'd never asked her to walk with him to Freshwater before, but he wanted to talk without the risk of being overheard. They followed the twisting bridle path through the woods until the sea came into view, glittering in the sunshine.

They'd arrived at low tide, and walked out on the golden sand until they reached the water's edge. The sea reflected the blue sky, and a small fishing boat sat at anchor. Bethan cursed as an incoming wave soaked the hem of her gown.

Robert put his arm around her slender waist, the first time he'd dared to, as there was no one to see. 'You know I could never marry you.'

'I know.' She stared out to sea. 'And I know you can't take me to London.'

'I shall have to live with my mother, until I have my inheritance.'

'Do you think you'll come back to Lamphey?' She wiped a tear from her cheek.

The glimmer of hope in her eyes troubled Robert's conscience. 'I shall miss you, Bethan.' He held her close. 'I've never been happier than here at Lamphey, but it's time to go and seek my fortune.'

Sir Robert Dudley welcomed them to Leicester House in the Strand, but he looked tired, and his face was grim. 'I'm afraid your mother isn't here. She's at our house in Wanstead, caring for our son. Your sister, Penelope, is with her.'

Robert couldn't ignore the haunted look in his stepfather's eyes. 'I'm sorry to hear your son is unwell.'

Sir Robert nodded. 'I fear it's serious. Our physicians are at a loss, so all we can do is pray for his recovery.' He studied Robert for a moment. 'I will help you prepare for your audience with Her Majesty. In the meantime, there is ample accommodation for you and your household here.'

'Thank you.' Robert took a deep breath. 'I'm afraid I shall need more funds for my expenses—'

'Of course. We must buy you doublets and coats. I want you to look your best for our meeting with the queen.'

Gelly accompanied Robert to visit his stepfather's tailors in Cheapside, a short walk from the Strand. The wide street of Cheapside ran east–west between the Great Conduit at the foot of Old Jewry to the grand cathedral of St Paul's, and was lined with impressive buildings up to five stories tall.

Robert had never seen so many shops, with open shopfronts set out with attractive displays of luxury goods, from Venetian glass to Flemish tapestries. He stopped to try on a pair of Italian leather riding boots. They fitted him perfectly, and he decided to buy them. This was the first time he'd been able to explore the city with money in his purse, and he resolved to make the most of it.

The tailor's shop was one of the grandest, with dark wood-panelled walls and a colourful display of satins and silks. The tailor, an elderly man with a white beard and a foreign accent, measured Robert and took notes of his requirements.

'I shall make you the talk of London, my lord.'

'I don't want to appear too extravagant.' Robert frowned as he thought what his grandfather would say.

The tailor held his hands up in the air. 'You are tall and, if I may, my lord, quite striking in appearance. You will stand out at court whatever you wear,' his voice became conspiratorial, 'but you will be judged by the quality of your doublet, particularly by Her Majesty.' He opened a drawer and took out a button, which he dropped into Robert's hand. 'Silver. You'll need three dozen for a doublet.'

Robert rolled the silver button in his hand. 'Can you make me a doublet with wide sleeves and matching breeches from silver cloth?'

The tailor smiled and called for one of his assistants to bring a roll of cloth of silver.

'I have to tell you this is expensive, but will make you a doublet fit for a prince.'

'Perfect.' Robert felt the thickness of the material. Light yet strong, the cloth glittered with a silvery sheen. He chose black velvet for a second doublet, a fashionable ruff of Belgian lace, two pairs of kidskin gloves and a new cape, trimmed with gold braid. He also had Gelly measured for a new doublet, and told the tailor to charge the lot to the Earl of Leicester's account.

They turned down a lane towards the river, bustling with wherries and barges, and followed the road along the riverbank until they reached the Tower of London. Robert stared in fascination at the White Tower, still dominating the London skyline more than five hundred years after it was built by William the Conqueror.

A low roar greeted them as they approached. Robert turned to Gelly. 'Let's see the animals.'

'I heard you have to bring a chicken or a rabbit for the lions.' Gelly gave him a wry look.

Robert patted the purse of coins at his belt. 'We shall have the guided tour.'

They crossed the bridge over the dark-green moat and spoke to the yeoman guard at the gate, who called for the animal keeper. Robert paid them both, and followed the man down stone steps into an underground dungeon. The stale air carried a musky scent, and a deep growl startled him as a lion appeared at the bars, its fangs bared.

Robert studied the lioness as she skulked in the darkest corner of the cell. The creature's golden fur was matted, and he sensed her unhappiness.

Gelly turned to the keeper. 'Are the animals caged like this all the time?'

The keeper nodded. 'It's good enough for lords of the realm.'

Robert frowned at the thought, and resolved never to cross the queen. He'd heard the stories. Too many good men and women had vanished into the misery of the Tower dungeons. Even those who were lucky enough to be released were never quite the same again.

When they returned to Leicester House his stepfather's secretary was waiting for them. 'Lady Leicester sent for your stepfather, my lord. He had to leave straight away.'

Robert frowned 'Is it about his son?'

His stepfather's secretary nodded. 'I'm afraid it is, my lord. Your mother said it was most urgent.'

Master Richard Broughton, as the family lawyer, had the duty to bring the bad news. He wore a black gown, and had put on weight since they'd last met, and his face looked grim.

'The wheel of Fortune turns again, my lord. I must report the tragic death of your half-brother, Robert Dudley, Baron Denbigh.'

Robert sat in silence for a moment before replying. 'My mother must be devastated.'

'She *might* still have another male child, but she's forty-one. Quite frankly, I doubt it.'

'Does that make me Sir Robert Dudley's heir?'

Master Broughton raised an eyebrow in surprise. 'That would be his nephew, Sir Philip Sidney, and your inheritance will depend what provisions your stepfather has made in his will. But, *ceteris paribus*, you would do well to stay on the right side of your stepfather.'

'Should I visit my mother, or write to send my condolences?'

'It's not for me to say, my lord, but I understand your mother is in mourning at your grandfather's house.'

Robert frowned. 'I don't believe I could face staying with them at Greys Court, or living here at Leicester House at my stepfather's expense.'

'What do you plan to do?'

'If you can secure the funds, I would prefer to return to Lamphey for a while, then visit my brother in York, before committing to life at court.'

Master Broughton seemed to understand. 'I'll do what I can, but be sure to write to your mother – and your stepfather.'

Robert's uncle welcomed him, yet questioned his sudden return. 'I trust you've come back for the right reasons?'

'I couldn't wait to return to Wales.'

'Could it be because of Bethan?'

'I confess I had little choice, but I've missed Bethan, and wish to ask your consent for her to join my household.'

His uncle nodded. 'It could be good for her, as long as you take care with her reputation.'

'You have my word,' Robert smiled, 'and I'm pleased to tell you I've secured funds, and we shall celebrate Christmas and New Year in style.'

8

MARCH 1585

Robert rehearsed his stepfather's advice as he followed him down the corridor in Nonsuch Palace to be presented to the queen. He knew Sir Philip Sidney was admired for not being in awe of her, and Robert told himself that behind the mask of royalty was a woman like any other.

He was supposed to have returned from Lamphey before Lent, but found an excuse to stay longer, as he waited until his sister Dorothy's baby was born at Carew Castle. The birth proved difficult, but the child lived. A boy, he'd been named Thomas, after his father.

A stern-faced footman in royal scarlet-and-gold livery opened the door, and Robert took a deep breath. His new doublet strained tight across his chest, and his lace ruff tickled his neck. He removed his hat and copied his stepfather's deep bow, and looked into the queen's eyes.

They shone with amusement as she studied him, as if he were some new entertainment. Her gown had slashed sleeves lined with red taffeta, as well as long sleeves that hung down to the ground. The high gossamer collar of her robe was decorated with pendants of rubies and pearls, and so delicate it seemed to float in the air.

She wore a fine gold chain of bright red rubies and shining white pearls round her neck, and a matching garland of small rubies over her dark-red wig. More pearls hung on pendants over her forehead, and wobbled when she moved her head.

'Your Majesty.' Sir Robert smiled. 'I present my stepson, Robert Devereux, Earl of Essex.'

'Two sweet Robins!' She laughed, a good sign, revealing several missing teeth. 'How you've grown, my Lord Essex.' Her sharp voice echoed in the high-ceilinged room.

Robert smiled. 'I am ready to serve you, Your Majesty.'

The queen raised a painted eyebrow. 'You remind me of your late father. Do you know he begged me not to allow you to go to Ireland?'

'I'm willing to do whatever pleases Your Majesty.' He spoke softly, as if to a young girl, and saw the effect his tone had on her.

The queen turned to Sir Robert. 'Your stepson does you credit, Lord Leicester.' She laughed. 'You were right to remove him from his mother's influence.'

His stepfather ignored the slur and smiled. 'My Lord Burghley has seen to his education, as Master of Wards, and I understand Sir Philip Sidney trained my stepson to ride well at the joust. I take little credit, Your Majesty, but commend him to your service.'

The queen stared at Robert with new interest. 'Welcome to court, Lord Essex. Your sister Penelope is like a daughter to me – and you shall be like a son.'

Robert's mind raced with possibilities as they made the fourteen-mile ride back to Leicester House. He'd not been overawed by the queen, a woman past her prime, ten years older than his mother. Unlike his mother, Queen Elizabeth had the power to make or break him with a wave of her hand, and the challenge excited him.

In that one short meeting he'd learned he had something even Sir Robert Dudley couldn't compete with. His youth gave him unexpected power over the Queen of England. If he played his hand well, he could change his fortune, and become the queen's favourite.

He looked across at his stepfather. 'I must thank you for your help.'

'You did well, and I'm pleased you listened to my advice.'

Robert smiled. 'I have a lot to learn, and am glad to have you as my stepfather.'

Sir Robert looked surprised. 'Your father would have been proud to see how you've turned out. It will be good if we can help each other.' A haunted look flickered in his eyes. 'I fear there is a campaign to do great harm to my reputation.'

'Who would wish to do that?'

His stepfather gave Robert a wry smile. 'Walter Raleigh, for one, but there are plenty at court who resent my success. You'll learn soon enough there is a price for winning the queen's affection. Some people will stop at nothing to undermine you for their own gain.'

'I've yet to meet Walter Raleigh, but I wouldn't expect him to mount a campaign against you. He seems well liked by the queen, and there's talk he'll soon be knighted.'

'This is bigger than Raleigh. The Catholic faction are circulating a document they call the Leicester Commonwealth, which makes certain accusations against me.'

'What sort of accusations?'

'They say a Master of Arts from Cambridge accused me of the poisoning of your father in Ireland, and that I murdered my first wife.' The haunted look returned to his eyes, and he cursed the Catholics under his breath.

Robert frowned. These were both accusations he'd discussed with his sister Penelope, although he'd never put them in writing. 'Are they trying to implicate me?'

His stepfather shrugged. 'These people take a grain of truth and grow it into a web of lies. Worst of all, they say my son's death was God's punishment upon me.' He scowled. 'The document has offended the queen and greatly upset your mother.'

'Can't you track down the people behind it, and have them charged with defamation?'

He shook his head. 'They work in the shadows, anonymously, like the cowards they are.'

'Could we seize and destroy every copy of this document?'

'The queen has commanded the Mayor of London to suppress as many copies as they are able to. We could try to do more, but it might only serve to draw attention to these scurrilous allegations.'

'I'm sorry. I had no idea this was going on.' A thought occurred to Robert. 'How do you know the Catholics are behind this document?'

'They implore the queen to recognise Mary, Queen of Scots as her successor.' His stepfather shook his head. 'I thought I should be the one to tell you, as you'll hear about it soon enough.'

Bethan slipped into Robert's room once the rest of the household retired for the night. They'd managed to keep her visits secret since arriving at Leicester House. He'd chosen a room with access from a servants' narrow staircase, and there were so many maids that Bethan didn't attract attention.

He'd been waiting for her, and lay awake with a single

candle burning at his bedside. 'I've had a letter from my sister Penelope. She's staying with my mother at her house in Drayton Basset.'

Bethan pulled off her linen coif and sat on his bed to unplait her long hair. 'Are you going to visit her?'

'They are less than twenty miles from my boyhood home. As well as seeing them both, I thought to ride out to Chartley, to see it's being well looked after.'

She combed the tangles from her hair with her fingers. 'I'd like to see your mother. I've heard so much about her.'

'I wish I could introduce you, but my mother would see it as her duty to keep us apart.' He kissed her. 'I promised my uncle to keep our secret, for the sake of your reputation.'

She looked at him with confident eyes. 'I made my own choice, and the worst that can happen is that I'm sent back to your uncle. No one will think any less of you for bedding an innocent maid,' she gave him a coy look, 'and they care little in Lamphey for the scandals and gossip of London.'

Robert had to admit she was right, and pulled her close. 'I was going to travel light, with only Bagot for company, but you shall be part of my travelling household.' He smiled. 'I'd like you to see my sister Penelope, and I might even tell her about you.'

She kissed him. 'I promise to be discreet.'

'Then it's agreed.'

The strain of the previous year showed in his mother's eyes, but she looked pleased to see him. She wore a brocade gown with wide, slashed sleeves, embroidered with flowers. Her pearl necklaces reached her waist and, like the queen, she had a large pear-shaped pearl pendant on her forehead.

She embraced Robert and stared at him for a moment before speaking. 'A beard suits you – and you've grown so tall.'

'I'm sorry for your loss, Mother.'

'It's taken a long time to come to terms with your half-brother's death.' Her confident mask faltered. 'He was so full of life. I still can't really believe he's gone.'

'I heard he suffered with a fever.'

His mother nodded. 'The doctors told me not to worry, but a mother knows. At least he didn't suffer for long.'

'I wish I'd met him.' Robert wondered whether to embrace his mother, but thought better of it. 'I saw the picture he ruined, at Leicester House.'

'Your stepfather was so cross with him.' She smiled. 'He called him the noble imp.'

'I hope you understand why it's taken me so long to come and see you, Mother.'

'You have your own life to live, and it seems you've already made your mark at court.'

Robert was pleased his stepfather had given a good account to her. 'God willing, I hope to restore father's fortune, as well as his good name.'

His mother smiled. 'You have that same glint of ambition in your eyes that he did – and Master Broughton tells me you are just as extravagant.'

'I've lived on fresh air and the charity of others since leaving Cambridge.' Robert heard the defensive note in his voice, but he spoke the truth. He'd had no money of his own since graduating from university.

She studied his cloth-of-silver doublet and smiled. 'You seem to have done well enough on charity.' She patted him, as if he were a small boy. 'Be patient, and try to learn to live within your means.'

Penelope, who'd been watching, stepped forward. Like her mother, she wore a high lace ruff and rich gold brocade, decorated with pearls. Penelope embraced him, and Robert caught the scent of expensive perfume. 'It's good to see you again, dear brother. You look well.' She smiled. 'How is our sister, and her child?'

'I called to see Dorothy and her son before I returned to London. The birth took its toll on her, but she's recovered now, and asked me to tell you both she is well.'

Penelope nodded. 'It seems unfair her husband can take part in the tournaments as he pleases, yet Dorothy is banned from court.'

'She's happy enough with her new life. But what of you? It seems you've given your husband the slip.'

She gave him an innocent look. 'My husband has kindly granted me leave to visit my mother.'

Their mother smiled. 'I believe I make Baron Rich nervous, so he is not expected to visit often.'

Robert raised an eyebrow. 'I believe you make the Queen of England nervous, Mother.'

'It's true.' Penelope laughed. 'The queen has no idea how to deal with you, and neither does my witless husband.'

Robert woke early to visit Chartley Manor, a comfortable morning's ride through open countryside. He was surprised to see men working on the gatehouse at the approach to the moat, as they seemed to be making it more defensible.

Richard Bagot greeted him. 'Welcome, my lord. It's been a long time.'

Robert grinned. 'A great deal has happened since we last met.' He pointed to the workmen. 'Are you preparing to withstand a siege?'

Richard Bagot laughed. 'We are preparing for an important guest, who will guarantee the maintenance of Chartley for the foreseeable future.'

'Is it anyone I might know?'

Richard Bagot frowned. 'We'd better go inside.'

Robert followed Richard Bagot into the great hall where his life had changed on that fateful day, and felt as if he were travelling back into the past. The magnificent antlers of a stag his father killed in Chartley forest still graced the wall, but the Flemish tapestry was gone. Robert hoped his mother had taken it, and not one of the tenants.

Richard Bagot looked nervous as they sat by the empty hearth. 'We've been commanded by Her Majesty to prepare Chartley as the new home for her cousin.'

'Her cousin?' Robert frowned. 'You mean Mary, Queen of the Scots?'

'Yes, my lord. It will mean we can do whatever repairs we need to restore Chartley at the queen's expense.'

'People will think I'm supporting her – and there's a risk I'll never have Chartley back.'

Richard Bagot shook his head. 'In truth, we have no choice, my lord. The queen has made her decision, and you'll risk her anger if you refuse.'

'Then I'll take that chance.' Robert looked up at the Devereux crest above the fireplace. 'I've lost most of my inheritance to the Crown, and I'm not going to surrender Chartley as well.'

He crossed over to the family table, with his late father's chair still at the head, and ran his hand over the polished surface. 'I want you to remove all the furniture, including this table and the beds, to a place of safekeeping. I might not be able to stop this, but I'll try.'

∼

On his return to Leicester House, his stepfather seemed to think it would be easy enough to change the queen's mind. 'All we need to do is find somewhere more secure, such as a castle. It would not be good if the Catholics managed to free the queen's cousin.'

Robert scowled. 'I've written to my grandfather, asking for his help. Chartley is the only property not encumbered with debt. Richard Bagot should have consulted me before preparing for our new tenant.'

His stepfather nodded. 'I believe he thought he was doing the right thing.' He sat in silence for a moment, as if reaching a decision. 'How would you like to come with me to the Low Countries?' Robert was a little drunk from too much wine, but sat up at his stepfather's words.

'Do you think the queen will allow it?'

'The situation has changed. The Duke of Parma has taken Antwerp, and the queen appointed me commander of her army. My nephew, Sir Philip Sidney, sailed with an advance party to take up his post as Governor of Flushing.' He frowned. 'If we don't act soon the Netherlands will be a Spanish colony – and a Catholic stronghold, the ideal place from which to launch an attack on England.'

'Is the queen also meeting the cost?'

'I'll have to contribute my own funds, but I think of it as a good investment.'

'Like my father did in Ireland?' Robert couldn't keep the bitterness from his voice.

'Could you levy and equip your own company?'

Robert's pulse raced at the prospect. It would be dangerous, but could be the chance he'd been waiting for to make his name. 'I would need a commission from the queen.'

His stepfather looked thoughtful. 'I could recommend you to Her Majesty as General of the Horse.'

'I've never commanded men, and have no experience of cavalry.' The enormity of what he planned to do seemed overwhelming.

His stepfather smiled. 'We all have to start somewhere. You'll have Sir William Russell, an experienced man you can trust, as your second in command.'

'When do we sail?'

∼

The narrow sea surged with white-crested waves, and the rigging creaked with the strain of a brisk December breeze, hastening their fleet of fifty ships forward. Robert braced himself against the foremast and tasted the salty spray in the cold air. He'd secured the queen's commission to sail in a holy war against the Catholics.

They'd sailed from Harwich to the sound of drums and trumpets, cheered on by crowds, heroes before they'd even left England. It had been time-consuming and costly to raise his followers. His uncle brought a mounted division of cavalrymen from Pembrokeshire, including Dorothy's husband Sir Thomas Perrot. He'd joked they were untrained, but made up for inexperience with loyalty and enthusiasm.

Richard Bagot redeemed himself by raising soldiers from the Staffordshire militia. Two hundred of them were armed and trained with calivers, with a smaller bore than a musket and less accuracy, but quicker to reload, so in trained hands capable of firing three times a minute.

Robert received a stern letter of rebuke from his grandfather for sinking another thousand pounds into debt. He sensed a grudging admiration from the old man, who wrote, '*I do like very well your desire to see the wars, for your own learning, and do like your desire much the better, that you take the opportunity of honouring my Lord of Leicester with your service under him, but this might have been done without any wasteful charge to yourself.'*

A staunch defender of the Protestant faith, if he were younger, Sir Francis would no doubt have done the same. He ended his letter with the words, '*I beseech our almighty God to so assist you with his heavenly grace, that youthful wilfulness do not consume you before experienced wisdom shall have reformed you.*'

Most of the men brought their own horses and weapons, but Robert paid for their Essex livery, which included a doublet, a pair of breeches, a hat, two shirts, three pairs of stockings and three pairs of shoes for each man. The greatest cost was feeding his hungry army.

For the first time, Robert understood the dilemma his father faced in equipping and maintaining an army in Ireland. Queen Elizabeth was skilled at encouraging others to meet the costs, and slow to commit to reimbursement.

He turned at the sound of heavy boots on the deck behind him. Gelly looked striking in the shining new breastplate he'd persuaded Robert to pay for. He'd been appointed as a sergeant of the cavalry, and had already won the respect of the men.

'Many suffer with seasickness, Lord General.'

Robert raised an eyebrow at his friend's use of his rank. 'I'm no general yet, Sergeant Meyrick, but as long as the weather holds, we'll be ashore soon enough.'

Gelly scanned the horizon, and pointed a nail-bitten finger. 'Land!'

Robert squinted and made out the distant sliver of grey between the dark waves and the wintry sky. He'd put his affairs in order before he left, and lodged his will with Master Broughton, leaving such lands as he had to his younger brother Wat, apart from his estate at Lamphey, which he'd left to his Uncle George.

He found himself thinking of Bethan's tears when he said

farewell. He'd found her a place in his sister Penelope's household, but knew her well enough to see she worried for him. Robert imagined his father shared the same mix of excitement and foreboding as he left his family for a long sojourn in Ireland. The risks were as great and, whatever happened, he would be changed by the experience.

9

FEBRUARY 1586

The clatter of iron-shod hooves on cobblestones echoed in the narrow streets, and people cheered 'God save the queen!' as the army marched through yet another Dutch town. Robert glanced back. His company, in orange Essex livery with white sashes, stretched into the distance as far as he could see.

He was flanked by his second in command – the gruff lieutenant Sir William Russell, who'd fought in Ireland – and his Uncle George, appointed Captain of the Horse. Robert relied on them both, and was learning that fighting a war was mostly about waiting to discover their enemy, and being cheered by grateful Protestants.

At Rotterdam and Delft they'd been treated like royalty, welcomed by the local dignitaries with fireworks and fanfares of trumpets, long speeches and grand banquets. Robert enjoyed the spectacle, but feared they'd travelled to the Low Countries on a fool's errand.

His stepfather talked of an imminent threat, and an urgent need to stop the Catholics, but he'd stayed out of sight in his luxurious apartments at The Hague. Not one voice had been raised against them, yet Robert sensed the tension in the air, like iron-grey clouds on the horizon before a violent storm.

Robert turned to Sir William Russell. 'I worry we'll become complacent with all this parading.'

Sir William agreed. 'We should have some drills to keep the men mindful of why we're here, my lord.' He frowned. 'We announce our presence so well, we leave ourselves exposed to ambush.'

'Do you think the Duke of Parma could be planning to waylay us?' Robert scowled. They wouldn't stand a chance, and he'd be at the front, a prime target.

'We know little of their tactics, my lord, but I believe our presence here has been enough to stop their advance. All the same, it's as well to be prepared.'

His uncle overheard. 'You'll be surprised how quickly they'll turn into fighting men once they see the enemy.'

Robert smiled. 'I hope you're right, Uncle. We've not had sight of a single Catholic soldier since we sailed.'

The city of Utrecht welcomed them with a banquet in the old hall of the Knights of Rhodes. The irony of such use of a Catholic religious and military order wasn't lost on Robert, who had a place of honour at the top table. The rusting swords and shields of long dead knights graced the walls, and it seemed everyone of importance in the city came to welcome them.

Robert picked at a silver plate of smoked herring in a sweet sauce, and did his best to look interested in the long speeches, repeated in Dutch and English. He'd been seated next to the Mayor of Utrecht, who spoke little English, but his Uncle George sat at his other side, enjoying a platter of ripe figs.

He offered one to Robert and grinned. 'Who'd have thought you'd be growing bored of banquets?'

Robert smiled. 'The Low Countries have proved a disappointment.' He bit into the fig, surprised at the honey-like sweetness of its syrupy juice. 'I miss the green lanes of Pembrokeshire. This place is so flat the countryside looks much the same wherever we go.'

His uncle nodded. 'I prepared for hardship when we first came here, and I've a feeling we should make the most of this welcome, while we can.'

Robert agreed. 'Each day takes us closer to the Duke of Parma's forces, and who knows what might be waiting around the next corner?'

His uncle's reply was drowned by the scrape of a fiddle as the tables were cleared and a group of Dutch musicians began to play a dance tune. Many of the local dignitaries had brought their ladies, and Robert decided his uncle was right. He should make the most of this opportunity.

He chose one of the younger Dutch ladies, standing together in a group, and bowed, before taking her hand in his and leading her to the cleared area. He'd not expected his dancing lessons at Theobalds to be tested quite so far from home, but he'd been taught well, and soon mastered the simple steps.

His partner wore an embroidered blue velvet gown, cut low at the front, her plaited black hair covered by a netted caul adorned with small diamonds. He could tell from her jewels she was wealthy, and found her confidence attractive. She spoke only enough English to tell him her name was Lilde, yet her eyes shone when he complimented her.

For the next dance he had to place his hand around Lilde's slender waist. The soft warmth of her body aroused his interest, but he guessed she had a jealous husband or fiancé watching somewhere close by. She asked him a question and gestured outside, but he couldn't understand.

A young Dutchman who overheard explained. 'She asks if you'll be at the barricade after evensong, my lord.'

Robert still didn't understand. 'The barricade?'

The Dutchman swung an imaginary sword. 'A tourney, in your honour.'

Robert turned to Lilde. 'I will take part,' he smiled at her, 'if you will come to watch.' He wished he'd not drunk so much Rhenish wine, and hoped his long hours of training at Lamphey would stand him in good stead.

Robert tested the weight of the borrowed lance, and found it well balanced and lighter than he was used to, which might offer an advantage. Gelly helped him into his armour, and brought a scarlet cape, a touch of flamboyance for the evening's entertainment.

Scanning the crowd through the eye slit in his helmet, Robert was pleased to see Lilde wave a hand and smile. His opponent, a Dutch knight dressed in black armour with a plume of ostrich feathers on his helmet, raised a gauntleted hand to signal that he was ready. Robert took a deep breath and did the same.

Trumpets sounded a sharp fanfare, and Robert urged his horse forward, remembering to keep focused on his target. The clash brought a cheer from the drunken crowd, as both lances found their mark and shattered. Robert frowned at the jagged scrape on his new armour, then realised it would be a badge of honour, won in fair contest.

Unlike the jousts at Carew, where he'd run three courses, he now had to take on his opponent on foot, armed only with a sword. The old weapon had a blunted tip and edge, but could still wound if he was caught off guard. Again, his practice at

Lamphey, as well as the cheers of his supporters, gave him confidence.

He let his opponent take the initiative, and repeated Sir Philip Sidney's advice in his head. *The lunge is fast, but leaves you vulnerable. The pass keeps you upright, and in a strong position.*

After a few jarring clashes Robert struck, parrying his opponent's blade with a single action. He placed the blunt tip of his sword at the man's throat, and demanded his surrender.

His uncle appeared and clapped him on the back. 'Well done – you've beaten one of their best men.'

Robert shook the Dutchman's hand, and congratulated him on his skill. At the back of his mind was the suspicion he'd been allowed an easy win for the sake of diplomacy. Either way, he'd begun to make a name for himself, although he wasn't sure he could do the same when the real fighting began.

Gelly placed a tankard of Dutch ale in his hand, and they were settling down for an evening of drinking, when Anthony Bagot arrived. He frowned with concern and brought a message for Robert from his stepfather.

'The Duke of Parma has laid siege to Grave, in the Duchy of Brabant, my lord. Our orders are to leave for Nijmegen, ten miles north of Grave, where the Earl of Leicester will meet us with the Dutch reinforcements.'

Robert looked at his tankard and scowled. 'We must get some sleep and leave at first light. There's nothing to be gained by marching at night, and half the men have been drinking.'

They were in a sombre mood as they made the fifty-mile trek south-east to Nijmegen. Robert had woken at dawn, his head buzzing from too much drink – another lesson he'd need to remember. He smiled to himself as he thought of his young partner, Lilde. He'd not had time to say farewell to her, which was perhaps just as well.

Undaunted by a shower of rain, Sir William Russell had got the men ready and on the road as the sun was creeping over the far horizon. 'If we keep up this pace, we should be there by nightfall, my lord.'

Robert glanced back at the heavily laden wagons following in their muddy wake, and doubted it. 'Can Grave be held until we arrive, Sir William?'

Lieutenant Russell shrugged. 'We'll find out soon enough. Grave was relieved only last month by Sir John Norris and his men, so if the Duke of Parma knows we're on our way he might decide to attack, rather than wait for us to end his siege.'

Robert stared down the long windswept road, bounded by flat fields, stretching to the horizon. If the duke had lookouts, they would be hard to miss, and there was no cover. It would be impossible for them to be taken by surprise in such open countryside.

The rain returned, forming muddy puddles on the dirt road, but the cold trickle at Robert's neck helped him keep focused. He would lead by example, and set the pace. He glanced across at his uncle, who'd repeated a worrying rumour. It was said the queen was displeased at the Dutch treating his stepfather as if he were royalty.

'Such rumours are often based on the truth.' Robert frowned. 'I hope this doesn't mean we'll be recalled before we've seen action.'

His uncle nodded. 'If it's true, I hope it's not an excuse not to pay our costs. The men won't march on loyalty alone. Some have a fever, and several have already deserted. They must be paid, and soon.'

They reached the sprawling camp at Nijmegen by late afternoon to learn that Grave had fallen to the Duke of Parma. It seemed that the Governor of Grave, and commander of the garrison, Baron Peter van Hemart, had surrendered without a fight, in return for his freedom.

Robert found his stepfather in a large house he'd requisitioned from a Dutch merchant. The roaring fire in the hearth blazed with the same ferocity as Sir Robert Dudley's anger. He'd been drinking and paced the room as he spoke.

'We must make an example of those who threw away our advantage, or we'll have lost this war before it's begun.'

Robert frowned with misgiving at his stepfather's harsh tone. 'What are you going to do?'

His stepfather stopped pacing. 'They shall be tried under martial law – and you shall be on the jury.' He gave Robert a wry look. 'The experience will be good for you.'

Baron van Hemart stared at Robert's stepfather in disbelief as the charges were read out. Robert wished he was somewhere else, as the whole charade could only have one outcome. He sympathised with the two young captains at the baron's side. They followed the baron's orders, yet were charged with desertion.

'Is there anything you wish to say in your defence?' Robert Dudley's tone suggested that whatever was said would make little difference.

Baron van Hemart spoke in accented English, his voice faltering. 'We were outnumbered, my lord.' He stared at the ground. 'There was nothing we could do.'

'Yet you were released unharmed?'

'The Prince of Naples offered us his mercy, my lord, and I respectfully ask that you do the same.'

Robert Dudley scowled. 'Cowardice in the face of the enemy

will not be tolerated.' His raised voice betrayed his anger. 'Your surrender has set back our entire campaign.'

The court was adjourned for sentencing, and Robert saw his chance. He turned to his stepfather once they were alone. 'What would you have had them do?'

'They knew we were on our way with reinforcements soon enough. All they had to do was hold Grave until we arrived.' His stepfather frowned. 'I heard Baron van Hemart was more concerned with entertaining his mistress than keeping guard.'

'But his captains—'

His stepfather glowered. 'Should have known their inaction would have consequences.'

Robert could see he'd made up his mind, and followed him back into the makeshift courtroom for the passing of the sentence. He tried to avoid the pleading gaze of the condemned men, and considered absenting himself from the executions, but his stepfather left him no choice.

He said a prayer for their souls and closed his eyes as the headsman's sharp axe thumped into the wooden block three times. Baron van Hemart had been negligent, and his captains lacking in courage, yet their punishment was barbaric. Robert would not forget this day in a hurry, and knew that was the point.

'Essex!' The shout in a familiar voice made Robert turn to see Sir Philip Sidney, who rode up to his side. 'I hear you've been putting our lessons to good purpose.'

'I believe the Dutchmen let me win, Sir Philip.'

He grinned. 'That's not what I heard.'

'Well, I heard you are the hero of a real battle, and captured the town of Axel.'

'I was lucky – and Lord Willoughby should have the credit. He had the idea of sending men to swim the defensive ditch and open the gates for us. The garrison fought bravely, but we had the advantage over them.'

Robert guessed Sir Philip was being typically modest.

'And now you'll show us how to take the town of Zutphen?'

Sir Philip's face became serious. 'I believe we'll have a fight on our hands. Sir John Norris's scouts have seen the Duke of Parma's army heading to relieve Zutphen in great numbers.' He scowled. 'They are escorting a convoy of supply wagons. If we are to stand any chance of holding the town to siege, we have to stop them.'

They rode in silence through the swirling mist of a September dawn. Sir Philip Sidney was at the head of one cavalry squadron with Lord Willoughby. Robert commanded the Essex cavalry with Lieutenant Russell, his uncle, and his sister's husband, Sir Thomas Perrot. Between them marched some three hundred and fifty pikemen, under Sir William Stanley and Lord Audley.

Robert's pulse raced at the prospect of fighting for his life. The deadly lance he carried had a sharp tip, designed to kill a man and, in preference to a sword, he'd chosen to carry a long-handled battleaxe. The night before, he'd tested the sharp blade against a tree and it hacked deep into the trunk.

Sir John Norris led the infantry division of English and Dutch musketeers and arquebusiers. Although they were likely to be outnumbered by the Spanish, they could still have the advantage if they could take the supply convoy by surprise.

The first glimmer of autumn sunlight reflected from something bright ahead. Robert cursed at the sight of over two thousand Spanish cavalry, pikemen, and soldiers with muskets.

They'd ridden into the Duke of Parma's main force, and there was no turning back.

Sir Philip was first to react, and called for his cavalry to charge. The air filled with the rattle of musket fire as their horses galloped into the line of Spanish musketeers. The yells and shouts were joined by cries of pain as the two forces met.

Robert shouted for his men to follow and charged the Spanish soldiers flanking the convoy of wagons. A bullet skimmed off Robert's armour, buzzing like an angry wasp as he lowered his lance and chose his target. For the first time he aimed to kill, and had a fleeting sight of his lance striking a Spanish cavalryman in the chest and knocking him from his saddle.

Robert dropped his lance, and tugged his battleaxe from its leather holder, swinging it at the nearest Spanish soldier. The axe clanged off the man's helmet and he fell to his knees. Robert's horse carried him deep into the Spanish ranks, and he swung his axe again and again with all his strength, cutting a swathe through the ranks like a farmer harvesting corn.

More shots blasted, and he flinched as another bullet cracked into his plate armour, numbing his left arm. There wasn't time to think about the terrible wounds his axe was inflicting, or the great danger he was in. He'd reached the soldiers armed with pikes, defending the convoy of supply wagons. It seemed the men driving the wagons had fled, as they stood abandoned in the road.

Hopelessly outnumbered, he realised they would not be able to stop the convoy reaching the town. He turned to see several hundred more Spanish pikemen arriving from Zutphen, and knew his men would be surrounded if they stayed any longer. The battle for the convoy was lost, and their only choice was to withdraw.

· · ·

Robert's heroism at the height of the battle meant he wasn't condemned for ordering a retreat. He'd saved the lives of his men, but the order came for them to make the hundred-and-fifty-mile march back to Flushing and embark on a ship for England.

The news was met with a cheer from the men. Robert had no wish to hold Zutphen to a long winter siege, particularly now the town was reinforced and resupplied. The talk in camp was that the queen no longer had any appetite for continuing such a costly war. If true, she wouldn't thank him for staying in the Low Countries, however noble his reasons.

Robert's uncle was philosophical. He pulled his riding cloak around him and scowled at the drizzling rain that dripped from his hat. 'Your stepfather isn't the only one who has had enough of this miserable country.'

Robert agreed. 'I'll not be sorry to see England again, but first I want to pay a visit to Sir Philip Sidney.'

'They say his wound is serious.'

'He wasn't wearing full armour, and a bullet smashed his thigh bone.' Robert frowned. 'I've heard he might lose his leg.'

A young, blue-eyed woman greeted him as he entered Sir Philip's chambers. 'He's sleeping, so it will be best if you come and see him in the morning.'

She spoke softly, yet Robert could tell she was well educated, and saw she wore a silk brocade dress under her woollen cloak. With a jolt, he realised this must be Sir Philip's wife, Lady Frances, daughter of the queen's spymaster, Francis Walsingham. Her presence in Flushing could only mean his friend was not expected to live.

'Robert Devereux.' He took off his cap, and bowed his head.

'I was sorry to hear what happened, my lady. What do the doctors say?'

'I fear there's nothing they can do.' Her face was pale and she sounded close to tears. 'His wound is poisoning him.'

'I have to find a ship for England. Will you tell him I was here?'

She glanced at her sleeping husband. 'He speaks of you like a brother, my lord, and would not forgive me if I allowed you to leave without waking him.'

Robert watched as she crossed to the bed and placed her hand on Sir Philip's brow. He didn't move, so she shook him gently by the shoulder. His eyes fluttered open and he stared up at her, then across at Robert.

'Essex.' His rasping voice sounded weak, and it seemed that even speaking took an effort, yet he forced a smile. 'You've been made a knight for your bravery at Zutphen.'

'Only a knight banneret – and you left me no choice, once you charged ahead.'

'I saw how bravely you fought.' Sir Philip glanced at his wife. 'He was ferocious in battle. The enemy parted before him like the Red Sea.'

Robert shook his head. 'You trained me well with the lance and sword, but neglected to teach me how to use a battleaxe from the saddle.'

Sir Philip grimaced with pain. 'Remember me to your sister, Penelope, my Stella. Now fly, fly, my friend, I have my death wound, fly!'

He lay back and closed his eyes as the words, taken from Sidney's own poem 'Astrophel and Stella', struck Robert with the force of the goodbye they undoubtedly were.

Robert turned to Frances. She had tears in her eyes and, without thinking, he pulled her close, as he might comfort one of his sisters. She seemed to appreciate the brief embrace and, instead of pulling away, placed her hand on his back.

'Thank you for taking the trouble to visit.' She stared at Robert as if making a judgement. 'It means a lot to him.'

Robert stared out at white-crested waves. But for God's grace, he could be the one who lay dying, yet he'd survived the war unscathed. He thought of Lady Frances Sidney. They'd met under the worst of circumstances, and he'd been concerned about Sir Philip, but one of the lessons he'd learned since leaving England was to seize opportunities while he had the chance.

He gripped the rail with one hand to steady himself as the ship rolled in the heavy swell. Sir Philip was a fighter, yet even he knew the end was close. His wife would need to spend time in mourning, and didn't have a great fortune, but Robert had sensed a connection with her.

Frances was about the same age as him, and no one was closer to the queen than her powerful father, Sir Francis Walsingham. Robert lost Elizabeth Cecil by staying his hand too long. This time, he must let his interest be known to Frances, when the time was right.

10

FEBRUARY 1587

Robert shared a jug of ale with Gelly in the corner of a tavern frequented by costermongers from the nearby street market. He wore an old felt cap and a winter coat over his fine doublet, glad no one knew or cared he was the Earl of Essex. He'd warned Gelly not to call him *my lord* or *sir*, although he sometimes forgot.

He had to think about his future. His experience in the Low Countries cost him everything, and he had to rely on his stepfather's charity. Robert told no one, but he was haunted by the knowledge he'd led men to their deaths, and slaughtered their enemies like animals in the name of the queen, defender of the faith.

Although he'd done his best, and fought as bravely as anyone, he hadn't returned as a hero. Their campaign was thought by those who mattered as a costly and badly organised failure. He needed a new role and a sense of purpose. He watched as Gelly took the earthenware jug and refilled their tankards with the foaming ale.

'I'll be twenty-two in November.' He smiled at the thought.

'It's time to make plans for what remains of my inheritance – and get my household back together.'

Gelly looked pleased. Of Robert's once thriving household, only he remained, happy to serve without pay. 'Are we going back to Lamphey?'

Robert was tempted as he sipped the bitter-tasting ale. His Uncle George had long since returned to West Wales with his chaplain, Rhys Prichard. They could live at Lamphey until the autumn ... but he shook his head. 'I'm still waiting for Philip Sidney's funeral. I don't want to travel to Wales, only to find I'm summoned back again.'

Gelly nodded. 'It will soon be four months. Too long to keep a man from his maker, if you ask me.'

Robert put the sad memory of his last meeting with Philip Sidney from his mind. 'Master Wright has found work in Chelsea as a Latin tutor, but told me it's temporary – so he can return any time.'

Gelly agreed. 'Bagot will be finished at Chartley Manor soon. Bethan seems happy enough in your sister's household, but she'll come back in a trice, if you wish.'

Robert heard the question in Gelly's voice. 'I miss Bethan. I saw her during the Christmas celebrations, and she asked when she might come back, but my conscience troubles me about how I've led her astray.' He frowned. 'It's time she found someone who can take better care of her.'

Gelly took another drink of ale and wiped his mouth on his sleeve. 'Bethan's as sharp as a razor. She knows well enough you can never marry her.'

Robert gave him a wry smile. 'I've resisted my mother's attempts to find me a suitable wife.'

Gelly raised an eyebrow. 'Your lady mother is determined to see you married, and won't give in easily.'

'She means well, but I confess I'm in no hurry to take a wife, at least not until I've cleared my debts.' He thought again of Frances Sidney, and the unspoken sense of connection between them. She would still be in mourning, but he planned to keep an eye on her.

'Bagot said there'll be income from Chartley coming your way, once his father finds a paying tenant.'

Robert brightened at the news. 'I was annoyed when I learned the Queen of Scots was moved to Chartley as soon as I left for the Low Countries.' Robert shook his head at the memory. 'My first thought was that the queen only allowed me to go to war to get me out of the way.'

'Well, it's a good thing you weren't here to make a fuss. Bagot said Chartley Manor has been left in better condition than you could have hoped for. All the original furniture is back, and he says the improvements they made to the gatehouse and boundary walls make the old place more secure.' Gelly lowered his voice. 'What do you think will become of the Scottish queen?'

Robert shrugged. 'I was as surprised as anyone to hear she was found guilty of treason – and that the queen signed her own cousin's death warrant. They didn't have to torture Anthony Babington. He confessed that Lady Mary's letter encouraged his plan to free her and replace Queen Elizabeth, yet he still suffered a traitor's death.'

Gelly frowned at the thought. 'I heard the Scottish queen condemned herself by her own hand, and Sir Francis Walsingham has the evidence.'

'Well, Her Majesty seems in no hurry to see the sentence carried out.' Robert gave Gelly a wry look. 'We should be grateful the problem of what to do with the Queen of Scots distracts our queen from asking questions about our campaign in the Low Countries.'

. . .

The church bells clanged in discordant celebration early in the evening, and Gelly went out to learn the reason. He returned a short time later with an uncharacteristic frown on his usually cheerful face. 'The Queen of Scots has been executed at Fotheringhay Castle, my lord.'

Robert scowled. 'May God preserve us all. There will be repercussions. I'm grateful we were out of the country and had nothing to do with it.'

His stepfather returned from court in a sour mood.

'The queen has cast the blame on her hapless secretary. Davison has been sent to the Tower, and William Cecil is banished from court.'

'I confess to bearing a grudge against William Cecil, yet banishment is a poor reward for a lifetime of loyalty.'

'Don't worry about Burghley.' His stepfather shook his head. 'Her Majesty will find an excuse to forgive him soon enough. William Cecil has achieved what he wanted, and his son is lined up as Davison's successor.'

'Robert Cecil?' Robert recalled the last time they'd met. 'I hope Robert Cecil has mellowed a little. He wasn't easy to get on with ... but that was a long time ago.'

'You'll need his support, so do your best not to cross him.' His stepfather looked serious. 'I understand you might not count him as a friend, but he could make a dangerous enemy.'

Crowds of Londoners thronged both sides of the winding road to the old cathedral of St Paul's. Women clasped their hands in prayer, and men pulled off their hats and bowed their heads. The long procession passed with the rhythmic tramp of marching feet and the metallic clink of horseshoes on cobblestones.

In the old tradition, Sir Francis Walsingham paid for thirty-two poor men, dressed in hooded black robes, one for each year of Sir Philip Sidney's life, to lead the way. Behind them marched Sir Philip's grim-faced yeomen with drums rattling out a sombre beat in the chill morning air.

Sixty liveried servants, physicians and clerics followed, with Sir Philip's fine warhorse, ridden by his thirteen-year-old page Henry Danvers, who carried his master's broken lance and reversed battleaxe. Heralds carried Sir Philip's spurs and gauntlets, and four men carried tall banners with the Sidney coat of arms.

The black-draped coffin was carried high on poles by fourteen men, seven on each side. Sir Philip's younger brother Sir Robert Sidney, as chief mourner, rode at the side of Sir Robert Dudley. Robert rode behind his stepfather with Sir Henry Herbert, Earl of Pembroke, and all the lords who'd fought at the Battle of Zutphen.

The Lord Mayor of London and aldermen of the city led the grocers' guilds in full livery, and at the rear came the London bands, marching three abreast. Their shrill fifes sounded too cheerful, out of place on such a sad occasion.

There were too many to count, yet Robert guessed this must be the grandest funeral procession seen in London in his lifetime. A lone voice called out, 'God rest you, my lord!' but otherwise the crowd remained respectfully silent.

Robert shivered in the wintry air. He imagined Philip Sidney would have made some wry remark about being given such a funeral, after having to wait since the previous October. In a final act of generosity, Philip had bequeathed his best sword to Robert, which he now wore at his belt, a reminder of the sort of man he aspired to become.

After the prayers, his friend's coffin was laid to rest, and Robert flinched at the sound of gunfire as the musketeers made their final salute. His sister, Penelope, asked him to tell her how Philip died, yet like all those who knew the truth, he kept his silence about what really happened at the Battle of Zutphen. The people needed a hero, and who better than the warrior poet, Sir Philip Sidney?

Robert Dudley pulled off his starched ruff and cursed as he tossed it to one side, massaging the red mark on his neck. He called for his servant to bring strong drink, and slumped into his favourite chair. He would be celebrating his fifty-fourth birthday before the end of the month, but his worry-lined face made him look older.

Robert knew the signs of another unsatisfactory meeting with the queen. 'Is Her Majesty still blaming the council?'

Nearly four months had passed, yet it seemed the consequences were far from over.

'She plays with us, like a cat with a mouse.' He sipped the warming spirit and nodded appreciatively. 'Burghley was clever, making sure the whole council shares the blame, as Her Majesty can't send all of us to the Tower.'

'What's happened now?'

'She accused me of allowing you to write to King James of Scotland to intercede on behalf of her secretary.'

'That was my own idea. There was no reply, but Davison's life has been spared.'

Robert Dudley frowned. 'You must take more care who you choose to support. I know to my cost how quickly our queen can withdraw her goodwill.' He shook his head. 'You are liable for your father's debts to the Crown. What would you do if the queen called them in, to teach you a lesson?'

'My intention was honourable. If I could prevent an innocent man from being executed for doing his duty, it's worth the risk.'

'A noble sentiment.' His stepfather gave him an appraising look. 'Davison's life has been spared, but he's been ruined with a fine of ten thousand marks.' He took another deep drink. 'Our queen has given me a task which she knows I cannot achieve. I've been sent back to the Low Countries, with a fleet of ships and three thousand men, to prevent the fall of Sluys.'

'I was planning to return to Lamphey. Do you wish me to come with you?'

'You must remain here and protect our interests. When I return, no doubt having failed, my enemies will be queueing up to finish me.' The bitterness in his voice was unmistakable.

Robert's relief was mixed with concern for his stepfather. 'I'll do my best, but I have no role at court.'

His stepfather managed a smile. 'I've recommended that you are made Master of the Horse, a post I've held long enough. It will make you part of the royal household. Her Majesty likes to ride every day, and the position has an allowance of one and a half thousand a year – but remember to look surprised when she tells you.'

'Why is that?'

'The queen is sensitive to the thought of anyone conspiring behind her back, however honourable their intentions.'

A shaft of bright June sunshine lit up the queen's privy chamber, glinting off the jewels in her orange wig. Queen Elizabeth looked pale, and fidgeted with her long necklace of pearls. More pearls decorated her wide sleeves and the edge of her ornate lace ruff, which reached to her shoulders.

She studied Robert as he bowed, her gaze raking his body, as if noting every detail. Her eyes rested on his silver-handled dagger, in a scabbard engraved with the Devereux motto, then she smiled at some whispered comment made by one of her ladies. It seemed her mood had improved since his stepfather's visit. Robert returned her smile with one of gratitude. He knew the reason for the summons.

'Is that a new doublet, my Lord Essex?' The challenge in her voice hung in the still air, like the exotic scent of her perfume, teasing Robert's senses.

'A gift from my stepfather.' He gave her a disarming smile. 'He thought I should look my best for Your Majesty.'

She raised an eyebrow. 'You are fortunate. He always was such a generous man – but can we trust him,' her eyes sharpened, 'after he married your mother without permission?'

He held her gaze, trying to read the look in her eyes. She was ten years older than his mother, and her blatant stare suggested more than admiration. This was a test, and one he'd prepared for. 'The Earl of Leicester is your most loyal servant.' He smiled. 'As am I.'

'We need men we can trust – now more than ever.'

'I am at your service, Your Majesty, to do whatever you command.'

Her eyes flashed with amusement. She was pleased with his answer. 'Good. My lord of Leicester recommends you to replace him as Master of the Horse.'

'I would be honoured, Your Majesty.' He'd forgotten to act surprised, but it didn't matter. His pulse raced at the possibility of being closer to the queen. At a stroke, his money worries would be solved, and the role carried some influence. His stepfather delegated the role to others, but Robert planned to take his advice, and make the most of this opportunity.

. . .

The nightwatchman gave Robert a questioning look when he returned so late to Leicester House. He'd tried not to drink too much, but the queen was insistent and the rich wine was the finest he'd tasted. They'd played games of cards, shared a fine supper of roasted venison, and talked until long after midnight.

One by one, her ladies made their excuses until only her most trusted servants remained. Robert was surprised at how entertaining she could be, and soon relaxed, speaking freely about his hopes for the future. His stepfather would have urged caution, but he had nothing to hide from his queen.

He saw behind the mask of royalty. Elizabeth was a lonely woman, with only her ladies and self-serving courtiers. Before they parted, he took her fingers in his and kissed them. She'd been in no hurry to withdraw her hand, and he'd held her gold-ringed fingers for long enough for an understanding to pass between them.

Robert enjoyed his new life as the queen's favourite. Over the past weeks, the thrill of his power over the queen developed into a bond of mutual affection as close as any mother and son. He'd discovered her wicked sense of humour as she whispered amusing, insightful, and sometimes outrageous observations about her courtiers.

He'd also witnessed how her mood could change like a weathercock in the wind. If a maid spilled wine, or an Italian ambassador failed to bow, they could be dismissed with a shouted reprimand and never seen again. Like her father, Queen Elizabeth used her power with threats they knew she would carry out.

Anthony Bagot was impressed by Robert's change of fortune as he helped Robert pull on his polished riding boots. 'You've become a man of status at court, my lord. I've written to my father that whenever the queen is abroad, there is no one closer to her than my lord of Essex.' Bagot fastened the long row of small silver buttons on Robert's doublet, and stood back to admire his work. 'It seems you've also become Her Majesty's favourite dancing partner.'

'Those long hours spent on dancing lessons at Theobalds prepared me well, Bagot.' Robert smiled. 'The queen announced that she will dance with no one else. I know what the gossips of court say but, frankly, I don't care. What troubles me is Her Majesty's affection for scoundrels like Raleigh.'

Bagot raised an eyebrow. 'I'm sure the queen must see he's not to be trusted.'

'Raleigh is not the only one I need to watch. The queen spends too much time with Francis Drake, who is little more than a pirate. He offers the queen gold and caskets of pearls, then stirs up her anger at the Spanish, and talks of an attack on their fleet at Cadiz.'

'Sir Robert Dudley said he has little enough chance of trying to broker a peace, without Drake's help.'

'True, Bagot, but he asked me to safeguard his interests while he is away, and I've promised to do my best.'

The first stop of the royal progress was at Theobalds, and Robert enjoyed escorting the queen as the guest of a much-humbled William Cecil. He was saddened to see Lady Mildred looking frail, and walked with her in the rose gardens while the queen rested. They stopped for her to recover her breath at her wooden bench seat, shaded from the setting sun.

Robert turned to Lady Mildred. 'I used to sit here with your daughter Elizabeth, long ago.'

'You are still not yet engaged, my lord?'

'I miss your daughter, and would have married her if I'd been a little older.' He could see the ghost of Elizabeth in her eyes. 'She taught me the hardest lesson of my life. Seize the day.'

Lady Mildred looked wistful. '*Carpe Diem*. A lesson for us all.'

The next stop on the progress was North Hall in Hertfordshire, the manor house of Robert's stepfather's elder brother, Sir Ambrose Dudley, Earl of Warwick. Robert's sister Dorothy contrived to visit Lady Warwick when the royal party arrived, and he hoped to use his new influence to bring her back to favour.

'Your sister?' The queen eyed Robert with suspicion. 'She is even worse than your godless mother. I have no wish to see her.'

'It would mean much to me if Your Majesty would allow my sister a second chance—'

'We shall not!'

Robert knew the queen would be in better spirits once she'd rested after their long ride, but he decided to make one more attempt, for his sister's sake. 'My sister's only crime was to marry for love, Your Majesty, as was my mother's.'

The effect on the queen made even the grim-faced yeomen at the door flinch. 'Your mother is a vixen, who was lucky not to be thrown in the Tower for her disloyalty!' Her shrill voice raised to a shout and her eyes blazed like coals on a fire. 'Leave us! Find Sir Walter, and tell him we wish to see him.' She dismissed him with a flick of her hand, as if he were her errand boy.

Robert's anger flared at the insults. 'That knave Raleigh is a consummate flatterer! He insults Your Majesty with his platitudes—'

'You *dare* to speak with such disdain about our loyal

servants?' Elizabeth glowered at him, and Robert turned to leave. 'Do *not* turn your back to us, Essex!'

He'd forgotten, and bowed, retreating backwards before she could say any more. He found Walter Raleigh and Robert Cecil, now the queen's secretary, waiting in the outer hall. Their stern faces told him they'd heard every word, so as well as ruining his sister's chances of redemption, he'd angered the queen and made at least one, if not two, enemies at court.

Robert stormed to his room, calling for Gelly and Bagot to pack and have their horses ready. 'We're leaving to join the Earl of Leicester. Sluys has fallen, but all hope is not lost and I might redeem myself.'

Bagot frowned. 'It will be dark before we reach the coast—'

'We have to return to London to collect my weapons and armour.' He cursed at the sudden reversal of fortune, and clenched his fist. 'I cannot remain here any longer, but might be able to retrieve my reputation if I can meet with the Duke of Parma.'

Bagot gave him a look which suggested he doubted it, but began packing ready for their return. Robert went to find his sister. She saw the dark look on his face, and placed her hand on his arm.

'I'm sorry, Robert. I should not have asked you to plead for me.'

He placed his hand on hers. 'If there is any fault, it's mine, for not choosing my moment with more care.' He looked into her eyes, and wished he had better news. 'We have to leave. Her Majesty will not change her mind.'

'I'll visit Mother, and Penelope. You know our sister has a son?'

Robert's black mood momentarily lifted. 'Penelope has named her little boy after me. I'd like to see him, but first I must make my fortune in the Low Countries.'

'Take care,' Dorothy embraced him, 'and be sure to visit us in Wales when you can.'

They left London at first light on the eighty-mile ride east to Sandwich, where Robert hoped to find them a passage on a ship to Flushing. They were close to Maidstone, where they planned to rest the horses overnight, when Gelly spotted a fast rider in pursuit.

Robert reined in his horse and turned as the rider hailed them. He recognised courtier Robert Carey, the youngest son of the queen's cousin, Sir Henry Carey. Carey's horse was in a lather, as if he'd raced to catch them.

'I have a message from Her Majesty, my lord. The queen commands you to return to court.'

'For my punishment?' Robert frowned and glanced at Gelly and Bagot. Carey rode alone, and wouldn't be able to force all three of them to return against their will.

'Quite the contrary, my lord. You are forgiven by Her Majesty.'

Robert couldn't believe his luck. 'Another day and we would have been at sea.'

Carey nodded. 'I had orders to pursue you to the Low Countries, if necessary.'

'Then I must thank you for your haste, Master Carey. Ride with us, and we'll find a tavern to drink a toast to our gracious queen.'

11

APRIL 1588

She called him 'sweet Robin', a name he knew she'd used for his stepfather, and allowed him to call her Bess in private. Her hand caressed his thigh under the table, and she whispered secrets, even though the queen's sharp-eyed ladies missed nothing. Robert learned to indulge her games, a small price to pay for such great reward.

'We bring out the worst in each other.' Elizabeth made it sound like an accusation.

Robert smiled at the thought, and whispered back. 'I would have it no other way.'

He loved her, but not as a lover, and not like he loved his mother or sisters. Robert loved her power, he loved her girlish admiration, and being envied as the favourite of the queen. He loved the sense of danger in teasing a woman who could have him thrown in the Tower of London. He loved the sense of being at the centre of everything, and loved knowing her fears and vulnerability.

He'd been made Master of the Horse, elected a Knight of the Garter, and granted lodgings at York House, the impressive mansion in the Strand with private access by a watergate to the

River Thames. He could come and go at all hours by wherry without being observed, other than by the trusted staff of his own household.

As well as dining with the queen, he sat at her side like her consort during the tedious business of state, and at the lively dances and court entertainments. Robert hunted with her in the royal parks, they walked together in her gardens, and he was often last to leave her chambers.

They were hardly ever alone, but her ladies looked the other way, and her servants bowed their heads. Robert thought he sometimes had a knowing look from her yeoman guards, man to man, but could rely on their discretion as he left her chamber, buttoning his doublet.

He knew his growing list of enemies called him her peacock, a popinjay – and worse. He'd heard that Raleigh called him a cuckoo in the nest, but Elizabeth laughed when he told her, and dismissed his concerns. In normal times, the gossips of court would have talked of little else, but these were not normal times. The country was preoccupied with the threat of invasion by Spain.

Lord Burghley, still holding on to his role as Treasurer, tried to warn her. 'I appreciate your faith in a peaceful solution, Your Majesty, but Walsingham's intelligence is that the Duke of Parma prepares a flotilla of barges to transport his army to England.' He frowned. 'I must counsel Your Majesty to invest in more ships—'

Elizabeth raised her voice at William Cecil as if he were a stable boy. 'You, of all people, should know how Ireland has drained our coffers. If you are so concerned, my lord, find me the funds to fight the Spanish!' Her shout echoed in the high-ceilinged chamber, and even her ladies, who'd heard her shout often enough, looked down at their needlework.

Anthony Bagot shook Robert awake. 'A royal messenger is here, my lord. He says it's urgent.'

Robert rubbed his eyes and cursed at the sound of Bagot pouring cold water from his ewer into the wash bowl. For a moment it seemed he was back in his attic rooms at Cambridge. Then he realised something serious must have happened.

'What reason did the messenger give for waking me at such an ungodly hour?'

'Only that Her Majesty requires your presence.' Bagot looked at him, as if he were going to make some comment but thought better of it. 'I'll fetch a fresh shirt, my lord.'

Robert clambered from his comfortable bed and splashed cold water in his face. He could be in trouble. Since the incident at North Hall he no longer took the queen's goodwill for granted. If he needed a reminder of how the queen could turn on her most devoted subjects, he need look no further than his own mother and stepfather.

Bagot helped him dress in his best doublet. Rich food and good living meant the gleaming silver buttons were harder to fasten each time.

'You've never been summoned so early in the morning, my lord. Do you think the Spanish war fleet have been sighted?'

'If they have, I shall ask the queen's permission to fight alongside my stepfather at Tilbury.' He brightened at the prospect. 'Her Majesty can't refuse if the beacons burn along the coast.'

The dawn tide on the choppy River Thames was in their favour as the surly boatman rowed him upriver to Richmond Palace. Robert frowned as a dead rat floated past. The river had seemed cleaner when he was a boy, but now the rapidly growing population treated it as an open sewer.

A red-liveried footman led Robert to the queen's private apartments, and Elizabeth's ladies made a discreet exit as he entered. The queen was dressed simply, in black embroidered with silver stars, with a necklace of glistening pearls. She looked up at Robert with tired eyes, and gestured for him to sit close to her.

'A letter has been delivered from Lord Admiral Howard.' She handed the square of unsealed parchment to Robert.

He unfolded the note, written in a confident hand.

'For the love of Jesus Christ, madam, awake thoroughly and see the treasons round about you against Your Majesty, and your realm, and draw your forces round about you, like a mighty Prince to defend you. Truly, madam, if you do so there is no cause to fear, if you do not there will be danger.'

'I am plagued by vivid nightmares.' She spoke softly, as if making a confession. 'I dreamed the Spanish sailed up the Thames into the heart of London, and there was nothing we could do.'

Robert refolded the letter, and looked into her dark-brown eyes. 'Your fleet guards our coast, and our militia is defending the estuary at Tilbury.'

She stared at him without speaking for a moment. 'There is still hope of peace. Our ambassador in Paris has been sent to tell the Duke of Parma we might surrender Flushing, if he will agree terms.' Her tone suggested she was beginning to have doubts.

'I fear it is too late for diplomacy.' Robert saw his chance. 'Let me assemble my company, and join the Earl of Leicester.' He held his breath, and stared into her dark eyes as she considered his request.

She took the Lord Admiral's letter and read aloud. 'Draw your forces round about you, like a mighty Prince.' Her mood seemed to brighten at the thought. 'We understand why you wish to fight. We shall accompany you, and your place is at our side.'

Robert arrived in Tilbury ahead of the queen, who'd been rowed down the River Thames from Greenwich Palace on her gilded barge. Promoted to her General of the Horse, a post last occupied by Sir Philip Sidney, he wore his best armour, and had sunk even deeper into debt recruiting and equipping his company.

A hundred and twenty musketeers and arquebusiers marched under his command, and he rode with two hundred cavalrymen. Few had experience of fighting, yet they looked magnificent, carrying new lances and banners, all dressed in the Essex livery of orange and white.

His stepfather, who'd been made Lieutenant General of the army, gave him a warm welcome, yet looked pale. 'I've suffered with a fever from the marshes, and can barely control my frustration at the way I've been treated by the queen's ministers.' He cursed Burghley and Walsingham. 'They've left me no choice but to pay the militia from my own pocket!'

'As they did with my father.' Robert frowned. His stepfather, now fifty-six, looked older. 'I will choose my moment and make sure the queen is made aware of this.'

Robert Dudley gave him a wry look, as if he doubted it would make any difference. 'I've had to reinforce a Roman fort as my headquarters. We're poorly equipped, and men have deserted. I fear this enterprise will cost me more than my good health. I expect Burghley and others are opposed to my appointment as Lieutenant General, and I might never be recompensed.'

. . .

Soon after the arrival of the queen, the Earl of Cumberland brought the welcome news that the Armada had been scattered, after cutting their anchors to escape fireships off Calais. Pursued by the English fleet, King Philip of Spain's Armada fled north, leaving the Duke of Parma unprotected.

The threat of invasion was over, yet Elizabeth was determined to turn the failure of the Spanish invasion to advantage. Sir Robert Dudley accompanied her as she inspected troops and made a speech from horseback, greeted with rousing cheers from her army.

Robert watched in awe. Elizabeth had memorised her speech, and this had been her plan all along. Her talk of a negotiated peace provided the perfect excuse to allow others, including himself and his stepfather, to meet the expense of her ships and land army. She had faced real danger, and become a victorious warrior queen. Now they called out, 'Gloriana, Gloriana, Gloriana!'

Despite being denied his fight with the Spanish, Robert led the celebratory march through the crowded streets of London. Behind him rode his cavalrymen, immaculate in their orange livery. Drummers and fife players were followed by his company of musket men and arquebusiers, who hadn't fired a single shot.

Elizabeth watched from a high balcony with his stepfather at her side. The crowds cheered, and called out, 'God save the queen!' when she raised a hand in acknowledgement. The celebrations served to remind her grateful people how she'd led them to victory, and saved them from the Spanish invaders.

'You have a rival for Her Majesty's affection, my Lord Essex.' Raleigh's companions laughed at his provocative comment.

The courtiers watched to see how he'd respond. Robert knew better than to rise to Walter Raleigh's taunt, yet cursed under his breath. He knew they spoke of Charles Blount, who'd arrived at court at the same time as Robert. Charismatic and talented, Blount was talked of as the true successor to Sir Philip Sidney – and, now, as the queen's new favourite.

Robert envied Blount, whose skill at the tournament was rewarded by the gift of the golden queen from Her Majesty's personal chess set. The talk of court was of how Charles Blount wore the queen's gift on his sleeve, fastened with a bright red ribbon, for all to see.

Robert turned to Raleigh. 'Now it seems every fool must wear a favour.'

Raleigh's companions laughed even louder, and Robert wished he'd kept silent, as somehow the joke seemed to be on him. He knew they envied him, and there was a price to be paid for being the favourite of the queen.

Gelly frowned with concern. 'Duelling is forbidden, my lord. It's a dangerous way to settle disagreements. Can I ask you to find some way to offer your apology?'

'Too late, Gelly. Charles Blount delivered the challenge in person, demanding satisfaction for being publicly offended, and I had to accept. What of my reputation if I were to withdraw now?'

'You could be killed, or charged with his murder.'

'Then I shall let God decide, and you shall be my second.'

He managed to achieve a note of bravado, yet too many summers had passed since Sir Philip Sidney taught him sword fighting at Lamphey. The last time he'd fought anyone with a sword was for entertainment, at the city of Utrecht. He'd won easily enough then, but had no idea how skilled Charles Blount would be, although he seemed to excel at all he turned his hand to.

Soft dawn light filtered through the trees of Marylebone Park, named by the locals after the church of St Mary at the Bourne. The deer park was the property of the Crown, within the manor of Tyburn, where so many had lost their lives. They arrived early, and found the park deserted. Robert began to hope the whole thing had been a joke at his expense when Charles Blount and his second arrived on fine black horses.

'You've not brought a physician?' Charles Blount nodded to Gelly, then turned to Robert. 'You may give quarter at any time, Lord Essex.'

Robert resented the note of arrogance. 'The same for you, Master Blount.'

This was the moment to beg his challenger's forgiveness, but he knew the story would be told in palace corridors for years to come. He drew his sword from its scabbard, and did his best to recall Sir Philip Sidney's advice.

Charles Blount was four years older, and although Robert had a height advantage, he'd enjoyed good living. Gelly helped him strip off his doublet, to fight in his shirt for ease of movement, and Blount did the same. Robert said a silent prayer as he adopted his stance, within a sword's length of Blount.

Blount pointed his rapier at Robert's throat in a show of confident bravado. 'I've no wish to harm you, Lord Essex.'

Something about the natural ease with which he handled his sword reminded Robert of Sir Philip Sidney. He recalled how he'd said to strike and parry your opponent's blade with a single action.

Robert struck, driving Charles Blount back, relying on his strength rather than technique, thrusting forward with reckless aggression. He no longer saw Blount in front of him, but Walter Raleigh's grinning face, and the sound of his court followers laughing in derision.

Their blades clashed again and again, with a ring of sharp steel. Robert remembered his training, and kept his guard, but Blount proved light on his feet. He parried increasingly vicious blows with apparent ease, yet didn't attack. Robert stepped back and the two of them circled, each making a judgement about the other's strengths and weaknesses.

Robert knew he was tiring, and must finish the fight. He lunged at Blount's sword arm, but his thrust was side-stepped and he glanced down as a sharp pain stabbed in his left thigh. Charles Blount was too quick for him, and the spreading bloodstain looked serious.

'Quarter!' Robert shouted and dropped his sword, raising his hands in surrender to prevent further injury.

Charles Blount stepped back and gestured to his second. 'It's a flesh wound. My man has brought linen, and will tend to you.'

Robert put pressure on his bleeding wound with his hand, and grimaced with the pain. 'I regret any offence I might have caused.' The wound was an honourable one, bad enough to stop the fight, yet he knew Blount might have disfigured him, or maimed him for life.

Blount watched as his second bandaged Robert's thigh. 'I consider honour satisfied, and regret your injury, my Lord Essex.'

Elizabeth was in good spirits as they planned a late summer progress. As Master of the Horse, Robert helped devise the itinerary, deciding which horses they would take, and how many mules and carts would be needed. Elizabeth teased him by changing her mind about which courtiers would accompany them, and which she would like to honour with her company.

The wound in his thigh was healing, yet ached when he put weight on his leg, and he walked with a limp. The queen insisted he made his peace with Charles Blount, who'd become an unexpected ally against Raleigh and his rowdy followers. He heard that, far from being angry at their duel, the queen was amused, and said it was time someone taught him better manners.

They were interrupted by a dour-looking Lord Burghley, who asked to see the queen in private, and gestured for Robert to leave. Robert waited in the anteroom, and heard the door of the queen's private chamber slam shut. He recognised the signs. There would be no more planning her progress until her mood improved.

Lord Burghley looked grim-faced as he emerged from the queen's apartments. 'It is with great sadness that I must inform you the Earl of Leicester is dead.'

Robert stared at him in shocked disbelief. His sense of loss was greater than when his own father had died, and it took him a moment to compose himself. He'd had no idea his stepfather's illness was so serious, and his mind filled with questions.

'How did it happen?'

'He was on his way to Buxton to take the waters. He'd been told it might effect a cure, but he fell ill with the return of his fever, and pains in his stomach. There was nothing his physicians could do, but I can tell you he died peacefully, with your lady mother at his side.'

Robert found a bench seat in the gardens, and sat alone, overwhelmed by grief. He remembered how, as a boy, he'd resented Robert Dudley sitting in his father's chair at Chartley

Manor, yet his stepfather always seemed to understand. He would miss his wry advice, his generosity and encouragement.

His hand went to the silver dagger he wore at his belt. The gift meant more to him now than ever, a connection with a man who'd succeeded in replacing his father, and who'd taught him so much. He rubbed his eyes and took a deep breath before returning to the queen's apartments. The doors were locked. Baroness Cobham, a Lady of the Bedchamber, approached Robert and curtseyed.

'Her Majesty has asked to be left alone, my lord.'

Robert understood, relieved to have an excuse to leave. 'Please tell the queen I returned to offer my condolences.'

He took a wherry to the Strand and found his mother, who'd returned to Leicester House. 'I've just heard—' His voice choked.

His mother wore mourning dress yet seemed stoical. 'You must be chief mourner, Robert, and take charge of the funeral arrangements.'

Robert stared at his mother in surprise at her matter-of-fact tone. She seemed to have already accepted being widowed for the second time.

'I would be honoured.'

'What did the queen say when she heard the news?'

'I don't know. She shut herself away.'

'He wrote to her, a long letter from his sickbed.' His mother sounded bitter. 'She'll have me out of here, you know.'

'Is Leicester House mortgaged to the Crown?'

His mother looked around her grand stateroom, with the gilded candelabras and magnificent portraits, as if seeing it for the first time. 'Everything is.' Her voice softened. 'He left you his best armour, and his Garter chain, but most of our property will be sold to silence his creditors.'

Robert recalled his stepfather's words at Tilbury, and clenched his fist. 'He said Burghley and others were opposed to his appointment as Lieutenant General, and that he might never be recompensed.'

'William Cecil is only the instrument of the queen, yet he bears a grudge, and drained my husband's fortune like a leech, until there was nothing left.'

'I shall speak to Her Majesty—'

His mother gave a scornful laugh. 'Do you *never* learn, Robert?' She shook her head. 'Your precious queen will take great pleasure in having me thrown on to the street.'

He knew in his heart she was right. 'Chartley is mine now and, although there are tenants, I shall have Master Bagot serve them notice and prepare our home for you.'

His stepfather's wish was to be buried close to his son, Lord Denbigh, the noble imp. As chief mourner, Robert led the funeral procession of a hundred men from Kenilworth, six miles south, to the Beauchamp Chapel of the church of St Mary the Virgin in Warwick.

Sir Robert Dudley's sword and helmet lay on top of the black-draped coffin, carried on a wagon pulled by four black horses. There were no crowds lining the cold October streets, only the gaze of the curious as the sombre procession made its way to the chapel.

By tradition, Robert's mother stayed away from the funeral, as did his sisters, but at his side rode his younger brother Wat. Now a celebrated scholar at Oxford, Wat had recently married Margaret Dakins, his fellow student from his time at the King's Manor in York.

Robert had made one last attempt to see the queen, who still refused to speak to anyone. Raleigh persuaded William Cecil to order her doors to be broken open, and Robert decided to leave while he still could.

His mother warned him of the whispered scandal – which had somehow reached her, as scandals always did.

'They say I poisoned your stepfather,' she'd scowled at the thought, 'with some secret potion in his medicine.'

'Why would anyone say such a thing?' Robert's anger at the chattering courtiers returned. 'He caught a fever in the Tilbury marshes, as did many of his men.'

'They said your stepfather murdered his first wife so he could marry the queen, and that he poisoned your father so he could marry me.' She'd looked defiant. 'There never was any proof or substance in the rumours, but he's no longer able to defend his good name, and people love to repeat a scandal.'

After the funeral Robert remained in the now silent church, and kneeled alone before the high altar. In all the excitement of his life at court he'd neglected his faith. For the first time in months, he clasped his hands together and prayed for the soul of Sir Robert Dudley, a good man, taken before his time.

12

MARCH 1589

Robert's grandfather, Sir Francis Knollys, looked stern and frowned at the sight of Robert. 'I know you to be honourable in your intentions, but I have a duty to urge discretion in your dealings with Her Majesty, for her own sake, as well as the reputation of our family.'

Robert stared at the old man, not sure what to say. His grandfather, now in his mid seventies, belonged to another era. A devout Protestant, he always wore black and was the self-appointed upholder of moral standards for his family, and at court. His eyesight was failing, but his mind was sharp. He'd always spoken kindly to Robert, yet this sounded like a reprimand.

'I'm careful never to forget my place, but you know how demanding Her Majesty can be.' Robert looked at his polished boots, rather than meet the old man's eyes.

'Indeed.' His grandfather frowned. 'As Treasurer of the Royal Household, I oversee the list of New Year gifts to Her Majesty. Your gift was described as a naked man in a flower of gold.'

Robert smiled as he remembered her reaction. 'A jewelled trinket, of no great value.'

He gave Robert a look of disapproval. 'I've long tried to counsel Her Majesty's better judgement in such matters. I've seen how she encourages flatterers who, in my view, are responsible for most of her difficulties.'

Robert resented the implied criticism. 'I've also tried to warn Her Majesty – although my efforts seem to have had the opposite effect. Men like Drake and Raleigh take liberties, yet Her Majesty indulges their scheming.' The note of frustration sounded in his raised voice.

His grandfather placed a hand on Robert's arm. 'I'm asking you to take care. For your mother's sake.'

'My mother will never be welcomed back to court.'

'Which is why she takes such great pride in your achievements, Robert, now more than ever.'

'She's never told me—'

His grandfather smiled. 'Nor will she, but it's the truth.'

Troubled by his grandfather's admonishment, Robert formed a plan to prove his worth. He discovered the queen had agreed to send six ships and two pinnaces, and invested sixty thousand pounds in Drake's ambitious scheme of an English Armada, to put an end to the threat from Spain.

He approached Sir Francis Drake, who was at Richmond Palace for a private meeting with the queen. 'I wish to sail with you, as commander of one of the queen's ships, Sir Francis.'

Drake gave Robert a suspicious look, and seemed in a hurry, unwilling to discuss his plans. He dressed in fine clothes, with a pleated ruff, and wore a thick collar of black fur with a heavy gold chain, like a noble – but when he spoke, his broad Devon accent betrayed his humble origins.

'We have no need of more commanders, my Lord Essex,

unless they have experience of fighting at sea, and can pay their way.'

Robert couldn't miss his implication. Although the queen granted him the tax on sweet wines, previously the right of his stepfather, he was still deep in debt, and Drake no doubt knew it. He needed money, and if the English Armada was successful, all who sailed with Drake would have a share of any prizes.

'I fought the Duke of Parma's army in the Low Countries, and was ready to do so again at Tilbury. Like you, Sir Francis, I have unfinished business with the Spanish.'

Drake gave him an appraising look. 'I'll consider your request, my lord, but be sure to have permission from Her Majesty.' He turned and left.

Robert scowled at the stocky sea captain's abrupt manner. Elizabeth would never be persuaded to let him sail with Drake. His plan risked banishment from court, the loss of York House, and possibly his life, but he'd grown tired of the gossipers saying he'd won his place on his stepfather's coat-tails.

He had to prove them wrong, and this might be his best chance. He'd learned that one of the queen's ships, the three-hundred-and-fifty-ton galleon, *Swiftsure*, was commanded by Sir Roger Williams. A fellow Welshman, from Monmouth, they'd fought together in the Low Countries, and Sir Roger would have no qualms about having him aboard.

It took three days of hard riding to reach the Cornish fishing port of Falmouth, stopping at dusk and starting again at first light. Robert couldn't help glancing back down the road for the first hundred miles, but saw no sign they were being pursued.

Gelly surprised him by announcing he would be unable to sail, as he was returning to Wales. 'I wish I was coming with you, my lord, but your Uncle George has proposed me to stand as Member of Parliament for Carmarthen.' He grinned with pride. 'Who'd have thought of such a thing?'

Robert wished him well, but would miss his cheerful Welsh companion, as they'd been together since his Cambridge days. He decided Anthony Bagot should remain at York House, and do his best to keep up a pretence that Robert was in residence, for as long as possible.

Instead, Robert's brother Wat, and John Reynolds, his hunting groom, rode with him. Like Robert, this could be Wat's best hope of making his fortune, and he'd fought with Sir Roger Williams in France. Reynolds wouldn't be sailing with them, as he would return with the horses, as well as the small brass key to Robert's writing desk in his study at York House.

Before he left, Robert had written letters explaining his actions, and Bagot had strict orders only to send them when Reynolds returned with the key. As well as letters to the queen, his mother and sisters, he'd spent the longest time on the wording of a letter to his grandfather. He wished to convince his grandfather of his honourable intentions, and included a clue to the name of his ship:

Sir, What my courses have been I need not repeat, for no man knoweth them better than yourself, and my debts are at the least two or three and twenty thousand pounds. Her Majesty's goodness hath been so great as I could not ask more of her, and have no way left to repair myself but mine own adventure, which I had much rather undertake than offend Her Majesty. If I should speed well, I will adventure to be rich; if not, I will never live to see the end of my poverty. And so, wishing that this letter, which I have left for you, may come to your hands, I commit you to God's good protection.

Your assured friend, R. Essex.

. . .

The *Swiftsure* was ready and waiting to set sail when they arrived, and Sir Roger greeted Robert with a grin. 'I trust you know what you're letting yourself in for, my lord?'

Robert grinned. Exhausted, stinking of horse sweat, hungry and thirsty, he had never been happier, and took a deep breath of fresh sea air. 'I'm grateful to you, Sir Roger. Now let's be under way while we can.'

They gave Plymouth a wide berth, heading out to sea to avoid being spotted by Drake's fleet. Salt spray lashed Robert's face and white-crested waves warned of a lively passage, but the *Swiftsure* kept a steady course on the choppy sea. Only now did Sir Roger confess he had no idea of Drake's plan.

'We know Spanish spies noted our preparations, and we encouraged the impression we're returning to Cadiz – but I suspect the Captain General has something quite different in mind. A successful attack on the Spanish treasure fleet would make rich men of us all.'

Robert worried about what Drake would do when he found out about his subterfuge. 'We can't join the rest of the fleet before we're too far out to be sent back.'

Sir Roger nodded. 'If I know Drake, he'll bluster and curse when he finds I have you aboard, but he needs every ship, and won't wish to spare the *Swiftsure*.'

After a week at sea without sight of any other ships, a sail appeared on the far horizon. A fat-bellied galleon with a high sterncastle, she flew a colourful Spanish pennant, and sailed without an escort. Sir Roger called the ship to action. Men scrambled to clear the deck and prepare the twenty-nine powerful guns.

Shouts rang out as gun crews loaded heavy cannonballs and chain shot. The *Swiftsure* was well named. Fast and manoeuvrable, she sped towards the stern of the Spanish merchant ship, presenting the smallest possible target.

Robert clambered down to the cramped gun deck to watch as they came within range. The gun captain studied the Spanish ship through the gun port, then called to the crewmen to place the lighted fuse to the touch hole. A sharp boom shook the ship as the heavy culverins roared, filling the cramped gun deck with the acrid tang of sulphurous gunpowder, and making Robert's ears ring.

The gun leapt back until stopped by the heavy restraining ropes attached to the inside of the parapet. Robert rushed back on deck in time to see the musket men preparing to provide covering fire, and ordered them to open fire with a fusillade as they drew alongside the Spanish galleon. The bullets cracked into the brightly painted timbers, sending splinters into the air.

They were rewarded by the sight of a white flag, fluttering in frantic surrender. The Spanish captain wore a scarlet coat and a broad-brimmed hat. He drew his sword and lay it on the deck as a gesture of surrender, to a rousing cheer from the English gunners. Robert couldn't believe their luck. They'd taken their first prize without a fight.

The crewmen of the *Swiftsure* threw grappling hooks and hauled the two ships together. In a show of bravado, Robert was first to board the Spanish merchant ship, and snatched the captain's sword from where it lay. The captain took off his hat and mopped his brow, speaking rapidly in Spanish.

Robert couldn't understand a word, but gestured for the Spanish captain to lead the way to his cabin. Small but well organised, his cabin had a narrow bunk with red velvet coverings. A finely crafted brass astrolabe sat on the chart table, under a shelf full of leather-bound books. He took the captain's astrolabe, locked him in his cabin and pocketed the key.

He still carried the captain's sword, and it gave him an air of authority as he ordered his men to make a thorough search of the hold. The Spanish watched with nervous concern as their cargo was plundered, and Sir Roger appeared from the hold, carrying a silver candlestick and looking pleased.

'The cargo is mostly grain, but we have a haul of spices, my lord. Worth a small fortune in London – a good prize to placate the Captain General.'

Robert handed him the key. 'I locked their captain in his cabin, but what will we do with the Spanish crewmen?'

'We'll set them ashore at the first opportunity – but now we must find the rest of our fleet, before we encounter a Spanish man-of-war.'

They sailed on for another three weeks in worsening seas and gusting, easterly winds. Sharp squalls of stinging rain made it unpleasant to remain on deck, yet Robert busied himself learning as much as he could. He climbed to the topmast to help keep a lookout, and took his turn on night watches.

After another week of sailing, the sea conditions improved, with a cool breeze taking them further south. Robert knew the stories of Drake's daring raid on Cadiz in 1587. He looked forward to his chance to fight the Spanish, but was concerned about Wat, who spent most of his time leaning over the side.

'Fix your eyes on the horizon. They say it'll help you find your sea legs.'

Wat looked doubtful. 'How much longer must we suffer, do you think?'

Robert shrugged. 'We have to wait for Captain General Drake, although I wonder what he'll say.'

. . .

At last, the welcome sight of the English Armada appeared on the horizon. They hove to, and lined up on the deck to welcome the Captain General. Robert had no idea how Sir Francis might react to his presence, but knew Drake dealt harshly with those who dared defy his authority.

Drake was rowed across from his flagship, the *Revenge*, to the *Swiftsure* in a pinnace. He scowled at Sir Roger Williams as he climbed aboard, then turned to Robert. 'You've displeased Her Majesty, Lord Essex. Sir Francis Knollys and the Earl of Huntingdon were sent to stop you, and I have orders to send you back to England.' He turned to Sir Roger. 'You, sir, should be removed from command, and charged with insubordination, or Her Majesty will have me answer for it.'

Robert was about to argue his case, and defend Sir Roger, but recalled his friend's words. Drake wouldn't want to lose a good ship or a commander with Sir Roger's experience. For once, he remained silent, bit his lip, and said a silent prayer.

Sir Roger replied for them both. 'We respect your wish to send us back, Captain General, but north-easterly winds are against us.' He glanced back at their prize galleon, now flying the flag of St George. 'My men of the *Swiftsure* have proved their worth, and our only wish is to fight the Spanish, under your command.'

Drake bristled and cursed under his breath, but there was a twinkle in his eye as he made his decision. 'You're right, Sir Roger. We've sailed too far to send you back. You've missed one battle, at Coruña, where we burned the town and many Spanish ships. I can tell you now we have Don Antonio aboard, and our plan is to make him King of Portugal in Lisbon.'

Robert could hold his silence no longer. 'Let me be the first ashore when we reach Portugal, Captain General.' He wasn't sure if Drake smiled because of deference or his impertinence, but he nodded.

'You shall lead the men to the gates of Lisbon, my Lord Essex, and, if God wills it, redeem yourself.'

The shock of the cold sea took Robert's breath away as he leapt from the boat, wading chest-deep in breaking waves, which threatened to knock him from his feet. He carried Sir Philip Sidney's sword above his head, to keep it clear of the water, and called for his men to follow.

They'd landed sixty miles north of Lisbon in the surf of the sweeping sandy beach at Peniche, and the thrill of adventure surged through Robert's veins. First to reach the shore, he felt truly alive for the first time since leading the charge against the Duke of Parma's army at Zutphen.

He heard shouts of alarm and looked back to see one of their overloaded longboats swamped by a breaking wave. Some twenty men were pitched into the churning sea, and several were dragged under by the current. Robert cursed the reminder of how easily their lives could be lost, but was relieved to see his brother Wat standing soaked but safe on the beach.

Sir Roger Williams landed with the other half of their men a short distance away, and raised his sword as the signal to launch the attack. There was no time to rest. Their plan was to take the clifftop fortress before the Portuguese used the shore battery against Drake's ships.

The deep boom of a cannon meant they were too late. Robert flinched as a second shot blasted over his head. The Portuguese gunners were aiming at the *Swiftsure*, anchored a safe distance offshore, and the heavy cannonballs splashed harmlessly into the sea.

Sir Roger led his men up the road to the fort, while Robert's followed him in a run up a winding path under the cover of steep dunes. They arrived at the gates of the fortress in time to outflank the Portuguese garrison, who'd come out to attack Sir Roger's soldiers.

Robert charged, yelling at the top of his voice. One of the Portuguese soldiers raised his musket and fired at close range, but the bullet cracked on the ground at Robert's feet. The garrison commander shouted the order to retreat towards the town, and his men fled.

Sir Roger produced the flag of St George from inside his tunic, and it soon flew from the fort's flagpole, from where it could be seen by Drake's approaching fleet. Robert searched the abandoned fort, and found a breastplate engraved with an eagle and a Portuguese lance as his reward.

They smashed the locks on cavernous storerooms filled with weapons and armour, casks of gunpowder, cured hams, flagons of wine and barrels of beer. Sir Roger grinned as he handed Robert a tankard of Portuguese ale.

'They ran so fast we didn't even have the chance to tell them we have their new king with us!'

Robert's clothes were still soaked from wading through the surf as he took a deep drink of the bitter ale. 'They robbed us of a fight, Sir Roger – but we shall redeem ourselves by accepting the surrender of Lisbon!'

Sir John Norris grudgingly spared Robert and his brother horses, unloaded with difficulty from the ships. 'You're to follow my orders, Lord Essex.' General Norris seemed annoyed to have missed the skirmish. He eyed Robert's engraved breastplate. 'The Captain General insists there is to be no looting. He wishes the people to welcome Don Antonio as their new king.'

'Of course, Sir John.' Robert mounted his horse, and tested his looted lance for balance. He'd seen Don Antonio, a sly-looking man with a straggling beard, and thought him a poor choice as Portugal's new ruler.

General Norris turned to Sir Roger. 'Your men are to remain here to guard the fortress and the beach. The fleet will sail around the coast while we march to Lisbon.'

Robert rode at the side of his brother Wat, who'd recovered from his seasickness. They stopped overnight at the town of Torres Vedras, some thirty miles from Lisbon, and occupied the ancient stone keep of the Moorish fortress.

Wat lay his bedroll on the dusty floor next to Robert. 'Don Antonio promised three thousand supporters would be waiting to welcome us, but there are fewer than forty.'

Robert nodded. 'I tried to ask them where the rest are, but none spoke English.' He frowned. 'Only a few have horses, but General Norris says he expects more will join us soon enough.'

He found it hard to sleep, so close to their objective, and heard a stifled cry, followed by an echoing neigh and the clatter of galloping horses. He'd slept in his clothes so only had to grab his eagle breastplate and sword before rushing to investigate.

He found General Norris bent over the body of one of their guards. 'They've murdered our sentries.' The general cursed. 'Cut their throats, and stolen one of our supply wagons.'

'I heard horses.' Robert peered into the darkness. 'They can't be far away. Let me take thirty cavalrymen, and we'll see if we can catch them.'

The general nodded. 'If we find they are Portuguese, then Don Antonio was mistaken when he told Her Majesty he'd be welcomed as their king.'

Robert woke Wat and Sir Roger. 'This is our chance to redeem ourselves – but we must be quick.'

Minutes later they were on the road with two dozen hand-picked riders. They were halfway to Lisbon before they saw the flickering light of a torch on the road ahead. As they drew closer,

Robert heard men talking and laughing, but couldn't understand what they were saying.

He led his cavalrymen in a charge, and swung his sword in a savage blow at the rearmost rider, hacking him from his horse, before turning on the next. The darkness worked to their advantage, as the enemy seemed to have no idea how many were attacking them.

The last two men surrendered and were taken back to the camp as prisoners, although Robert already knew the answer to the general's question. The Portuguese rejected Don Antonio, and would rather be ruled by the Spanish.

The next day the air filled with the tang of burning timber. In revenge for the attack on the sentries, General Norris had ordered the burning of barns used to store corn. The flickering glow and smoke from the fires continued until nightfall, and extra sentries had to be posted all night with their weapons to hand to guard against the threat of further attacks.

In the morning, they rode the last few miles to Lisbon, where Wat stared up at the high city walls. 'The Portuguese know we won't be able to hold them to siege. We don't have enough men or supplies.'

They had no choice other than to return, and it was little consolation to Robert to be appointed the commander of the rearguard as they withdrew. Before they left, he cantered to the city gates and plunged his lance into the thick oak, calling out a challenge.

'Accept Don Antonio as your king, or live with the consequences!' There was no answer. Yet again, he'd been robbed of his chance of fame and glory.

The men were cheered to learn that Drake's flotilla plundered a good many Spanish merchant ships, some laden with copper. They would all have a share of the profits once the ships and cargos were sold in London, but storms and gales prevented any voyage to the Azores in search of Spanish treasure ships.

As well as those who drowned in the landing, one man hanged for looting, and a few who died after drinking poisoned water, many more were now dying of a strange fever. Robert would be glad to see the green fields of England, and thanked God he and his brother survived their Lisbon adventure unscathed.

Robert was surprised to be welcomed back as a hero, and at how easily he was forgiven by the queen. Despite her threatening letters, she wanted to hear every detail of his adventures in Portugal. He gave her the looted Spanish astrolabe, and she looked as pleased as if it were made from solid gold, rather than brass.

He decided not to confess to her that, far from making him rich, their adventure had increased his debts by some ten thousand pounds. The sale of prize ships and cargos failed to cover the costs. Many of Drake's men died of a mysterious illness on the voyage home, and the expedition was deemed a financial and military failure.

Robert also had to keep secret the news which might send the queen into another of her black moods. One of the letters waiting for him at York House was from his mother. She had married Robert's late stepfather's Master of the Horse, Sir Christopher Blount. A devout Catholic, he was sixteen years younger than Robert's mother, and he thought it an unhappy choice.

His late stepfather warned him once that Sir Christopher secretly spied for Francis Walsingham. Robert Dudley made light of it, but he thought this was how the queen seemed to be so well informed about his life after he left her court.

Robert decided it would be best to stay away from his mother's household. His failure to visit or write was rewarded by another letter chiding him for '*being somewhat sparing of your pen,*' and was signed, '*Your mother that more than affectionately loveth you.*'

He sat at his desk, surprised at how deeply he'd been moved by his mother's words, and thinking about his family as he stared at his mother's neat writing. His brother Wat had proved a good companion, but he shouldn't have neglected his sisters. There was no point in resenting his new stepfather, and the time had come to think about a family of his own.

Robert smiled as he thought how the queen would react when he found a wife, but he needed a son, and Elizabeth would not live forever. He brightened as an idea formed in his mind. His plan was not without risk, but he sharpened his quill and took a fresh sheet of parchment. He began to write to the man most likely to be his future benefactor, King James of Scotland.

13

APRIL 1590

Robert noted the faded velvet and worn gilding on the ornate arms of the chair as he waited for Lady Frances. Walsingham House in Seething Lane, by the Tower of London, looked grand from outside, but there seemed to be few servants and the rooms were cold, with rush matting floors, and moth-eaten tapestries.

He'd called out of courtesy, to offer his sympathy on the death of her father. He could have written, but thought he should see Frances in person, out of respect. He'd not forgotten the connection he'd once sensed.

The door creaked open and Lady Frances appeared in the doorway. Robert had expected her to be in mourning dress, but was surprised at how well her black gown showed off her figure, with a fan-shaped ruff, open at the front and a laced bodice with a carcanet of gauze.

Two small spaniels entered with her, and one went bounding up to Robert for attention, licking his hand, its tail wagging furiously. The other dog stared at him with too-knowing eyes, as if making up its mind whether he was welcome.

'Eris!' Frances called her boisterous dog to heel, but it ignored her.

Robert smiled as he recalled his tutor's lessons. 'Eris was the Greek goddess of chaos, strife and discord.'

Frances gave him a warm smile. 'They are sisters, but could not be more different.' She looked down at the dog hiding in her skirts. 'This one's called Harmonia, goddess of harmony and concord.'

She called for her maidservant to take the dogs outside and turned to Robert. 'Thank you for coming. I hear much about you these days, my lord.'

He remembered the reason for his visit, and took off his hat as he stood to bow. 'I'm sorry for your loss, my lady. Her Majesty said her life will never be as safe without your father.'

A flicker of sadness showed in her cornflower-blue eyes. 'Father loved his work, but it cost him dearly.'

'I know he suffered with poor health these past months.'

'I pleaded with him to stay at home and rest, but he told me the queen showed little sympathy, and insisted he must return to work.'

Robert nodded. 'Her Majesty is the most demanding of mistresses.'

'Father had to meet the costs of his network of agents from his own pocket.' Frances frowned. 'He worried about his debts, and having so little to show for all those years of loyal service. He was buried in haste, at midnight, to outwit his creditors.'

'I truly had no idea.' Robert shook his head at yet another example of the queen taking advantage of those who served her. He'd not attended the funeral at St Paul's Cathedral. 'I will speak to Her Majesty on your mother's behalf. It's only right she should clear your father's debts to the Crown.'

Frances nodded. 'My mother will be most grateful. I know she worries about how we will cope without my father.'

'And you, Frances, are you provided for?'

'I'm fortunate that I have few expenses.' She forced a smile. 'Mother has left for Barn Elms, our house in Richmond. Will you do me the honour of keeping me company for supper?'

'I have no other plans for the evening.' Again, she'd surprised him. 'It would be my pleasure.'

He followed her into the dining room, where a warming log fire burned in the grand fireplace under a flattering portrait of the queen in her youth. He stared into the painting's dark eyes and cursed under his breath. His father, his stepfather, and even Sir Francis Walsingham, had all been crippled by debt as a reward for their loyalty.

The supper proved surprisingly good – a simple meal of succulent beef tenderloin, roasted in butter with rosemary, followed by almond gingerbread, rich with ginger and cinnamon. Frances opened a cask of her late father's excellent wine, and Robert raised his glass in a toast.

'To your father's memory. We'll not see his like again.'

Frances nodded and raised her glass. 'He did his best for us all, and we shall miss him.'

Her servants cleared the table and withdrew, and she gestured for Robert to join her on a comfortable seat by the fireside. She didn't seem in any hurry to see him go, and proved a good listener, witty and knowledgeable, with many questions he was happy to answer.

'I heard how you defied the queen to sail to Portugal with Captain Drake.' Her eyes twinkled in the firelight.

Robert smiled at the memory, and loosened a few buttons of his doublet. He enjoyed the unexpected attention, and her tone seemed flirtatious.

'I doubt my grandfather will ever forgive me. He was ordered to ride through the night to Plymouth to bring me back, only to find I'd sailed from Falmouth.'

Frances smiled. 'Yet Her Majesty forgives you?'

'I thought I might be banished, like my poor mother, but your father was good enough to speak on my behalf, and Her Majesty confessed she needs me.'

Frances raised an eyebrow. 'For what, exactly?'

Robert hesitated, not sure if she was teasing him, but knew he could trust her discretion. 'She says I make her feel young again.'

Frances refilled their glasses with the rich wine. 'The potent elixir of youth.' She took a sip, and gave him a meaningful look. 'What do you think she'll do if you ever decide to marry?'

He smiled at her question. 'It's not a crime.'

'But if you were to ask her permission?'

'She'd find some reason to refuse.' He'd drunk a few glasses of wine but didn't miss the implication of her question. His eyes drifted to the revealing carcanet over the uplifted curves of her breasts, and his pulse raced with longing. 'I should tell you I once asked your father if I could be your suitor.'

'He told me.' She spoke softly, and looked deep into Robert's eyes as if trying to read his thoughts. 'He said he gave you his blessing.'

'I'm sorry I didn't tell you before. I wasn't ready for marriage.' Robert stared into the flames as he remembered the joy of dancing with his first love, Elizabeth Cecil, and how Bethan seduced him with her dark-brown eyes, sparkling with mischief. He'd seen Bethan when he visited Penelope, and an understanding passed between them as their eyes met. He still loved her, but nothing could ever come of it.

'Father also told me about your letters to the King of Scotland.'

Robert's good mood evaporated in an instant, and his mind filled with questions. 'What did he say?'

'Your Scottish messenger, Richard Douglas, was one of my father's informers, and Father soon worked out your code. You should have come up with something more imaginative than 'Venus' for the queen – and 'weary knight' for yourself.'

'He told you that?' Robert had underestimated Frances, and her father. 'Did he tell Her Majesty?' He held his breath, feeling his future hanging in the balance.

'If he had, you would know by now. Father kept few secrets from Lord Burghley, though, and Robert Cecil called here with his men the day my father died, and took away all his papers.'

Robert sat back, numb with shock. They knew everything. He'd been foolish enough to put it in writing, and involved Penelope too. It would look like a conspiracy, and the queen would not forgive him easily. It seemed Robert Cecil had enough evidence to have him and his sister charged with treason. He would have to take more care.

A shower of hail rattled against the leaded windowpanes, breaking the silence. Frances stared at him for a moment, as if reaching a decision. 'I've kept you late, and the weather has taken a turn for the worse. If you like, I can have a room made ready for you.'

'I would be grateful. The thought of taking a wherry in this downpour doesn't appeal to me.'

Frances rang a bell and her maidservant appeared. 'Lord Essex will be staying for the night, so the guest room needs to be prepared.' She glanced at Robert. 'I shall show his lordship to his room, so will have no further need of you this evening.'

She watched her servant leave, then turned to Robert. 'I'm curious. I would expect a man like you to marry for money, or love – yet I have no money of my own, and you've paid me scant attention at court since Philip died. Why did you consider me? Was it because of some promise you made to my late husband?'

'In truth, I thought to marry you to have an heir, and I would have been glad of your father's protection.'

Frances stared into the fire. The flames had died down but the glowing logs lit up her face, reflecting in her eyes with a strange intensity. 'I was barely sixteen when my father arranged my marriage to Philip. My husband was a dreamer, and I always knew he loved your sister, Penelope. I lost a child, a boy, through miscarriage, but my daughter, Elizabeth, is five, so I could give you an heir.'

Robert smiled at her frank honesty. 'This evening has not turned out as I expected. You seem to have a talent for surprising me, Frances.'

She stood, and led him to the door, then turned, and spoke softly. 'This evening is far from over, my lord.'

He followed her up the creaking wooden staircase and through a narrow hallway lined with gloomy, gilt-framed portraits. The guest room was at the back of the house, with dark-oak panelling and mullioned windows of diamond leaded glass.

Frances closed the door behind her and turned the key in the lock with a soft click. Beeswax candles in silver holders lit up a velvet canopied bed with a warm yellow glow. Robert kissed her hand, before undoing the rest of the silver buttons on his doublet and pulling it off, followed by his shirt.

He saw her blue eyes widen at the sight of his bare chest. He'd put on a little weight through good living, but since losing his duel with Charles Blount he'd worked to improve his fitness. He was in his prime, firmly muscled, and his broad chest was well-toned.

Neither of them spoke as Frances undressed, taking off her silk shoes, then the fan-shaped ruff and her gauze carcanet, before unlacing the sleeves of her gown. She deftly unfastened the hooks at the front of the bodice, then stepped from her skirt and farthingale, and removed her petticoats and stockings, until she wore only her thin linen chemise.

Robert sat on the bed, kicked off his shoes and undressed. Conscious of her eyes on him, he stripped off his breeches and hose, pulled back the damask coverlet and climbed into the bed. He relaxed on to the down-filled pillows, and beckoned Frances to join him. She hesitated for a second, then took off her chemise and stood before him naked.

Her pale body seemed to glow in the soft candlelight, and Robert remembered she was a year younger than him, although he'd thought of her as older. Her figure had lost the girlish look of youth, but the sight of her bare breasts aroused him. He smiled as he took her hand and pulled her closer.

'Has anyone told you how beautiful you are?'

'Not for many years.' She kissed him softly on the cheek, then with passion, and they forgot about the world.

The black-robed minister cleared his throat, and sounded nervous as he asked if anyone knew of good reason why they should not be joined in marriage. They waited in silence for any answer, but the echoing chapel was empty except for Lady Walsingham, Robert's sister Penelope, his lawyer, Master Richard Broughton, and Anthony Bagot, who'd come to witness the wedding.

Robert knew of a good reason. He'd not dared risk the queen's anger by asking her permission, and there would be consequences. They had discussed their options, but he agreed with Frances. The risk of the queen finding some way to stop them was too great, and now it was too late.

He smiled at his sister, who held one hand over her middle, heavy with her second child. She shared their secret, as only his sister and his new mother-in-law knew Frances also carried a child, too small yet to be noticed under her loose gowns. They'd already agreed, if it was a boy, they would name him Robert – or Ursula, after her mother, if the child was a girl.

Robert's life became one of subterfuge from that day on, as he made excuses to visit Frances in Seething Lane, but took care to spend as much time as he could at the whim of the queen. He made great show of returning to York House, only to slip away in the night on the next wherry.

Lady Walsingham welcomed him as the son she'd never had, and little Elizabeth already called him *Father*. A pretty miniature of her mother, she spoke to him in French and played simple tunes on her virginal. Robert could see something of her true father in her amber eyes, and hoped he could learn to be good enough for her.

Elizabeth ran to welcome him when he arrived early, and shrieked in delight as he reached down and swept her off the ground. 'Where is your lady mother? I have news to share with her.'

Frances must have heard her daughter's shriek, as she appeared in the hallway with her two dogs at her heels before he'd removed his cloak. 'Good news, I hope?'

'Her Majesty has agreed to cancel your father's debts to the Crown – and has granted you a pension of three hundred pounds a year.'

'Thank the Lord. I confess I thought we'd be in penury for the rest of our lives.'

'Well, Her Majesty might change her mind once she learns what we've done.'

'Which means my news is even more important.' She glanced back over her shoulder. 'Your lawyer, Master Richard Broughton, is here.'

Robert followed her to her late father's study. The dark-panelled room was served by a window so small a lamp had to be kept burning on the large desk. Richard Broughton stood as they entered, and raised his cap.

'Good day, my lord. Your arrival is timely, as I have some proposals for you.'

Robert sat in one of the leather chairs. 'Have you found a way to redeem my father's debts, an end to my money worries?'

Richard Broughton gestured to the pile of ledgers on the desk in front of him. 'Your records are incomplete, but it seems you still have debts of some three and twenty thousand pounds, including three thousand owed to the Crown.'

Robert had hoped the sum was less, but trusted his lawyer's assessment. 'The expedition to Lisbon proved costly, and I've been mortgaging property to tide me over.' He regretted the defensive note in his voice. In truth, he'd been gambling vast sums.

'Indeed, and now there is nothing left to mortgage.' Richard Broughton consulted his notes. 'Chartley Manor, and Keyston in Huntingdonshire remain unencumbered, and the mansion in the Strand.'

'I thought Leicester House was forfeit to the Crown?'

'I've checked the deeds, and the lease belongs to you by default from your late stepfather's estate, my lord – or, at least, the income from rent does. If you offer Keyston Manor to the Crown estate, I see no reason why you should not be permitted to retain your property in the Strand.'

'Well, that alone is good news.' Robert gave him a wry look. 'I shall rename it Essex House and install my mother. Her new husband can oversee the upkeep.'

Richard Broughton nodded. 'Your main income is from revenues and patronage as Master of the Horse. You might appoint a clerk to record these, so they can be taken into account. I also believe we can increase your income from the tax on sweet wines.'

Robert brightened. 'Is money owed to me?'

Richard Broughton shook his head. 'Imported wines are taxed, two or three shillings a tun. Sweet wines are supposed to be taxed at double, but it seems easy enough to get away with paying the lower rate.'

'And you can do something about that?'

'The wine importers could be reminded of the law.'

'You've done me good service, Master Broughton. Keyston Manor might be the saving of me yet.' He stared at the pile of ledgers. 'Will you find me a good clerk, and prepare the necessary legal papers?'

'Of course, my lord, and might I inform your mother that she can return to London?'

Robert thought for a moment; he'd forgotten Richard Broughton was also his mother's lawyer. 'I should do so myself, but I've learned that her new husband might be an informant for Robert Cecil, so the longer we can delay him learning of my new circumstances, the better.'

'How *dare* you!'

The shout echoed, causing even the queen's most experienced ladies to flinch. She counted off his crimes on her long fingers, her eyes blazing. 'You wed without our consent, to a woman beneath your station, who is not well born, who failed to provide Sir Philip Sidney with an heir, then you both conspire to conceal the truth from us!'

Robert had always known this was coming, yet he'd never seen the queen so angry, and the mention of conspiracy made his heart thump in his chest. There had been a difficult conversation with Robert Cecil, who seemed to enjoy having such power over him, but had agreed to keep their great secret – for now, at least.

He kneeled before Elizabeth, begged forgiveness, and waited to learn his fate. It didn't surprise him that someone had revealed his secret. He'd been careful at the beginning, but Elizabeth's courtiers loved to gossip. A thought occurred to him, a possible way out.

'The Countess of Essex will live in retirement at her mother's house, Your Majesty, and I shall serve you in France, fighting for the Protestant cause.' He looked up at her with pleading eyes. 'If God wills it, I will return victorious.'

Elizabeth stared at him, seemingly confused by his offer. 'You might have married his widow, but I'll not have you throwing your life away as Sir Philip Sidney did. I *forbid* you to go to France, and if you dare defy me again, you will suffer the consequences.'

'Thank you, Your Majesty.' There was nothing else to say for now but, if he could persuade the queen, he might yet be allowed to make his name in France.

14

JANUARY 1591

The musicians struck up the stirring opening bars of la volta, Robert's favourite, and he bowed as he took the hand of the prettiest girl in the room. Wine flowed freely at the New Year's Day celebrations, and he'd drunk too much, but knew who smiled at him from behind her jewelled mask.

Elizabeth Southwell was the queen's newest maid of honour, and daughter of Lady Southwell, one of the senior ladies-in-waiting. Her youthful figure had caught Robert's eye, and an idea formed in his mind. He'd been teased once too often about being the queen's puppet, and decided it would be good to show Her Majesty he was free to dance with whoever he chose.

They began with a galliard. After three quick hops with alternate feet, Robert jumped, landing with one leg ahead of the other. Then they danced la volta. He placed his hands on either side of her waist. She put her hands on his broad shoulders, and he lifted her into a high leap, her skirts flying.

An accomplished dancer, Elizabeth Southwell reminded him of Elizabeth Cecil. She leapt as if she weighed nothing, and moved with effortless grace, with a gift for anticipating his steps in a way the queen never had. A space cleared around them, and the onlookers applauded their elegance and skill.

Robert smiled at her as he recalled how, as a boy, he'd looked forward to the day he might dance for the Queen of England. It seemed only natural to choose Elizabeth Southwell for the next dance, and the next – until, at last, he asked to rest and recover his breath.

She fanned her face with her hand. 'I feel the need for fresh air, my Lord Essex. Would you escort me?'

Robert agreed. The queen suffered chills in winter, so log fires blazed in every grate, and with their exertions he would be glad of some cool air. He followed her down the long corridor and out through a side door into the queen's formal gardens.

The cool night air was refreshing, a respite from the noisy carousers. She removed her mask, and Robert did the same, as they walked together down the gravelled pathway. He felt comfortably at ease, as there was no need to impress her, or be anything other than himself.

'Her Majesty left early. I hope she was not displeased with us, my Lord Essex.' Elizabeth's tone sounded conspiratorial, even flirtatious.

Robert smiled. 'Her Majesty is fifty-seven. I believe she tires more easily now.'

They walked in silence until the sounds of music faded. A bright sliver of moonlight lit their way, and the night sky twinkled with stars. He sensed her flinch as a screech echoed in the darkness. His instinct was to put a protective arm around her waist, and she moved closer to him.

'My mother tried to prepare me for this, but I confess they scare me.'

Robert peered into the darkness. 'I believe it was only an owl.'

She laughed. 'I meant the courtiers. There are so many

complicated rules about what I'm supposed to do and say, I find I'm scared of saying the wrong thing.'

'You don't seem scared of me.'

'You're different, my lord.' She kissed him on the cheek. 'A true gentleman.'

Robert woke with a headache. He'd drunk too much wine, and now must pay the price. He rubbed his eyes and remembered. They'd returned for more drinking and dancing, and no one paid them any attention when he spirited her away with his black velvet cloak around her shoulders.

He'd had no idea of the time, but the ink-black River Thames was strangely silent and deserted except for their wherry. She laughed as he almost fell on the slippery riverside steps in the darkness, and he'd smuggled her through the back door of York House. If any of his servants noticed, they knew to look the other way.

Elizabeth Southwell lay sleeping at his side, and Robert's life had become much more complicated. He stared at her in wonderment. A day ago, he'd hardly spoken to her, yet being with Elizabeth was like being given a second chance with his first love, Elizabeth Cecil, but with the passion and mischief of Bethan.

Beautiful and fun to be with, she was the woman he'd dreamed of finding. She understood him, and if only he'd waited a little longer, she would have made the perfect wife. He hadn't seen Frances since before Christmas, as she'd been in her confinement with her mother at Walsingham House; their child was due in a week or so.

Elizabeth opened her eyes and reached out to playfully trace a finger down his cheek and caress his beard. She smiled, a twinkle in her eye. 'Does this mean I've become your mistress?'

Her question sounded innocent enough, yet she'd proved herself far from innocent in her encouragement of him.

Robert leaned across and kissed her. 'Only if we do this again.'

'I would like that.' She returned his kiss, and climbed on top of him.

Robert knew he should remind her he was a married man with a child due soon, hopefully the son and heir he longed for. He should apologise, and say they must never do anything like this again, for the sake of her reputation. Instead, he surrendered to her, body and soul, with no concern for the consequences.

St Olave's Church, in Hart Street, across the road from Walsingham House, was where his stepdaughter, little Elizabeth, had been christened five years before. Robert studied the impressive stained-glass windows celebrating the queen's visit, while she had still been Princess Elizabeth, after her release from the Tower of London.

It seemed strange to think she'd been imprisoned by her half-sister, Queen Mary, on a charge of plotting against the Crown. He'd heard she'd been held in comfort in the queen's former apartments, and released after two months, on the anniversary of her mother Anne Boleyn's execution.

The newborn baby squealed as the stern-faced minister plunged him into the water of the font and named him Robert Devereux. Frances remained in her bed, recovering from her ordeal, but her mother, Lady Ursula, couldn't have looked prouder of her grandson.

Robert's mother outshone them all in her finest gown for her new role as godmother. The birth of his son had brought them together again, but her Catholic husband tactfully stayed away. Her father, Sir Francis Knollys, seemed pleased to have been asked to act as the child's godfather, and gave him a leather-bound prayer book.

For his sister's sake, Robert agreed that Penelope's long-suffering husband, Lord Rich, could also be godfather. Penelope watched, clutching her six-month-old son, Henry Rich. Their other son, little Robert Rich, now nearly four years old, had his mother's red hair, and stared up at the new baby in fascination.

If Frances had a view about Robert's choice of godparents, she kept it to herself. He'd spoken to Penelope about them all moving to the newly renamed Essex House. There were more than forty rooms, and access to the river by a private watergate. He thought it time Frances and Penelope should forget their differences over Philip Sidney; they would be good company for each other.

After the service he held his new son in his arms for the first time. He stared into little Robert's wide eyes, and promised before God to be a good father. He would double his efforts to persuade the queen to let him make his name in France. He would clear his late father's debts, and ensure the third Earl of Essex had the best possible future.

Robert fanned his cards and frowned. He held a losing hand, and the stakes were high. The queen threw down a knave of hearts. Robert followed with a seven, and saw her brown-toothed smile. A good sign. He held his breath as he lay down an eight of diamonds, and made a show of despair when she beat him with a ten.

He'd lost a small fortune that evening, yet he needed her in a good mood. 'Well done, Bess.' He gave her his warmest smile. 'I'm ruined.'

She laughed at his exaggeration. 'You might have better luck in the next game.'

'In that case, shall we raise the stakes?' He gave her a challenging glance. 'If I win, you permit me to fight for you in France – and if I lose, you have my word I'll not ask again.'

Elizabeth shuffled the cards. 'Going to France was supposed to be punishment for your sins, so I win either way.' She lay down a queen of diamonds, and sat back looking pleased with herself.

Robert won with a king, followed by the queen of hearts. His pulse raced as she lost the hand, and he lay down the knave of diamonds. France looked within his grasp. The proceeds of the sale of Keyston Manor were intended to reduce his debts, but he was already planning his new livery as Lord General of the queen's army.

Instead of plain orange and white, his new colours would be bright orange and gold. He would wear a cloak of orange velvet, embroidered and trimmed with gold braid. His saddle and harness would be orange, decorated with gold and studded with jewels, and he would send six trumpeters, like royal heralds, to announce his approach.

Elizabeth lost the next two hands, then scowled and lay down her cards. Their game was over. 'Your luck has changed, Robin. It seems you have your wish.'

She didn't look happy about losing but, after so many stern refusals, the queen had relented. In an instant, he saw a brighter future for his growing family. Unknown to Elizabeth, he'd already met with the French ambassador, who'd told him he would also have the gratitude of King Henri of France.

'I shall make your people cheer your name, and Gloriana will be shouted once more.'

She smiled at the thought. 'I shall put conditions on your expedition – and woe betide you if you dare to ignore them.'

It took longer than he'd planned to raise three thousand soldiers and some four hundred cavalrymen, and easterly winds kept them waiting in Dover harbour. After a risky crossing in heavy seas, they'd arrived in the port of Dieppe to find Robert's old friend from the Lisbon campaign, Sir Roger Williams, had already left.

Three weeks passed and Robert cursed his promise not to advance until King Henri agreed the queen's terms of a treaty. They'd pitched their sprawling encampment in fields outside the town, which the rains turned to muddy marshland. Supplies were running low, and the men were growing restless.

His brother Wat seemed to be regretting his decision to join the venture. 'What will we do if there's no answer from King Henri to your letters?'

'King Henri needs us more than we need him.' Robert smiled. 'Have faith, Wat. When we take Rouen, there will be reward enough for us all, and we shall return as heroes.'

Their lookout shouted. 'Riders are coming, my lord!'

Robert and Wat went to see the dozen men approaching down the stony track. They rode at a fast canter, and one carried the flag of St George. Their leader raised a hand as they came within hailing distance. 'My Lord Essex!'

'Sir Roger!' Robert grinned. 'Have you brought news from the king?'

Sir Roger nodded. 'Good news – and bad news, my lord.' He dismounted and handed his reins to one of his men. 'Let's find a jug of ale and I'll tell you.'

They made their way to Robert's tent, where Sir Roger took a deep drink and wiped his mouth on his sleeve. 'The King of

France invites you to meet him, but it will mean riding to Compiègne, a hundred miles east of here.'

'We'll leave in the morning, once you've had some rest – and tasted the pottage we've had to live off!'

Sir Roger frowned. 'I said there was bad news. The Catholic League, under the command of Admiral de Villars, waits to waylay us, so the journey is not without danger.'

'They didn't stop you.' Robert had delayed long enough, and was ready for a fight.

'We travelled light, and were lucky.' Sir Roger took another drink. 'Choose your best riders, and we'll leave at first light.'

They rode hard and fast, a hundred cavalrymen thundering through the flat countryside. Each rider was hand-picked, but most lacked fighting experience. Sir Roger's men acted as an advance party, scouting the road ahead, with Robert leading the main body of riders and his brother Wat commanding the rearguard.

Sir Henry Unton, grandson of Sir Edward Seymour, Duke of Somerset, rode at Robert's side. Sir Henry was a veteran of the ill-fated Battle of Zutphen, and had been knighted there. Now the new ambassador to France, his task was to win the agreement of King Henri to the treaty.

Robert's heart pounded with the thrill of action, but he doubted the queen would understand why he'd left Dieppe against her orders. He carried a sharp battleaxe as well as his sword. Neither would be much use if they were ambushed by musketeers, so they relied on speed, and hoped to reach Compiègne before lookouts of the Catholic League spotted them.

After three days of riding from dawn to dusk, they stopped for the final night in the cover of the Compiègne Forest. Robert found it hard to sleep, and realised that in his haste to leave for Dover he'd neglected to say farewell to Frances. At least when he returned victorious, there would be rewards.

In the morning, Robert had his men wear their orange-and-gold livery. Anthony Bagot, promoted to Robert's squire, carried the Devereux standard on a gilded pole. They were met on the road by a nobleman wearing black armour with a sash of white silk, and an escort of the king's lancers.

He introduced himself with passable English. 'Armand de Gontaut, Baron de Biron, Marshal of France.' He smiled. 'King Henri welcomes you, my Lord Essex, and thanks you for riding to Compiègne.'

Robert returned his smile. 'We've been tested by the journey, Baron, but I trust it has been worthwhile.'

They followed the baron to a towering castle on the outskirts of the town of Compiègne, where they were greeted by King Henri. Good humoured, with a white beard, he spoke poor English so Robert had to address him in French.

'Your Majesty should know I am under orders not to advance on Rouen until the treaty is agreed.'

King Henri replied in French. 'All in good time, my Lord Essex. First, we dine, and I want to hear all about your queen.'

The castle was furnished like a palace, and the banquet proved fit for a king, with servants bringing silver platters of venison. The main course, a roasted wild boar with gilded tusks, was followed by rich delicacies, and fine wine flowed freely. The king proved skilful in avoiding talk of the treaty, and surprised Robert by becoming quite drunk before being led away by his attractive young mistress.

The next morning Sir Henry Unton discovered the truth. 'The king is preparing to leave, my lord. It would seem he's riding east, and has no intention of agreeing the treaty, or joining us to besiege Rouen.'

Sir Roger scowled. 'We've been outmanoeuvred. The French have been playing some game with us.'

Robert felt a sinking feeling in his heart. 'What do you mean? Why would the king wish to trick us?'

Sir Henry broke the silence. 'While our army remains in Dieppe, Admiral de Villars' Catholic League are forced to defend the territory to the west of Rouen, leaving King Henri free to negotiate with other allies.'

Robert cursed. 'There is one way to secure the agreement of the King of France. We will ride to Rouen, and win a great victory without him.'

Sir Roger agreed. 'I must support Marshal Biron with the siege of Gournay, but then I will bring my men to help, and ask the marshal to join us.'

Robert faced a dangerous journey back, and the wrath of the queen for his fool's errand to Compiègne, but success was still within his grasp. He'd told the queen people would cheer and call her Gloriana. She'd replied with a warning of consequences if he dared to ignore her orders.

The crack of musket fire shattered the silence and one of his men yelled out in pain. A second shot hit one of the leading horses in the flank, causing it to throw its rider. The Catholic League chose the ground for their ambush well. Robert's men were caught in the open by an invisible enemy.

Robert shouted. 'We'll have to make a run for it!'

'What about the wounded?' Wat looked back to where several horses and riders sprawled.

'They have to understand. It's every man for himself.'

He called for his men to follow as he urged his horse into a gallop. There was nothing he could do for the injured, but he hoped Admiral de Villars would show them Christian mercy. If not, their lives would be on his conscience.

His shirt clung to his back, soaked in sweat, and his voice sounded hoarse as he called for Bagot to bring water. Hungry, thirsty, and exhausted, they'd arrived in near darkness at the town of Pont-de-l'Arche, twelve miles south of Rouen, after some twenty hours in the saddle.

Robert sent a rider with orders for the rest of his army to join them. When they arrived he'd been concerned to find so many suffering with a fever from the mud and stink of the camp in Dieppe. They also brought a dispatch from the queen, which arrived while he was in Compiègne.

He'd read the letter to Wat. 'Her Majesty orders me to send King Henri to England – and she has travelled to Portsmouth to meet him!'

Wat shook his head. 'How will you reply?'

'I shall tell her as it is. We've had no choice other than to advance on Rouen. With luck Sir Roger will soon be here with reinforcements – and Marshal Biron's French army.'

He also wrote to Lord Burghley, asking him to defend him in his absence. He signed his letter with an apology for his poor handwriting, but failed to mention how illness had sapped his strength and kept him in his pallet bed for days.

Still weak from the fever, he peered out through the flap of his tent. They'd advanced up the River Seine to within a few miles of Rouen, and were camped in the river valley. Cooking fires flickered and smoked, but Robert could tell something was wrong. An air of despondency hung over the camp like a black cloud.

Robert called for his brother, and Sir Henry Unton

appeared. He looked tired, and frowned as he approached. 'I'm glad to see you are improving, my lord, but I regret I have grave news.' He gestured for Robert to return to his tent, and followed him inside.

'Your brother led a skirmish to the walls of Rouen, and was killed.'

Robert slumped back on his pallet bed, unable to come to terms with the news. 'How?' His voice sounded flat. 'I want to know.'

Sir Henry hesitated. 'A bullet struck him in the cheek. He died instantly.'

Robert stared at Sir Henry and choked back tears. 'Have they brought him back?'

'His body has been sealed in a lead casket, my lord.'

'Then we shall carry him, as Sir Walter Devereux, through the gates of Rouen when we are victorious.'

After Sir Henry left, Robert kneeled and clasped his hands to pray for his brother's soul, but grief overcame him. He wept as he remembered how Wat always followed him around as a boy at Chartley, wearing his oversized hand-me-downs. Wat had followed him to Rouen, and now he would have to explain to their mother, and his brother's widow, how he'd allowed him to die.

15

SEPTEMBER 1591

'The French are coming!'

Robert roused himself from his flea-infested bed at the lookout's cry, and thanked God the waiting was over. His head ached, but he could feel his strength returning after his fever, and was looking forward to some action. He'd been in a black mood, but resolved to avenge his brother's death, even if it must be at the cost of his own life.

As the riders cantered into the camp, he recognised Marshal Biron's English-speaking infantry captain, and raised a hand in greeting. 'Does this mean you've taken Gournay, captain?'

The French captain dismounted and brushed the road dust from his cloak. 'The people of Gournay are stubborn, Lord Essex.' He frowned. 'They've resisted our siege for two weeks, but we cannot have a Catholic town at our back when we hold Rouen to siege, so Marshal Biron requests your support.'

'I cannot come myself, captain, but I can let you have my musketeers and a division of cavalry. Victory at Gournay will restore their spirits – and, with luck, they'll return with much-needed supplies.'

He ordered his men to prepare, and invited the captain to

join him for a drink. The captain looked grateful as Bagot poured them both a cup of wine. 'Marshal Biron sends his word we will return as soon as Gournay has fallen, and we shall take Rouen together.'

After the captain left, Robert drafted another letter to the queen. She had been demanding his return to England, and he was running out of excuses.

'My most dear Lady, whom I love and trust more than I do all the world.'

He decided to be direct.

'I am much grieved Your Majesty thinks my faith, and my humble affection so small.'

Robert cursed his bad luck. The queen tied his hands behind his back. She criticised his efforts to secure the treaty with King Henri, and accused him of exceeding his authority, and taking unnecessary risks. He dipped his pen in fresh ink and did his best to explain his circumstances.

'I find Your Majesty's indignation threatens the ruin and disgrace of him that has lost his dearest and only brother, spent a great part of his substance, ventured his own life and any of his friends, in seeking to do Your Majesty's service.'

He signed the letter, *'Your Majesty's servant, miserable by his loss and affected with your unkindness. R. Essex.'* Then he added a postscript. *'I have heard from Marshal Biron, he would fain take Gournay, and sends to me to that end, and stands well to victual us. I have refused to go to meet him, fearing to offend Your Majesty.'*

He sent for Robert Carey, commander of one of his regiments, and handed him the letter. 'I need you to deliver this and plead on my behalf. Tell Her Majesty we are close to victory – and at what great cost to me. If I must, I will return, but tell her my shame will be such I will retreat to West Wales, and never show my face again at court.'

Captain Carey frowned. 'I will go, my lord, but if your answer incurs the queen's displeasure—'

Robert anticipated his objection. 'Her Majesty told me only to bestow knighthoods in the field on the most deserving.' He forced a smile. 'Do this for me, and you might turn the tide of the siege of Rouen.'

Bagot fastened the worn leather strap of the borrowed helmet, and looked doubtful. 'You'll fool no one, my lord, and you've told the queen you refused to go.'

The faded orange livery was spattered with mud, and his iron breastplate had seen better days, yet Robert grinned. 'I didn't come to France to sit in my tent – and who would expect a general to carry a pike?'

Bagot gave him a disapproving look and muttered to himself as he went to fetch their horses. The town of Gournay was a thirty-mile ride to the east, and they would have to leave soon to be there before sunset.

They heard the deep boom of the French cannons before they arrived, and stopped as they crested a hill to take in the scene before them. Marshal Biron's army encircled the town, and all the roads were barricaded. The orange livery of Robert's men glinted alongside the blue-and-white livery of Sir Roger Williams.

The cannons blasted the high town walls again and again, the gun crews reloading without a rest. Shards of stone flew high into the air with each direct hit, and the acrid smell of gunpowder drifted on the wind. The walls were cracked and crumbling, and would not last much longer.

Robert hefted the long pike. The wooden shaft had worn smooth with use and a sharp steel tip had been fitted to the end. He saw Bagot's frown of concern.

'Don't worry. There's not much skill in using a pike, and I have my dagger and sword.' He headed for the men in orange livery, feeling happier than he had for a long time.

The Frenchmen cheered as Marshal Biron gave the order to advance through the breaches in the walls. The cover of the fading light suited Robert, allowing him to become just another pikeman among the many who stormed into the town, glad the overlong siege was finally over.

The town was in chaos. Blood-spattered bodies were trampled in the street, and houses set on fire, the acrid smoke and roaring flames adding to the confusion of clashing weapons, gunfire, screams and shouts. The soldiers defending the town fought bravely, firing muskets at close range, and a man close to Robert died with a bullet in his unprotected throat.

A rider cried out a threat in French as he charged and hacked at Robert, his axe clanging a glancing blow on the borrowed helmet. His ears ringing, Robert took a firm grip on his pike and thrust it at the rider's chest. He had a glimpse of the man's alarmed face as he was unhorsed, then Robert abandoned his pike and drew his sword.

He was ready to fight but, on the signal of a trumpet blast, the soldiers of the Catholic League withdrew to gather in the town square, where they threw down their weapons. The townspeople held up their hands and waved white cloths in surrender. Robert followed his men, going from house to house, evicting anyone they found, and looting anything of value.

He rode back to Rouen at the side of Marshal Biron, followed by their victorious armies and several wagons laden with fresh supplies, looted from the town. Once they reached his camp, he invited the marshal to join him for a drink.

'Now we besiege Rouen, marshal?'

The marshal nodded appreciatively as he sipped his wine. He unfolded a parchment map of the area and spread it out on Robert's table. The sweeping curve of the River Seine was coloured blue, and the main fortifications of Rouen's city walls were shown in black. He tapped the village marked with a cross to the east.

'We'll occupy the village of Darnétal, three miles from here, and closer to the walls.'

'That will be our headquarters for the siege?' Robert wished he'd thought of that before, and realised his inexperience had cost his men dearly.

The marshal smiled as he looked up at the sagging canvas of Robert's tent. 'We might be there for some weeks, so let's have some comfort.'

'The men will be glad of it. Too many have died from fevers brought on by the poor conditions in our camp.'

'Well, there is much they can do to prepare. The walls of Rouen are strong, but there is a weak spot – St Catherine's Castle, on the Dieppe road. Your men can make themselves useful digging trenches within musket range, and preparing scaling ladders for the attack.'

'With luck, captain, this siege will be over before Christmas. But first, I must plead to my queen for permission to remain.'

Marshal Biron raised an eyebrow. 'Would your queen have you leave your post so close to achieving our objective?'

'Let us hope she would not.'

Marshal Biron frowned. 'Let us pray you are right, my Lord Essex. There is nothing worse than a winter siege.'

Robert called for Bagot. 'Another letter has arrived from the queen, demanding my return without delay. I sent Captain Carey to plead my case, but it appears he was unsuccessful.' He cursed. 'I have no choice but to plead in person, so we must leave for Dieppe at dawn.'

He had a restless night, troubled by the knighthoods he'd awarded to his loyal followers. He'd disobeyed the queen's orders, gained nothing for himself, and lost his only brother. The easiest path would be to remain in France, but the queen's last letter threatened he would answer with his utmost peril if he failed to return.

At dawn he rode to the highest point above the camp for one last look at Rouen. The city flickered with bright pinpricks of light, like fireflies in the morning mist. Within the walls slept some six thousand men of the Catholic League, and Admiral de Villars. If they could take the city before the Duke of Parma arrived, his future would be assured – yet first he must appease the queen.

They rode hard at sunrise, and found a fast skiff at Dieppe to carry them across the Channel. The weather was fair in France, but once under way strong winds buffeted their bows, as if willing them to turn back. Robert stared at the dark thunder clouds gathering over England, a bad omen.

He braced himself against the wooden rail, oblivious to the salty spray which stung his eyes, and watched as the royal dockyard of Rye in East Sussex drew closer. He had no idea what he could say to the queen, but if she didn't allow him to return to Rouen he would not remain in disgrace at court.

He'd planned to surprise his wife and see his infant son, but he'd arrived too late, and decided to stay at Essex House overnight before his audience with the queen. He woke his sister Penelope, who'd moved in with her two sons.

'I have to tell you that our brother Wat has been killed in battle at Rouen.'

Penelope held him close in a moment of shared grief. 'Robert Carey told me. He said our brother died a hero.'

'He was fearless,' Robert fought back tears, 'and would still be alive if I hadn't asked him to go to France.'

Penelope looked into his eyes. 'You can't blame yourself.' She frowned. 'You've lost weight, and Robert Carey told me you suffered with a fever, and they feared you might die.'

'I sent Robert Carey back to plead for me. Do you know if he saw the queen?'

'He did. He said she flew into a rage when she saw your letter, yet somehow he persuaded her to relent, so I am surprised to see you here.'

Robert swore. 'I was too hasty to return to England. No doubt Carey is arriving in Rouen now, to tell me I have permission to remain.'

'Don't be too quick to throw your life away in some heroic gesture, Robert. You're my only brother now, and you have two sons to think about.'

'Two?' He didn't understand.

'Did you not know your mistress has given you a son?'

'You mean Elizabeth Southwell?'

'How many mistresses do you have?'

Robert frowned. 'As God is my witness, I had no idea Elizabeth carried my child.'

'There was quite a scandal. Thomas Vavasour took the blame, and is imprisoned in the Tower for his sins.'

He stared at Penelope in disbelief. 'I must do what I can to have him set free. Thomas Vavasour fought with me in the Low Countries, but why would he risk his career to protect my reputation?'

She gave him a knowing look. 'You had better ask that question of your mistress.'

'Is she here?'

Penelope shook her head. 'I felt sorry for her, and sent her to mother's household in Drayton Basset. She was certain you are the boy's father.'

'But the queen doesn't suspect?'

'If she did, it's you who would be languishing in a cell at the Tower of London.'

Robert kneeled on the cold tiled floor before the queen. He'd not been sure what to expect, but her unwelcoming coldness worried him. Wearing a gown of black brocade with a fan-shaped ruff, the queen looked as if she could be in mourning. He had done what she asked, and returned as quickly as he could, yet she made no move to dismiss her ladies, and glowered at him.

Robert stared at her black silk slippers, and noted how the embroidery of fine gold thread was becoming unravelled, as was his career as her favourite courtier. He said a silent prayer while he waited, his future in the balance, and regretted his hasty decision to return from France.

When she spoke, her voice was harsh. 'You claim to be our most loving subject, yet disobey the simplest request, Lord Essex.'

Robert knew better than to argue in front of so many observers. 'I beg forgiveness, Your Majesty.' He looked up at her, hoping to see some sign that she was pleased to see him returned safely. Her face was stern, like a judge about to pass sentence. 'I suffered with a fever, and could not even walk. It was impossible to make the voyage back until I recovered.'

She stared at him as if suspecting some trick. 'We hear how little the French king regards the hazards of our men, and how you, our general, at all times refuse not to run with them – like a common soldier in hope of a battle.'

'My only wish is to serve Your Majesty to the best of my ability.' He spoke softly, for fear of betraying his true feelings.

'Our army in France has been deceived, and we will have no more of it!' Her shout echoed with accusation.

Robert bit his tongue. If he'd been younger, he might have pointed out that she sent her army before any agreement was in place with King Henri. Now he bowed his head, and waited for her to calm a little, as she surely would.

Her slender fingers toyed with the large pearls of her necklace as if they were rosary beads, and when she spoke her voice had softened. 'We shall draw up a list of our grievances against King Henri of Navarre – and you, my lord, shall be required to deliver it in person.'

Robert couldn't believe his luck. She was allowing him to return. 'I shall do as you command, Your Majesty.'

He returned to Essex House and told Penelope. 'She plays her games with me as if I were a court jester.'

Penelope smiled. 'There are worse positions at court.'

'You mock me?' Robert had hoped for sympathy from his sister.

'Jesters get away with saying whatever they wish – and, in my experience, are never as foolish as they seem.'

'I deserve better, and am aggrieved by the way she treats me. Her Majesty seems determined to ruin me, even though I humble myself and yield to her will.'

Penelope placed her hand on his arm. 'You might be the general of the queen's army, but you are still my little brother and should listen to my counsel. Be glad you have what you want. She has allowed you to return.'

Robert grudgingly had to agree. 'It's the manner of her doing it—'

'Don't you see?' She looked exasperated. 'Her list of grievances to the King of France is her way to save face. I believe she wants you to have a second chance, and you should seize it with both hands.'

Robert recalled their conversation as the quayside of Dieppe emerged from the sea mists. He'd been offered another chance, and was determined to make the most of it. He had intended to visit his wife and son, then go to see his mother and Elizabeth Southwell, but there was no time.

He'd ridden through the night to Dover and been lucky to find them a place on a Dutch merchant ship. They made their way to the village of Darnétal, arriving at dusk. The place should have been lively with his men, but looked deserted.

They rode up to the guard. 'Where is everyone?'

'The fever has come back, my lord, and many of the gentlemen have returned to England.'

'How many are left?'

'I cannot say, my lord, but a good number of the men have abandoned us.'

Robert cursed his luck, and swore to deal with the deserters but, for now, he had to rally those who remained. He found Sir Roger Williams, who'd taken one of the larger houses in the village, and joined him for a meal of salted pork on a trencher of rye bread. Sir Roger listened to his account of his meeting with the queen, and poured them both a tankard of beer.

'I've not been back to England for a good while, my lord.' Sir Roger took a deep drink of beer. 'If you wish, I can ask the council for reinforcements and supplies.'

Robert agreed. 'I fear our numbers have been greatly reduced, so anything you can do is most welcome.' He sipped his beer. 'Where is Marshal Biron?'

'He left soon after you did, my lord.' Sir Roger frowned. 'He led a force of cavalry and a brigade of infantry east to harass the Spanish, who've been spotted close to the border with Picardy.'

Robert cursed. 'He promised to help us take Rouen. I never dreamed this siege would take so long, and involve so much waiting.'

Sir Roger nodded. 'But if we can take Rouen, we'll control the Seine from Paris to the sea.'

'We will all be heroes – and wealthy men, Sir Roger.'

The muddy trench had been dug to the height of a man, and provided the perfect firing position. Robert took aim with a primed and loaded musket, and remembered to breathe out, as he'd been shown. The soldier guarding the top of the wall stood out in silhouette against the skyline, oblivious to the danger he was in.

Robert pulled the trigger and was half blinded by the flash as the weapon fired. He peered up at the wall. 'He's gone, but I can't tell if he's been hit.'

Edward York, lieutenant of his infantry, grinned. 'If not, you've given him a fright, my lord.'

Robert stared up at the wall. 'I've heard they send out skirmishers. Have you seen any?'

'They come at night, my lord, which is how they manage to elude us.'

'Choose your best men, Lieutenant York, and tell them to be ready at sunset. The Catholic League are not the only ones who can see in the dark.'

. . .

Robert shivered in the frosty night as they waited, his breath freezing in the cold air. He'd expected to see the enemy skulking through the trees, but the attack was sudden and ferocious. Enemy soldiers charged from the darkness, but Captain York's men were ready, and fired a deadly salvo of bullets.

A dozen attackers fell dead, including their commander, and several more were wounded and cried out in agony. Robert drew his sword and ordered his men forward. They pursued the rest to the city gates, where he called out a challenge in French to Admiral de Villars to engage in personal combat.

The men on the battlements jeered and shouted in French, insulting the queen and all who served her. Robert cursed. He'd promised he would only remain in France if he believed there was a chance of taking Rouen, but their siege was futile without King Henri's support.

In his pocket was a terse note from the queen, giving him permission to return, and saying it was not befitting an earl and knight of the realm to be employed on so futile a task. As he turned and led his men away, he remembered Marshal Biron's warning. *There is nothing worse than a winter siege.*

16

JANUARY 1592

Frances looked pale as she signalled for her maidservant to leave, then turned to Robert.

'I've missed you.' She studied his face with a frown of concern. 'It seems Normandy has taken its toll on you.'

'I'll not be going back.' He forced a smile. 'I've had enough of fleas and foul pottage.'

'I'm glad to hear that – but what do you plan to do now?'

'In truth, I don't know. I put my name forward as Chancellor of Oxford University, but I find Lord Buckhurst has beaten me to it.' He scowled. 'While I've been risking my life in Normandy, others are rewarded for sitting safely at home.'

Frances reached out and placed her hand on his arm. 'Don't be bitter about things over which you have no control.'

'The chancellorship would have brought much-needed income, as well as patronage and influence.'

She smiled. 'We have a bright future, despite our debts. You should aim higher than to be a chancellor. You are well placed for one of the great offices of state.'

'I wonder if I have the patience needed for statecraft. I've seen how the queen treats her ministers, even your father, who could not have been more loyal.'

'My father used to have a saying. *Scientia potentia est*.'

'Knowledge is power.'

She nodded. 'Robert Cecil has taken over my father's network of informers, but I am still in contact with some of the best.'

'You mean I should have my own spy network?'

'Think of them as providers of information which you might use to advantage.'

He stroked his newly trimmed beard as he thought. 'Your father's network made him indispensable to the queen, but at a cost.'

'Let me send for Master Francis Bacon.'

'The lawyer? I've seen him at court. Francis and his brother Anthony Bacon are both Trinity men, but I had no idea Francis Bacon worked for your father.'

She gave him a meaningful glance. 'Anthony Bacon has recently returned from France, and is lodging at his brother's chambers at Gray's Inn.'

'And both now work for Robert Cecil?' The bitterness returned to his voice.

'They are his cousins, through his late mother, but Anthony once joked about Cecil's crooked back, and he's never forgiven him.'

He stared at his wife. How much did she know that she wasn't telling him?

'If I'm to become a statesman, a good lawyer with knowledge of statecraft will be most useful.'

Before he left, Robert called at the nursery. He found Robin's room empty, but on hearing loud squeals from outside Robert crossed to the mullioned window and peered out into the rear courtyard, where his son played in the snow with Elizabeth.

He watched as his stepdaughter, now seven, scraped snow from the ground to make a snowball, and threw it at her infant half-brother, who squealed with delight.

'Your turn now, Robin.' Elizabeth showed him how to scoop the snow in his hands and make a ball, but he didn't seem to understand.

As Robert watched, he saw another game being played. He was like little Robin, taking his first, faltering steps, with so much to learn. Elizabeth was like the queen, wiser than her years, and glad to have someone to amuse her. Somehow, he would have to show the queen he'd grown up in Normandy, and should not be treated like a child.

The snow continued to fall as the passing bell tolled for Wat's funeral, the first time Robert's family had been together since they'd left Chartley. His mother, swathed in black furs against the cold, hugged him in an unexpected show of affection, and stared at him with sadness in her eyes.

'I was heartbroken when I had the news of your brother, but I thank God you have come back home safe to me.'

'I believe the experience has changed me, Mother.' He nodded to Sir Christopher Blount, who waited tactfully behind her. 'I wish to spend more time with my family, and it's time I got to know my new stepfather.'

They stood in the arched doorway of the old church, sheltering from the sleet as they welcomed the mourners. Robert's grandfather, Sir Francis Knollys, escorted Wat's young widow, Margaret. He wore a heavy black cloak, and walked with a stick, his back stooped, yet he asked to read from the Bible at the service.

Next came Penelope, snowflakes glinting like diamonds on

her black shawl, with Lord Rich at her side. Robert sensed the depth of her grief as her eyes met his. They didn't need to speak. He dug his fingernails into his palms as he struggled to remain composed.

He'd not expected to see his sister Dorothy, as snowstorms must have made the journey from Wales difficult – dangerous even. She arrived without her husband, Sir Thomas Perrot, but was escorted by their Uncle George and their chaplain, Rhys Prichard, from Lamphey.

'Thank you for coming.' Robert was touched to see them, and pleased his uncle looked so well.

Rhys Prichard shook his hand. 'If you will permit me, my lord, I would like to officiate for at least part of the service.'

Robert nodded. 'Thank you, Master Prichard, and I hope to speak to you afterwards. My family has need of a chaplain.'

Behind them followed his old friend, Gelly Meyrick, now a successful merchant and still Member of Parliament for Carmarthen. He wore a sprig of rosemary in his hatband, in the old tradition, and placed his hand on Robert's shoulder.

'Your brother was a fine man, my lord. We shall all miss him.'

Robert struggled to find his voice. 'Thank you, Gelly. You must join us afterwards at Essex House, and we shall drink to my brother's memory.'

Richard Bagot had ridden from Chartley with Anthony Bagot, who looked unusually smart in his black mourning clothes. Robert shook hands with his old tutor, Master Wright, and their family lawyer, Master Broughton. He hadn't seen either of them for some time, and their grey beards reminded him of the passing years.

The mournful clanging of the church bell stopped, and Robert took his mother's arm and led her up the nave of the church to where the black-draped coffin waited. They stopped to look at his brother's sword and helmet on the coffin, then took their place in the front pew, next to his grandfather and Wat's widow, Margaret.

Robert stared at his brother's coffin as Rhys Prichard began the service. This could have been his own funeral, but for luck and the grace of God. There'd been so many times when a stray bullet could have ended his life. They said Wat's death was sudden, and he would not have suffered. Robert thanked God for that one small mercy.

He contrived a moment alone with his mother after the wake. He embraced her, holding her close. For a moment he could imagine he was a child, safe in his mother's arms again. He'd had a few glasses of wine, and was in a mellow mood.

'I wanted to carry Wat's coffin into the city of Rouen, and hold his funeral in the cathedral.'

His mother shook her head. 'I believe he would have preferred to return home, so we could say farewell.'

'I swore to avenge his death, but the queen ordered me to return before my work was done.'

She stared at him, as if remembering a time long ago.

'You remind me so much of your father.'

'You mean his debts, or his long absences?'

'Both. And you share his dry sense of humour.'

'I remember Father as a serious man.'

'He could be quite mischievous. Richard Bagot used to despair of him.'

Robert smiled at the thought. 'Anthony Bagot says he despairs of me.'

'From what I hear, the queen can scarcely bear to have you far from her side. It seems you've done rather better for yourself than your father.'

'That's what I wish people to believe. In truth, I'm deeper in debt than ever. I had to pay my men from my own pocket.'

'As your father did.' She shook her head. 'None of you *ever* learn.'

Robert took a deep breath. He would soon have to return to his guests, but had a difficult question to ask her. 'Penelope said she sent Elizabeth Southwell to you.'

His mother raised an eyebrow. 'I told Penelope to keep the matter secret, but I should have known; the two of you were always inseparable, even as children. Did she tell you your mistress says you are the father of her child?'

Robert nodded. 'A boy. Are they still at your house in Drayton Basset?'

His mother glanced at the closed door. 'It seems Elizabeth Southwell might be accepted back at court.'

'And the child?'

She smiled. 'The boy's presence in my house must be kept our great secret, unless you wish to incur the wrath of the queen.'

'Thank you, Mother. I'll send money for his upkeep when I can.' A thought occurred to him as he was about to return to his guests. 'What name has he been given?'

'Walter, after your brother – and your father.'

At sunset Robert climbed down the worn stone steps to the river to come to terms with the change in his mother. All his life, he'd thought of her as remote and uncaring. He couldn't recall her ever saying he'd made her proud, or that she loved him.

The bear-baiting pit on the opposite bank stood silent and empty, to reduce the spread of the plague, but he'd not forgotten Elizabeth Cecil's words, all those years ago.

Bear-baiting. Father says it's a barbaric sport.

He'd been so naive, a country boy on his first visit to London; he'd thought they were pulling his leg. Elizabeth's brother, Robert Cecil, a man of the world even then, soon put him right. Robert had hoped they would become close friends. Now it seemed they were rivals, each trying to build their network of informers, and be the first with information of value to the queen.

Robert picked up a stone and threw it into the middle of the river, where it vanished without a splash. He went to see the bear-baiting once, out of curiosity, and agreed with Elizabeth's father. The sight of the magnificent creature being torn to shreds sickened him, and he'd not been back since.

He watched as a wherry rowed past, the rhythmic creak of the oars telling of the boatman's struggle against the incoming tide. The well-dressed passenger had a protective arm around an attractive young lady at his side. He looked much older than her, and Robert wondered if she was the man's wife or his mistress.

He guessed Frances had found out about Elizabeth Southwell. She was the daughter of a spymaster, after all.

His first thought had been to find an excuse to let a little time pass before having to explain himself to his wife. He chose a larger stone, and hurled it out into the river. The stone hit the water with a thump. He would do his best to be a good father to his son, little Walter, and try to give his mother a second chance.

Francis Bacon removed his wide-brimmed hat and bowed. 'My Lord Essex, this is my elder brother, Anthony.'

'I understand we shared the same tutor in Cambridge.'

'Master Whitgift is Archbishop of Canterbury now.'

Robert nodded. 'The Church's gain is Trinity's loss.'

Anthony Bacon walked with a limp and complained of gout, although he was only in his mid thirties. He wore an elaborate ruff of white silk and had a pointed black beard. His dark eyes shone with intelligence and studied Robert as if seeing his soul.

His brother Francis, by contrast, was sallow-faced, and dressed in a lawyer's plain black robes. His way of speaking was abrupt, as if he were annoyed about something, but Robert could see why he'd gained a reputation as one of the sharper lawyers in London.

He led them into his study, which had once belonged to Robert Dudley; the colourful Leicester coat of arms still graced the marble fireplace, and a large portrait of Robert's mother dominated one wall. He closed the heavy oak door and invited the brothers to take a seat.

He turned to Anthony Bacon. 'I understand you've recently returned from France. What news is there of King Henri?'

'I had an audience with him last month, my lord,' he spoke with a soft, cultured voice, 'and can share a great secret with you, which might help prove my usefulness. You are no doubt aware King Henri has a mistress.'

'Mademoiselle Gabrielle d'Estrées?' Robert smiled. 'I met her at a banquet I attended with the king in Compiègne.' He remembered the calculating woman, with striking blue eyes and pink ribbons in her golden hair. 'She looked young enough to be King Henri's daughter.'

Anthony Bacon leaned forward in his chair. 'The lady is an agent of the Catholic League, and has wormed her way into the king's affections, as young women do.' He sounded disparaging.

Robert sat back in his chair as he considered the consequences. If true, Roger Williams and his men could be in great danger. 'Does she plan to poison him?'

'In a manner of speaking. She has poisoned his faith, and

persuaded King Henri that converting to Catholicism will secure the French Crown.'

Robert recalled how the devious king had tricked them all at the siege of Rouen. 'Her Majesty will be furious, after investing so much in her alliance.'

Francis Bacon nodded. 'You could be the one to inform her, if it does come to pass.' He studied Robert with the confident gaze of a man who knows he is right. 'Such knowledge is beyond value to Her Majesty, and can make a *good* statesman into a *great* one, my Lord Essex.'

Anthony Bacon continued. 'Even more pressing is the need to order the return of our army from Rouen. Don Alexander Farnese, Duke of Parma, is on his way with thirteen thousand infantrymen, and over four thousand cavalry. It's only a matter of time before our forces are overwhelmed.'

Robert needed no persuading. 'I would like to invite you both to join my household. What do you say?'

Francis Bacon glanced at his brother, who nodded. 'We would be most honoured, my lord, and can recommend certain others who were formerly in Sir Francis Walsingham's service.'

Robert frowned. 'I need to take care. In truth, I can't afford to have many agents on my payroll.'

Anthony Bacon smiled. 'Some of our contacts have access to information which can make you a rich man.' He paused and glanced at his brother.

Robert sat up, his curiosity aroused. 'How?'

'We have an agent in the court of the King of Spain. He recently sent a coded note, naming Irish nobles who are plotting a Catholic revolution.'

Robert's pulse raced. As a boy he'd dreamed of one day avenging his father's death in Dublin, and now the means to do so could be within his grasp. 'They mean to overthrow the English occupation in Ireland?' He'd raised his voice with the excitement of the news, and saw Francis Bacon's frown of concern.

Anthony Bacon put his finger to his lips, and spoke softly. 'This is most secret, my lord, but how many lives could be saved if the knowledge is used wisely?'

The great hall of Sudeley Castle was transformed into a magical woodland glade for the entertainment of the queen. Laurel branches framed the raised stage, decorated with ferns and trailing ivy. Elizabeth was in a good mood, and Robert sat in pride of place at her side, pleased to be back in favour.

The musicians played a haunting refrain as a young girl danced on to the candlelit stage in a diaphanous green gown which revealed her shapely body. Her long dark hair was worn down, a sign of her purity, and she spoke in a clear, well-educated voice.

'I am Daphne, a nymph, daughter of the river god Ladon, in Arcadia, and am *determined* to remain unmarried and untouched by any man.' She gave Robert a mischievous glance, and smiled as she caught his eye.

The queen laughed and applauded. Robert stared, enchanted by the young girl playing Daphne. She had the innocence and grace of his first love, who'd taught him to dance so long ago at Theobalds. Elizabeth Cecil had been attractive, but Elizabeth Brydges was beguiling. The daughter of Baron Chandos, whose father was granted Sudeley by Queen Mary, she had become the queen's youngest maid of honour at seventeen.

The drums struck up a sinister beat as Daphne was pursued by a muscular man, wearing a loincloth, who announced he was Apollo. On the point of being captured, she prayed to Gaia, her mother, who transformed her into a laurel tree, before she escaped to seek the protection of the queen.

She came so close to Robert her long hair brushed his hand as she kneeled before the queen and presented her with the victor's laurel wreath. Her flimsy costume left little to the imagination, and would have caused a scandal if she'd not been a player in a pageant.

He dreamed of Elizabeth Brydges that night, and woke early, a risky plan to see her again forming in his mind. His competitive spirit was aroused, and he'd sensed that, despite her innocence as Daphne, she would not be sorry to learn she'd made his life even more complicated.

17

FEBRUARY 1593

Francis Bacon's dark-panelled study at Gray's Inn had become Robert's second home. The small windows meant they worked by the light of tallow candles, and legal books, including works by Plato and Hippias, were heaped on the dusty desk. A log fire crackled in the hearth, keeping the winter chill at bay.

Anthony and Francis Bacon tutored Robert in the art of statecraft, and helped to plan his future as a privy councillor. Parliament was to meet for the first time in four years to agree funding for war with Spain, offering Robert his best chance to make his name as a statesman.

Francis checked his notes. 'The date has been set, my lord. Shrove Sunday, the twenty-fifth of this month. You shall take the oath of supremacy, and of a privy councillor, at the council board.'

'I'd hoped it would be before the opening of Parliament, not after it.'

'The wheel of Fortune turns slowly in government, and it's soon enough. You've done well to convince Her Majesty in so short a time, and you'll be in the House of Lords at the official opening. I've been returned for the county of Middlesex, and

Anthony as the member for Wallingford, so we shall be in the Commons. How many other supporters can we rely on?'

Robert counted them on his fingers. 'There's my stepfather, Sir Christopher Blount; my grandfather, Sir Francis Knollys; and our former tutor, Archbishop Whitgift – as well as my uncle, Sir William Knollys, member for Oxford, and my loyal members from Wales.' He grinned. 'And my tenants who we've been able to raise to the Commons. Together, we are more than a match for Lord Burghley's faction.'

Francis looked up from his notes. 'Your grandfather will always vote with his conscience.'

'As will I.' Robert smiled. 'Which means we are unlikely to concur with Lord Burghley.'

Anthony Bacon nodded. 'We must keep our powder dry, my lord,' he gave Robert a cautionary glance, 'and not alert Burghley to our plan. We've learned he's invited Her Majesty to visit him at Burghley House before the new Parliament, and intends to win her support for his proposals.'

'Your informer in his household is costly, but earns her keep.' Robert understood why Sir Francis Walsingham had died in debt. His growing network of agents had already cost him over nine hundred pounds. Information was an expensive commodity, but he hoped to see rich rewards for his investment.

Anthony placed a fresh log on the fire. The sap in the unseasoned wood crackled and spat bright sparks as the flames caught. 'Let this also be a lesson, my lord. We suspect a man in your kitchens at Essex House works for our good Lord Burghley.'

Robert cursed. 'Tell me his name. I'll dismiss him straight away.'

'They will simply find another, my lord.' He gave Robert a mischievous look. 'We might see an opportunity to pass him misleading information.' Anthony winced as he returned to his chair. 'It's better for us to keep our secrets within these four walls.'

'Your pains have returned?' Robert watched him with concern. They played a dangerous game, as newcomers challenging the established power and influence of William and Robert Cecil, and he relied on them.

'I'm in constant pain from my gout, my lord, despite the pills and medicines. The doctor tells me it's a stone, but our mother calls it God's punishment for my sins.'

'*Si vitam puriter egi.*' Francis smiled as he trimmed the nib of his pen with his knife. 'If you had led a pure life.' He held his nib up to the light to inspect it, then looked across at Robert. 'My brother's past will catch up with him one day, and *then* he shall know God's punishment.'

Robert shivered in the wintry air, despite his furs, as he watched the gilded royal barge arrive at the Westminster steps. The herald's trumpets broke the silence with a sharp fanfare, yet there was no cheering. The riverbank should have been thronged with Londoners, but fear of catching the plague kept them at home.

The cold weather meant the dreaded plague was less virulent, but those who could, abandoned the city. Frances, once again with child, had taken his stepdaughter and little Robert to live at Barn Elms, her mother's house in the countryside. Penelope took her boys to their grandmother's house in Drayton Bassett.

The once lively Essex House stood silent, except for the few servants who had no choice but to stay and take their chances. Even Hampton Court seemed strangely empty without the chattering courtiers, foreign ambassadors, and queues of the hopeful, waiting for royal favours.

Robert had attended the service of dedication in Westminster Abbey that morning, and said a private prayer for those he loved to be spared the plague. He prayed to be guided on the right path in his new life as a statesman. With luck, he might clear his debts, earn the respect of his peers, and the gratitude of his queen.

Queen Elizabeth looked magnificent in her scarlet, ermine-trimmed cloak, the winter sunlight catching her gold necklace, glittering with precious diamonds and rubies. Her ladies made her look younger than he remembered, and she gave him a brief smile as their eyes met – confirmation he was still her favourite.

She wore her gold coronet as she declared the opening of Parliament. A good few of the lords stayed away because of the plague, including Robert's grandfather, and Archbishop Whitgift, but he was pleased to see so many of his supporters.

The new Lord Keeper of the Great Seal, Sir John Puckering, Speaker of the House of Commons, made a speech stressing the imminent threat of a Spanish invasion. He proposed the need for a subsidy to meet the expenses of preparing for war.

Elizabeth spoke in a clear, commanding voice, without the need to refer to notes, instructing both houses. *'Only confer upon speedy and effectual remedies against these great and fierce dangers, and do not spend time devising new laws and statutes.'*

For the first time since he'd watched her address the troops at Tilbury, Robert felt a surge of pride in his queen. In the shortest of speeches, she controlled the business of both houses of Parliament in her own interests. He studied her with renewed respect. There would be consequences for anyone who dared to defy her instruction.

. . .

After all the weeks of preparation and planning, Robert swore his oath as a privy councillor, and attended his first meeting of the most powerful men in the land. The Chancellor of the Exchequer, Sir John Fortescue, agreed to appoint a subsidy drafting committee, and Robert was the first to volunteer his services.

In the Commons, Robert Cecil showed his hand with a proposal to double the subsidies for the queen, before Francis Bacon stood to make a speech setting out the counter arguments. As planned, Robert's men supported the vote. They'd defeated Robert Cecil, but there were consequences, as several of Robert's loans from the Crown were called in.

Once in the privacy of Gray's Inn, Robert confronted Francis Bacon. 'Our plan has displeased Her Majesty. Our success seems less of a victory if it's at the cost of our reputations – or my finances.'

Francis sat back in his chair. 'An unintended outcome, my lord – but I doubt anyone saw through our subterfuge.'

'I'm going to have to support Lord Burghley.' Robert scowled. 'He leaves me no choice.'

Francis shook his head. 'There are always choices in politics, my lord. Return to the subsidy drafting committee, and persuade them to agree an increase.'

Robert explained to the committee that he'd concluded the subsidy was inadequate, and spoke of his experience of keeping an army fed, equipped and paid. Privy councillor Charles Howard, Lord High Admiral, spoke up in his support, and told of how his ships had been starved of ammunition, even as the warships of the Spanish Armada approached England.

Lord Burghley argued in favour of his son's proposal, but was at a disadvantage. Despite all his years of experience, William Cecil had never been to war in France or Spain, or to sea in a fighting ship. There were gasps of surprise from the lords when Robert proposed a triple subsidy, and his supporters won the day.

Lord Charles Howard congratulated Robert, with a twinkle in his eye. 'In one Parliament, you've established yourself as a statesman to be reckoned with, prepared to put the interests of queen and country before your own.'

Robert returned to Essex House from a long day at Hampton Court Palace to find Anthony Bacon waiting for him with a tall, middle-aged man, with fair hair and beard. The stranger removed his cap and bowed to Robert.

'Anthony Standen, at your service, my lord.'

'I've heard of you, Master Standen.' Robert frowned. He was tired, and needed a drink. 'What brings a Catholic agent to my house?'

'In truth, I feared for my life in France, my lord.'

'Well, you must know the plague is rife in London. Everyone knows somebody who has died of it.'

Anthony Standen gave him a wry look. 'Better a quick death of plague in London than a slow one at the hands of the Spanish.'

Anthony Bacon turned to Robert. 'Master Standen was Sir Francis Walsingham's agent at the Spanish court. He provided useful information about the preparations for the Armada, and now wishes to join us, my lord. My brother has offered him lodging in his chambers at Gray's Inn.'

Robert nodded. 'Your timing is good, Master Standen. Her Majesty might never forgive your service to her cousin, Mary,

Queen of the Scots, but any advantage your knowledge and contacts might give us, however slight, will be useful.'

Anthony Standen bowed. 'Thank you, my lord. I bring information about a possible threat to the queen, from her physician, Doctor Lopez.'

Robert frowned. 'I've known Doctor Lopez for years. As well as Her Majesty, he has treated me, as well as my late stepfather, the Earl of Leicester. I've never had reason to distrust him.'

Anthony Standen looked him in the eye. 'A Portuguese man named Ferrera da Gama is spying for Spain, and might be persuaded to expose the truth about Doctor Lopez.'

Robert turned to Anthony Bacon. 'We shall have Ferrera arrested for questioning – and have men ready at the southern ports to intercept any incoming letters from Portugal.'

Anthony Standen nodded. 'You won't regret it, my lord.'

'We shall see, Master Standen, we shall see.' Robert smiled to himself as he imagined what the queen would say when she found out, as she surely would. His network of agents and informers was growing, and would now rival that of Lord Burghley.

Gelly Meyrick, invited to act as Robert's squire, helped him into his sable armour for the Accession Day tilt in the grounds of Windsor Castle. The ornate black armour was finely crafted, and thinner than battle armour to keep it light, with many straps and fastenings for ease of movement.

'Just like the old days at Carew, my lord.' Gelly grinned, pulling one of the leather straps a little tighter.

Robert nodded. 'It's good to have you back, Gelly. Now Sir Thomas Baskerville has been elected as member for Carmarthen, will you return to London as my chief steward?'

'I would be honoured, my lord. In truth, I'm tired of travelling between London and Carmarthen.'

'You'll not regret it, Gelly. I need men I can trust more now than ever.'

The theme of the day was St George and the dragon, and Gelly helped Robert put on a white tabard, with the red cross of St George, over his armour. Robert's supporters wore the same, and his powerful black destrier was caparisoned in flowing white silk.

There had been no Accession Day tilt the previous year because of the plague, but the deadly disease had yet to reach the town of Windsor, and many courtiers had been glad to rent houses in the town and attend the celebrations.

A high wooden platform, painted red and gold, with banners fluttering in the breeze, had been built for the queen and her ladies overlooking the tiltyard. For once, the late November weather was in their favour, with bright autumn sunshine and a cloudless sky.

Vendors selling ale and pies called out to customers, and a troupe of minstrels added a festival atmosphere to the occasion. Heavy horses cantered down the list as knights made practice runs, and a rousing cheer went up as the heralds sounded their fanfare to announce the start of the tourney.

Sir George Clifford, Earl of Cumberland, the queen's champion, led the procession of competing knights in pairs, carrying flowing silk pennants on their lances. Sir George had styled himself as the Knight of Pendragon Castle, with the crest of the red dragon on his livery.

Robert rode at the side of his uncle, Sir Robert Knollys, the member for Breconshire, and was followed by Sir Robert Radclyffe, Lord Fitzwalter, and another of Robert's supporters in Parliament, Sir Carew Reynell. The last two riders were the ambitious young jouster, Sir Thomas Gerard, and Robert's one-time rival, but now close friend, and his sister Penelope's lover, Sir Charles Blount.

Each rider dipped his banner in salute before the queen, and her ladies presented them with gold buttons as a token of her appreciation. When it came to Robert's turn, he was surprised to see Elizabeth Southwell was one of the queen's ladies, back in royal favour.

The crowd cheered as the Master of the Joust called for the heralds to sound their trumpets. Lord Fitzwalter was first to ride, against Sir Carew Reynell. Robert flinched as Sir Carew was unhorsed on his second pass, crashing to the ground. He wasn't injured, and both riders made a show of continuing the fight on foot, their blunted swords clanging to the delight of the crowd.

Robert was next, riding against his uncle, Sir Robert Knollys. Gelly handed him the lightweight lance, and he lowered the visor on his helmet. His duties on the Privy Council meant he'd not had time to practise jousting. Although this was only for show, his pulse raced at the thought of imminent danger, and he said a silent prayer.

Gelly called out in his strong Welsh accent, 'St George for England and Her Majesty the queen!'

The Master of the Joust gave his signal, and Robert charged. The lance was too light, and he struggled to keep it steady before his uncle's lance crashed into his shoulder. He swore, as he failed to score a hit on such an important day, in full view of the queen and her ladies.

Gelly took the reins of Robert's horse and led him to the turning area. Robert cursed at the sight of the jagged scar on his armour where he'd been struck by his uncle's lance. He lifted his visor and pulled off his gauntlet as Gelly handed him a leather flask of beer. He gratefully took a sip. He wasn't used to such exertion, and his shoulder ached.

They watched as Robert's stepfather, Sir Christopher Blount, rode against Sir Thomas Gerard. Both accomplished and experienced jousters, they rode hard and fast, and the crack of breaking lances brought cheers and applause.

Robert's last ride was against another of his uncles, Sir William Knollys. He saw the marshal's signal and urged his destrier forward in a fast canter, his iron hooves digging deep into the Windsor turf. Couching his lance under his arm, he focused on his target, determined not to miss this time. The clash of the impact knocked him back in his saddle and the air filled with sharp splinters.

The crowd roared, and he saw the queen raise a hand in acknowledgement as he pulled up his visor. His shoulder and arm felt numb, but he'd proved he was the only privy councillor who could still ride at the joust. His eyes were drawn to Elizabeth Southwell, the mother of his child, staring at him from behind the queen. He was glad to see her back in favour, but if Robert Cecil ever learned her secret, it could mean banishment, or even the Tower.

The great hall at Hampton Court was festooned with laurel leaves, holly and ivy, and lit by a thousand candles for the feast of St Stephen. Edmund Tylney, Master of Revels, had organised an extravagant programme of masques and dancing for the twelve days of Christmas.

Robert was determined to show the court he was a statesman, and had brought a secret weapon to keep him on the right path – his wife, Frances. Out of confinement after giving birth to their daughter Penelope, Frances played her part well, in a gown of dark crimson silk and an elaborate winged ruff of shimmering silver lace.

He doubted anyone would guess they had hardly seen each

other all year. He'd been working long hours on parliamentary committees and royal commissions. Frances remained at her mother's country home, overseeing his son's education, and preparing his stepdaughter Elizabeth for marriage and a life at court.

On Christmas Day they'd both risen early to attend morning prayers with the queen in the palace chapel, and spent the day in religious devotion, until the final evening prayers. Robert found his mind wandering during the overlong sermon, and stared up at the chapel's vaulted ceiling, a legacy of the queen's father, King Henry.

Robert's grandfather, Sir Francis Knollys, had been granted his estate at Rotherfield Greys, and his fine manor house, Greys Court, for his service to the old king. He'd only been a few years older than Robert at the time. His grandfather rarely spoke of those days, but Robert had heard enough to know where Queen Elizabeth had inherited her mercurial temperament.

Unlike her father, Elizabeth clung to her estates like a dog with a bone, and granted him only a few unprofitable properties. His lawyer, Master Broughton, tut-tutted when he studied the deeds, and pointed out they were more likely to incur Robert costs than provide an income.

Robert took care not to drink the free-flowing wine at the St Stephen's Day feast, and sat between the queen and his wife. Elizabeth's hand no longer strayed to his thigh under the table, but there was a twinkle in her eye when he'd complimented her on the morning's hunt.

She'd ridden well, but turned sixty in September and, Robert noticed, had little appetite, picking at a plate of larks in ginger. Robert found himself thinking of the succession. He'd not dared to write to King James of Scotland for some time, but he needed to think of the future.

After the tables were cleared, the great hall echoed to the

sound of hunting horns as the huntsmen entered for the traditional ceremony of St Stephen. They brought a frightened fox in a purse net, tied to one end of a staff, with a cat tied to the other. The audience cheered and applauded as they were followed by nine young hounds, who were set upon the unfortunate animals.

The musicians began playing as the yapping dogs were led away and an army of servants descended to clean the blood from the floor. Robert needed a drink. Despite the horrors he'd witnessed in France, the old tradition sickened him. He signalled to a young serving girl to fill his glass with wine, then took a sip and felt the warmth in his throat. He saw Frances watching and smiled.

'It's Christmas time. One glass will do no harm.'

Whenever Robert danced the pavane he remembered Elizabeth Cecil, laughing at his clumsy steps long ago at Theobalds. The simple dance had only two single steps and one double step, moving forwards or backwards in a solemn procession of couples, retreating and advancing in time to the rhythmic music.

Frances rested her hand on his back, yet her touch seemed formal, without affection, a sign of the distance between them. Robert smiled at a pretty girl on the opposite side of the circle. She wore a fashionably revealing gown and there was something familiar about her. It came back to him as she returned his smile.

Elizabeth Brydges looked even more striking than when he'd seen her as Daphne in the play at Sudeley Castle. He tried to put the memory of her long hair brushing against him from his mind, yet when he looked across at her she gave him a knowing look. One lesson he'd learned from his year in politics was that he could achieve whatever he wished, if he put his mind to it.

Late after midnight he reached into the pocket of his doublet and took out a laurel leaf, put into his hand by Elizabeth Brydges. Laurel was given to the winner in Pythian games, held to honour Apollo, who lustfully pursued Daphne. Her message was clear to anyone who knew the game of courtly love.

18

JANUARY 1594

Robert had been waiting for this moment. She laughed, and her ladies applauded, as she beat him at cards yet again, and he judged the queen to be in the mood to grant him a favour.

'I'd like to remind Your Majesty of my proposal that Francis Bacon be appointed to the position of Attorney General.'

Elizabeth glared at him with a look of disdain. 'We have not forgotten, my Lord Essex. There are better men for the post, and Lord Burghley proposes Sir Edward Coke.'

Her good humour had vanished in a heartbeat.

Robert cursed inwardly. The Cecils had seen their chance to outwit him. Only a month before, he'd persuaded Robert Cecil not to object to Francis Bacon's appointment, but he'd said nothing about his father. He'd been tricked again, and struggled to contain his frustration at being misled.

'Sir Edward Coke is Lord Burghley's man. If you can grant me this one request—'

'Francis Bacon is *your* man.' She wagged an accusing finger at him in reproach.

'I would not recommend him if I did not judge him to be the best man for the position, Your Majesty.'

'It is time you understood that the wisdom of age is to Lord Burghley's advantage.' Elizabeth's voice had an icy edge, as frosty as the winter dawn. 'We will be advised by men whose good judgement has been proven – and you must not presume on our affections, for we will not be badgered by a young man's whim.'

She swept from the room, her long skirts swishing on the tiled floor, followed by her silent ladies. Robert stared after her, trying to think of a retort which would not make his position worse. Despite all he'd achieved, the queen still treated him like a naive boy.

He summoned Francis Bacon to Essex House to tell him the news. 'We've made the mistake of underestimating not only the queen, but also William Cecil.' He shook his head. 'Neither has forgotten your speeches to the Commons, and now it seems there is a price to be paid.'

Francis frowned as he listened to Robert's account of his meeting with the queen, but he had a new proposal.

'Might Her Majesty take a different view if we were to expose a serious threat to her life?'

'Another Catholic plot?' Robert heard the scathing note in his raised voice. 'When I said her personal physician could be involved in a plot, she accused me of making trouble for him.' He scowled at Francis Bacon. 'I should have been told Doctor Lopez was spying for Lord Burghley.'

Francis ignored his outburst. 'Antonio Pérez has confirmed Anthony Standen is right. The man he named, Ferrera da Gama, is a Portuguese spy. He's only an intermediary, but he could lead us to the rest of a network planning to cause harm to Her Majesty.'

Robert was intrigued by Antonio Pérez, but the charming and devious Spaniard had once served as the King of Spain's

Secretary of State. He liked the Catholic, Anthony Standen, who was already proving his worth. He'd warned Robert he suspected Antonio Pérez was spying on them for Lord Burghley, although he'd yet to prove it.

'Her Majesty disapproves of Antonio Pérez. She says a man who so easily betrays his own sovereign might have little compunction about betraying another. Before I can go back to her, I'll need proof – preferably in writing.'

Francis Bacon agreed. 'We shall make it our business to uncover the truth.'

'If Pérez is right, this could restore your reputation – and allow us to outmanoeuvre Lord Burghley.'

Francis nodded in agreement. 'The double agent lodges with the queen's physician, Doctor Lopez.'

'Then we will soon have the excuse we need to question the good doctor.' Robert sensed a major coup might be within their grasp. 'The queen says she will be advised by those who have proven good judgement, so we shall provide her with that proof.'

A glint of hope showed in Ferrera's dark eyes. A middle-aged man with a tanned face, he'd been imprisoned in the cold, windowless basement of Essex House, threatened and cajoled for days, but now he'd begun to tell them what he knew.

'The plot is not against your queen.' He spoke with a strong Portuguese accent, and Robert struggled to understand.

'If not the queen, then who?'

'The pretender, Don Antonio.' His voice was edged with contempt.

Robert recalled Don Antonio, a sly-looking man with a straggling beard, who they'd once planned to make King of Portugal. It didn't surprise him that the Catholics wished to silence him, but Don Antonio was of little consequence, and might be used to distract them from the plotters' true purpose.

'I need evidence.' Frustration made his raised voice echo in the dark basement. 'Tell us what you know, or you'll be taken to the Tower.'

Ferrera's eyes widened. 'A man named Gomez d'Avila is expected from Flanders, with letters for Doctor Roderigo Lopez.'

'Letters which will be evidence of a plot?' Robert's pulse raced at the thought. At last, he would be able to show the queen he was a worthy successor to Sir Francis Walsingham.

Ferrera shrugged. 'I only know he is coming.'

Anthony Bacon stepped forward and spoke to Ferrera in rapid Spanish. Ferrera sounded imploring as he replied, also in Spanish, but the questions and answers were too fast for Robert to follow.

'What has he told you?'

Anthony Bacon beckoned Robert up the basement stairs, out of earshot of their prisoner. 'He's described Gomez d'Avila, who is due to arrive at Sandwich on a merchant ship. With your permission, my lord, I can have him arrested and brought here.'

Robert nodded. 'If he does carry letters, can you translate them from Portuguese? I don't trust Ferrera.'

'Don Antonio is lodging with his son at Eton. He's guaranteed to tell us the truth of these letters.'

Robert recalled Ferrera's pleading voice 'What was Ferrera asking you?'

'He wants to know if he'll be set free, in return for helping us.'

Robert frowned. 'I doubt it – but let's offer him a little hope until we have evidence of a conspiracy.'

Anthony Bacon smiled. 'He also offers us a little hope, my lord, as he begged me to take the news of his arrest to Doctor Lopez.'

Don Antonio looked thin and grey, a shadow of the man Robert recalled from when they'd last met. Gomez d'Avila had been arrested at Sandwich, and a search uncovered the single letter in front of them. Written in a confident hand, with a flamboyant signature, Robert could only pick out the words, *pela graça de Deus*. By the grace of God.

'What does it say?'

Don Antonio ran his fingers through his grey beard, and frowned. 'The writer is unknown to me, Lord Essex, but the letter seems to concern a commercial transaction.'

'Is the queen's doctor implicated?'

Don Antonio shook his head and read aloud, translating the Portuguese into English. '*The bearer will inform your worship in what price your pearls are held. I will advise your worship presently of the uttermost penny that can be given for them. Also, this bearer shall tell you in what resolution we rested about a little musk and amber, the which I determined to buy, but before I resolve myself I will be advised of the price thereof, and if it shall please your worship to be my partner, I am persuaded we shall make good profit.*'

Robert cursed. 'Who would be addressed as *your worship*? Could it be a code for Doctor Lopez? I know Antonio Pérez has a liking for musk and amber, and it wouldn't surprise me if he was involved in some way. Her Majesty is always wearing pearls – but so does everyone at court, including me.'

'This is no code I can decipher, Lord Essex,' Don Antonio frowned, 'but my life might depend on it.' He looked at Robert with vengeful eyes. 'I believe it's time Ferrera was taken to the Tower and shown the rack.'

Robert clenched his fist in frustration. 'We will try one last trick, Don Antonio. Compose a note from Ferrera, warning Doctor Lopez to stop Gomez d'Avila coming to England, as he has knowledge which would implicate him in treason against the Queen of England. We shall see how he replies.'

~

Lord Burghley agreed with Robert. 'You should take these findings to Her Majesty.' He sounded as if he felt sympathy for Robert. 'You realise you are damned if you do, and damned if you do not?' He frowned. 'Either way, I doubt Her Majesty will thank you.'

Robert knew only too well. 'We've all placed our trust in Doctor Lopez; not only Her Majesty, but myself as well. My sister Penelope swears by his potions, and recommends him to anyone who will listen.'

'Well, you would be wise to secure Her Majesty's approval before having her personal physician arrested and questioned.'

'And what do we do if she refuses?'

Lord Burghley studied the doctor's letter a second time. 'Lopez incriminates himself by replying to Ferrera's note. He admits he tried to prevent the arrival of Gomez, and would spare no expense to do so – but he would only be guilty of a plot to rid us of Don Antonio.'

'A plot is still a plot, my lord.' Robert sensed he was being undermined. 'Don Antonio has the protection of the Crown, and who can know what else is being planned?'

'Emanuel Tinoco, for one. It is regrettable your men had to threaten torture to obtain his name as the author of the letter. Tinoco has served as my agent for some years, and his letter is evidence of nothing. All the same, I shall summon him to England, so we can question him before you inform Her Majesty.'

~

Robert lay restless and awake in the darkness, and heard Frances stir at his side. The ropes supporting their mattress creaked as she turned to face him. Her hand reached out and caressed his chest, the first sign of tenderness from his wife in a long time.

'You've hardly spoken since you returned from your meeting with the queen.' Her soft voice had a note of concern.

'Doctor Lopez has powerful friends, but I'm certain he's a danger to her.'

'He was my father's physician, and—'

Robert placed his hand on hers and held it tight. He decided to tell her what troubled him.

'Doctor Lopez has been spreading a malicious rumour that he'd been treating me for the pox.' He gave her hand a squeeze. 'There's no truth in it, of course, but you know how they love to gossip at court – and how damaging such a rumour could be to my reputation.'

Frances lay in silence for a moment. 'You need firm evidence against the doctor, or people will say you are trying to have your revenge, and wish to silence him.'

'Lord Burghley and I questioned Emanuel Tinoco when he arrived from France. He confessed he'd been told to win Doctor Lopez to the service of Spain. When we searched his papers, we found a large sum of money in bills of exchange, as well as curious letters in Portuguese, like those found on Ferrera.'

'What did you do?'

'What could we do? I met with Admiral Howard and Robert Cecil to discuss what action to take. We secured permission to question Doctor Lopez, while Robert Cecil's men searched the doctor's house in Fulham.' He cursed under his breath. 'Robert Cecil could hardly wait to tell the queen they discovered nothing to incriminate her physician.'

'That was why she summoned you?'

'Her Majesty called me a rash and temerarious youth, to accuse the poor man whose innocence she knew well enough.' He heard the bitterness in his voice. He didn't tell Frances, but he'd been so furious he'd shut himself away in his rooms, and considered returning to France to fight as a soldier of fortune.

Frances sat up in bed. 'You can't back down now, Robert. There's too much at stake.'

'I fear the queen has tired of my efforts, and always sides with Lord Burghley.'

'You must uncover proof of the doctor's guilt. As her doctor, Roderigo Lopez has every opportunity to poison the queen.'

'I'm at my wits' end, Frances. I believed his letter trying to stop Gomez d'Avila coming was proof enough of his guilt, but the queen doesn't agree, and I'm running out of options.'

'Ferrera de Gama was willing to talk when shown the rack. Question him again.' In the darkness she sounded like her father, speaking from the grave.

Their breath froze in the dank air, and the passage to the dungeon in the Tower of London echoed to the sound of their boots. Robert shivered at the thought of the ghosts of those who'd died there. He had to obtain some useful information from Ferrera. They laughed behind his back at court, no doubt encouraged by Robert Cecil.

Anthony Bacon cursed as he hobbled down the narrow passageway ahead of Robert. He could no longer conceal the fact that he was crippled in both legs by gout. He needed to use a stick to walk, and confessed that every step caused him agony.

The surly guard jangled his keys as he found the right one and unlocked the heavy iron door. Furnished with a table, two chairs, and a pile of old sacking that served as a bed, the cell stank of stale urine. Robert frowned at the sight of the leather bucket in the corner, the source of the unpleasant smell.

Ferrera sat slumped in one of the chairs, and shielded his eyes from the glare of the lantern Robert carried. His fine doublet and boots were gone, and his shirt was torn and soiled, making him look more like a beggar from the backstreets than a Portuguese nobleman.

Robert set the lantern on the table and waited for Anthony Bacon, who'd brought his pen and parchment, to be ready to note what was said. Also there was Sir Michael Blount, Lieutenant of the Tower of London, who'd agreed to attend as a witness.

'This is your last chance to make a full confession of what you know about Doctor Roderigo Lopez.' Robert shook Ferrara by the shoulder when he didn't answer. 'Do you understand?'

Ferrera looked at Robert with the blank expression of a man who no longer cared if he lived or died, yet when he spoke, a note of anger sounded in his voice.

'I received a letter from Doctor Lopez ten months ago, promising to do whatever the King of Spain required.'

'Where is this letter?'

'Burned, my lord.' He spat the words out, as if pleased to deny them what they wished.

Robert cursed. 'What do you believe the King of Spain might tell Doctor Lopez to do?'

'I believe he was willing to poison your queen, as well as Don Antonio – and the traitor Antonio Pérez.' Ferrera scowled. 'The doctor received a precious jewel as a token of favour, and undertook to kill your queen by poison for fifty thousand crowns.'

Robert turned to Anthony Bacon and Sir Michael Blount. 'You will both sign as witnesses to this confession, and I shall take this news to Her Majesty.' He frowned. 'Doctor Lopez must now face the consequences for his disloyalty.'

The death of Dorothy's husband was no surprise – Sir Thomas Perrot had been ill for some years – but Robert raised an eyebrow at the speed of his sister's remarriage. At least she was reconciled with the queen, and had consent to marry Henry Percy, Earl of Northumberland.

One of the wealthiest nobles at court, handsome and talented, Henry Percy was the same age as Dorothy. His reputation for his keen interest in alchemy and astrology was shared with his new neighbour, the court astronomer, Doctor John Dee.

The wedding at the old chapel in the grounds of their new home, Syon House, was a welcome respite from the intrigues of the Portuguese plotters and, once again, their family was reunited for the occasion. His mother looked formidable, with a magnificent gossamer ruff framing her red hair. She embraced Robert before chiding him for not visiting her. His stepfather, Sir Christopher Blount, smiled as he looked on. He'd supported Robert at every vote in Parliament, and they'd become friends.

Robert's sisters, Penelope and Dorothy, turned heads in matching gowns of shimmering silk, and Robert's young stepdaughter, Elizabeth, acted as Dorothy's bridesmaid. Robert wore a new doublet of gleaming silver, fastened with pearls, and Frances wore a new gown of silver brocade.

He bowed to Dorothy. 'Congratulations, Countess of Northumberland, I've never seen you look happier.'

Dorothy placed her hand on his arm. 'And you seem to be the talk of court, my Lord Essex.' She had a mischievous twinkle of disapproval in her eye.

Robert forced a smile. 'If only they would talk of me for the right reasons.'

Young Henry Wriothesley, Earl of Southampton, a friend of the groom and well known to Robert, cornered him at the reception. He carried a glass of wine, and looked as if he'd already had too much to drink.

'I'm curious, Lord Essex.' He took a deep drink of his wine. 'Why did the queen decide to stay the executions?'

Robert frowned, as he'd rather forget. 'Her Majesty summoned Doctor Lopez out of prison to treat her, and I believe he took the opportunity to tell her his confession was achieved using torture.'

'They say you put him to the rack.'

'You will do me a service by reminding anyone who repeats such gossip that there was no need. As soon as Lopez was shown the manacles, he made a full, written confession of his crimes.'

'I don't blame him for trying to avoid a traitor's death.' Henry Wriothesley scowled at the thought. 'Hanged, drawn and cut into quarters. A sight, my Lord Essex, I fear I'll never forget.' He drained his wine and stared into his empty glass. 'Did you know the doctor professed his innocence to the end?'

'You witnessed the executions?' Now Robert was curious. He'd stayed away, but there were many stories circulating among the gossipers at court. 'I heard Tinoco swung a punch at the executioner.'

'Emanuel Tinoco almost managed to escape after he was cut down.' He shook his head at the memory. 'The crowd went wild, but he never stood a chance.'

'In truth, my conscience troubles me about Tinoco. He came to England on a promise of safe conduct, but was arrested as soon as he landed in Kent.'

Henry Wriothesley gave Robert a knowing look. 'If you hadn't acted when you did, they might have poisoned Her Majesty.' He smiled. 'You saved our queen, although I doubt she will admit she owes you her life.'

~

Robert and Gelly studied the list of riders for the Accession Day tilt, to be held at Whitehall Palace. Robert smiled as he pointed to his first ride. 'I have a score to settle with my uncle, Sir Robert Knollys. He knew I was out of practice, yet showed me no quarter last year.'

Gelly pointed to a name in the list. 'Then you'll ride against another skilled jouster, Sir Thomas Vavasour.'

Robert nodded. 'Thomas Vavasour fought with us in the Low Countries, and I owe him a favour – he served a spell in the Tower to protect my reputation.'

He showed Gelly the fine crystal ball in a bag of white taffeta he'd bought from Doctor John Dee. 'My Accession Day present for the queen. He says it helps you see the truth.' He hoped she would appreciate its symbolic significance as he peered into its murky depths.

Gelly studied the crystal and frowned. 'Well, its secrets are safe from me – all I can see is my own reflection.'

The great chamber at Whitehall Palace was filled with the nobility of England for the great banquet on the anniversary of the queen's accession, thirty-six years before. The queen sat resplendent on a golden throne under her cloth of estate, under three flags taken by her troops from the Spaniards in Brittany.

Robert had done well at the joust, and won the respect of the crowd on the second day, when he took on all comers. Then a lance struck his gauntlet in a chance accident, breaking his finger and forcing him to withdraw.

A fanfare of trumpets announced the proclamation by Richard Lee, the Clarenceux King of Arms.

'Most high mighty princess, whereas there was a challenge to be run, it has been most nobly and well performed. There are two prizes to be given, the one for him that broke most staves in four courses, the other for him that ran most fairest. The judgement rests in your sacred Majesty to be pronounced and delivered at your pleasure.'

The honours went to Robert's uncle, Sir Robert Knollys, who was presented with a jewel of gold set with precious stones. Robert was given one of the queen's gloves, which he took as a reference to his injured hand. His sister Dorothy had sent for her physician from Syon House. Her doctor bound the broken finger with a wooden splint, and told him he'd been lucky.

He smiled to himself at the thought. The queen seemed angry at him, the Cecils outwitted him at every turn, his marriage was a sham and his debts continued to mount. He raised his glass in the toast, and raised his voice in the hope she might hear him above the others. 'To Her Majesty, Queen Elizabeth of England. Long may she reign!'

19

MAY 1595

Anthony Bacon lived in the wood-panelled wainscot apartment at Essex House, at the top of the stairs leading to the third floor. His gout had worsened, and his doctor's cure of rubbing rancid goose fat, mixed with wax and flour of rye, into his joints made little difference.

Robert liked to keep him close, rather than with his mother at the Bacon's family home at Gorhambury Manor, and Anthony helped keep an eye on the Essex household in lieu of rent. He was waiting to greet Robert when he arrived from Hampton Court.

'Have you seen a copy of the book about the succession, my lord?'

Robert loosened the buttons fastening his doublet, and called for a servant to fetch him a drink. 'Everyone is talking about that accursed book, which cannot be a good sign.'

'I don't think any of them can have read it.' Anthony Bacon held up the leather-bound book for Robert to see. 'I have acquired a copy from a contact in Amsterdam.'

Robert scowled. 'Owning such a book could see you in the Tower. Worse still, you bring it into my house!'

Anthony Bacon raised an eyebrow at Robert's angry tone. 'I had to see for myself if the rumours I'd heard about you were true, my lord.'

'What rumours?' Robert had learned how Anthony Bacon liked to reveal his secrets in riddles.

'I suggest you might like to read the dedication.' He handed the book to Robert.

The heavy book was prefaced by a formal dedication, several pages long. Robert stared at his name, his pulse racing as he read. 'The author claims I have done him and his friends favours – not only me, but my father and grandfather – yet I've never heard of him.'

Anthony Bacon nodded. 'I believe the author is Robert Parsons, an outspoken Jesuit writing under a pseudonym. Are you sure you didn't meet him during your campaigns in France?'

'No!' Robert's mind raced with the consequences. He knew he was innocent, but there was no way he could think of to prove it. 'Her Majesty will believe I'm involved in some way, however much I protest.'

Anthony Bacon nodded. 'Others are already drawing that conclusion. This is a deliberate attempt to discredit you, my lord.' He took back the book and read aloud from the foreword.

'No man is in a more eminent place than yourself, or in favour with your prince, or high liking of the people, and consequently no man can like to have a greater part in deciding this great affair, than your honour, and those that will assist you are likeliest to follow your fame and fortune.'

Robert's servant brought him a large glass of wine, and he drank most of it as he considered what to do. 'When the Cecils hear of this, they could say it is treason.'

Anthony Bacon looked sympathetic. 'The book sets out a balanced argument, although it is disparaging about King James of Scotland, and predicts civil war after the death of the queen.'

Robert cursed his bad luck. 'Can you imagine what my enemies at court will make of this? At best I'll be a laughing stock, and at worst arrested by the Yeomen of the Guard.'

Anthony Bacon closed the book. 'I was thinking, my lord, you would be well advised to see Her Majesty as soon as possible, and swear on your word that you have nothing to do with the book, or the author, whoever they might be.'

Robert suffered a restless night, troubled by the unexpected turn of events he could do without. The queen would enjoy having sport with his predicament. Worse still, Robert Cecil could have already used the scurrilous dedication to poison her mind against him. He'd also overheard talk at court that Henry Wriothesley was the queen's new favourite. Robert noticed how she tolerated the young earl and indulged his impertinence, as she had his own.

He called for Bagot to bring his doublet and breeches of silver cloth, the red velvet gown with a broad gilt belt with tassels of gold and silk, and his best cape. He put on his jewelled gold Garter collar, with the medallion of St George, and chose his black hat with a white ostrich feather plume.

Bagot gave his boots an extra polish. 'Important meeting, my lord?'

'Let us hope I find the queen in good spirits, Bagot, in which case my meeting will be a mere courtesy.'

He stared up at the sky as he took the wherry to Richmond Palace. They'd had a long winter, and he'd hoped for spring sunshine, but a chilly breeze made him shiver, and threatened to take his hat. Although he claimed he wasn't superstitious, the dark storm clouds gathering overhead seemed ominous, and he said a silent prayer.

. . .

Robert could tell something was wrong as he entered the palace. The footmen avoided his eye, and two of the queen's maids of honour passed without speaking. He was kept waiting for half an hour before being granted an audience, and found the queen standing in the middle of the room, with her ladies at a discreet distance.

She looked striking in a satin gown embroidered with moons and stars in thread of gold, with wide sleeves and a ruff of delicate silver lacework that seemed to form a halo around her head. Her ornate red wig glistened with jewels, making her face look paler than ever, and her eyes flashed with anger when she saw him.

Robert bowed, his well-rehearsed speech forgotten.

'I'm sorry, Your Majesty.' He'd become a small boy again, caught out and knowing he'd be punished. He recalled Anthony Bacon's advice. 'I swear on my honour that—'

'Honour?' Her sharp retort sounded like the shrill cry of a hunting hawk. 'You know nothing of honour, my Lord Essex.'

He knew how jealously she prevented talk of the succession, yet it hardly seemed a matter of honour. 'I can only surmise that the author is an agent of the Catholics, seeking to cause trouble between us.' He looked her in the eye. 'I give you my word I had no part in that book.'

'That book?' She frowned. 'We've seen a copy of that seditious book, and do not believe you had any part in it.'

'Then how do I offend Your Majesty?'

'We have discovered that you, my lord, are the father of Elizabeth Southwell's child – not Thomas Vavasour.'

Robert stared at her, his heart pounding, unable to think how best to respond. Denial would achieve nothing, but he would dearly love to know who had betrayed him. He'd feared his secret would one day reach the queen, and the timing could not be worse.

'I had no idea until I returned from the siege of Rouen. There was nothing I could do, Your Majesty.'

'Yet you allowed an innocent man to be imprisoned in the Tower?' She scowled. 'We have been lied to by all parties involved, for four years!'

'A moment of indiscretion, Your Majesty, which I deeply regret. It was never my intention to betray our great friendship—'

'You *test* our friendship, Lord Essex.' She dismissed him with a wave of her hand. 'Go, while I consider your position.'

He knew better than to remain within her sight. He cursed as he headed for the watergate where his wherry waited. The dark clouds turned to a heavy shower of rain, as if even nature was against him. He'd barely spoken to Elizabeth Southwell since that fateful time, and had never even seen their son.

Robert languished in his bed. He'd suffered sleepless nights, the thought of imprisonment in the Fleet or, worse, the Tower of London, swirling in his head. He replayed his meeting with the queen. Too late, he realised he should never have allowed her to dismiss him without defending himself.

He drifted into a fitful sleep, dreaming of the first time he met the queen. He'd been in awe of her as a small boy. His mother warned him only to speak if Her Majesty asked him a question. The worry had kept him awake that night, but the queen simply stared at him with sharp eyes. Little had changed. He was still in awe of her.

Bagot threw open the shutters and bright June sunlight streamed into his bedchamber.

'Good morning, my lord.' He studied Robert with a frown of

concern. 'You should be up to break your fast.'

Robert groaned and shielded his eyes from the light with his hand. 'I've no appetite, Bagot, and close those shutters. I suffer with an ague.'

'You must eat, and will feel better when you're up and dressed. Master Francis is here and wishes to see you.'

'Why so early?'

Bagot shook his head. 'It's mid morning, my lord. I thought it best to leave you to sleep.'

Robert rubbed his eyes. 'I shall see Francis Bacon.'

'I'll send him up, my lord, and will see what cook can find to tempt you.'

Robert slumped back on his pillows, and despaired at how little his life had changed. Even Bagot treated him as if he were still a boy, back in the attic room at Trinity College.

The door opened and Francis Bacon entered, carrying a writing slope and a lawyer's case.

'I hear you've succumbed to self-pity, my lord. Sit up for me, if you will.' He arranged the pillows for support, placed the writing slope on the bed in front of Robert, and then took papers, quill and ink from his case.

'I understand Her Majesty might be receptive to a well-worded letter of apology.'

'How do you know such things?'

'I make it my business, my lord. My information comes from Henry Wriothesley. Her Majesty told him to find out what ails you, and he came to me.'

Bagot returned with a platter of cold meats and cheese, freshly baked bread, butter, and a cup of small beer. 'If this doesn't restore your appetite, my lord, I shall gladly eat it myself!'

Robert watched him go and turned to Francis. 'You are right. I shall spend the day writing letters – to the queen, my mother, and my wife.' He took a sip of the beer. 'Thank you, Francis. I am sorry I failed you.'

'My lord?'

'I promised you the position of Attorney General – and now it looks unlikely you will even become Solicitor General, but I shall make it up to you. I still have lands within my gift.'

Francis Bacon held up a hand. 'I would rather not be obligated, my lord. You have my loyalty, and all I ask is that you heed my advice.'

Bagot opened the shutters on another fine day and turned to Robert. 'One of the queen's cooks has arrived, and is in your kitchens, my lord.'

Robert saw the glint of amusement in Bagot's eye. 'Is this some trick to get me to rise from my bed?'

Bagot smiled. 'She says Her Majesty is calling to visit you.'

'Kindly inform Her Majesty I suffer with an ague, and am unable to receive visitors.'

'If you wish, my lord.'

Robert lay back on his pillows and closed his eyes. There was some truth in what he'd said. He'd woken in a sweat in the night, his body aching, and he worried his old fever had returned. He didn't blame Bagot for trying to trick him into getting out of bed, but he couldn't recall when he'd last had a full night's sleep.

The door opened and a matronly woman entered carrying a bowl of soup. Behind her followed the queen, dressed simply, with a look of concern in her eyes. Elizabeth took the chair at the side of Robert's bed and placed her hand on his brow.

'They say you are refusing to eat. You must recover your strength, my Lord Essex. We need you at court.' Her voice was soft, like a mother calming her son.

All the bitterness he'd felt about this complicated woman evaporated in an instant. Despite her harsh words, taunts and shouted threats, she truly cared about him, and he loved her for it. Robert stared at her, as if seeing her for the first time.

'I'm grateful to you for coming to see me, Your Majesty.'

He found it hard to believe the queen was in his bedchamber. He watched as she took the bowl of soup. He might have been having a strange dream, but the subtle scent of the queen's perfume was too real to be imagined. She took a spoonful of soup and offered it to him. A long-forgotten memory came to mind of his mother doing the same, when he'd been a child. He tasted the soup, surprised at its rich, spicy warmth.

'Good.' She kept her eyes on his, as she fed him another spoonful. 'God willing, you'll be on your feet soon enough.'

Robert swallowed again. Francis Bacon was right. He'd succumbed to self-pity, and his letter of apology must have won the queen over. He decided he would grant lands in Tottenham to his friend, whether he wanted it or not. Francis Bacon talked of returning to Cambridge, or even travelling abroad, and Robert needed him now, more than ever.

He looked into the queen's eyes. 'Elizabeth Southwell was innocent—'

'Not innocent, but she is forgiven.' She fed him another spoonful.

Robert was glad to hear Elizabeth would not be punished. 'Thank you. Will she be permitted to remain at court?'

She nodded. 'On condition she marries within the year.' Her tone suggested some deal had been done.

He wondered who had seen the opportunity to secure Elizabeth Southwell as a bride, and hoped she'd not been persuaded to pay too high a price. Francis Bacon might help him discover who betrayed their secret. He took another spoonful of soup, rather than reveal his thoughts.

She smiled. 'The Earl of Leicester once gave me a present of a handsome young stallion.' Her eyes shone at the memory. 'It was magnificent, but too spirited, and would not be broken in. I never rode him without worrying he might throw me from his back.'

Robert could guess what became of the stallion. 'Am I forgiven?'

She took another spoonful of soup and put it to his lips. 'When you are well enough, you shall deal with our foreign correspondence.' She smiled. '*Fac et aliquid operis, ut semper te diabolus inveniat occupatum.* You must be kept busy, to keep you from mischief, and your talents should be put to better use.'

Robert's mother swept into Essex House like a galleon in full sail, followed by her entourage of servants. She still used the title Countess of Leicester, and kept her apartments at Essex House, although she'd been remarried for six years.

She whispered in his ear as she embraced him. 'It's good to see you well again. I have a surprise for you.'

She turned, and a small boy stepped forward. He stared up at Robert, wide-eyed.

'Father?'

'Yes, I am your father.' The words caught in his throat as he kneeled before his son. 'Has anyone told you what a good-looking boy you are?'

Little Walter shook his head. 'No, sir.'

'Well, I am proud to be your father.' Robert stared at his son in wonder. 'How old are you now?'

'Four, sir.'

'You are tall for your age, Walter.' He smiled. 'Do you ride?'

'Only in a carriage, sir.'

'Then I shall teach you to ride – and you shall have a fine pony, as I had when I was your age.'

After supper he visited his mother's chambers. 'Thank you for bringing little Walter. I've decided to rewrite my will, and acknowledge him properly.'

'I thought it would be good for you to see what a fine boy he's become.'

I shall have to tell Frances about little Walter, now the secret is out.'

She put her hand on his arm. 'Frances has always known.'

'Are you sure?'

'She is her father's daughter. Surely you've been married long enough to understand? No one is quicker to know the truth than a wife.'

Robert had the honour of organising the Accession Day celebrations at Whitehall. He'd commissioned Francis Bacon to write a play, and met with the players to rehearse. His old tutor, Master Wright, with his white beard, would play a hermit, representing contemplation, a thinly veiled reference to Lord Burghley.

Gelly was to play an old soldier, representing fame, and made a passable impression of Sir Roger Williams, with some choice Welsh curses and a battered iron breastplate. Bagot played Robert's squire, wearing his orange livery.

'We need someone to play the part of the secretary of state, representing experience.' Francis Bacon turned to Robert. 'Who better than my brother, Anthony?' He smiled. 'Although it might annoy Robert Cecil.'

'So much the better. This is only a play, to amuse Her Majesty.'

Francis Bacon handed them each a copy of his short play. 'You, my lord, meet with an old hermit, a secretary of state, a brave soldier, and a squire. The hermit presents you with a book of meditations.'

Robert frowned. 'It must not look like the seditious book. I don't want that raised again, even in a play.'

Francis Bacon agreed. 'Master Bagot, let's hear your opening address.'

Bagot cleared his throat. 'Most excellent and glorious queen, give me leave to offer my master's complaint and petition. Coming to Your Majesty's most happy day, he is tormented by a melancholy dreaming hermit, a mutinous soldier, and a tedious secretary. His petition is that he may be as free as the rest, and troubled with nothing but how to please and honour you.'

Francis Bacon turned to Robert with a smile. 'The secretary offers you political discourse, and the soldier tales of bravely fought battles. They each try to persuade you to take their course in life, and you, my lord, make a speech in praise of the queen.'

On Accession Day over a thousand spectators crowded into every available space around the tiltyard. Robert had decided he should be first to ride, against Sir George Clifford, Earl of Cumberland. Sir George wore gilded armour and, once again, dressed his horse as a red dragon, but Robert wore dazzling white over his armour, with a white lance and helmet, signs of knightly purity.

The queen watched from a high window, flanked by the Lord Admiral, Sir Charles Howard, and Edward de Vere, Earl of Oxford, the Lord Chamberlain. Robert was pleased to see her laughing, and calling to the gentlemen in the tournament below.

His play was planned as the highlight of the evening entertainment, in the presence chamber before the queen, and a crowd of her courtiers gathered to watch. Some of the more drunken courtiers jeered and pleaded with Robert to leave his vain following of love, in favour of meditation.

They laughed at the secretary's argument in favour of Robert remaining as a privy councillor, and cheered Gelly's blustering parody of a drunken old soldier, waving his sword in the air and encouraging Robert to seek glory in battle. At the end, they stood and applauded when Robert made his rousing speech.

'I shall never forsake the love of my mistress, whose virtue makes my thoughts divine, whose wisdom teaches me true policy, whose beauty and worth at all times make me fit to command armies.'

Master Wright, disguised as the hermit, stepped forward. 'He shows all the defects and imperfections of our times, and therefore thinks his course of life to be best in serving his mistress.'

The courtiers called for more, and patted the players on the back, but the queen seemed more interested in discussing something with Master Caron, the resident Dutch agent, and left early. The celebrations of the thirty-seventh year of her reign had been a success, yet left Robert wondering what it would take to impress her.

He had never arranged a funeral before, particularly one so grand, at St Paul's Cathedral. His old comrade in arms, Sir Roger Williams, who'd taken great risks in battle, had died suddenly in his bed, and left him all his worldly goods.

Robert stared at Sir Roger's black-draped coffin as the dean,

Alexander Nowell, read the long sermon. He found himself remembering the breathtaking excitement of their escape from Falmouth on the *Swiftsure*, and the unconvincing rage of Sir Francis Drake when he found out.

He could imagine Sir Roger cursing in his broad Welsh accent at the thought that all his gold and silver plate, his fine horses, and even his home, had been sold to pay the expenses of his funeral and memorial. A long line of fifty-five poor men, all dressed in black robes, one for each year of Sir Roger's life, had been paid to lead the procession.

Robert rode behind the funeral hearse at the head of a full cavalry division. He'd made sure they were all men who'd been proud to fight at the side of Sir Roger in many battles to defend the Protestant cause, from the Low Countries to the long siege of Rouen.

Despite the hardship and danger, foul pottage and flea-infested bedding, part of him longed to be back on the battlefield. The life of a privy councillor was too dull and, despite his best efforts, there'd been scant recognition for his work as a spymaster.

Sir Roger's polished sword and helmet gleamed on the top of his coffin in the light of a hundred candles. Robert had learned some hard lessons about how to lead men in battle. If he had the chance, he would gladly show the doubters he was older and wiser, and a worthy military commander.

There were rumours of a second Armada, with the fears and excitement of seven years before. Sir John Hawkins and Sir Francis Drake had raised a fleet of twenty-seven ships to attack the Spanish in the West Indies. They'd sailed from Plymouth at the end of August, and Robert wished he was with them, risking his life to take the fight to the Spanish.

20

MAY 1596

The crisp spring air of Plymouth harbour filled with the sounds of ships being loaded with supplies. Men shouted orders and curses as barrels of ale, gunpowder and shot, and sacks of grain and salted pork were hoisted on to the waiting galleons.

Heavy rains, early frosts, and the ravages of pestilence meant the harvests for the past two years were the worst in living memory. Provisioning the fleet of twelve thousand men for five months proved expensive, and drove Robert further into debt, with no guarantee of reimbursement from the Crown.

The queen's ship, *Elizabeth Bonaventure*, had docked at Milford Haven with news of the death of Sir John Hawkins at sea off Puerto Rico, followed in January by the death of Sir Francis Drake off the coast of Portobello. Their final mission was a failure, and they'd both succumbed to a deadly fever at sea.

Undaunted, Robert secured the queen's permission to sail on a raid on Cadiz, the great seaport of Spain, and home of the Spanish fleet. His new flagship, the *Due Repulse*, was a fast, forty-gun galleon. Her master, Captain Thomas Grove, had an experienced crew of two hundred and seventy-four mariners ready for her maiden voyage.

Then came news that Calais, the last foothold of England in France, was under siege from the Spanish army of the Count of Salazar. Robert raced to Dover with an army of six thousand men to relieve the siege, but his plan was frustrated. The queen revoked his orders just as they were all embarked and about to sail to France.

Precious time had been wasted and, back in Plymouth, Lord Admiral Charles Howard, commander of the fleet, summoned his officers to a meeting. Robert commanded a squadron of warships, as did the Lord Admiral's brother, Vice Admiral Sir Thomas Howard, who'd commanded the *Golden Lion* against the Spanish Armada.

Sir Francis Vere, who'd fought with Robert in the Low Countries, oversaw the land forces, and brought two thousand battle-hardened soldiers, from Holland and France, to boost the army which had marched from the abandoned Calais campaign.

Robert's old rival, Sir Walter Raleigh, was chosen as the fourth commander, and remained at Deptford to oversee the delivery of the ships which had yet to join the fleet. Raleigh had regained the queen's favour, and Robert resolved to put their differences behind him.

Admiral Howard studied their faces. 'First, I have good news, gentlemen. The Admiral of Holland, Jan van Duvenvord, is bringing his fleet of twenty-four Dutch warships to support us in Cadiz.'

Robert made a quick calculation. 'If Raleigh brings the ships we've been promised, that brings our fleet to a hundred and fifty ships, half as many again as sailed against the Armada – but I suspect you also have bad news?'

Admiral Howard nodded. 'I fear we might be on course to replay events at Dover. Her Majesty desires me and my Lord Essex to return to court.'

Robert cursed. 'For what reason?'

The admiral handed him the latest dispatch from the queen. 'It seems we are too dear to Her Majesty, and such persons of note, as she cannot allow us to sail.'

Francis Vere frowned. 'Does the queen know our preparations here in Plymouth are at your own expense?'

Robert nodded. 'That's how it's always been, even in my father's time. We work hard to ready the fleet, pay the crews and find supplies, while men like Robert Cecil plant the seeds of doubt in the queen's mind.'

Admiral Howard agreed. 'Our only hope is that you can persuade Her Majesty that we must sail, with her good wishes.'

'I've spent the past six months planning and provisioning this expedition, and have no intention of surrendering now.' He smiled. 'The die is cast, gentlemen, and I shall not return to court.'

On the last Saturday in May, the queen sent Sir Fulke Greville, Treasurer of the Navy, with her licence for the fleet to depart. As well as confirmation of Admiral Howard's command, Robert was commissioned to the rank of admiral and, alone in his cabin on the *Due Repulse*, he read her personal letter. She had written a prayer for their success, and added a note, in her own hand.

'*I make this humble bill of requests to him that all makes and does, that with his benign hand he will shadow you so as all harm may light beside you, and all that may be best hap to your share, that your return may make you better and me gladder. Let your companion, my most faithful Charles, Lord Howard, be sure his name is not left out in this petition. God bless you both, as I would be if I were there, which, whether I wish or not, he alone doth know.*'

He called his men to assemble on deck and, flanked by his trusted companions, Gelly Meyrick and Sir Anthony Standen, who'd recently been knighted, held the letter in the air for the men to see. 'We have the blessing of Her Majesty, a prayer made by the queen for our departure, which I shall now read to you.'

The men cheered, and several called out, 'God save the queen, God save the queen!'

Robert waited for them to settle, then read the queen's prayer in a clear voice so all could hear.

'Most omnipotent maker and guider of all our world's mass, that searches and fathoms the bottom of all our hearts' conceits, hath bred the resolution of our army. We humbly beseech with bended knees, prosper their work, and with best forewinds guide their journey, speed their victory, and make their return the advancement of thy glory, the triumph of their fame, and surety to the realm, with the least loss of English blood. To these devout petitions, Lord, give thou thy blessed grant, Amen.'

The men cheered again, and called out 'Amen!' and 'Long live Her Majesty!'

Gelly stood at Robert's side as the fleet sailed from Plymouth Sound. 'I've never seen such a sight, my lord.'

Robert turned to stare back at the line of warships following in their wake, pennants streaming in the stiff north-westerly breeze. 'We've done it, Gelly, although I believed we might be on our way to France.'

'How did you change the queen's mind?'

'I wrote to my fellow privy councillors. I reminded Lord Burghley that the Crown has invested thirty thousand pounds in this venture, and I played the one high card left in my hand.' Robert smiled at the thought. 'Her Majesty has a great fondness for her Treasurer of the Household.'

'Your grandfather is the last of his kind, my lord.'

'I fear he has not long on this earth, Gelly, but he was kind enough to grant me this one great favour.'

Gelly stared out at the white-crested waves and churning seas ahead. 'I'm no mariner, my lord, but it looks as if we're to be tested on this voyage.'

Robert had to agree. The sails flapped as the wind veered, and a rogue wave crashed against the side, sending a shower of spray high into the air. 'God willing, the *Due Repulse* is more than a match for these conditions.'

As if to prove him wrong, they plunged into a deep trough, and the ship heeled over to one side. They heard shouted curses as another high wave sluiced the deck, soaking the men who were struggling to reef the sails. Robert took a firm grip on the rail as he studied the fleet in their wake. 'Some of the older ships are making heavy going.'

Gelly pointed at the Lord Admiral's flagship, *Ark Royal*, as she fired a cannon. 'That's the signal to turn back.'

Robert cursed. 'Another day wasted. Every day we wait in port costs me a small fortune in provisions. Let's hope this is just a passing squall.'

Bright June sunshine meant Robert had to shade his eyes as he studied the distant horizon. They'd had to wait two long days in Plymouth, but the stormy weather passed and although there was still a heavy swell, they'd made good time, with the wind in their favour.

The Dutch fleet appeared like ghosts in the night, as promised, sounding trumpets and firing muskets in the air, to the cheers of the English crews. Robert breathed the fresh sea breeze as they sailed in formation, the greatest fleet any of them had seen. He sensed, at last, this voyage would make his reputation.

The alarm was sounded one night when an approaching galleon was spotted, but it proved to be an Irish merchantman, bound from Cadiz to Waterford. The captain told them there were only four Spanish warships and some twenty galleys in Cadiz, the rest being the merchant fleet, laden with goods for the West Indies.

It seemed they could be unaware of the approaching fleet, as the Irishman had seen no sign of the Spanish preparing their defences. The garrison of Cadiz might have four thousand men, and a division of cavalry, but the odds were in favour of the English and Dutch.

A light flickered on the skyline, and Robert's heart pounded as he made out distant buildings and the masts of ships. Cadiz was the jewel in the Spanish Crown, and the spoils of war could make him rich. Nine years before, Sir Francis Drake had trapped the Spanish fleet in the port of Cadiz, and their plan was to do the same.

The *Ark Royal*, supported by the Dutch fleet, would keep the Spanish ships in the port, while the English troops were landed to the west of the town. The attack would be made by land and sea, and Robert hoped to take the Spanish garrison by surprise.

When they agreed the plan, he hadn't imagined the huge waves breaking on the shoreline. Few of the men would be able to swim, and they would be in armour and carrying weapons. Landing would be risky and dangerous, so he consulted Master Tom Grove.

'We can't risk running aground, but we need to get the boats within wading distance.'

Tom Grove studied the rolling waves. 'The wind is offshore, my lord, which causes those breakers.' He frowned. 'I suspect the seabed shelves steeply. If we had more time, I could send men to take depth soundings, but the wind's freshening. Your soldiers will have to take their chances.'

Robert watched as Gelly counted eight soldiers into the first barge, which pitched and tossed alongside the *Due Repulse*. He raised a hand, recalling the men drowned trying to land at Peniche, north of Lisbon, seven years before. 'Take care, men – and God speed!'

The barge lurched wildly in the ocean swell, then sped forward through the surf as the rowers heaved on their oars. They lifted on the crest of a wave and crashed on to the shore. The soldiers scrambled for cover as musket fire rattled from the trees, and one of the oarsmen was hit in the back as he struggled to turn the boat around.

Robert cursed. 'The Spanish must have been expecting us, after all.'

They watched as the barge, now lighter with only the oarsmen, turned side on to the swell and flipped over, dumping the men in the water. The second barge had barely set out when a wave broke over the bows. The soldiers began frantic bailing with their helmets, but the next wave swamped them and the barge capsized.

Most didn't have a chance, and vanished into the waves, weighed down by their armour, but one yelled, 'God help us!' as he clung to a floating barrel.

Before Robert could stop him, Gelly leapt into the flyboat and rowed towards the drowning man. He disappeared behind a monstrous wave, but the flyboat reappeared, bobbing on the water like a cork. Rowing with all his strength, he reached the lone survivor and pulled him to safety, risking his life to save the man in the heavy seas.

Robert prayed they'd get back safely as more shots rang out, and he saw that, instead of returning, the little boat was headed to the dangerous shore. Gelly called out in his Welsh accent, and bullets struck the water as the men who'd landed waded out to him. They'd abandoned their armour and weapons, and managed to turn the boat in the surf before leaping aboard.

The men watching cheered as they made it back to the *Due Repulse* and struggled up the rope ladder, soaked and exhausted. One man was bleeding from a wound, but all looked glad to be alive. Robert raised a hand in acknowledgement to Gelly, who grinned as he wrung a pint of seawater from his cap.

The urgent clanging of church bells drifted across from the town, a sign they'd lost the element of surprise. Robert decided to anchor in the shelter of the headland and join the rest of the fleet in the morning. One man had been shot in the back and a dozen drowned. If not for Gelly's bravery they could have lost more men with their failed landing attempt.

The seas calmed overnight, and the four Spanish warships moved to anchor in a line across the entrance channel to the port. The roar of the Spanish guns made Robert's ears ring as one fired a broadside, but the cannonballs splashed harmlessly into the sea.

The huge cannons at the fort were a different matter. Designed to protect the port, they roared like the crack of thunder. The gunners found their range as a jet of water sprayed twenty feet into the air close to Raleigh's ship, the *Warspite*, another fine new galleon with a crew of three hundred men.

Gelly brought Robert his steel helmet and breastplate. 'Best put these on, my lord.'

Robert's answer was drowned by a deafening explosion. He turned to see a pall of thick grey smoke rising from the fort. 'Luck is with us today, Gelly. It looks as though the Spanish have destroyed their own gun!'

He watched as the *Warspite* positioned herself alongside Vice Admiral Sir Thomas Howard's warship, *Mere Honour*. The *Due Repulse* had been ordered to stay in reserve but, after the disaster of the landing, Robert needed to prove what his crew could do. He said a prayer for luck as he ordered the guns to be made ready.

Against orders, they sailed straight for the Spanish warships, presenting only their bows as a target until they made a sharp turn to starboard. The master gunner shouted in his deep voice, 'Have a care!'

Robert felt the deep boom of their cannons as they reverberated through the hull. The Spanish warship's stern shattered in splinters, and a gaping hole appeared close to the waterline. The air filled with the sulphurous smoke of gunpowder. He flinched as a Spanish cannonball thumped hard against the hull of the *Due Repulse*, but the new timbers withstood the assault.

Not to be outdone, Raleigh ordered his gunners to open fire, and the salvo of the *Warspite*'s guns echoed across the water. Like the *Due Repulse*, his flagship was armed with the latest cannons. The rigging of the second Spanish warship hung in shreds, and billowing smoke appeared as her crew began to abandon ship.

Master Grove stood watching with Robert. 'I'd say the crew have set her ablaze, my lord.' He pointed at the last undamaged ship, as flames leapt high into the air. 'Looks as if they've robbed you of your sport.'

The crackle of the flames and smell of burning tar and timber drifted across the water. Two of the Spanish ships were on fire – with men jumping into the sea, risking death by drowning to escape the flames – while the remaining two were deliberately run aground so their crews could leap on to the muddy bank.

Robert turned at the crack of musket fire, and cursed as he

saw the Dutch soldiers taking potshots at the escaping Spanish crews. If they'd been English, he would have sent orders to cease firing, but he had no authority over the Dutch. He scowled and turned to Tom Grove.

'Find us somewhere safe to land, Master Grove. It's time to get our men ashore.'

Gelly helped him into his armour, and he thought of his brother, and Sir Philip Sidney, as he strapped on his best sword for luck. The familiar mix of nerves and excitement made his pulse race. There was a danger he might be killed or suffer a terrible injury, but he would avenge his brother's death.

'There are letters to Her Majesty, my wife and my mother in my cabin, Gelly. I wish you to deliver them in person if anything happens to me.'

Gelly grinned. 'You can count on me, my lord, but God willing, we'll all return safe and sound – and laden down with Spanish booty!'

~

The sheltered bay was deserted, but they faced a three-mile march to Cadiz. Robert regretted wearing full armour, and swigged warm beer from his leather bottle. He'd chosen his stepfather, Sir Christopher Blount, to prevent Spanish reinforcements reaching the town, and Colonel Sir John Wingfield to lead a diversionary attack.

Gelly agreed to take a dozen hand-picked soldiers to scout ahead of the main army and provide early warning of Spanish troops. Armed with the latest muskets, they were the best shots and trained to be the fastest at reloading.

Cadiz looked bigger than it had from the sea, with high walls and lookout towers. The bells of the churches clanged in a warning as Robert led the main body of men out of sight of the sentries. Colonel Wingfield marched on to create his diversion, with orders to fall back as soon as the Spanish gates were open.

The muffled boom of cannons from the port fell silent. The sea battle was over, but yells and gunfire told them the shore-based attack had begun. Gelly returned with his men, a look of concern on his face.

'They've opened the gates and sent out a whole division of cavalry. Sir John Wingfield is wounded, my lord.'

Robert cursed and turned to his commanders. 'Have your men ready to advance.'

The sharp fanfare of trumpets signalled the attack, and the Spanish scattered at the sight of Robert's army. The high gates were barred, leaving some forty cavalrymen to face two thousand soldiers. Most were pulled from their horses, but Robert spotted some escaping through a gap in the walls. He drew his sword and yelled for Gelly and his men to follow.

The Spanish darted for cover, but one aimed his musket and a bullet clanged from Robert's breastplate, leaving a dent. He charged the musket man, who dropped his weapon and ran. Robert joined Gelly and his men as they fought their way to the gate.

His sword clashed on a Spaniard's helmet, and shots rang out as Gelly's musket men opened fire, scattering the last of the soldiers guarding the gate. They slid the heavy locking bar and pushed the high iron gates open. The rest of Robert's men swarmed through, chasing the defenders down narrow side streets.

Robert led his men into the marketplace, where a division of Spanish soldiers put up a determined fight. More had found high vantage points in buildings overlooking the marketplace, and bullets struck several of Robert's men, killing some and wounding others.

Something hit him in the back and he went down, striking

his face on the ground, his best sword clattering to the cobbles. Dazed, he tasted blood in his mouth, and stared up to see Spanish soldiers armed with swords. His men were gone, and his only hope was to surrender.

The men looked back at the sound of trumpets, and Robert feared Spanish reinforcements had overcome his stepfather's division. Instead, hundreds of English soldiers burst into the marketplace, shooting and killing the men standing over him.

Robert found his sword, and struggled to stand. He recognised Sir Walter Raleigh, and raised a hand. 'I've never been more pleased to see you.'

Raleigh grinned. 'We've won, Lord Essex.' He took Robert's hand and helped him to his feet. 'Are you wounded?'

Robert unfastened the leather strap and pulled off his helmet. He'd cut his lip when he was knocked to the ground, and wiped the blood with his hand. 'I'm lucky to still have my front teeth.' He saw the bloodstained bandage on Raleigh's leg. 'You are wounded, though.'

'I'll live.' He grimaced. 'Hurts like hell, but it's only a flesh wound.'

'I was told Colonel Wingfield has a serious injury. Have you seen him?'

'I'm afraid Sir John Wingfield is dead.' Raleigh spoke softly. 'He was shot in the head, and killed instantly.'

Lord Admiral Charles Howard took the castle as his headquarters, and called his officers to a meeting. 'I've learned that the commander of Cadiz was an old adversary – the Duke of Medina Sidonia.' He frowned. 'He's managed to escape, but offers a ransom of two million ducats if we release his merchant fleet.'

Robert cursed. The duke, commander of the Spanish

Armada, would have been a great prize to take back to England. 'The men have looted anything of value. We need those ships as reward for our risk and investment.'

Admiral Howard nodded. 'You disobeyed orders, Lord Essex, but fought bravely, so I'm prepared to overlook your actions. As for the duke, I agree. We've only destroyed four warships, but shall return with the merchant fleet as our prize, and strike a blow far greater than its monetary value.'

Robert saw the others agreed. 'I'd like to occupy Cadiz, as governor. This town can become our new Calais. We'll show the Spanish who controls these seas.'

Admiral Howard shook his head. 'Her Majesty's orders are clear. We are to return, after our comrade, Colonel Wingfield, has been buried with full honours, then we shall lay Cadiz to waste.'

Robert woke to the clanging of bells, and called for Gelly as he reached for his sword in the darkness. 'The Spanish must have launched a counter-attack. Rouse the men!'

He crossed to the window and stared at the scene before him. The entire port was ablaze, with bright orange flames roaring twenty feet into the night air. A muffled explosion boomed as a gunpowder store caught fire, and the mast of a merchantman toppled and crashed into the sea as the stays burned through.

Gelly joined him, his face lit up in the eerie orange light of the blaze. 'There goes our fortune.'

Robert stared in silence for a moment. 'Not just ours, Gelly. The Crown will never recover its investment, and we'll all face the consequences.'

Robert was wrong. He stood alone, in solemn silence as the queen berated him in front of the whole court. 'Is it not enough, my lord of Essex, that we invest fifty thousand pounds in your venture?'

He could have pointed out that it was more like thirty thousand, that he'd made no profit and had increased his debts in her service. He should have pointed out that the Lord Admiral commanded the venture, and that he'd come close to losing his life in the attack on Cadiz.

He might have added that on the voyage home, his plan to find the Spanish treasure fleet was overruled by Lord Admiral Howard. After their return to Plymouth, they'd learned the unescorted treasure fleet, laden with gold, silver, and precious jewels, was only two days' sailing behind them at Lisbon.

Instead, he allowed her to reprimand him for knighting his gentlemen adventurers after the battle. He gritted his teeth and drew on every ounce of self-control as she called him a wastrel and a disappointment. It was worth it, to reward Gelly's bravery and see his pride at becoming Sir Gwyllyam Meyrick, a knight of the realm.

Worst of all, Frances suffered another miscarriage, and withdrew into herself, like a snail into its shell, barely acknowledging him. She'd always been resilient. Even after the sudden death of her father she took control. He worried about her, and didn't know what to do.

He'd also been absent from a family funeral. His grandfather could have joined his wife – Robert's grandmother, Lady Catherine Carey – in Westminster Abbey but, with typical humility, chose to be laid to rest in the family chapel at Rotherfield Greys in Oxfordshire. Gelly once said Sir Francis Knollys was the last of his kind. Robert would miss him.

21

MARCH 1597

Frances raised an eyebrow as she read the advice from Francis Bacon about how Robert might win back the queen's affection. 'He says not to underestimate Her Majesty, as she has the keenest political mind of anyone he knows.'

Robert gave her a wry look. 'If that's so, why can't she see I serve her best interests?' He pushed the door closed, not wishing to be overheard by servants, or the Cecils' spies. 'She changes her mind too often for Master Bacon's advice to be of use.'

She looked up at him, and for a moment he saw the woman he'd married, before the familiar disapproval darkened her eyes. 'You asked to see me in private, and I don't believe you only want me to see this.' She handed back Francis Bacon's notes.

Robert sat back in his chair. He regretted the distance between them, but had only himself to blame. 'The queen tried to take my share of the ransom from Cadiz – so I told her I made no other profit from the venture.'

'Is that not true?' She raised an eyebrow.

He took the blue velvet bag he'd brought, and slid it across the table to her. 'You're going to help me make my words true, Frances.'

She stared at the bag, then pulled the cord securing the neck and poured some of the contents into her hand. Gleaming rubies and gold jewellery spilled out. She emptied the rest on to the table, and picked out a sparkling diamond ring, turning it in the light from the candle.

'A king's ransom?'

Robert smiled. 'I want you to have it all.'

Frances tried the ring and found it fitted her finger. 'I wonder what became of the owner of this?'

'The Dutch had a score to settle with the Spanish, but I give you my word we treated the women, children and elderly with respect, and set them free.'

Frances scooped the gold and jewels back into their velvet bag and retied the neck. 'I'll offer you a piece of advice in return, worth more than all these looted jewels.' She stared into his eyes. 'Learn from your mistakes.'

'I do!' He'd not meant to raise his voice, but her words annoyed him.

'You do not. You never have.' She thought for a moment. 'The Lord Admiral is old and tired. He stood in your way, and lost you the Spanish treasure fleet. You should lead your own fleet. Finish what you began.'

'The queen said she will never allow it.'

'And what did you do?'

He gave her a sheepish look, and hesitated before replying. 'I had to concede I've had my chance.'

'You did not. I know you threatened to return to Wales, until the queen called you back.'

'What would you have me do, Frances?'

'Surround yourself with good men you can trust, like your stepfather, and your uncle. Win the support of the Cecils, and make your peace with Raleigh.'

'Robert Cecil schemes behind my back, and Raleigh cares only for himself.'

'Robert Cecil is Secretary of State, and the queen often dines at Burghley House. You need his support, and Raleigh might have to save your life again.'

Robert studied her with new respect, and smiled. 'You forgot to add that I should never underestimate my wife.'

He woke the next morning fired with enthusiasm, and wrote letters to Raleigh and Robert Cecil, inviting them to Essex House. Despite the short notice, he expected they would come, if only from curiosity, and decided this was the time to serve his best wine.

Raleigh was first to arrive. He wore a gold chain over his embroidered doublet, and a gilded dagger at his belt.

'What are you up to now, my Lord Essex?'

Robert smiled. 'How is your wound?'

Raleigh grinned. 'An honourable one, but my doctors tell me I was lucky not lose my leg.'

Robert Cecil arrived next, dressed in black, his hunched back more pronounced than ever. 'I find myself wondering what I have done to deserve this unexpected honour, my lord.'

Robert invited them into his study, where Bagot poured them each a glass of wine. 'To the queen.'

They both raised their glasses. 'The queen.'

'This wine is from the Duke of Medina Sidonia's cellar in Cadiz.' Robert smiled. 'I thought I might return to Spain and bring home some more.'

Robert Cecil frowned. 'I believe you might find the costs excessive, Lord Essex.'

'That's why I've invited the two of you here. Everything we need is ready. The ships are refitted, the crews rested and ready for action, and our commanders rich with experience, if not the spoils of war. All we need is the approval of Her Majesty. What do you say?'

Raleigh sipped his wine before answering. 'You can count me in, Lord Essex. The thought of the Spanish treasure fleet slipping through our fingers keeps me awake at night.'

Robert Cecil looked thoughtful. 'My information is that the Spanish war fleet is preparing to sail to Ireland, to establish a base for the invasion of the West Country. It would seem prudent to prevent them.'

'We shall learn from Cadiz, gentlemen.' Robert sipped his wine. 'I wish to put my name forward as overall commander.'

Raleigh frowned. 'Lord General? Lord Admiral Howard will have something to say about that.'

'I thought to recommend his brother, Lord Thomas Howard, as my vice admiral – and you, Sir Walter, as rear admiral.'

Vice Admiral Thomas Howard, Earl of Suffolk, raised his hat and welcomed Robert aboard his flagship, *Mere Honour*. 'I wish to thank you, Lord Essex. I heard Her Majesty refused your proposal for me to sail with you.'

'It's Lord Burghley you should thank. He said we needed a firm hand at the tiller. We were fortunate to have his support. Yet again, Her Majesty considered calling the whole thing off.'

Lord Howard looked concerned. 'I've put my own money into this venture. We need to be under way as soon as we can.'

Robert agreed. 'I've had our sailing orders. We will attack the Spanish fleet, thought to be at the port of Ferrol. If they've sailed for Ireland, we are to pursue them, but I hope not at the expense of a visit to the Azores.' He smiled. 'You shall have your investment back tenfold if we apprehend the treasure fleet – and I'll let you into a secret. We plan to occupy the Azores, and end the flow of gold and silver to the King of Spain.'

Robert prayed for an improvement in the weather. He'd battled into the teeth of a squall, sailing down to lead the fleet. Unfavourable winds and slate-grey skies meant leaving Plymouth was a risk, but it was time to roll the die. Progress would be slow, but anything was better than sitting in port.

His flagship, the *Due Repulse*, had been refitted with heavier guns, and he'd made his cabin more comfortable, with a good mattress on his bunk, which doubled as a bench seat, and a table large enough for dining and meetings with his officers. In addition, there was a chart table, which also served as a writing desk, with a shelf above holding his books.

The sea chart of the Bay of Biscay was spread out on the chart table, and he studied the planned route, marked by his navigator. They would have to tack until the winds changed, but there was still a chance of catching the Spanish.

A confident knock sounded on the door, and his friend Charles Blount appeared. Knighted in the field after victory at Cadiz, and now a Garter Knight, Penelope's lover had become a regular visitor to Essex House. He had recently become Baron Mountjoy, on the death of his elder brother.

'It seems I've offended our marshal, Sir Francis Vere.'

'I know he was displeased to hear you command the land forces, but your appointment as Colonel General was approved by Her Majesty.'

'I told him to stop his press gangs.'

'You were right to do so. We have enough volunteers.'

'The Lord Admiral stood them down, so Sir Francis Vere ordered men to be taken by force from their families. They've no experience of fighting, and few have ever sailed on a warship.'

Robert frowned. 'The men on this voyage earn their share of any treasure, so let us hope that knowledge makes them loyal servants of the Crown.'

The flash of lightning ripped across the night sky, followed by a deep rumble of thunder. Robert cursed his luck. The fleet had sailed from Plymouth in promising winds, yet no one would sleep this night. The *Due Repulse* lurched in the heavy sea, and several of Robert's precious books clattered from the shelf to the floor of his cabin.

As he picked them up, he heard the ship's timbers groan and cries of 'God save us!' from the crewmen outside. The bell clanged for the middle watch, and he pulled on his waterproof cap and stepped out. A torrent of icy rain thundered on to the deck, running from the sails like rivers. A few flickering pinpricks of light astern were the only sign the fleet still followed in his wake.

Lightning flashed again, and Gelly appeared from below decks, dripping with water. 'The pumps are coping, my lord, but it's hard work for the men.' He looked down at his soaked boots. 'They say the caulking has sprung a leak. We've taken quite a pounding.'

The sharp crack of thunder directly overhead made Robert flinch. 'We have to ride this storm out, but I worry about the older ships, with inexperienced crews. It's only a matter of time before the fleet is scattered.'

Gelly peered into the rainswept night. 'I can count a dozen. I'll not be surprised if some have turned back for home.' He sounded as if he wished he could do the same.

Robert looked up in alarm as they rode down the trough of a building wave, rising high above the bows. It broke, pounding over the deck. It seemed they might be swamped, but the *Due Repulse* was designed for heavy sailing, and the water ran from the scuppers in a torrent.

The first light of dawn revealed they were alone. Tired and disheartened, Robert scanned the horizon but couldn't see a single mast in any direction. 'What's our position, captain?'

'We've been blown off course, my lord, five leagues off the coast of Cornwall.' He pointed up at a broken yardarm. 'We've rigged it as best we can, but we're still taking on water, my lord. I have to tell you we must land for repairs, or face the risk of sinking.'

Robert cursed. 'What's our nearest port?'

'Falmouth, my lord.'

After two days and nights of hard sailing in storm-force winds and heavy seas, they were further away than ever. Their English Armada suffered the same fate as the Spanish, and Robert knew he would be blamed for setting out in bad weather. He had no idea how many ships and men had been lost, or whether they would be able to continue after repairs were made.

Gelly rode with him for company to Plymouth, where a dozen warships sat at anchor. They could see the *Warspite*, Raleigh's flagship, but no sign of Sir Francis Vere and his soldiers. They found Charles Blount drowning his sorrows in a waterside tavern, and Robert joined him while Gelly took care of the horses.

Charles Blount called for a beer for Robert. 'Thank God you're safe.' He smiled. 'We cheered when we had your message from Falmouth, as we feared we might have to sail under Raleigh's command!'

Robert took a grateful sip of his beer. 'In truth, our pumps came close to being overwhelmed. The *Due Repulse* is a good ship, but the storms tested her.'

Charles Blount nodded. 'Several ships were dismasted but, as far as I know, none are lost.'

'What of our general?'

'Sir Francis Vere sent a messenger to tell us his squadron is anchored at the groyne, and will sail here when the weather settles.'

Charles Blount took a letter with a dark wax seal from his pocket and handed it to Robert. 'From Lord Admiral Howard. I was going to allow another day before sending it to Falmouth.'

Robert drained his beer before reading the letter, dreading the prospect of being recalled to court to be harangued by the queen. It irked him that the Lord Admiral had no doubt taken some pleasure in being proved right. He broke the wax seal and read.

'*To the Earl of Essex. The comfort we have received by a letter from Sir W. Raleigh of your arrival into Falmouth is to us, your true friend, unspeakable, and do give God deep thanks for it. The like weather at this time of the year was never seen by man.*'

Robert looked up at Charles Blount. 'There was no need for Raleigh to be in such haste to report to Her Majesty.' He read on in silence. '*I did never see more comfort than Her Majesty when she saw by Sir W. Raleigh's letter that your person was safe. She showed the dear love she beareth you, for with joy the water came plentiful out of her eyes.*'

He struggled to remain composed as the strain of the past week caught up with him. He refolded the letter and watched as Charles Blount refilled his tankard from a jug. 'Our venture is not lost.'

Blount frowned. 'This storm has tested not only our ships. Many of your gentlemen have had enough and departed for home.'

'Their loss is our gain, Charles. The storm has sorted the wheat from the chaff. When we take the Spanish treasure fleet, we'll have a greater share of the reward.' A thought occurred to him. 'Will you arrange for the pressed men to be released from service? They can have eight pence each for their troubles – and if we can do it before Francis Vere returns, so much the better.'

The reduced fleet of sixty ships slipped from Plymouth in bright July sunshine. The winds were so light the *Due Repulse* had to be towed from the harbour behind a rowing tug. Robert said a silent prayer that after all the work, expense, and hardship, they were finally under way.

Short of provisions, he'd raced to Greenwich Palace with Raleigh to offer the queen his account of their situation. Appeased by his promises of a fortune in gold and silver, she'd allowed them to sail with her blessing.

A gust of wind filled the sails, and the fleet followed in close formation. So much time had been lost Robert doubted they would find the Spanish waiting for them at Ferrol, so lookouts watched for the enemy, and the guns were kept ready for action.

Although they'd waited for good weather, the blue skies of Plymouth turned an ominous grey as their journey progressed. He called for the captain. 'Should we sail closer to the shore, in case we need to seek shelter?'

The captain studied the wind. 'We're in the Bay of Biscay, my lord. Many ships have been lost on a lee shore. I recommend we set a course straight for Ferrol.'

Robert retired to his cabin to write his report to Lord Burghley, and left instructions to be called if the wind changed. He woke with daylight streaming through the small porthole, and thanked God. The air felt warmer, a sign they were close to Spain, but the ship's timbers creaked and the thick rope stays strained in heavy seas.

Gelly banged on the door, a concerned look on his face. 'The captain says we should reach Ferrol by noon, but another storm is on the way.'

'Well, there's no going back now.' Robert pulled on his waterproof cape. 'Let's see how the fleet is doing.'

The line of ships was losing formation, with the smaller carracks falling behind. He raised his voice to be heard over the wind as he studied the sky, trying to read the clouds. 'With luck, we'll beat the storm to Ferrol.'

He repeated those words in his head as the winds rose, and monstrous, white-crested waves battered the fleet. One of the sails ripped loose, flapping wildly as men fought to bring it under control. Robert gasped as cold seawater splashed in his face, and he had to grab the handrail to keep his footing on the slippery deck.

He heard a rending crash over the noise of the storm as the mast of the *St Matthew*, one of the Spanish prizes taken from Cadiz, toppled into the sea. The crew hacked at the stays with axes, and her commander, Sir George Carew, raised a hand as they turned back for home.

A distress cannon fired close by, and he turned to see the main yardarm of Raleigh's ship, the *Dreadnought*, broken off and swinging in the gale. The *Dreadnought* heeled alarmingly in the heavy swell. There was nothing he could do to save them, as Robert's crew battled with the pumps to keep the *Due Repulse* afloat.

After a day of dangerous storms, the wind eased but, with the fleet scattered, Robert reluctantly ordered the captain to head for their rendezvous off Cape Finisterre. Only twenty-eight ships had made it, less than half the fleet. They spotted the galleon of his uncle, Sir Robert Knollys, and sent a boat to ferry him to the *Due Repulse*.

Sir Robert cursed as he lost his footing and almost fell into the sea as he clambered aboard.

'I'm too old for this.'

Robert led his uncle to his cabin, where he poured them both a cup of wine. 'Have you seen the *Dreadnought*, or any ships of Raleigh's squadron?'

His uncle shook his head. 'No, but I've never seen such a storm. It's a miracle any of us made it here.'

'Unless they show up soon, there's no hope of an attack on Ferrol with this easterly wind.' Robert frowned. 'We might find ourselves the target of the Spanish.'

His uncle agreed. 'Our best hope is to head for the Azores, before we run out of water and provisions.'

'My concern is that Raleigh has stolen a march on us. I'd not be surprised to find he's set off in search of the treasure fleet – or, worse, returned home to give his own account of our venture.' Robert sipped his cup of wine. 'I need someone I can trust to take my dispatches to court, and provide a fair report on our progress.'

His uncle nodded. 'I'll be pleased to see my family again, although I doubt I'll be granted an audience.'

Robert took a letter he'd written, added a footnote, and then signed it, *R. Essex, Cape Finisterre.*

'Make all speed to court and tell Robert Cecil you have a letter from me to Her Majesty. When you are admitted into her presence, present my letter and inform her of what happened since leaving Plymouth.'

'I'll do my best.' His uncle raised his cup. 'To better fortune – and fairer winds.'

Robert smiled. 'When we find the Spanish treasure fleet, which I'm sure we will, I give you my word you shall have your fair share.'

22

AUGUST 1597

The clanging alarm bell brought the *Due Repulse* to action stations. Robert was busy writing a letter to Lord Burghley, and dashed out on deck where he saw the dark shape of a warship headed straight for the fleet. Men shouted orders and gun ports banged open as the crews prepared to open fire.

All eyes were on the approaching ship. Robert held his breath as she drew closer. This was his first test as a commander of a sea battle, but the ship was too far off to see how many more followed. If the Spanish war fleet had come for them, they wouldn't stand a chance.

The lookout pointed and called from his high platform. 'They're English, my lord! The *Dreadnought*, from Rear Admiral Raleigh's squadron!'

Robert laughed with relief at their mistake. The *Dreadnought*, twenty-four years old, with thirty heavy guns and twenty sails, was one of the queen's first great warships. Her commander, Sir William Brooke, was a friend, and one of those knighted by Robert at the siege of Rouen.

Sir William was rowed across and raised a hand as he climbed aboard. 'It's good to see you safe, my lord Essex!'

'We feared the *Dreadnought* was lost with all hands in the Biscay storms.' Robert smiled. 'Have you seen the *Warspite*?'

Sir William nodded. 'I've brought a message for you from Rear Admiral Raleigh. He was driven west, together with the *Swiftsure* and the *Bonadventure*, and is making repairs at the Azores.'

The news presented Robert with a dilemma. His orders were that all important decisions had to be recorded, with the names of those advising noted. He raised the flag to summon his commanders for an urgent conference.

'I thank God Raleigh is safe, but he has sailed to the Azores, and will have some explaining to do.'

Vice Admiral Howard nodded. 'Without his squadron, it would have been foolhardy to risk the rest of the fleet in an attack on Ferrol.'

'Raleigh disobeyed his orders.' Sir Francis Vere scowled. 'He hopes to beat us to the treasure fleet – and take the greatest share and the glory for himself.'

Robert unrolled his chart of the Azores on the table in front of them. Looted from a Portuguese merchantman, and illustrated with fanciful drawings of whales and sea monsters, the English names for the nine islands and principal towns had been added in black ink.

'Our orders were clear, gentlemen. If we could not destroy the Spanish fleet at Ferrol, we were to prevent them sailing to Ireland.' He smiled. 'Our failure to do so might be overlooked if we return with our holds full of Spanish gold.'

Vice Admiral Howard studied the chart. 'Most of these islands are settled by the Portuguese, but I believe the Spanish have their main fortress at Tercera.' He tapped his finger on the island in the centre. 'If Rear Admiral Raleigh alerts them to our presence, we might never take the treasure fleet by surprise.'

Robert agreed. 'We're low on water, and many of our ships

need to make repairs. My proposal is to avoid the Spanish at Tercera, and make for the Bay of Flores, to the west.' He smiled. 'My captain tells me Flores has good anchoring and fresh water – and with luck we'll find the natives are friendly!'

After his commanders returned to their ships, Robert sent for Gelly. 'I'm sending the *Dreadnought* back to Raleigh, with a message to meet us at Flores. I want you to sail with her, and note what he says and does.'

'What do you suspect he might do, my lord?'

Robert frowned. 'Who knows, Gelly, but if Raleigh deliberately ignores orders, there will have to be consequences.'

Robert had never sailed as far as the Azores, and his pulse raced at the sight of verdant hills on the shimmering blue horizon. They'd left the rain squalls behind, and playful dolphins leapt in the blue water ahead of the *Due Repulse*. The fresh, easterly winds which had slowed the fleet now sped them to the islands with a sense of urgency, a good omen.

He studied the high cliffs of Flores as they approached. The natural inlet, sheltered from the winds, led to a narrow beach with a wooden landing jetty. A shearwater soared and wheeled low over the waves, and the yellow flowers the island was named for gave the distant hills a golden glow. Keen to be the first ashore, he ordered boats to be made ready and led his fleet into the calm waters of the bay.

The captain proved right. The deputation of wary Portuguese settlers who came to greet them carried muskets, but were reassured by Robert's promise not to mistreat them. They showed his men the way to a spring of fresh water, and traded bread and fruit for iron tools.

Charles Blount hacked apart a ripe pineapple with his knife

and offered Robert a slice. 'Seems we've found our paradise on earth, my lord.'

Robert tasted the sweet yellow flesh, a delicacy after so long at sea. 'I'll be happier when we sight the treasure fleet – and Rear Admiral Raleigh.'

∽

Robert sent out patrols to search the channels between the other islands for Spanish ships or Raleigh's missing squadron. It wasn't long before they found him, at anchor off the island of Fayal. Raleigh was unrepentant, and said he'd been busy with repairs to the *Warspite*.

Robert summoned Raleigh to the *Due Repulse*, and gave him a formal reprimand in front of the other officers. 'Your orders were to join the fleet off Cape Finisterre.' He looked Raleigh in the eye. 'Some are saying your failure to do so is mutiny. A hanging offence.'

'We needed fresh water, and had to make repairs, my Lord Essex. Every beam and bulkhead, and even the bricks from the stove, shook loose in the storms.' Raleigh frowned. 'We came under fire from the fort as we landed. One of our boats foundered on the rocks, and only by the grace of God did none of us drown.'

Robert needed Raleigh's support, and had no wish to make an enemy of him. He turned to Sir Francis Vere.

'I propose you take La Gratioza, with your Dutchmen, while Baron Mountjoy and Sir Christopher take St Michael's to the east.' He nodded to Raleigh. 'We will occupy Fayal. Keep vigilant, and watch for the Spanish, gentlemen. With luck the treasure fleet will sail right into our hands.'

. . .

Tired of waiting for Raleigh's squadron to complete repairs and take on water, Robert ordered the *Due Repulse* to sweep in a wide arc around the west of the Azores. Robert hoped to spot the treasure ships, but they saw nothing. When they finally arrived back at the island of Fayal, they were hailed by Gelly Meyrick from the *Dreadnought*, anchored in the bay.

Robert called out to him. 'Where is Rear Admiral Raleigh?'

'Gone ashore, my lord, with all his men.' Gelly pointed. 'Shots were fired from the fort.'

Robert had wished to lead the attack, and regretted not giving Raleigh orders to wait for him to arrive. 'Send an order for them to be recalled – and Rear Admiral Raleigh is to report to me on the *Due Repulse*.'

He became more irritated as he waited. Raleigh's insubordination challenged his authority, but he could face the question of any punishment when they finally returned home. He summoned Gelly and Charles Blount as witnesses, and was surprised to see that Raleigh appeared pleased with himself.

'We've brought back a good collection of booty, my Lord Essex, and taken several Spaniards as prisoners.'

Robert frowned. 'Are you aware it is forbidden to land troops except on my orders?'

Raleigh looked confused. 'You told me to take Fayal with you, Lord Essex. We waited all afternoon and all night for you to arrive. In the morning we saw the Spanish digging defensive trenches and evacuating the town, no doubt taking anything of value with them.'

Gelly looked uncomfortable, and cleared his throat. 'What the Rear Admiral says is right, my lord, although I asked if we could wait a little longer—'

'We waited for as long as we could, Lord Essex.' Raleigh glowered at Gelly, then turned to Robert. 'I believe you would have done the same.'

Robert had to accept he was right. Yet again, Raleigh made him look an ineffective leader, taking the glory and looted property for himself. He'd heard enough.

'Take a shore party and burn the town, then do what you can to despoil the fort. We're finished here, but at least we can make sure Fayal cannot be used against us.'

Robert despaired of ever seeing the fabled treasure fleet but, after another week of patrolling, a dozen Spanish ships were spotted at dawn near the island of St Michael's. The men cheered, and were in good spirits as they set off in pursuit, but the Spanish had a head start, and raced for the safety of the fortified port at Tercera.

Robert called another meeting of his commanders. 'I propose we land our best men to attack the fort from the rear, while the fleet engage the attention of the gunners.'

Charles Blount agreed. 'I'm prepared to lead the shore-based assault. We could land at night, to increase our chances of surprising the guards at the fort.'

Vice Admiral Howard shook his head. 'I admire your spirit, Baron Mountjoy, but in my view the risks are too great.'

Sir Francis Vere looked across at Robert. 'A land attack would be reckless. We lack the men or munitions to attack such a well-defended harbour. All we can do is wait for them to make a run for Spain, which they surely will.'

The patrols continued for a week, then three Spanish ships, a fine galleon and two frigates, were intercepted. No match for the *Due Repulse*, they hoisted white flags of surrender without a shot being fired. Robert was disappointed to find they were merchant ships. The largest belonged to the Governor of Havana, and carried a cargo of wine and cochineal. The rich red dye would fetch a good price, but he wanted Spanish silver and gold.

They took the Cuban galleon and frigates as prizes, and headed for the Bay of St Michael's, where Robert formed a plan to land at night, a short distance from the town of Vila Franca. Once the town was secured, they would march across the island to the capital, Punta Delgada, while the fleet remained as a diversion.

The barges were launched at midnight, and Robert led them into the town. A dog barked as they searched the main street, but Vila Franca was deserted, with signs the inhabitants had made a hasty escape. Robert chose one of the best houses, and the men busied themselves ransacking the town, many becoming drunk on looted Spanish wine.

The settlers had left little of value, but as well as a barn full of sacks of grain, they found a cellar stacked with fleeces, which would fetch a good price in England. Robert also discovered a collection of old Latin books, which he decided to take back for Francis Bacon, and a Portuguese flag, which he kept as a trophy.

Several days passed before Charles Blount returned from his scouting mission, looking despondent. 'It's no good. The mountains are too high and the roads are little more than goat tracks, with many places where we could be ambushed by the settlers.'

Robert cursed. 'We need to take on water, and be gone from here before the winter storms. With luck our few prize ships will cover the cost of this mission, but I fear Her Majesty will have harsh words for me when we arrive in England empty-handed.'

An ominous column of grey smoke rose into the sky as they approached the waiting fleet, and the sweet scent of burning sugar and spices drifted on the wind. A burning ship lay beached on the rocky shore, the bright orange flames gaining hold from bow to stern. Raleigh rowed across from the *Warspite* to make his report.

'We saw a Spanish carrack sailing into the bay, and hoped to surprise her.' He scowled. 'They didn't seem bothered by the sight of us, but one of the Dutch warships ignored my order, and opened fire.'

Robert stared at the burning hulk. He guessed she was more than one and half thousand tons, and would have been a good prize. 'It looks as if her crew ran her aground.'

Raleigh nodded. 'I sent a boarding party, but she was set ablaze as the Spanish made their escape, and there was nothing we could do.'

Robert called another meeting of his commanders. Storm clouds were gathering, and the rough seas were a sign of worse to come. Robert gave the reluctant order for the fleet to return to England. Gales scattered their ships yet again, and men on the pumps of the *Due Repulse* worked day and night to keep the bilges free of water.

Battered by storms, they limped home with only two ships of the Dutch fleet for company. Robert's mood darkened as he arrived in Plymouth some days after Raleigh, exhausted and short of food. Robert was unsurprised to find a sealed letter from the queen waiting for him, and groaned when he read her message.

'*We do wish the safe return of you and our fleet under your charge, as a prince that knows the value of such our dear and beloved servants, but when we do look back to the beginning of this action which hath stirred so great expectation in the world and charged us so deeply, we cannot but be sorry to foresee already how near all our expectations and your great hopes are to a fruitless conclusion.*'

His only hope of redemption came from reports of an

Armada of sixty Spanish warships, with as many support vessels, a few leagues from Falmouth. One had been captured, and it seemed he had a final chance of glory. Rather than reply to the queen, he wrote to Lord Burghley, offering to set out with as many men as could be mustered.

While he waited for an answer, news arrived that the Spanish fleet had been scattered by the savage autumn storms. The threat of invasion was over, and Robert could delay no longer. The time had come to return to court in Westminster Palace to face the recriminations.

The queen stared at him without speaking as he made his excuses. He blamed bad weather, the delays, his leaky ships, and even the adventurers, like Raleigh, who'd been nothing but a hindrance. Robert knew what they said behind his back. He'd failed in his mission, and risked the English fleet while the Spanish escaped to fight another day.

Robert could not bear to stay in Westminster, although he had duties on the Privy Council, and rode with Bagot and his stepfather, Sir Christopher Blount, to Wanstead Manor, in Essex. His mother looked more like the queen than ever, and embraced him.

'I want to know every detail of what happened.'

Robert shook his head. 'I fear I'm in no mood to speak of it, and will not be allowed to command a fleet again.'

His stepfather was quick to come to his support. 'We braved the worst storms I've ever seen. No one could have done more.'

Robert's mother smiled. 'I prayed for you both every day, and could not be happier to see you safe and sound.' She turned to Robert, a glint of amusement in her eye. 'There is someone else here who prays for you.'

'My son?'

'Walter is six now, and grown into a fine boy, although he is a challenge to his tutors, much like you were at his age.' She nodded to a waiting servant who returned with Walter.

He bowed to Robert. 'Good day, Father.'

Robert kneeled. 'I would have come to see you earlier, but I've been away at sea.'

As he looked into his son's sharp eyes he had a memory of his own father returning with the same apologies from Ireland. He'd been in awe of him then, but his father had remained a stranger. Robert had forgotten his promise to be a better father, and a wave of guilt overcame him.

After he returned to Essex House, Robert struggled to decide what to do about his future. The strain of the islands voyage had taken its toll and his feverish ague returned. He languished in his bed until noon, when Bagot knocked and entered carrying a freshly laundered shirt.

'Your sister, Lady Penelope, has arrived, my lord. She asked me to rouse you as she has returned from court with surprising news.' Bagot had a twinkle in his eye, as he often did when Penelope visited.

Robert groaned. He'd had enough of Queen Elizabeth's games, or the gossiping of her self-serving courtiers, but his curiosity was aroused. He dressed and followed Bagot to his study, where his sister waited.

'You have more lives than a cat!' She smiled. 'It seems you are back in favour with Her Majesty.'

Robert struggled to understand. 'How can it be?'

'That's what I said.' She gave him a mischievous look. 'How can my errant brother redeem himself so easily?'

He brightened. 'Tell me what you've heard.'

'One of your commanders, Sir Francis Vere, returned to court and was summoned to provide his account of your conduct. I only have it second-hand, but it seems he painted quite a different picture from the others. He walked with the queen in her garden. It's said he told her the storms you encountered were the fiercest he'd ever seen, and far from treating Sir Walter Raleigh badly, you showed true leadership and understanding.'

'The queen likes to play us against each other. In truth, I never liked Francis Vere. He sent the press gangs out in Plymouth without my approval, and resented Charles Blount's appointment.'

Penelope smiled at the mention of her not-so-secret lover. 'I believe that's why the queen trusts Sir Francis Vere's word. She knows he wouldn't lie for you.'

'I'll not return to court unless I'm ordered to.' Robert shook his head at the thought. 'The queen rewarded my greatest critic, Lord Admiral Charles Howard, by making him Earl of Nottingham for sitting safe at home!'

Penelope gave him an exasperated look. 'Lord Admiral Howard is an old man, at the end of his career. It's not a slight against you.' She placed her hand on Robert's arm, and gave him a comforting squeeze, as she had when he was a boy. 'Return to court while you can, and make the most of this opportunity.'

23

FEBRUARY 1598

Robert wiped the sweat from his brow and laughed. 'I concede. You could have let me win, for once.'

Charles Blount swished his racquet through the air. 'I might have, but did you not see we had an audience?' His voice echoed in the tennis court, built for the queen's father, but never used by the queen.

Robert glanced up at the viewing gallery, disappointed to see it empty. 'I was too busy trying to win.'

'Your secret is safe with me, my Lord Essex, but you will not be surprised to know Lady Elizabeth Brydges came with a lady companion to watch you play.'

Robert bent to retrieve the tennis ball and tossed it into the leather bucket with the others. 'How do you know it wasn't *you* they came to see?'

'My life is complicated enough, without the attentions of the queen's maids of honour.'

'Your life is a fresh spring breeze compared with my stormy existence, Lord Mountjoy. I confess I enjoy their attention – but regret there is no opportunity to do anything about it.'

'I might have some sympathy, Lord Essex, were you not the

queen's favourite, and now Earl Marshal of England, ranking above the Lord High Admiral himself.'

Robert grinned. 'That was a poke in the eye to my critics. Robert Cecil has even made me secretary, while he's off on his fool's errand in France.'

'You don't have much hope for his chances?'

'King Henri is a wily old fox, not beyond forgetting his promises. Robert Cecil will do his best, and I wish him well.' Robert pulled a cape over his tennis clothes. 'He persuaded the queen I should have the cochineal we brought from the Azores at a discount. I'll clear seven thousand pounds in profit.'

'A drop in the ocean towards your debts – and I'll wager Robert Cecil has asked for some favour in return.'

'Only that I'll keep his best interests in mind while he's away – which, of course, I would have done anyway.'

Robert stepped out into a cool shower of rain, refreshing after his exertion. He'd not fully recovered from the ague which had plagued him for months, and Charles Blount, a skilled tennis player, had tested his stamina. They hastened through the doors and made their way down the wood-panelled corridors of Westminster Palace.

He turned to Charles Blount before they parted. 'My mother is staying at Essex House for Saint Valentine's Day, as well as both my sisters.' He gave him a knowing look. 'You are welcome to join us.'

Robert's mother presided over the festivities like a queen surrounded by her subjects. It was her idea to recreate the feast of Lupercalia, the original Valentine's Day celebration. Gelly and Bagot had been busy decorating the great hall to resemble a

Roman villa, with wooden pillars painted to look like marble, and a raised balcony.

The men dressed as senators, with tunics and togas of white linen, and the ladies in high-waisted gowns, with colourful sashes, and laurel wreaths in their hair. Minstrels played soft music on lutes as the servants brought platters of sugared delicacies and ewers of wine. The tables were arranged around an open area for the highlight of the evening, a special performance by the Lord Chamberlain's Men.

Robert sat between his mother and his wife, and had already drunk too much. He'd been surprised Frances accepted his mother's invitation, as she rarely visited Essex House. She made an attractive Roman lady, with a red velvet cape over her shoulders, and a gilded laurel wreath in her hair.

For once she was talkative. 'What do you plan to do now you are the queen's secretary?' Her eyes sparkled in the candlelight, reminding him of happier times.

Robert shrugged. 'I've not given it any thought.'

'Well, perhaps you should.'

'It's only temporary, until Robert Cecil returns from his mission to France.' He took a drink of his wine, resenting the sharp edge to her voice, but finding himself curious. 'What do you suggest?'

His mother replied for her. 'Could you find a way for me to be accepted back at court?'

Robert turned to her in surprise. 'I would have thought that ship sailed long since.'

His mother shook her head. 'Others who were banished have been forgiven for greater sins.'

Frances nodded. 'I heard Elizabeth Brydges and Mistress Russell were banished from court for three days, simply for going through the privy galleries to watch men playing tennis.'

Robert was keen to change the subject. 'I can ask, if I find the queen in a good mood, but caution you not to raise your hopes.' He frowned as he saw his mother brighten. Like the queen, she only heard what she wanted to. 'A gift of some sort might help.'

'I have just the thing.' His mother picked a sugared comfit from her plate. 'A jewel which belonged to my lord of Leicester.' She glanced at her husband. 'I have no further use for it.'

Robert leaned closer to Frances. 'How are the children?'

'You should come to see them.' Frances sipped her spiced wine. 'I understood when you were away at sea, but they are growing up fast. Elizabeth will soon be thirteen, and we shall have to start thinking of a suitable match for her. I hear the queen has tired of Elizabeth Southwell's indiscretions, and agreed her engagement to Barentyne Moleyns.'

Robert frowned. His wife baited him, like a bear in a pit, and he would not let her have the satisfaction of seeing his irritation. The queen had chosen the most unsuitable husband for Elizabeth Southwell out of spite. Moleyns was ugly and boorish. He had no money, and had suffered disfiguring wounds after fighting on the Continent.

He chose a heart-shaped sugared pastry from his plate and took a bite before replying. 'How is little Robert?'

'Robin will be seven years old this year, and needs a father.'

Again, he resented her sharp tone towards him, but knew the reason. He'd seen more of little Walter than his legitimate son, his daughter Penelope, or his stepdaughter Elizabeth. His conscience troubled him, but there was no point in making excuses.

'What do the doctors say about little Penelope?'

'She's a constant worry to me.'

'And to me.' Robert spoke softly. 'I shall come to see her, as soon as I am able to.' His mood evaporated as he thought of his little daughter, a sickly child who clung to life.

He looked across at his sister Penelope, laughing happily at some comment from Charles Blount. He envied their open affection for each other. Lord Rich no longer visited Essex House, and seemed resigned to his reduced role in their pretence of a marriage.

Frances shook his arm. 'Your sister Dorothy is sitting on her own. I worried for her, when she married Northumberland. They seemed an unlikely match.'

'Henry Percy is a secret Catholic. His father was a sympathiser of Mary, Queen of Scots—'

'And died in the Tower.' Frances glanced across at Dorothy. 'You should speak to her. Did you know she's carrying the earl's child?'

'No, I didn't – but that might be a good thing.'

A drum roll demanded their attention, and Will Kempe, narrator of the Lord Chamberlain's Men, stepped into the centre of the floor. Dressed as a senator, he gave them a flamboyant bow, and produced a scroll, which he unrolled and read aloud.

'My lords, ladies and gentlemen, we present for you a tale of...

Two households, both alike in dignity,
In fair Verona, where we lay our scene,
From ancient grudge break to new mutiny,
Where civil blood makes civil hands unclean.
From forth the fatal loins of these two foes,
A pair of star-cross'd lovers take their life...'

Robert watched the overlong play, and found himself thinking Elizabeth Brydges would have made a more convincing Juliet than the sallow boy who called from Gelly's makeshift wooden balcony. He also thought of Elizabeth Southwell's engagement to Barentyne Moleyns, and silently cursed their cruel queen.

About to refill his empty wine glass, he glanced at Frances and saw a tear glisten on her cheek. The tragedy of the players' ill-fated lovers had touched her more deeply than him, but he reached out and took his wife's hand. She responded with a familiar squeeze, a sign he hoped meant he'd been forgiven.

He kissed her, and lay back on the bed, his pulse racing. The years hadn't diminished his love for her, or his desire. 'I'd never imagined we would be together like this again.' He reached out and pulled her close, so he could look into her eyes. 'I wish we hadn't waited so long.'

She kissed him back and smiled. 'I've missed you.' She gave his beard a playful tug. 'Tell me what happened between your mother and the queen.'

'It wasn't amusing for my poor mother.'

She laughed at his stern look. 'Your mother, of all people, should have known what to expect.'

'My mother believed she'd been punished enough. She'd had a new gown made for the occasion, but was made to wait like a servant in the privy gallery for half the morning.'

'I heard the queen didn't see her after all.'

'She pretended to be too busy – but my mother persuaded me to ask the queen a second time.' Robert frowned. 'She agreed to attend a dinner, and we spent a small fortune on the preparations, then she cancelled at the last minute. They did meet in the end, but my mother is not welcome at court, so all I've achieved is to irritate them both.'

'You should know the queen's games by now. It's cruel, how she likes to show her power over us all.'

Robert stroked a strand of her long hair away from her eyes.

'You cannot marry that scoundrel Barentyne Moleyns. He's despicable.'

Her bright eyes darkened at the thought. 'The queen leaves me no choice.'

'I'm sorry, but I believe she meant this as a punishment for me, as well as you.'

The row began at a meeting of the queen's advisors to agree who should be the new Lord Deputy of Ireland. Robert suspected the previous deputy, Lord Burgh, had been poisoned the previous winter, just like his own father, but would never be able to prove it.

'My nomination is Sir George Carew.' Robert was surprised at their frowns.

The queen shook her head. 'Carew is no friend of yours, my Lord Essex. We suspect you wish him out of the way.' She held up her hand, to stop him replying, but he continued, scowling at the queen.

'Why does my opinion matter so little to you?' He heard someone gasp at his tone.

'Your opinion serves only your ambition!' The queen's strident reply echoed in the chamber.

'Then why ask for my counsel, if you plan to ignore it?'

His frustration at the way she treated him, insulted his mother, and cruelly punished his mistress added a sharp edge to his raised voice.

'Go to the devil!' she shouted, loud enough to be heard by the whole palace.

Robert struggled to control his rage. He opened his mouth to reply but saw the concern on the councillors' faces, and decided to leave. As he turned to go, the queen stepped forward and struck him on the side of the face.

'Do *not* turn your back on us!' Her shout was like the screech of a hunting hawk.

Instinct at the shock of her insult made his hand fall to the hilt of his sword. Sir Charles Howard stepped forward and placed himself between Robert and the queen.

'Stay your hand, sir!'

Robert saw the glint of triumph in Charles Howard's eyes, which infuriated him further. He pushed Howard back and glared at the queen. 'I would not take such insults from your father!'

'You should be hanged for your insolence!'

He stormed from the chamber, his future and reputation in ruins, with her words ringing in his ears. In all his time at court he'd never seen the queen strike anyone – but, then, he'd never seen her spoken to with so little respect.

He waited to learn the consequences at Essex House, expecting to be arrested or banished.

'I'm done for now, Bagot.' He stared out of the high window.

'Perhaps an apology, my lord?' Bagot looked at him with concern. 'A letter, begging forgiveness?'

'I think I must lie low for a while, Bagot. I'm not well. I might seek refuge at my mother's house at Wanstead.'

He turned back to the window and looked down the wide street. With a word, the queen could order his arrest, and have him locked up in the Tower dungeons. He regretted his outburst, but was determined he would not be the first to give in. This time, the queen would have to beg *his* forgiveness.

Robert bowed his head and clasped his hands in prayer as he listened to the dean read the service, his dour voice echoing to the high-vaulted roof of Westminster Abbey.

'I am the resurrection and the life, saith the Lord, he that believeth in me, yea, though he were dead, yet shall he live. And whosoever liveth, and believeth in me, shall not die forever.'

Lord Burghley had been ill for months, but Robert was surprised at how deeply the news of the old man's death affected him. They'd often disagreed, but Lord Burghley had always been an important part of his world, and would be missed.

Robert's last memory of William Cecil was at a council meeting where they'd argued about making peace with Spain. Lord Burghley stared at him with his one good eye, and accused him of wishing for war. He'd produced a prayer book and read, *'Bloody and deceitful men shall not live out half their days.'*

The irony of the old man's words was not lost on him as they'd set out in bright August sunshine from Cecil House. Robert was glad of his anonymity in the sombre procession of five hundred black-garbed mourners through London streets thronged with silent crowds.

He glanced across at the crooked shoulders of Robert Cecil, now carrying an extra burden of responsibility. As expected, Cecil's mission to France was a failure, as King Henri struck a deal with the Spanish, yet Robert Cecil would be rewarded. His father had ensured he would become the new Lord Privy Seal, and inherit the valuable role of Master of Wards.

Robert planned to put his own name forward for the newly vacant post of Chancellor of the University of Cambridge. He'd already written to his former tutor, Archbishop Whitgift, and was confident of securing his support, but to be sure of the queen's agreement, he would have to somehow resolve his problems at court.

His uncle, Sir William Knollys, stepped in as peacemaker,

possibly at the queen's suggestion, urging Robert to attend to his duties on the Privy Council. He wrote, '*I fear the longer your lordship doth persist in this careless humour of Her Majesty, the more her heart will be hardened.*'

Robert stayed away, and there'd been no word of any punishment. He'd agonised for days over the wording of a letter to the queen, yet she'd not replied, or sent any message. He imagined what was being said about his absence by the gossipers of court. He hoped he'd earned respect for standing up for himself, and not become a laughing stock.

He looked up as the Dean of Westminster read Psalm 39 from the Book of Common Prayer. '*I will take heed to my ways, that I sin not with my tongue. I will keep my mouth with a bridle, while the wicked is before me.*'

Robert took the sacred words to heart. His fellow privy councillor, Lord Keeper of the Great Seal, Sir Thomas Egerton, wrote telling him to learn to conquer himself. Insulted, he'd replied with angry questions. Cannot subjects receive wrong? Is earthly power infinite?

Only now did he see such words could be construed as treason. Good men had been locked up in the Tower dungeons for challenging the divine authority of the queen. He'd enjoyed her protection as her favourite for so long he lacked a proper sense of restraint, and left himself vulnerable to his enemies.

After the service the coffin was carried back out through the high-arched doors. Lord Burghley had asked to be taken to Stamford, Lincolnshire, in a coach draped in black, for burial in St Martin's Church. With typical economy, he'd asked for the costs to be kept under a thousand pounds, and his funeral cortège to be no more than twelve men.

Francis Bacon sat alone at the back of the congregation, and caught Robert's eye as he was leaving after the service. 'Did you receive my letter, my lord?'

Robert was surprised to see him. Francis Bacon had run out of funds, and had been staying with his mother at Gorhambury Manor for some months. Then he recalled that Lord Burghley was once married to Francis Bacon's aunt, and he'd previously been employed by him.

'Your letter about the situation in Ireland?'

'Ireland is worse than ever now, my lord. If you are returning to Essex House, I could accompany you.'

Robert nodded. 'You are welcome, although you'll find me poor company. I've been unwell.'

'I heard what happened at court,' Francis Bacon gave him a sympathetic glance, 'which is why I'm keen to share my thoughts on a solution, my lord.'

Robert waited until they were alone before raising the question nagging in his mind. 'Have you been at court?'

'I have, my lord. I wished to see the lie of the land.'

'What do they say about me?'

Francis Bacon frowned. 'Forgive me for speaking plainly, my lord. Some ask if you've been banished, and others question why you have not.'

Robert cursed. 'I've offered even the most dim-witted of my opponents enough excuse to blacken my reputation – but what does the queen say?'

'Nothing, as far as I am aware.'

'Nothing?' The thought was another slap across the face. 'To not even be spoken of is the worst insult.'

Francis Bacon shrugged. 'I am, of course, not party to all the queen says, only that which is repeated by gossipers.'

'You believe I should look to Ireland to redeem my fortune?'

'The situation there is worse than I predicted. The English army in Ireland is routed. Two thousand are dead, including the Lord Marshal, and many are injured or have deserted. The rebels have seized control of Ulster, and hammer at the gates of Dublin.'

Robert frowned. 'In truth, I've lost the will to fight for our queen. Why should I risk my life for her, when she treats me like a dog?'

Francis Bacon counted the reasons on his fingers. 'You are Lord Marshal of England. You can choose your commanders, and lead the greatest army ever seen in Ireland. You can ask for your debts to be cancelled. If not for our queen, win a great victory for our country – and avenge your father.'

Robert stared at him in silence for a moment. 'You are right, Francis. I shall put my name forward to lead the new campaign in Ireland, and finish what my father started. What is there to lose?'

24

JANUARY 1599

Robert chose his moment well, as the Twelfth Night celebrations at the Palace of Whitehall were under way. Loud music played, and many of the guests danced a galliard. A few onlookers noticed his arrival, some nodding, others whispering, but most looked too drunk to care.

He stood, taking in the sights and sounds of the world which was once his. He missed the excited buzz of chatter, the lively dance music, and the clink of wine glasses. The happy laughter of the young, bright-eyed ladies dancing in swirling gowns filled him with regret.

The queen sat talking to a handsome, well-dressed man Robert guessed must be the visiting Ambassador of Denmark. She smiled as she spoke, a good sign, and looked surprisingly attractive in a wide-sleeved gown and a necklace of iridescent black pearls. Her silver tiara gleamed as sparkling diamonds caught the light when she turned her head.

The dance ended and the floor cleared. Aware of everyone watching him, Robert strode across the open space to the queen. The last time he'd been to court she refused to see him, and he had no idea how he would be received. He took a deep breath and bowed to the queen.

'May I have the great honour of the next dance, Your Majesty?'

The queen gave him an appraising look. She seemed about to decline, then the musicians began to play the stirring drumbeat signalling the start of la volta, and dancers took their places. She laughed and spoke to the ambassador in Latin.

'I shall accept my Lord Essex's request in your honour, ambassador, so you might report to your king that the Queen of England is not decrepit.'

Robert held her slender fingers lightly in his as they danced, and thanked God the queen had shown him mercy. They were the centre of attention, and he was glad to see the queen smiling again as he took her waist. She embraced his broad shoulders, and laughed like a girl as he lifted her into the air.

After the dance she led him back to her gilded seat. The ambassador had gone, and she invited Robert to take his place next to her.

'I confess we've been concerned by your absence from court.' She placed her hand on his, as a mother might with her child. 'It's good to have you back, Robin.'

He enjoyed the familiar warmth of her touch, knowing few would miss her sign he was truly back in favour.

'I've not been well, Your Majesty. My doctors told me to rest.'

Her eyes narrowed with concern. 'You seem well enough now.'

Robert leaned close to her, and looked deep into her dark eyes. 'Your Majesty's divine company would raise the most melancholy of spirits.'

She brightened at his rare compliment. 'Are you certain you are well enough to lead the campaign to Ireland?'

'The Irish believe they have the better of you, and I see it as my duty, Your Majesty, as your Lord Marshal, to assert your sovereignty.'

Robert smiled as he saw her reaction to his words. He'd listened to the advice of Robert Cecil about what might please the queen. His instinct had always been to avoid any form of flattery, yet the queen's secretary knew her weakness.

It had seemed he might be too late. Lord Mountjoy was the queen's choice, but Robert Cecil – no doubt keen to solve two of his most pressing problems – persuaded her to make Charles Blount Robert's deputy. He'd been granted an advance of twelve thousand pounds to begin the preparations, and was already making plans.

The queen gave him a cautionary look. 'For once you shall abide by our instructions, and not grant knighthoods to every man who follows you to Ireland.'

Robert walked in his wife's garden with his stepdaughter, Elizabeth Sidney. A February breeze whistled through leafless rose bushes, and he was glad of the riding cape he wore. Elizabeth looked older than her years in a hooded cloak trimmed with fur, and was now the same height as her mother. Frances told him to explain matters to her, but he didn't have the first idea how to begin to tell Elizabeth his news.

'You remind me of your mother, when I first met her.'

Elizabeth spoke in a clear, well-educated voice. 'Mother says you've chosen a husband for me.'

Robert stopped walking. She didn't call him *Father* or *sir*, like her half-brother, or even *my lord*. He took her gloved hand in his. 'Roger Manners is the Earl of Rutland. He will be a good husband for you,' he smiled, 'and you will be a countess, like your mother.'

'I am only thirteen—'

'Old enough.' He didn't know when she'd be fourteen, but Manners couldn't be more than ten years older.

She gave him a concerned look, and seemed close to tears. 'When?'

'I wish the marriage to take place as soon as possible. Before I leave for Ireland.'

'Why do you have to leave so soon? Can you not stay for another month?'

'The queen ordered me to deal with the Irish rebels, and each day I delay will make my task more difficult.'

Elizabeth frowned. 'Mother says Ireland will be dangerous.'

'I'm taking the greatest army we can muster, and will return with a great victory.' His boast sounded hollow, but he managed a smile. 'I've done my best to secure your future. My advice, Elizabeth, is to make the most of the hand you've been dealt.'

Calls of 'Good luck, my lord!' and 'God save you!' came from crowds of curious onlookers lining the London streets. Robert rode his grey charger, Suleiman, with Gelly at his side, at the head of five hundred orange-liveried cavalrymen. All the knights carried flowing banners, and the clatter of hooves echoed like drumbeats on the cobblestoned streets.

There was no going back. He'd made his will, and said his goodbyes. His stepdaughter's wedding was a rushed ceremony in St Olave's Church, close to Walsingham House. She'd said her vows, but stared at him with the same expression as her mother, as if she might never trust him again.

Frances warned him that, one way or another, he would learn his destiny in Ireland. Her ominous words echoed in his mind as he heard the distant thunder. He scowled at the darkening clouds as the first drops of rain spattered the ground. The deep rumble of thunder boomed over their heads, and Robert turned to Gelly.

'We'll be soaked before we leave London.'

'You sound as if you'd rather stay at home, my lord.'

'Too late, Gelly. I've rolled the dice, and must live with the consequences, although even Francis Bacon advised me to find an excuse to stay.' Robert frowned. 'The preparations took longer than planned, and the queen refused my stepfather a place on the Council of Ireland – and ordered me not to appoint Henry Wriothesley, Earl of Southampton, as Master of the Horse.'

The rain turned to hail which stung his face, as if nature were trying to send him a message. He thought of his father, poisoned while dining at his house in Dublin. The rebels had no honour, and lurked in the shadows. They would not be defeated in a fair fight, but Robert doubted they knew he had so little to lose, and swore to avenge his father's murder.

The queen's ship *Popinjay*, a solid, eighty-ton pinnace, strained against her anchor off Beaumaris, on the Welsh island of Anglesey. They'd waited in gales for two long days for the weather to improve, and Robert's captain, Master George Thornton, knew the route well and advised against putting to sea.

By the third day Robert summoned him. 'The men grow restless, Master Thornton. Each day is costing us, and I have to order them to embark.'

'We've missed the morning tide, my lord. It would mean sailing through the night.'

'Then so be it. Tell the men to be ready to sail with the

evening tide. Better to make the crossing by night, and be in Ireland by morning.'

Great waves crashed against the rocks, making the loading of the horses dangerous in the failing light, but they'd had enough of waiting. The crossing to Ireland took thirteen long hours, and most men suffered with sickness as the ships pitched and rolled in the churning, grey-green seas.

They anchored in the restless waters of Dublin Bay at mid morning, and had to wait for the tide before unloading the men and horses for the ride to the castle. Robert wore his silver armour, with an embroidered white surcoat, velvet hose and riding boots of polished Spanish leather. He also carried his good luck charm, the fine sword bequeathed to him by Sir Philip Sidney.

They'd landed a mile from the city gates, and sounded trumpets as they marched with drums, their banners flying. As they entered, their path through the throng of people had to be cleared by a vanguard of men with pikes and shouted threats. Robert thought they'd come to see him, then realised these were English settlers, seeking the security of the city.

He turned to Gelly. 'I had no idea Dublin was such a sprawling, stinking place – with so many people.'

Gelly frowned at the severed heads on pikes. 'It seems they've found ways to keep the numbers down.'

'Our first sight of rebels.' Robert looked away from the grisly trophies, blackened and rotting, their eyes pecked out by crows. He'd seen heads often enough on London Bridge, but swore to find better ways to assert the queen's authority in Ireland.

The mayor waited with the dignitaries of Dublin to greet them, and bowed. 'Welcome, your excellency. We present you with the keys to the city.'

Robert took the keys, and held them up for everyone to see. 'I thank you, Lord Mayor.' He looked back at his army. 'My men have suffered greatly in the crossing, and need food and lodgings. I will make the castle my headquarters.'

The mayor frowned. 'The castle is a foul, damp place, fit only for prisoners, your excellency. May I suggest you take the house of the late Lord Deputy, Lord Burgh? It's of a fair size, and well furnished.'

Robert smiled. 'I'll be glad of a dry bed and a hot meal, Lord Mayor.'

In the morning, Robert was presented with the Irish sword of state and sworn in as the new Lord Lieutenant. At his first meeting of the Council of Ireland he looked around at their dour faces, recognising some, and making mental notes as the others introduced themselves.

'My orders are to proceed north to Ulster, and arrest Hugh O'Neill, Earl of Tyrone.' He saw several members of the council frown at the news, and the Bishop of Meathe shook his head, as if the idea was foolish.

Sir Conyers Clifford, who'd suffered a disfiguring white scar from his forehead to his chin, spoke up for them. 'With respect, my lord, I caution against such action.'

'For what reason?' Robert expected the council to be difficult, but not obstructive. 'I command the largest army ever brought to Ireland, with more than sixteen thousand infantry and one thousand three hundred cavalrymen.'

Sir Henry Harington, an experienced commander, nodded. 'The rebel army of the Earl of Tyrone has much the same number – but they are battle-hardened fighters, who know this country. Am I right in thinking that few of your soldiers have ever fought in Ireland, my lord?'

Before Robert could answer, Secretary of State Sir Geoffrey Fenton intervened. 'I propose this council signs a letter to Her

Majesty, asking for another two thousand men, and more supplies, to tip the balance in your favour, Lord Lieutenant.'

'Reinforcements could take months to recruit, and I doubt they'd be experienced men.' Robert studied their faces. 'We can't sit here in Dublin and do nothing, while the rebels do as they will.'

Sir Conyers Clifford agreed. 'We should march west through Leinster. The rebels are expecting an attack to the north, and might be taken by surprise.' He smiled. 'The experience will be good for your men, Lord Lieutenant.'

Robert rode from Dublin at the head of his army on a fine May morning, the knights with their banners flying. He'd been saddened by a letter from Frances. She mourned the loss of their infant daughter, Penelope, who'd finally succumbed to her mystery illness. His daughter had never been a strong child, but he knew his wife would be devastated.

The road ahead became narrow and rubble-strewn, ideal for a rebel ambush, and he began to understand why the council had been so concerned. A well-placed fallen tree would stop his entire army, and there was good cover on each side. He decided to send a scouting party ahead, and told his men to be on their guard.

They reached Kilcullen in the late afternoon. The fast-flowing River Liffey ran through the village, with a single rickety bridge. Many of the cottages were abandoned, and some fit only for pigsties, but Robert commandeered one of the largest, and Gelly made him a bed for the night from straw bales.

In the morning he went for a walk in the dawn mists to clear his head. A blackbird broke the silence with its tuneful call, and the hedgerow was filled with wild flowers. Ireland reminded him of happier times at Lamphey Palace in West Wales – so close, he could see the shadow of the land across the sea ... yet a world away.

They rode to the market town of Athy, where the castle built to protect the bridge over the River Barrow was held by rebels. Robert studied the towering, slab-sided castle, and was agreeing a plan of attack when a great number of cavalry and foot soldiers appeared in the distance.

Sir Henry Harington recognised their banners. 'The Earl of Ormonde, from Kilkenny, my lord, with his Irish regulars.'

'Can they be trusted?' Robert watched as the riders approached. They looked like rebels, and many carried bows and quivers of arrows.

Sir Henry Harington nodded. 'They know this region, so we should welcome them.'

The Earl of Ormonde raised a hand in greeting. 'Welcome, my lord. We've come to oust the rebels.' He glanced up at the castle. 'Their leader is James Fitzpierce, and I'll be first to place his head on a spike.'

Robert frowned. 'We haven't the time or equipment for a siege. We'll encircle the castle and demand their surrender. Your men can help by guarding the bridge.'

No flag flew from the castle, but a white sheet was hoisted soon after they'd blocked any chance of escape. James Fitzpierce shouted from the battlements that he asked only for his life to be spared, and they would find a good supply of provisions in his cellars. Robert had him taken into custody and escorted back to Dublin, while his men stripped the castle of everything of value.

A group of some three hundred rebel horsemen appeared on the opposite bank of the river as they marched on to the next castle. The wild-looking men waved spears as they shouted insults, but turned and galloped away when Robert's musket men opened fire.

The woodland on either side thickened into dense forest, and Robert recalled his concerns about the danger of a rebel ambush. The trees closed overhead like a green tunnel, cutting out the May sunshine. He turned to Sir Henry Harington, riding at his side.

'We need somewhere safe to camp tonight. How far do these woods extend?'

Sir Henry Harington smiled. 'From sea to sea, my lord, and they harbour every kind of beast.'

Robert thought he saw movement in the shadows, and imagined sinister shapes skulking in the dark undergrowth. 'Could there be wolves?'

Sir Henry nodded. 'Wolves and worse, my lord. Traitors and vagabonds—'

His reply was interrupted by a cry of alarm as rebel archers fired a shower of arrows from the cover of the trees. More rebels burst from the undergrowth, yelling fierce Irish curses, some with swords and others throwing sharp spears with deadly accuracy at such close range.

An arrow struck one of the horses in the flank, causing it to rear in panic and throw its rider. A spear clanged off the steel breastplate of one of the men, and another arrow flew past Robert's ear. He drew his sword and charged their attackers, slashing at them left and right with all his strength. The fight was brutal but short.

Henry Wriothesley fought bravely, hacking at the rebels with no care for himself. The other knights followed his example, and the rebels melted back into the undergrowth. Many on both sides lay dead and bleeding from deep wounds, and Robert's heart pounded at the exertion of fighting for his life.

He decided to accept the Earl of Ormonde's offer for his men to recover at his castle in Kilkenny, although that meant marching even further south. The people of the town cheered and waved handkerchiefs, and scattered herbs and rushes in the streets as the army rode through. The earl provided a fine banquet, but Robert suffered with the return of his fever, and took to his bed early.

They progressed from castle to castle, each time forcing the garrison to surrender and replacing them with their own men, mostly without incident – except for when a bullet shattered the leg of Sir Henry Norris, who died in agony. The sight of Sir Henry Danvers, shot in the face in a skirmish, reminded Robert of his brother Wat.

In revenge, the next castle to be taken was burned and razed to the ground. Robert regretted his anger when he saw the severed heads, piled in the grass. Some were grey-haired old men, who would have been glad to surrender. Others were fresh-faced, and one was a woman, her long hair tangled, her glassy eyes staring.

Sickened, he ordered a Christian burial for them, and cursed the savagery of his men. This was not what he'd come to Ireland for, yet he understood how his predecessors had been changed by this country. His own father's fate might have been Irish vengeance for harm done by the English in the name of their queen.

The weather turned to a cold, clammy fog, which soaked them to the skin, and the road grew so boggy that progress halted. There seemed no way forward, but he couldn't go back to Dublin. The queen's orders were clear but, too late, he realised he'd made them impossible to achieve with this fool's errand to the south.

Robert's army suffered few fatalities, but a good many were left to garrison captured castles. Supplies were running short, and an increasing number of his men were sick or wounded. Unless reinforcements arrived soon, his army would be outnumbered, an easy target for the rebels.

As dusk fell he wrote to the Privy Council, setting out the details of their campaign, explaining the sorry state of Ireland and the challenges he faced. He also wrote personal letters to the queen and Frances, hinting of his fears he might not return. He called for Gelly, and handed him the sealed letters.

'I have to ask you to deliver these in person.'

'You're sending me home?'

Robert nodded. 'I shall miss your company, Gelly, but there is no one I trust more.'

'Take care, my lord.' Gelly frowned. 'I don't believe the rebels can be beaten. The best you can hope for is to secure a truce.'

Robert smiled at Gelly's naive wish for a truce with the rebels. It seemed unlikely, after the savage way both sides treated each other, but the idea might offer him a way to avoid disaster. He watched his friend vanish into the swirling fog, and said a silent prayer. At least one of them would have a chance of returning safely to England.

25

AUGUST 1599

Camping for the night by the coastal town of Dungarvan, Robert called his commanders to a council of war. The meeting had barely begun when they were interrupted by a commotion outside. A dishevelled soldier, covered in mud, burst into the tent, causing several to draw their swords, before he announced he brought a message from Sir Henry Harington, sent to garrison Wicklow.

Robert scowled as he read the scribbled note, and turned to the others. 'Grave news. Sir Henry's division has been defeated by a band of rebels at the pass near Arklow.' He stared at the messenger. 'How did this happen?'

'Ambushed, my lord. The rebels had blocked the pass, and were upon us before most could draw their weapons. Some two hundred and fifty of our men were killed and more wounded.' He looked down at his feet. 'We were greatly outnumbered, and some of our men threw off their livery and ran.'

'Sir Henry Harington lives?'

The soldier nodded. 'He wished you to be alerted to his plight, as a matter of urgency.'

Robert turned to face his commanders. 'I propose to take

three companies of foot and two of horse to see what has become of Sir Henry Harington – and take any deserters into custody.' He took a deep breath. 'After that, I must abide by the queen's order to head north and confront the Earl of Tyrone.' He saw their grim faces but no one opposed him. 'The time has come, gentlemen, and it must be done.'

A brisk September breeze welcomed what remained of his army to Louth, where Robert received a message from the Earl of Tyrone. He agreed to meet Hugh O'Neill, man to man, at the nearby ford of the River Lagan at Bellaclynth. His men thought the risk of being captured was too great, but he recalled Gelly's words, and saw no alternative.

'The rebels outnumber us two to one, they know this godforsaken country, and live off the land. Our best hope is to agree a truce, and we will not engage them in battle unless they leave us no choice.'

He put on his best black armour for the meeting, but left his sword and helmet, and carried only his fine silver-handled dagger in the scabbard engraved with the Devereux motto: *Virtutis comes invidia*. He allowed one division of cavalry to follow at a distance, but told them to keep well back.

He'd not been sure what to expect, and was surprised to find the earl was a thick-set man of about sixty, with dark eyes and a long grey beard. Hugh O'Neill waited on a fine black horse at the far side of the wide river crossing, and rode out into the fast-flowing water as Robert approached.

'Good day to you, Lord Essex.' He spoke with an educated Irish accent, and sounded more like a friend than a rebel enemy.

'You are the Earl of Tyrone?'

Robert looked behind the earl. A group of riders waited at a distance, but the entire rebel army could be waiting just out of sight.

'At your service.' Hugh O'Neill smiled and touched his cap in a salute. 'My man said you might agree a truce?'

Robert nodded. 'I wish an end to this fighting. Too many good men have died for little gain.'

Hugh O'Neill gave him an appraising look. 'They call me a rebel, yet I served with honour at the court of Queen Elizabeth, and spent six years in the household of the Earl of Leicester – a good man.'

Robert nodded. 'Sir Robert Dudley was my stepfather.'

Hugh O'Neill looked wistful. 'I was created an earl, as you were, and we share the same wish.'

'Then you will agree to a truce?'

'I cannot speak for the whole of Ireland, any more than you can speak for all England, but I ask you to take a message to your queen, if you will.' He looked across at Robert. 'You will be replaced by another, so tell Her Majesty for every Irishman who is killed, another two stand ready to take his place.'

'I shall have a peace treaty drawn up, which we will review every six weeks.'

Hugh O'Neill nodded. 'I thank you, Lord Essex – and have a safe journey home.' He touched his cap once more, and turned his horse, leaving Robert alone on the opposite bank.

Heavy rain made the trek back to Dublin difficult, and several horses slipped and were injured on the muddy roads. He tried not to imagine what the queen would say about his truce, but news of Sir Conyers Clifford's murder by the rebels served as proof for Robert of the futility of his mission. His fever had returned, and his only wish was to board a ship for home.

His last duty was to deal with the court martial of Sir Henry Harington and the captured deserters, at a special meeting of the Council of Ireland. The members of the council, even the sanctimonious Bishop of Meathe, were in favour of executing the commanders and hanging the deserters. Robert had seen enough death, and proposed that Sir Henry Harington, a member of the council, should be taken back to London for punishment.

'One of the officers will be executed, and one in ten of the deserters will be drawn by lot and hanged as an example, but I exercise my right to pardon the remainder.'

He recalled their grumbles of discontent as he boarded a ship. He'd been tempted to ask the council members which of them could have done better than Sir Henry Harington, who'd otherwise served with distinction. Robert would speak in his defence in London, if he was allowed the opportunity.

He'd received another stern letter written by the queen, forbidding him to return and warning him not to agree a 'hollow peace'. There was no way she could have learned of his agreement with the Earl of Tyrone, or of the men he'd knighted in the field. There was also a letter from the Privy Council approving his request for reinforcements. He turned to watch Dublin vanish into a swirling grey mist, as if the entire venture had been a bad dream.

Robert took a deep breath, knowing his future hung by the slenderest of threads. The queen was in residence at Nonsuch Palace, and he had to see her to explain his actions before anyone else did. He stood the risk of being arrested and thrown in the Tower dungeons, but this might be his only chance.

He smiled at the guards on the doors to the presence chamber, who recognised him and allowed him to pass without challenge. Robert rushed through to the privy chamber, only to find the room deserted. His plan was foiled, but there was still a chance of seeing the queen, if she was in her bedchamber.

He tried the gilded handle, half expecting to find it locked, but the door swung open and he saw the queen in her nightdress. He hardly recognised the plain, half-naked woman as the queen. He'd never seen her without her wig, and her long hair hung in thin golden strands to her shoulders.

The room was dominated by a magnificent canopied bed, on which her gowns and petticoats for the day had been arranged. The queen's elderly lady-in-waiting gasped, and looked about to raise the alarm, but the queen dismissed her with a wave of her hand. Her brown eyes looked softer without her usual make-up, and she stared at him in amazement.

Robert fell to his knees and took her hands in his. 'Forgive me, Your Majesty.' He kissed her fingers, and waited for her to shout for her guards.

She placed her hand on his head. 'Robin. You never cease to surprise us.' Her soft voice had no hint of rebuke.

'I did my best to serve Your Majesty.'

'We prayed for you each day.' She stroked his hair, like a mother might, to calm a spoiled child.

'I believed I could defeat the Irish rebels, but the people there will not be tamed.'

'Does your return mean you have captured the Earl of Tyrone?' Her question had a harder edge.

'The Earl of Tyrone speaks of Your Majesty with great respect, and recalled when he served in your court.' Robert looked into her eyes. 'I decided Your Majesty is better served by having such a man to parley with in Ireland, than to make him a martyr to his followers.'

She bent and kissed him on the forehead. 'We shall think on

this – and you must change your clothes. You've brought the mud of the road into my bedchamber.'

Robert apologised and took his leave before his intrusion was discovered. His daring gamble had worked. As far as he knew, no man had been alone with the queen in her bedchamber, or seen her in a state of undress. She'd welcomed him with greater kindness and understanding than he could have hoped for.

Nonsuch was one of the royal palaces where Robert had his own chamber, and he was pleased to find a change of clothes remained, despite his long absence. He washed and changed, then lay on his bed as he waited, rehearsing his excuses.

When he was summoned, the queen was fully dressed in a formal wig and gown, with reddened lips and pale, powdered cheeks, demanding to know every detail of his adventures in Ireland. Beginning with the perilous sea crossing, he described the stinking streets of Dublin, the dreadful state of the castle, and the churlish attitude of the council.

Her eyes widened as he told her how the rebels fought with bows and arrows, throwing spears like savages as they ambushed his army in the forests. 'Many were the times I feared for my life, Your Majesty, but my army fought bravely to assert your sovereignty.'

At dinner he sat with Charles Blount and regaled the ladies of court with outrageous stories of his Irish expedition. The queen sat with her secretary, Sir Robert Cecil, the Lord Admiral, and Robert's other old adversary, Sir Walter Raleigh, and seemed to be deep in conversation about some serious matter.

When they were finally alone, Charles Blount shared his worrying news. 'Her Majesty has summoned the Privy Council to an urgent meeting to discuss your conduct in Ireland.'

Robert cursed. 'I believed I might be forgiven, but I should not be surprised my enemies see their chance.'

Charles Blount agreed. 'I should also tell you my name has been put forward as the next Lord Lieutenant of Ireland.'

'That's no surprise, but I don't envy you the task. Dealing with Ireland is like trying to remove a nest of wasps by hitting it with a stick. The consequences are equally predictable.'

Charles Blount looked serious. 'I'm not sure which is worse, dealing with the Council of Ireland or the rebels.'

A messenger from the queen arrived to tell Robert he was to remain in his chamber until summoned. He turned to Charles Blount. 'I believe I shall learn my fate soon enough but, whatever happens, I wish you well in your new duty.'

'Take care with what you say if you are called before the Privy Council, my lord.' Charles Blount shook his head. 'Our *friends* on the council here are as likely to set up an ambush as any rebels in Ireland.'

Robert cursed his luck. An armed guard was posted outside his door, and although he'd not been deprived of his sword and dagger, he expected that would come next. He had a headache and feared his fever raged. He was just considering taking to his bed when Francis Bacon knocked and entered.

Robert was surprised to see his friend looking prosperous, his drab lawyer's robe replaced by a velvet doublet and hose, and a wide ruff collar of white filigree lace. The last time they'd met, he'd ignored Francis Bacon's advice, and now their roles were reversed.

'I wish we were meeting under better circumstances, Francis.'

'Indeed, my lord, which is why I must speak with you.' He

lowered his voice to a whisper. 'In your absence, I sought to gain the confidence of the queen.'

Robert realised that, not for the first time, he'd underestimated his friend. 'What do you plan to do?'

'I hope to convince the council that I am no longer of your affiliation, so I might better protect your interests.'

'The consequences could be serious if you fail—'

Francis Bacon held up a hand. 'I don't have long. I don't wish them to know I offer you advice, but do nothing to antagonise Her Majesty and, particularly, do not speak of your private dealings with Hugh O'Neill.'

Robert frowned. 'It's too late for that.'

Robert felt even more unsettled after Francis Bacon left. He'd hoped the queen's disfavour was like the mist in Dublin, quick to appear, yet just as quick to vanish without any trace. Francis was a shrewd man, not one to misread a situation, and was preparing for the worst.

The summons came the next morning, and Robert found himself in front of the Privy Council, his head uncovered, to be brought to account. Uncertain how to conduct himself, he bowed. Sir Thomas Egerton, the Lord Keeper, dismissed the clerks, and waited for them to close the heavy doors before consulting his notes.

'My Lord Essex, you are charged with being in contempt of Her Majesty's instructions in returning to England without permission.' He glanced up at Robert. 'You are also charged that many of your letters from Ireland have been presumptuous, and that you departed from the instructions given before you left England, that your flight from Ireland was irresponsible, that you were overbold in forcing entry to Her Majesty's bedchamber and, finally, that you created an unjustified number of idle knights while in Ireland.'

Robert took care with his words as he replied to the charges. 'I admit, my lords, to returning on my own judgement, and accept my failure to carry out Her Majesty's wishes. A great number of my men were sick with marsh fever, as am I, or dispersed to garrisons, or wounded. The enemy outnumbered our forces to the extent I judged a winter war to be unwinnable.'

He studied their faces, taking some comfort from nods of understanding, before continuing. 'I did not force access to Her Majesty. I was welcomed, and I had no written instruction not to award knighthoods in the field, which was my right as sworn Lord Lieutenant of Ireland.'

Sent back to his chamber to wait, he took to his bed and shivered with the fever. He'd served on the Privy Council long enough to know how they worked. Each man cared only for himself, and would find the easiest path to rid themselves of the tricky problem he had become.

He woke with one of Raleigh's men shaking him. 'My lord! You are to come with us to York House, where you are to be detained by the Lord Keeper at Her Majesty's pleasure.'

Robert groaned. 'I am not well enough to ride...'

The man gestured for him to rise, and looked ready to use force if necessary. 'A coach has been made ready for you, my lord.'

Life at York House became a dull routine, marked only by occasional visitors permitted by the queen. Robert Cecil, one of the first to call, declared he bore Robert no malice, and would do his best for him. His next visitor was equally unexpected. Gelly studied him with a look of concern.

'Her Majesty has ordered your household to be dismissed, my lord, with only Bagot to oversee Essex House.' He forced a smile. 'You were allowed one servant to support you.'

'You have appointed yourself to that role?'

'Of course, my lord – and I bring a crumb of good news. You have a new daughter, and with your blessing Lady Essex shall name her Frances Devereux.'

Robert looked at him in astonishment. He could hardly recall when they last lay together, so much had happened since. 'How is she?'

'A good strong girl, by all accounts.'

'I meant my wife, Gelly. How is Frances?'

'She dressed in mourning black and visited the queen at Richmond Palace to plead for your release, and to be permitted to visit you, my lord.' Gelly shook his head. 'Her Majesty declined to give her an audience, and banished her from court.'

Robert groaned. 'I must see her, before it is too late.'

Gelly frowned. 'You've lost weight, my lord, and I hear your fever has returned.'

Robert nodded. 'You will understand that sleep does not come easily, and my fever troubles me. The queen sent several of her doctors, but I refuse their potions.' He stared at his old friend. 'Tell me how it is, Gelly. What are they saying?'

'They sing songs of your exploits in the taverns, my lord. Your enemies say you never drew your sword but to make knights, and that you went to Ireland like a hasty messenger, then went away before you had done your errand. It is also rumoured that you are dead.'

Robert managed a smile. 'It would suit many if I were, but I shall deny them that satisfaction, for a while at least.'

Gelly glanced at the door, and reduced his voice to a whisper. 'Others say the queen knows not what to do with you – or that you are to be committed to the Tower. Your friends came to me with a plan. They've sent letters to King James of Scotland and, if that fails, intend to contrive your escape.'

Robert held up a hand. 'Tell them to stop, Gelly. The risk is too great, and I cannot bring down any more than I have already.'

~

Sir Thomas Egerton looked concerned. 'How are you, my lord?'

'Close to death.' The Lord Keeper was a good man, and Robert once counted him as a friend, although he must resent his unhappy role as jailer, and the use of his home as a prison. 'I wish to receive communion.'

Too weak to rise from his bed, he'd slept fitfully, his head full of troubling dreams. The fever made him sweat so much that each day he had to be lifted so the bed sheets could be changed. His head ached and, worst of all, he'd lost the will to live.

'Her Majesty has charged me to ensure your welfare. You should rise from your bed and eat, Lord Essex.' Sir Thomas spoke softly but his voice was firm. 'I will send for your chaplain, but I came to tell you Her Majesty, in her mercy, has agreed you can be visited by the countess.'

'My wife?'

Sir Thomas Egerton nodded. 'Your wife has been most persistent, and I should not be surprised if Her Majesty might visit you herself.'

Robert made the effort to eat a bowl of warm broth, but remained in his bed. He asked for writing materials and struggled with the wording of a letter to Henry Wriothesley, apologising for any trouble he'd caused and asking him to take no action.

The door opened and Frances entered. She still wore mourning black and stood, for a moment, staring at him. Then she crossed the room and placed her hand on his forehead. 'It's true. You are feverish.' She frowned. 'Have you seen a doctor?'

Robert nodded. 'Too many. The queen even sent her own physician, Doctor Brown. They tell me what I already know, that I have the Irish flux, and must rest.'

Frances dragged a heavy chair closer to his bedside and sat, arranging her skirts with unnecessary care, as if not sure what to say. She reached out and took his hand in hers. 'We have another daughter.'

'Gelly told me she is named Frances, after you. I was saddened to hear of little Penelope. I never had the chance to know her.'

'Your friend, Henry Wriothesley, stood as godfather. I pray you will be recovered soon, and I can bring your new daughter for you to see, as well as young Robin. He is much like you, quite a handful now, and often asks after you.'

'What have you told him?'

'That you are ill, and need time to recover.'

Robert lay back on his bed. 'I confess I care little enough for myself, but I regret the lack of attention I've shown our children – and you, Frances. I am deeply sorry I've not been a better husband.'

Frances gave his hand a familiar squeeze. 'I shall stay for as long as I am allowed, and you must rest, to recover your health.'

She leaned forward and kissed him. Robert saw the glisten of a tear run down her cheek.

'If Her Majesty sees fit to set me free, we shall move to Chartley and live out our days in the country. Just you, me, young Robin and little Frances.'

He shut his eyes and surrendered to the much-needed sanctuary of sleep.

26

FEBRUARY 1600

Sir Robert Cecil appeared through the servants' door, a grey cloak over his fine clothes. 'You look well, my lord, for someone I am told is close to death.'

Robert was surprised to see him, and smiled at his visitor's wry tone. 'My fever passed, thanks be to God – and to the credit of my wife, who tended me well. But I'm tired of this prison.'

Robert Cecil crossed to the fire blazing in the hearth to warm his hands. 'The imposition on Lord Keeper Egerton weighs heavily on him since the death of his wife. He complains to Her Majesty, and has yet to return to court.'

'When am I to be brought to trial?' The question burned in Robert's mind every waking moment, and haunted his dreams.

'That's the reason for my visit so late in the evening. A date has been set for the Star Chamber. I've come in secret, but wish to honour my promise to you.' Robert Cecil studied him for a moment, as if deciding how much to reveal. 'If you write a letter to Her Majesty, expressing contrition, I will present it at an opportune moment.'

'That is more than I might ask of you.' Robert couldn't

believe his luck. He'd lost all hope of support from the queen's secretary. 'Can you wait while I write the letter?'

'There is no time like the present, Lord Essex.'

Robert prepared a fresh sheet of parchment and sharpened the nib of his pen. 'What news is there from court?'

'Your sister, Lady Penelope Rich, has petitioned the queen on your behalf. She writes Her Majesty letters, sends jewels and presents, and begs to be allowed to see you.'

'To no avail?'

'I understand her letters are read, and her presents received, but no leave has been granted, although your other sister, Lady Northumberland, was granted an audience.'

'Do you know what my sister Dorothy asked?'

'Lady Northumberland complains of the little means she has to live.'

Robert frowned. 'I thought her husband was a wealthy man?'

'The Earl of Northumberland is a poor gambler, and spends much of his time with Sir Walter Raleigh at cards.'

Robert began to write his note to the queen. '*Be pleased to remember how humbly and unfeignedly I have acknowledged mine offence, and how patiently I have undergone your indignation. I again acknowledge mine offence, and beg that this cup may pass from me.*'

He looked up. 'I heard Lord Mountjoy sailed for Ireland.'

'I regret to tell you the truce in Ireland is broken.' Robert Cecil shook his head. 'The rebels attack the English Pale every day. You've not left Lord Mountjoy an easy commission.'

'I voyaged to Ireland with little knowledge of what we might find there. We were outnumbered by the rebels, and not reinforced until too late.' He saw Robert Cecil's frown at his defensive tone, and softened his voice. 'Lord Mountjoy has the advantage of our experience, and is a good man, who will lead our army well.'

'I trust you are right, Lord Essex. Lord Mountjoy's army is one quarter less than yours was, and the queen will not accept another failure.'

After his visitor left, Robert sat staring into the fading red embers in his hearth, his mind full of questions. Had he misjudged Robert Cecil? What kind of friend had to slip through the servants' door, for fear of being seen? Had the letter been a ruse, when in fact he'd been sent by the queen to see if he was fit to stand trial?

Essex House was cold and echoing without the hordes of servants, guests and visitors he'd always known. Robert's new jailer, old Sir Richard Berkeley, the white-bearded former Lieutenant of the Tower of London, escorted him from York House.

'You are permitted your steward, who will also act as porter, but I regret to say you must not have any visitors, my lord.'

'Not even my wife?'

'It seems Her Majesty is offended by the efforts of your friends who petition for your release, but I shall ask that the Countess of Essex may attend you.'

'Do you have news of my trial, Sir Richard?'

'The public hearing set for the Star Chamber in February was cancelled, but I don't know the reason, my lord.' Sir Richard gave him a rare smile. 'There was quite a commotion, as a good number turned up, not realising there was nothing to see.'

Robert could imagine his enemies jostling for the best seats to witness his downfall. His hopes of the queen's mercy increased with each passing day. He said a silent prayer of thanks to his unlikely saviour, Sir Robert Cecil – if it had been him, and whatever his reason.

Sir Richard Berkeley seemed content to let him roam the

forty-odd rooms of Essex House as he pleased, and take exercise in the extensive gardens leading down to the River Thames. Gelly came up with a plan to escape by boat from the watergate, but Robert disagreed.

'I take comfort from the delay of a public hearing, and Her Majesty might feel I've been punished enough. I also need to be mindful of Sir Richard Berkeley. He's shown me kindness, and I fear he would pay the price if I escape.'

'Think on it, my lord, while you still have your liberty. A boat at night can take us downriver unobserved, and I can have post horses waiting.' Gelly looked serious. 'This might be our only chance.'

Frances arrived early one morning with their infant daughter for Robert to see. 'You have to thank Sir Richard Berkeley.' She smiled as she placed their new baby, swaddled in a woollen shawl, in his arms. 'He's given his personal assurance.'

Robert stared in wonderment into his daughter's large eyes. 'There was a time when I believed I'd never be allowed to see you again, let alone the children. Are you allowed to bring Robin?'

'Robin has started his first term at Eton. I miss him, but my mother insisted on paying the fees.'

'Your mother is too quick to interfere, Frances. I'm sure she means well, but I want my son to go to Trinity.'

'My mother swallowed her pride and begged the queen to permit me to see you.' Frances sounded hurt. 'She told me the queen humiliated her, despite my father devoting his life to her service.'

Robert's daughter smiled up at him as he handed her back. 'Thank your mother for me, Frances. Your care for me at York House saved my life.'

'Mother isn't well. I think the strain has taken its toll. She's returned to Barn Elms, and I must go and see her after—'

'After I'm consigned to the Tower?' He heard the bitterness in his voice. 'I see it in your eyes, Frances.'

'I was going to say after our child is born.' She spoke softly, but with an edge to her voice. 'I was waiting to tell you when I was certain, but I'm sure enough.'

'I'm sorry, Frances. I had no idea...'

'I confess I was surprised, but perhaps we can take some hope from this.' She smiled, but her eyes were full of sadness, and she looked close to tears. 'I shall pray for you, Robert, and don't lose hope, for who can know God's will?'

Robert waited like a servant for half an hour outside the heavy oak doors of the great hall at York House. He hadn't expected to be back there again, and feared he might never return to Essex House. At the same time, he was relieved to finally be tried, after waiting so many months.

The doors opened and the sergeant-at-law called his name in a stern voice, as if Robert were some common criminal. He entered and saw the hall arranged like a courtroom, with knights, clergy and judges, including his uncle, Sir William Knollys, his former jailer, Lord Keeper Egerton, and Sir Robert Cecil.

He stood at the end of the long table, waiting for someone to acknowledge him. The only one who gave any sign they knew him was someone Robert had not been expecting to attend the hearing. Their eyes met, and Francis Bacon gave him the briefest nod, then looked down at his papers.

Although he'd made a good recovery from his fever, Robert hoped someone would offer him a chair. He couldn't stand like a statue for the long hours this hearing might take, and was grateful when Archbishop John Whitgift ordered a clerk to fetch a stool for him.

The Lord Keeper declared the hearing open, and the Attorney General, Sir Edward Coke, set out the substance of the charges in a self-important voice. He'd had to fight for his post when Robert argued for Francis Bacon, and now he had the opportunity to take his revenge.

Robert wasn't listening to the facile allegations. They spoke as if he'd committed treason, yet any of them might have done the same in his position. He studied the stern faces of each of the men around the table, counting those he thought might support him.

Of the eighteen courtiers, he'd crossed swords at one time or another with more than half. The only ones he could call friends were Francis Bacon, the old Master of Trinity, Archbishop Whitgift, and his uncle. There would be little question of the outcome if it came to a vote, regardless of anything he might say.

They didn't ask him questions, or offer him the chance to defend himself. Worse still, the hearing strayed into a general indictment of his conduct, as well as the behaviour of his family. Sir Edward Coke held up a letter, and seemed so incensed he could hardly continue.

'The accused's own sister, Lady Rich, wrote to Her Majesty in an insolent tone.' He held the letter as if it might burst into flames. 'Such contemptuous actions aggravate the stated offences, and show disrespect for the queen and the loyal members of her council.'

Robert remained silent as the Solicitor General made a speech about how the Earl of Tyrone had been emboldened by the truce, and posed a serious threat to the peace of the nation. He said nothing about the chain of castles now with English garrisons, or how Robert's inexperienced army was short of supplies, and outnumbered by the Irish rebels two to one.

Sir Robert Cecil spoke next, and surprised them all by pointing out that this was not a trial, but a court of enquiry and, for him, the only crime was one of error.

'My Lord Essex was persuaded by the Council of Ireland to take his army southwards, instead of following Her Majesty's instruction to capture the Earl of Tyrone. He then compounded this error with his unlawful return.'

Judge Sir Thomas Walmsley, a bluff-speaking veteran of the courts, agreed. 'I would compare my lord's coming home to the act of a shepherd, leaving his flock to the care of a dog!'

Lord Keeper Egerton called the meeting to order, and invited Francis Bacon to present his evidence. Robert hoped for some redemption, and recalled their brief conversation at Nonsuch Palace. Francis had been a loyal friend, and hadn't borne a grudge when passed over as Attorney General. He looked self-assured in his lawyer's black robes, yet avoided looking at Robert as he spoke.

'I ask all present to note that any loyalty to my former master, the Earl of Essex, is laid aside, and I thank Her Majesty for permitting this hearing to be held in private session.' He consulted his notes, then read out damaging passages from Robert's letters to the queen.

Robert clenched his teeth to stop the protest he could barely contain. This was not what Francis Bacon referred to at their brief meeting. He knew how dangerous the words were, out of context, and he delivered them with consummate skill. There was no need to ask who could speak so ill of the queen. The letters were in Robert's hand, and bore his signature and seal.

At last, Robert was asked what he had to say. He stared at them, silently cursing Francis Bacon for his disloyalty; Sir Robert Cecil, who'd done little to help him; his uncle, Sir

William Knollys, who'd not said one word to defend him; and the elderly archbishop, John Whitgift, who'd merely asked for a wooden stool.

He fell to his knees, and spoke with calm sincerity. 'The inward sorrow laid privately upon my soul, between God and my conscience, for the great offence towards Her Majesty, is more than any cross that could befall me.' He looked directly at the Attorney General, Sir Edward Coke. 'I would never excuse myself from crimes of error or rashness which my youth, folly or infirmities might lead me to, but I must profess loyalty, unfeigned affection and desire to do Her Majesty the best service I am able to.'

His words echoed in the room, and seemed to have struck a chord. His speech had the compelling ring of truth. Although he'd not prepared a proper defence, he found himself going through each of the charges, making excuses and blaming others, until Lord Keeper Egerton held up a hand to silence him.

'There is no question of your loyalty, Lord Essex, but the charges are serious, and you should be sent to the Tower.' He took his quill and made a note on his papers, then looked back up at Robert. 'For now, my lord, you must return to your imprisonment at Essex House while we make our report to Her Majesty.'

Robert showed Gelly the note from Francis Bacon. 'He sends an apology, then offers to show the queen letters between me and his brother, as proof of my loyalty.'

Gelly scowled. 'I don't trust him. He's done you no favours. He's up to something, my lord.'

'I don't blame Francis Bacon; he's a clever man and covers all his options. I don't believe the queen ever doubted my loyalty, although I confess it's being tested now.' Robert screwed up the letter and tossed it into the hearth. 'I worry these charges mean my profit from sweet wines is under threat. Without that, I'll have no income, even if I'm allowed to retire.'

'What about King James?'

Robert frowned. 'King James could succeed the queen, but you can bet men like Robert Cecil will waste no time in poisoning his mind against me.'

'We could escape to Wales—'

'I've told you, Gelly. I can't live the rest of my days as a fugitive, in Wales or anywhere else.'

The terse summons to see Sir Robert Cecil at York House threw Robert into a quandary. Gelly told him to plead illness, or find some excuse not to go, worried the meeting could be a trap. Sir Richard Berkeley, who was to escort him, was of the opposite view.

'If they wish to arrest you, my lord, they will send guards from the Tower.'

Robert brightened. 'Of course. You are right, Sir Richard and, with luck, this might mean Her Majesty has finally relented.'

They chose to walk the short distance to York House in pleasant August sunshine, taking the back road to avoid attention. When they arrived, they were shown into the Lord Keeper's study, a wood-panelled room, where Sir Robert Cecil was flanked by Lord Keeper Egerton and Lord Treasurer Buckhurst, who offered them a seat. Cecil turned first to Sir Richard Berkeley.

'Her Majesty has asked me to thank you for your service, Sir Richard. You will be pleased to hear your work is done, and you are granted permission to return to your family.'

Sir Richard Berkeley looked relieved. 'Thank you, Master Secretary.'

Robert Cecil turned to Robert. 'Her Majesty has decided you are no longer to be held under arrest, Lord Essex, but you are not to come to court.'

Robert saw the gleam of triumph in Robert Cecil's eye, and knew banishment was what he'd planned all along.

'Kindly inform Her Majesty I am grateful for her mercy, and intend to retire to the country.'

By the time he'd returned to Essex House, his good mood had turned to anger. He shut himself in his room and paced back and forth as he tried to think what to do. Gelly knocked at his door, and listened as he explained what had happened.

'Banishment is a cruel punishment for a man like me, and the queen has shown my mother how long she can bear a grudge. Sir Robert Cecil has what he wants – and there is nothing I can do about it.'

'Did they mention your profit from the tax on sweet wines, my lord?'

'No – but I've no doubt someone will be rewarded with my sweet wines income, and I will be ruined.' Robert scowled. 'My debts mean I can't retire to Chartley, or afford the upkeep of this place.'

'We could return to Lamphey Palace, my lord.'

'Frances is with child.' Robert smiled at Gelly's raised eyebrows. 'In truth, Gelly, I only lay with her once at York House. I could join her at Barn Elms—'

'Or you could write to King James.'

Robert sat in thought for a moment. 'You are right. It's only a matter of time before my creditors demand repayment of more than five thousand pounds, and I'll find myself in the debtors' prison. I shall take one last roll of the die, and write to Her Majesty, appealing against my banishment from her court.'

He crossed to the window, and looked out over the city. Many of the buildings appeared shabby after years of poor maintenance. The stunted spire of the great cathedral of St Paul's, struck by lightning during a violent storm before Robert was born, had never been replaced.

'London looks old and frail, like our queen. We need to be putting our energies into promoting the interests of her successor. I will write to King James, confirming support for his accession, and denouncing Robert Cecil and Walter Raleigh as men who should not be trusted.'

27

JANUARY 1601

Essex House buzzed like a hive with secret preparations, with more men arriving each night at the watergate. Robert worked with a new sense of urgency. His new daughter, named after his sister Dorothy, had been born at the end of December at Barn Elms, and he planned to see her soon.

His hand went, out of habit, to the black silk purse he wore on a silk cord around his neck. Inside was his touchstone, the brief note from King James of Scotland. The purse also held the key to a strongbox, hidden in his study, full of personal letters from the queen.

Henry Wriothesley came blundering in, cursing and shouting. The Earl of Southampton had always been a hothead and, at first, Robert thought he'd been drinking – yet this was different.

'For God's sake, Henry, calm yourself and tell me what's happened.'

'It's that bastard Thomas Grey. He's always had it in for me, and attacked me with his sword as I rode by Durham House.'

Robert saw the blue bruise on Henry's cheek, and the rip in the sleeve of his silk doublet. 'Are you hurt?'

'I'm not, but one of Grey's men cut off the hand of my servant, who might die of his wound.'

Robert scowled. 'I've never trusted Lord Grey. What caused the fight?'

Henry Wriothesley took a deep drink of the cup of ale Gelly brought for him. 'He says Lord Mountjoy has achieved ten times more than we did in Ireland, and that we spread falsehoods about Cecil plotting with Spain.'

'What did you say?'

'I told him to go to hell.'

The official summons for Robert to appear before the members of the Privy Council gave no reason, but wasn't unexpected. As before, Gelly argued that to do so was to walk into their trap. Robert agreed, and summoned his friends to discuss what they should do.

As well as Henry Wriothesley and Gelly Meyrick, he'd been joined by his stepfather, Sir Christopher Blount, his stepdaughter Elizabeth's husband, Roger Manners, Earl of Rutland, and Sir Ferdinando Gorges, who fought with him in France. His Uncle George, who was close to sixty and deep in debt, had ridden from Wales with two dozen armed men. Robert doubted they understood the situation in London, but was glad of their loyal support.

He showed them the summons. 'I shall say I'm unwell, to buy us time. Robert Cecil has made his move against us by having Lord Grey goad Henry into a fight.'

Henry Wriothesley nodded, his bruised face like a badge of honour. 'He wanted an excuse to finish me.'

'Cecil won't rest until we are all ruined.' Robert looked around the table at their faces. 'We have to act soon, and choose our moment when the queen is at the Palace of Whitehall. It's only twenty minutes' march from here, and the royal apartments are relatively unprotected.'

Henry Wriothesley grinned. 'You've secured a private meeting with Her Majesty before, and can do so again.'

Sir Ferdinando Gorges frowned with concern. 'I recall your last meeting with the queen didn't end well, my lord, and Raleigh has doubled the queen's guards.'

'We have some three hundred men armed and ready, and I hope as many again will join us when we show our hand, including the Mayor of London's militia.'

Sir Christopher gave him a doubtful look. 'And if they do not?'

'Then I would rather die fighting for our cause, than spend the rest of my days in the Tower dungeons.'

Robert Sackville, son of the Lord Treasurer, sat in Robert's study and sipped his glass of wine. He'd arrived alone, and said he needed to speak with Robert in private. Robert was intrigued, and keen to hear the news from court. He'd last seen Lord Buckhurst at York House, and wondered what he was up to.

'So, what brings you here on such a cold night?'

'My father spoke to Her Majesty on your behalf, my lord. He said I should tell you the meeting went well, but the queen is troubled by the company you keep.'

Robert raised an eyebrow. 'How would the queen know who visits me here?' He smiled. 'I would have thought Her Majesty has better things to do than concern herself with the comings and goings at Essex House.'

'Quite so, my lord, but as a friend, I feel obliged to remind you how she might view the way you entertain so many nobles here.' He gave Robert a meaningful look. 'Some might say you set up a court to rival her own.'

Robert laughed at the thought. 'Until Her Majesty prohibits me from entertaining my friends, I shall feel free to continue to do so.'

Robert Sackville drained his glass and stood to warm his hands by the fire. 'I don't usually listen to gossip at court, but there is talk of your steward, Sir Gelly Meyrick, bringing bands of men from Wales. It's easy enough to imagine how the queen might become concerned.'

'Well, you can thank your father, and reassure him I'm simply rebuilding my household, which he well knows was dismissed when I returned from Ireland.'

As Robert Sackville left, he turned to Robert.

'Take care, my lord.'

It sounded like a threat.

Frances and Penelope arrived unexpectedly, looking concerned when they saw the number of horses in the courtyard, and armed men guarding the entrance. Robert greeted them with mixed feelings, and tried to be dismissive. 'As you can see, Essex House has become so popular we have to limit the numbers.'

Penelope made light of it. 'I've brought my servants, and enough luggage for a week.' She hugged him. 'The queen is surely soon for the grave, and is not forgiven for the way she's treated our family – first our father, then Mother, and now you.'

Frances kissed Robert on the cheek. 'We heard so many stories, it's hard to know what to believe, so we had to find out for ourselves. Mother is caring for our daughter, so you will understand I cannot stay for long.'

. . .

When they were finally alone, Frances revealed the true reason for her visit. 'Come back to Barn Elms with me, Robert, while you can – at least until this all dies down.'

He stared at her in surprise. 'I cannot.'

'For the sake of our children, if not for me, I beg of you.'

'This has gone too far—'

'It has not, but you make so little secret of it. I know what you plan to do, Robert, as does half of London.'

'You can't know, because we haven't agreed anything.'

'You plan for your men to infiltrate Whitehall Palace, and seize control on a signal.'

He gripped her arms with both hands and stared into her eyes. 'Where did you hear of this? Who is the traitor in our midst?'

'You're hurting me, and as you have asked, most people would say it is *you* who are the traitor.'

'You're wrong. The people love me, and tire of our vindictive queen.'

'You're a fool, Robert.' She stepped back from him, as if afraid. 'You could have had everything, anything you wanted, but you throw it away, for what? To prove you are a better man than Robert Cecil, with his crippled back, or that arrogant peacock, Walter Raleigh?'

The lookout on the front gate called to Robert. 'More visitors, my lord. Sir William Knollys, with members of the Privy Council, Lord Keeper Egerton, Sir Edward Somerset, Earl of Worcester, and Lord Justice Popham.'

Robert cursed. 'Admit the lords by the wicket gate, but not any armed men in their company.'

As they entered, his uncle gave Robert a despairing look. 'What game are you playing?'

Robert resented his uncle's tone. 'I've done nothing wrong.'

'Secretary Cecil has men watching this house. He knows your steward has been recruiting men, and arming them with muskets – and now we see it for ourselves.'

Robert's pulse raced. They'd been careful, with men only entering and leaving at night, yet any one of Gelly's band of retainers could be a spy in Cecil's pay. 'Whatever you've heard, my intentions are honourable.'

Sir Edward Somerset scowled. 'They say you call the queen an old woman, as crooked in mind as in body.'

Robert had no answer. Cecil's spy must be even closer than he'd thought. One of the servants, or even one of his friends, playing for both sides. He *had* called the queen an old woman – and worse.

His uncle pointed to the guards at the gates. 'Why do you act like this, and fill your house with armed men?'

'I have to defend myself against those who plot my downfall, and threaten to murder me.'

Lord Keeper Egerton shook his head. 'If you have a grievance, Lord Essex, you should raise it in the proper manner, and allow the law of England to take its course.'

'I have many grievances. Lord Grey attacked my friend, the Earl of Southampton, and seriously wounded his servant.'

'Lord Grey has been locked up in the Fleet prison, as you will be, if you don't have a care.'

The men in the courtyard grew restless at Lord Keeper Egerton's threat, and some began calling out, 'Lock them up!' One of them pushed Lord Egerton in the back, causing him to stumble.

The Lord Keeper turned and shouted at them in defiance. 'I

command you all to lay down your weapons and depart, if you are good subjects of Her Majesty!'

The men called back. 'Throw them out!' Some drew their swords, and looked ready for a fight. Robert called them to order and turned to Gelly.

'Kindly escort these gentlemen to my study, and detain them there – for their safety.'

His uncle turned to him. 'The summons from the Privy Council was to reprove you for this unlawful assembly, and to wish you to leave the city and retire into the country, as you promised Her Majesty.' He scowled at Gelly. 'We're here in the queen's name, so detaining us will have serious consequences.'

The men waved their swords and jeered. Robert glanced back at the house, torn between making his peace with Frances and the excitement of his followers. The gates were thrown open and his men began assembling in the road. One of Gelly's men brought him Sir Philip Sidney's sword, his good luck charm.

Caught up in the moment, he drew the fine sword and raised it high in the air, to cheers from the men. 'To the queen! To the court!'

As he'd hoped, more men joined as they marched down Fleet Street. Women leaned out of windows to see the rare commotion on a Sunday. Some cheered and applauded, but others slammed their shutters. The faithful were leaving the cathedral of St Paul's as the rowdy procession passed, and many returned inside for sanctuary.

Robert called to his followers. 'To the sheriff's house, where we shall meet the Lord Mayor of London!'

One of his young grooms carrying his Devereux banner pushed through the ranks to march at his side, and Robert smiled as he saw him. Handsome and blue-eyed, he looked more like a noble than a servant. 'What's your name, boy?'

'Henry Tracy, my lord.'

'Well, Master Tracy, keep close by me, and you'll be rewarded by seeing history made today.'

They marched up to the sheriff's grand house, and Thomas Smythe met them on the steps. He spoke softly to Robert, so the others couldn't hear. 'Go home, my Lord Essex, before the queen's guards arrive.'

'I'm counting on your men to join us, sheriff, and wish to speak with the mayor.'

'Only my few servants are here, my lord, as it is Sunday, but they can serve you some refreshment while I send a message to the mayor.'

Robert dined at the sheriff's table, but the messenger returned without the mayor, and announced that the Ludgate was barricaded by a force of the queen's pikemen, and heralds were telling Robert's followers they would be pardoned if they dispersed, or called rebels if they stayed.

Robert laughed and turned to his groom. 'Did you hear that, Master Tracy, we're rebels now. Find us horses. We shall take the Ludgate, and march on Whitehall. Then they shall see we're no rebels, but loyal servants of the queen.'

There seemed fewer men outside, and their mood changed when they saw the heavy chains stretched across the road, and rows of men armed with pikes guarding the barricade. Robert decided the time had come to play his trump card, and he turned to Sir Ferdinando Gorges.

'Make haste to Essex House by the river, and tell Gelly Meyrick he is to release Lord Justice Popham, who is to tell Sir Robert Cecil the other three will remain as our surety.'

Robert's stepfather studied the barricade. 'Those aren't the queen's guard. They look like the lord bishop's men, but there's an experienced soldier at work here. I shall find out who is in command. We have to win them over, as we can't go forward, or back to Essex House, without a fight.'

One of his men primed his pistol, and fired a shot as Sir Christopher approached the guards. A fusillade of shots rang out from both sides, and there were yells of alarm as men were hit. A bullet skimmed Robert's hat, then another struck young Henry Tracy in the chest.

The boy gave a yelp of surprise and dropped his banner, then toppled from his horse, dead before he hit the ground. A pikeman gored Sir Christopher in the face, cutting open his cheek, and then struck him over the head. Several of Robert's men ran to his aid as he fell unconscious to the cobbles.

Henry Wriothesley called to Robert. 'To the river! It's our only way out!'

Robert hesitated. He should see his stepfather safe, but to do so would risk his own capture. His men hacked with swords at the guards before they were driven back. He watched Sir Christopher being dragged over the chains, his face bleeding from his wound. There was nothing he could do. He spurred his horse and galloped towards the Queenhithe river steps, praying for a boat.

Heavy furniture, boxes, and even Robert's precious books were piled behind the doors and windows of Essex House, with men armed with pistols and muskets posted at every vantage point. Robert called for Gelly when he found his study empty.

'Where is my uncle, and the others?'

Gelly looked surprised. 'Sir Ferdinando Gorges said you ordered them set free. He's taken them by boat.'

Robert couldn't blame anyone, other than himself. Sir Ferdinando Gorges must have seen his chance of redemption, and taken it. Robert never intended harm to his prisoners, but the consequences would be added to his growing list.

He took the key from the black purse around his neck and unlocked the strongbox in his study, throwing the contents and the purse on to the fire in the hearth. The note from King James, and the cherished personal letters from the queen, curled and blackened before bursting into flames. It saddened Robert to see them turn to ash, but it had to be done.

At dusk, the iron gates were smashed open and soldiers burst into the courtyard. Shots echoed, and several men fell dead, but more swarmed in, taking firing positions where they could. A bullet cracked a pane of leaded glass, killing one of Gelly's Welsh lookouts, and another thudded into the barricaded door splintering the wood.

Robert watched as Lord Grey, already set free, entered by the watergate with men armed with muskets and accompanied by Sir Robert Cecil and Sir Robert Sidney, who called for their surrender. 'Culverins have been sent for from the Tower, and we shall reduce Essex House to a pile of rubble if necessary!'

Henry Wriothesley called back. 'We'll die first, before we surrender to men such as Thomas Grey.'

After a silence, Robert Sidney called for them to let the women out. It meant the risk of removing the barricade from the door, but Robert was glad to see Frances, Penelope, and their ladies go. He'd planned a farewell speech, but only gave each of them a last hug as they prepared to leave. He'd not seen Penelope in tears since her wedding to Lord Rich.

Frances looked pale and frightened. She leaned forward and kissed him on the cheek. 'You must surrender, Robert. They have the house surrounded.'

'I've escaped from tricky situations before.' He forced a

smile. 'Thank them for freeing you – and be sure to tell them you were held against your will.'

As night fell, the house was ringed with the eerie yellow light of burning torches. Robert was prepared to go down fighting, but the lives of the others weighed on his conscience. He pulled the furniture and heavy boxes from inside the doors, scattering them without a care.

Henry Wriothesley opened a window and shouted into the cold night air. 'We surrender, on condition of a fair and proper hearing!'

The long silence tested their nerves, then the familiar voice of Sir Charles Howard, Lord Admiral and Earl of Nottingham, replied. 'So be it.'

Robert drew his sword from its fine scabbard, then pushed open the door and took a few paces before falling to his knees and offering his sword to Sir Charles with both hands. One by one, the others followed his example, and were led away by armed guards.

Robert took one last look at Essex House, and was taken to the bishop's palace at Lambeth. From his window he could see distant lights in the windows of Whitehall Palace across the water. He doubted they would wake the queen, but imagined Robert Cecil could not wait to tell her his news in the morning.

28

FEBRUARY 1601

He'd never seen the cavernous hall of Westminster so full. Motes of dust glinted in a shaft of bright winter sunlight shining on the dour, grey-bearded face of Lord Buckhurst. The Lord High Steward sat under a grand canopy of estate, flanked by black-robed lawyers, like crows waiting to peck the eyes from a dying lamb.

Robert had been allowed to send for his best black doublet and hose, with a cape against the winter chill. He wore, he was sure for the last time, his Garter collar of St George, on a ribbon of blue satin, but his cherished sword and silver dagger were taken from him, lost forever.

He'd spent his first night at the Tower in a surprisingly well-furnished room, although he'd had little sleep. His jailer, Sir John Peyton, Lieutenant of the Tower, told him Frances was safe with her mother at Walsingham House. Robert was distressed to learn his sister was under arrest for treason, but relieved to hear his stepfather had been treated for his wounds and recovered, a small consolation.

Henry Wriothesley stood at Robert's side and pointed out Lord Grey, sitting in judgement upon them. Robert noticed

Francis Bacon in his lawyer's robes on the benches for the prosecution. His former friend knew everything about him, but nothing about what had happened in the past days at Essex House.

The clerk read out the charges, his voice echoing.

'Robert Devereux, Earl of Essex, did conspire with Henry, Earl of Southampton, Roger, Earl of Rutland, and diverse knights and gentlemen, to deprive and depose Her Majesty from her royal state and dignity, to procure her death and destruction, to cause a cruel slaughter of Her Majesty's subjects, and change the government of her realm.'

The sergeant described the events in such detail Robert guessed one of his friends must have made a full confession to save himself. There was no point in pleading not guilty, yet he found himself doing so, trying to sound confident of his innocence. Henry Wriothesley followed his lead, as he'd always done.

The Attorney General, Sir Edward Coke, stood to explain the law of treason. His voice droned, and he soon forgot any pretence of neutrality. He wagged an accusing finger at Robert. 'The Earl of Essex, that stands now in black, should have worn a bloody robe!'

Robert struggled to contain his anger and called out, 'Will your lordships give us our time to reply to these slanders?'

The Lord High Steward scowled. 'First, we must hear the evidence against you, my Lord Essex.' He nodded to Lord Chief Justice Popham, next to speak.

Robert heard the gasps, muttered oaths, and even laughs as the self-important judge gave a colourful account of his detention in Robert's study. He claimed he'd feared for his life at the hands of the bloodthirsty rebels. Robert clenched his fists, digging his nails into his palms to stop himself from shouting as, one by one, men he thought loyal friends testified against him.

Sir Ferdinando Gorges claimed he'd been tasked by Robert to trick Sir Walter Raleigh into being captured, and had begged him to forget his dreams of rebellion and turn himself over to the queen. Robert couldn't contain his silence.

'My lords, can you not see this man has been made to bear false witness?'

Francis Bacon made an overlong speech, and looked him straight in the eye. 'All you can say in answer to these matters are but shadows. Confess, my lord.'

Robert stared at Francis Bacon in disbelief. He, of all people, knew how the queen needed to be protected from her self-serving advisors. He made their rebellion sound like the act of a fool – or, worse, a traitor.

His poorly thought out defence forgotten, he rambled, as he'd done to the enquiry at York House, accusing Francis Bacon of disloyalty, pretending to be his friend, and Sir Walter Raleigh of plotting to kill him. He saved his anger for Robert Cecil, who he accused of plotting to sell the Crown of England to the Spanish, so he could place the infanta of Spain on the throne.

Robert Cecil fell on his knees before the Lord High Steward, and begged to be allowed to defend his name. 'My lord of Essex, the difference between us is great. I am not a noble, but I am a gentleman. I'm no swordsman, but I have a conscience, truth and honesty to defend myself from such slander.'

Robert blamed himself as he listened to the theatrical speech, another dagger stabbed in his back, and twisted as a final insult. Robert Cecil must have anticipated his accusation and worked long into the night preparing his revenge, savouring each word, and counting the hours.

Robert and Henry were led from the hall for the lords to consider their judgement. They waited under armed guard in a cold antechamber, and heard raised voices, shouting in the crowded hall. They couldn't hear what was being said, but Henry Wriothesley looked hopeful.

'Someone is arguing for us, thank God.'

Robert doubted it. The voice he heard over all the others was Lord Justice Popham. From the moment he'd surrendered his sword to the Lord Admiral, he'd known there could only be one outcome. He glanced at Henry and understood the fear in his friend's eyes.

The sergeant-at-arms called on each of the lords to declare their judgement. All said the same. 'Guilty, my lord, of high treason, upon my honour.'

Robert was asked if he could offer any reason why he should not face a death sentence.

'I ask only for leniency for Earl Henry of Southampton. He was led astray by me, my lords, and bears no treacherous intentions towards Her Majesty.'

Lord Grey and his supporters shouted 'Lies!' The sergeant called the hall to silence, and all eyes turned to Lord Buckhurst, who had the duty of pronouncing the sentence. He stared at Robert and Henry, as if the weight of what he was about to say troubled him, then read from the sheet of parchment in front of him.

'You shall be drawn on a hurdle through the midst of the city, and so to the place of execution, there to be hanged by the neck and taken down, your bodies to be opened, your bowels to be taken out and burned before your face, your bodies to be quartered. Your heads and quarters to be disposed of at Her Majesty's pleasure, and may God have mercy on your souls.'

Numbed by the stark facts of a traitor's death, Robert overcame the dryness of his throat. The queen, in her mercy, would surely commute the sentence to a private beheading. He hoped death would be quick, and in a last act of bravado, made a joke of it.

'I shall die as cheerful a death as any man ever did.'

～

The straw pallet bed in Robert's cell, alive with fleas, kept him awake, and the bitter cold froze his breath in the moonlight. His request for a candle and writing materials was refused, his surly jailer pointing out he would not be held in his cell for long.

His head buzzed with ideas for how he might have better defended himself. He could have paid Francis Bacon to speak for him, or confessed to a lesser crime. A sincere apology for his actions would have helped. Instead, he'd fallen into their trap, like a bear blundering into a pit of sharpened stakes. Too late, he saw through the plan to goad him with a web of half-truths and lies.

Frances called him foolish, and so he had been, even though his life, and the lives of his friends, depended on him. He recalled the moment he'd decided to march to the city, instead of to Whitehall. The palace was so close the guards could have been taken by surprise. Instead, he'd led his followers on a wild goose chase, wasting precious time.

He pulled the thin blanket of grey wool around his shoulders and shivered in the cold, falling into a fitful sleep. The events of the past days haunted his troubled dreams. His young groom, Henry Tracy, wagged an accusing finger at him and shouted, 'You, my lord, should be wearing a bloody robe!'

Robert woke with a jolt and lay in the darkness listening to his own heavy breathing. For a moment he thought he was back at Essex House, and Bagot might come at any moment to open the shutters. He looked to the window and saw, instead of diamonds of leaded glass, a small opening with heavy iron bars.

He waited as the dawn turned to day, and a shaft of winter sunlight cut through the darkness. He recalled that prisoners could pay for better food, to be allowed visitors, and even to be moved to a better room. He crossed to the grill in his iron-studded door, and called for his guards.

'I wish to see my chaplain.'

He recognised Dean Thomas Dove, the softly spoken cleric. 'I asked for my chaplain.'

Thomas Dove nodded. 'Your chaplain has returned to Wales, but I can hear your confession.'

Robert noted he was no longer addressed as *my lord*.

'It must be my own chaplain.'

'Confess your sins to me, and I will give you absolution.'

'I have sinned, but not against the queen, or her servants. I defended my house, and detained members of the Privy Council and my uncle, for their own safety. They were released unharmed, and never did I, or any of my men, go near the palace of Her Majesty.'

The dean looked unsettled, as if uncomfortable with his task. 'Men died in fighting at Ludgate—'

'Not by my hand, and one was my own servant, a young groom. He was unarmed, and only carried my banner.' Robert frowned. 'I learned yesterday he was shot by a servant of his grace, the bishop.'

Thomas Dove shook his head. 'I should tell you, Lord Essex, I am charged to report everything you tell me to the council.' He turned to go. 'I shall send for your chaplain, and pray he arrives in time.'

'In time?'

'Her Majesty has signed your death warrant. Time is not on your side, Lord Essex.'

Robert's pulse raced. He'd secretly hoped, for the sake of the long friendship they'd shared, for a pardon or a commuted sentence of imprisonment. He couldn't believe the queen had been persuaded to sign his death warrant so soon. He pictured Robert Cecil, begging on his knees, or Walter Raleigh, exaggerating the threat of rebellion. For the first time, the back of his neck prickled with the frisson of fear.

He lay back on his creaking pallet bed, listening to the sounds outside. The clump of heavy boots on the cobblestones. Someone laughing – a cruel, humourless laugh, as if at someone else's expense. Robert guessed he would be the subject of wry jokes in taverns all over London. He'd seen how quickly his friends could turn, and how stories were exaggerated in the retelling.

A guard brought his food. Dry bread, a cup of small beer, and a bowl of pottage. Robert had no appetite, and pushed the pottage aside. He took a sip of the stale beer, then ate the bread, remembering the royal banquets of twenty courses, with gilded peacocks and endless goblets of rich French wine.

The door banged open and Robert's friend, the cleric Master Ashton, entered. Robert had lost track of the days, and fallen into the routine of waking at dawn and sleeping when daylight failed. His days were punctuated by the changing of the guard and the delivery of his meals.

'My lord, you have dishonoured your God, shamed your profession, and offended Her Gracious Majesty.' Ashton gave him a stern look. 'Worst of all, you have led good men to believe that you should be sovereign, and would have seized the Crown for yourself. I am here for you to make confession of your fault.'

Robert stared at him in bewilderment. Ashton had always been deferential, yet his tone seemed oddly demanding. 'Never in my life did I seek the throne – or show anything other than true loyalty to Her Majesty. All I hoped was to alert her to the dangerous plans of her advisors.'

Ashton held up a hand to silence him. 'My lord, you must remember you are going out of this world.'

'You don't believe me?' Robert's voice echoed. 'I swear, before God, I speak the truth.'

'Free your conscience, before God, of the burden of your sins.'

Robert kneeled on the hard floor and searched his soul. 'The fault is not all mine. Others gave me encouragement, as you well know, Master Ashton.'

'Confess, my lord, and I shall absolve your sins.'

Robert rambled, as he had at his trial, naming everyone who'd led him to his bleak cell in the Tower. He blamed his stepfather, and even his sister Penelope, for encouraging his impetuous actions, and told how those he thought his friends twisted his words for their own gain.

He looked into Ashton's eyes and saw a look of guilt.

'Even you, Master Ashton. You freely visited me as my chaplain, and prayed with me, but all that time were you reporting back to Robert Cecil?'

Ashton shook his head. 'I have to bear witness against you, my lord.'

Robert hammered on his cell door to summon his guard.

'I wish to see Sir Robert Cecil.'

The guard looked doubtful, but a few hours later the cell door opened and Robert Cecil entered with Sir Charles Howard. They looked taken aback by his condition. He'd not been eating or sleeping, and hadn't washed since arriving at the Tower.

Robert bowed his head. 'I confess I am a traitor. I planned to seize the queen and change the government.'

Robert Cecil raised an eyebrow. 'What is it you want?'

'Forgiveness.'

'Forgiveness for accusing me of plotting to sell the Crown of England to the Spanish?' His bitter tone showed he still bore a grudge.

'I was wrong, and humbly beg you to forgive me.'

Charles Howard glanced towards the door, as if he wished to go. 'What brought about this change of heart?'

'All I ask is to be forgiven – and to be allowed to die within the privacy of Tower Green.'

Robert Cecil nodded. 'I cannot say you will ever be forgiven, my lord. I shall ask Her Majesty to grant your request. But first we need your full confession.'

Sir John Peyton, Lieutenant of the Tower, brought quills and parchment, and handed Robert a sealed bottle.

'Ink, for you to write your confession, my lord.' He took one of the quills and a sheet of parchment. 'You must sign it as your full and true confession.'

Robert worked until the light failed, and woke to the sound of hammering. Someone cursed about having to work so early. A saw rasped back and forth on wood, and a deep voice complained about the cold. They were building a scaffold, and seemed in a hurry. Straining to see out of his window, he found he didn't have a view of Tower Green, only the empty courtyard, the cobblestones white with frost.

He asked the guard who brought his food to make sure his confession was passed to Sir John Peyton, and prayed his efforts were enough to satisfy Robert Cecil. He didn't want to face the public at Tower Hill – but if he had to, he would be ready.

His answer came sooner than he'd expected. Rector Thomas Mountford and William Barlow arrived with news. 'The sentence is to be carried out at dawn tomorrow, my lord. We've come to help you prepare, and are to ask you to keep your speech short.'

'I've made my full confession and, as for my speech, I believe enough has been said.'

He prayed on his knees, long into the night, and wept for his wife. Frances always did her best for him, but had been rewarded so poorly. His last memory of her was her eyes flashing with silent anger at his stubborn refusal to listen to her. She was right: he'd been foolish.

He wished he'd been a better father to his son Robin, and his daughters, Penelope, gone before her time, little Frances, and new baby Dorothy, who he would never see. He prayed for his friend Gelly Meyrick, and tried not to think of his cruel reward for a lifetime of loyalty.

Robert remembered his mother in his prayers, thanking her for taking care of his other son, young Walter. She would be saddened at how he'd blamed her husband, but prayed for her forgiveness.

At first light his Welsh servant, Williams, brought a clean linen shirt, his best black doublet, a satin waistcoat and breeches, and a new lace ruff, with a black velvet hat and cape. He looked apologetic. 'I'm sorry about the rain, my lord.'

Robert managed a smile. 'The weather is the least of my concerns, Master Williams, and no fault of yours.'

His servant helped him dress, then Sir John Peyton arrived with Thomas Mountford and William Barlow, all dressed in black robes. Robert took one last look at the room which had been his home and followed them out into the courtyard.

He savoured the cool rain on his face. At one time he would have cursed his luck at how the weather always spoiled his plans, yet now he welcomed the purifying rain. They turned the corner and his step faltered at the sight of the scaffold, on the spot where the queen's mother Anne Boleyn, Katherine Howard, and Jane Grey had all met the same fate.

He recognised Raleigh in the small crowd of about a hundred men standing in the rain. Most would have been ordered to attend, and refused to catch his eye. He thought Raleigh had come to gloat, then realised he would be there as captain of the Yeomen of the Guard.

Robert climbed the few steps of the scaffold. The fresh straw was wet and blowing away in the wintry breeze. The block looked too low, as if made for someone much smaller. He took off his hat and bowed.

'My sins are more in number than the hairs on my head. I have bestowed my youth in wantonness, lust and uncleanness. I have been puffed up with pride, vanity and love of this wicked world's pleasures.'

He sensed movement at his side. His executioner, wearing a black hood and carrying the axe, joined him on the scaffold. Thomas Mountford gestured for Robert to continue. They were in a hurry for the business of the morning to be over. Robert looked out over the waiting crowd, counting the moments with each thump of his pounding heart.

'I humbly beseech my Saviour Christ to be a mediator to the eternal Majesty for my pardon, especially for this, my last sin, this great, this bloody, this crying, this infectious sin, whereby so many for love of me have been drawn to offend God, to offend their sovereign, to offend the world. I beseech God to forgive me.'

Robert pulled off his wet cape and unfastened his ruff. He had to shout to be heard over the rain drumming on the wooden scaffold. 'The Lord grant Her Majesty a prosperous reign—' His voice faltered as he thought of the queen. 'And a long one, if it be his will!'

Turning his face to the grey winter sky, he said the Lord's Prayer, and forgave the executioner. Robert unbuttoned his doublet to reveal his last show of flamboyance – his bright scarlet waistcoat. He had to lie prostrate on the scaffold to place his head on the wooden block, wet with the cold rain, and stretched out his arms.

'Lord be merciful to thy servant. Into thy hands I commend my spirit.' He thought of his mother, of Frances, of his children, and cried out, 'Executioner, strike home!'

Well I used to have a home,
A place where sacred love was kept,
But I threw it all away
For a dream that turned to debt.
Now there's no way to pay my toll,
No going back to change my life.
The only thing I can do now
Is to return and forfeit pride.

So I'm finally going home,
I've been travelling so long.
It's been a long and weary journey,
But I know where I belong.
And I'm pleading for forgiveness,
For I know that I've done wrong.
I took a turn down sinners' highway,
But I'm finally, finally going home.

Katie Petersen

AUTHOR'S NOTE

Robert Devereux was the last man to be executed with an axe at the Tower of London, on Ash Wednesday, 25 February 1601. His executioner was Thomas Derrick, a man he'd pardoned for rape on the condition he became an executioner. Unfortunately, Derrick took three blows to sever Robert's neck, then held his head for the crowd to see, shouting, 'God save the queen!'

Henry Wriothesley, Earl of Southampton, was imprisoned for life in a comfortable apartment by the Tower's royal palace, and pardoned on the death of the queen two years later. Sadly, Gelly Meyrick fared less well, and suffered the horrors of a traitor's death before a large crowd at Tyburn on the 13 March 1601.

Countess Frances Devereux didn't see Robert again after she left Essex House, but she wrote an impassioned plea for clemency to Robert Cecil. Her son, Robert Devereux, became the third Earl of Essex, and King James awarded Robert the income from the tax on sweet wines.

He was a close friend of his illegitimate half-brother, Walter. They were both parliamentarians, and fought against the royalists in the English Civil War. Robert became a general, and his adjutant was Sir John Meyrick, Gelly Meyrick's nephew.

Author's Note

During the research for this book, I visited Tower Green, and the Chapel of St Peter ad Vincula at the Tower of London, to pay my respects. In front of the altar is a stone which reads, 'Near this spot lie the remains of Robert Devereux, Earl of Essex'. Close by are the remains of Queen Elizabeth's mother, Anne Boleyn.

I also saw the tower in which Robert was held prisoner. Not usually open to the public, the tower, in the north-west corner of the inner curtain wall, is now named 'The Devereux Tower' in his memory. I think he would have been pleased.

One of the surprising discoveries made during my research was that Robert lived at Lamphey Palace, and his sister Dorothy at nearby Carew Castle. I know both places well, as I once lived in Carew, and both are only twenty minutes from my present home. (My books are on sale in Carew Castle gift shop!)

I should mention the apocryphal story of the queen's ring, supposedly sent by Essex to the queen as a plea for mercy. The story is that the ring was wrongly delivered to the Countess of Nottingham, who allegedly confessed it on her deathbed to the queen in 1603. There is no evidence of this – it is one of many romantic myths, which include fanciful ideas that Elizabeth and Robert were lovers, which I doubt.

Much has been written about the life of Robert Devereux, and in the interests of historical accuracy, I relied on the comprehensive work by Walter Bourchier Devereux, *The Lives and Letters of the Devereux Earls of Essex*. I have included direct excerpts in italics.

I am also grateful to the work of Steven Veerapen, author of *Elizabeth and Essex: Power, Passion and Politics*, for providing a fresh perspective that cuts through many of the myths and misconceptions of the relationship between the earl and the queen.

Most of this book was written during the global pandemic of

Author's Note

2020, and the music of The Petersens was often playing in the background while I worked. One of their songs, 'Finally Going Home', resonated with how I imagined Robert Devereux felt at the end, and I would like to thank Katie Petersen for allowing me to use the extract from her original lyrics.

I would also like to thank my wife Liz, and my editor Nikki Brice, for their support during the research and writing of this book.

If you enjoyed reading this book, please consider leaving a short review. It would mean a lot to me. Details of all my books can be found at my author website www.tonyriches.com which also has links to my podcasts about the stories of the Tudors.

Tony Riches, Pembrokeshire
www.tonyriches.com

OWEN

Book One of The Tudor Trilogy

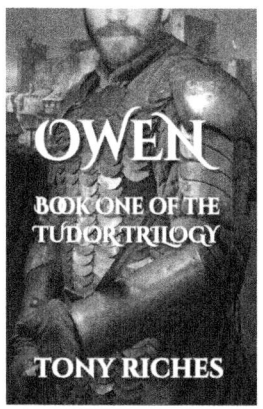

England 1422: Owen Tudor, a Welsh servant, waits in Windsor Castle to meet his new mistress, the beautiful and lonely Queen Catherine of Valois, widow of the warrior king, Henry V.

Her infant son is crowned King of England and France, and while the country simmers on the brink of civil war, Owen becomes her protector.

They fall in love, risking Owen's life and Queen Catherine's reputation, but how do they found the dynasty which changes British history – the Tudors?

Available as paperback, audiobook and eBook

MARY ~ Tudor Princess

Book One of the Brandon Trilogy

Midsummer's Day 1509: The true story of the Tudor dynasty continues with the daughter of King Henry VII. Mary Tudor watches her elder brother become King of England and wonders what the future holds for her.

Born into great privilege, Mary has beauty and intelligence beyond her years. Her brother Henry plans to use her marriage to build a powerful alliance against his enemies – but will she dare to risk his anger by marrying for love?

Meticulously researched and based on actual events, this 'sequel' follows Mary's story from book three of the Tudor Trilogy and is set during the reign of King Henry VIII.

Available in paperback, audiobook and eBook

DRAKE - Tudor Corsair
Book One of the Elizabethan Series

1564: Devon sailor Francis Drake sets out on a journey of adventure, and risks his life in an audacious plan to steal a fortune.

Queen Elizabeth is intrigued by Drake and secretly encourages his piracy. King Philip of Spain has enough of Drake's plunder and orders an armada to threaten the future of England.

Drake – Tudor Corsair continues the story of the Tudors, which began with Owen Tudor in book one of the Tudor trilogy.

Available in paperback and eBook

Printed in Great Britain
by Amazon